Staff Officer wuffled, snorting open his wet black nostrils and working his whiskers. "Traat-Admiral directs me to inform you that your request for transfer has been denied—"

"Traat-Admiral!" Ktiir-Supervisor rasped. "He is like a kit who has climbed a tree and can't get down, mewling for its dam!"

Staff Officer glared balefully. "He follows the strategy of the great Chuut-Riit, murdered through your incompetence—or worse."

"You nameless licker-of-scentless piss from that jumped-up creche-product Admiral, what do you accuse me of?"

"Treason."

Ktiir-Supervisor screamed. "Inner-worlds fops! You and Traat-Admiral alike! I urinate on the shrines of your ancestors from a height; crawl away and call for your monkeys to groom you with blow driers!" Hairdressers were a luxury the late governor had introduced, wildly popular among the younger nobility.

"You are not fit to roll in Chuut-Riit's shit! You lay word-claws to the blood of the Riit." The Riit was the family of the Patriarch of the Kzin.

"Chuut-Riit made *ch'rowl* with monkeys!" A gross insult, as well as fatal for the human.

The two orange shapes seemed to flow together, meeting at the arch of their leaps, howling. . . .

MAN-KZIN
WARS III

Larry Niven

with

Poul Anderson,
J.E. Pournelle,

and

S.M. Stirling

BAEN
BOOKS

MAN-KZIN WARS III

Copyright © 1990 by Larry Niven

A Baen Books Original

Baen Publishing Enterprises
260 Fifth Avenue
New York, N.Y. 10001

ISBN: 0-671-72008-2

Cover art by Steve Hickman

First printing, August 1990

Distributed by
SIMON & SCHUSTER
1230 Avenue of the Americas
New York, N.Y. 10020

Printed in the United States of America

CONTENTS

MADNESS HAS ITS PLACE, Larry Niven   1

THE ASTEROID QUEEN, J.E. Pournelle
  & S.M. Stirling   35

INCONSTANT STAR, Poul Anderson   167

MADNESS HAS ITS PLACE

Larry Niven

Chapter I

A lucky few of us know the good days before they're gone.

I remember my eighties. My job kept me in shape, and gave me enough variety to keep my mind occupied. My love life was imperfect but interesting. Modern medicine makes the old fairy tales look insipid; I almost never worried about my health.

Those were the good days, and I knew them. I could remember worse.

I can remember when my memory was better too. That's what this file is for. I keep it updated for that reason, and also to maintain my sense of purpose.

The Monobloc had been a singles bar since the 2320s.

In the '30s I'd been a regular. I'd found Charlotte there. We held our wedding reception at the Monobloc, then dropped out for twenty-eight years. My first marriage, hers too, both in our forties. After the children grew up and moved away, after Charlotte left me too, I came back.

3

The place was much changed.

I remembered a couple of hundred bottles in the hologram bar display. Now the display was twice as large and seemed more realistic—better equipment, maybe—but only a score of bottles in the middle were liquors. The rest were flavored or carbonated water, high-energy drinks, electrolytes, a thousand kinds of tea; food to match, raw vegetables and fruits kept fresh by high-tech means, arrayed with low-cholesterol dips; bran in every conceivable form short of injections.

The Monobloc had swallowed its neighbors. It was bigger, with curtained alcoves, and a small gym upstairs for working out or for dating.

Herbert and Tina Schroeder still owned the place. Their marriage had been open in the '30s. They'd aged since. So had their clientele. Some of us had married or drifted away or died of alcoholism; but word of mouth and the Velvet Net had maintained a continuous tradition. Twenty-eight years later they looked better than ever . . . wrinkled, of course, but lean and muscular, both ready for the Gray Olympics. Tina let me know before I could ask: she and Herb were lockstepped now.

To me it was like coming home.

For the next twelve years the Monobloc was an intermittent part of my life.

I would find a lady, or she would find me, and we'd drop out. Or we'd visit the Monobloc and sometimes trade partners; and one evening we'd go together and leave separately. I was not evading marriage. Every woman I found worth knowing, ultimately seemed to want to know someone else.

I was nearly bald even then. Thick white hair covered my arms and legs and torso, as if my head hairs had migrated. Twelve years of running construction robots had turned me burly. From time to time some muscular lady would look me over and claim me. I had no trouble finding company.

But company never stayed. Had I become dull? The notion struck me as funny.

* * *

I had settled myself alone at a table for two, early on a Thursday evening in 2375. The Monobloc was half empty. The earlies were all keeping one eye on the door when Anton Brillov came in.

Anton was shorter than me, and much narrower, with a face like an axe. I hadn't see him in thirteen years. Still, I'd mentioned the Monobloc once or twice; he must have remembered.

I semaphored my arms. Anton squinted, then came over, exaggeratedly cautious until he saw who it was.

"Jack Strather!"

"Hi, Anton. So you decided to try the place?"

"Yah." He sat. "You look good." He looked a moment longer and said, "Relaxed. Placid. How's Charlotte?"

"Left me after I retired. Just under a year after. There was too much of me around and I . . . maybe I was too placid? Anyway. How are you?"

"Fine."

Twitchy. Anton looked twitchy. I was amused. "Still with the Holy Office?"

"Only citizens call it that, Jack."

"I'm a citizen. Still gives me a kick. How's your chemistry?"

Anton knew what I meant and didn't pretend otherwise. "I'm okay. I'm down."

"Kid, you're looking over both shoulders at once."

Anton managed a credible laugh. "I'm not the kid any more. I'm a weekly."

The ARM had made me a weekly at forty-eight. They couldn't turn me loose at the end of the day any more, because my body chemistry couldn't shift fast enough. So they kept me in the ARM building Monday through Thursday, and gave me all of Thursday afternoon to shed the schitz madness. Twenty years of that and I was even less flexible, so they retired me.

I said, "You do have to remember. When you're in the ARM building, you're a paranoid schizophrenic. You have to be able to file that when you're outside."

"*Hah*. How can anyone—"

"You get used to the schitz. After I quit, the difference was *amazing*. No fears, no tension, no ambition."

"No Charlotte?"

"Well . . . I turned boring. And what are you doing here?"

Anton looked around him. "Much the same thing you are, I guess. Jack, am I the youngest one here?"

"Maybe." I looked around, double-checking. A woman was distracting me, though I could see only her back and a flash of a laughing profile. Her back was slender and strong, and a thick white braid ran down her spine, centered, two and a half feet of clean, thick white hair. She was in animated conversation with a blond companion of Anton's age plus a few.

But they were at a table for two: they weren't inviting company. I forced my attention back. "We're gray singles, Anton. The young ones tend to get the message quick. We're slower than we used to be. We *date*. You want to order?"

Alcohol wasn't popular here. Anton must have noticed, but he ordered guava juice and vodka and drank as if he needed it. This looked worse than Thursday jitters. I let him half finish, then said, "Assuming you can tell me—"

"I don't know anything."

"I know the feeling. What *should* you know?"

A tension eased behind Anton's eyes. "There was a message from the *Angel's Pencil*."

"*Pencil* . . . oh." My mental reflexes had slowed down. The *Angel's Pencil* had departed twenty years ago for . . . was it Epsilon Eridani? "Come on, kid, it'll be in the boob cubes before you have quite finished speaking. Anything from deep space is public property."

"*Hah!* No. It's restricted. I haven't seen it myself. Only a reference, and it must be more than ten years old."

That was peculiar. And if the Belt stations hadn't spread the news through the solar system, *that* was peculiar. No wonder Anton was antsy. ARMs react that way to puzzles.

Anton seemed to jerk himself back to here and now, back to the gray singles regime. "Am I cramping your style?"

"No problem. Nobody hurries in the Monobloc. If you see someone you like—" My fingers danced over lighted symbols on the rim of the table. "This gets you a map. Locate where she's sitting, put the cursor on it. That gets you a display . . . hmm."

I'd set the cursor on the white-haired lady. I liked the readout. "Phoebe Garrison, seventy-nine, eleven or twelve years older than you. Straight. Won a Second in the Gray Jumps last year . . . that's the America's Skiing Matches for seventy and over. She could kick your tail if you don't watch your manners. It says she's smarter than we are, too.

"Point is, she can check you out the same way. Or me. And she probably found this place through the Velvet Net, which is the computer network for unlocked lifestyles."

"So. Two males sitting together—"

"Anyone who thinks we're bent can check if she cares enough. Bends don't come to the Monobloc anyway. But if we want company, we should move to a bigger table."

We did that. I caught Phoebe Garrison's companion's eye. They played with their table controls, discussed, and presently wandered over.

Dinner turned into a carouse. Alcohol was involved, but we'd left the Monobloc by then. When we split up, Anton was with Michiko. I went home with Phoebe.

Phoebe had fine legs, as I'd anticipated, though both knees were teflon and plastic. Her face was lovely even in morning sunlight. Wrinkled, of course. She was two weeks short of eighty and wincing in anticipation. She ate with a cross-country skier's appetite. We told of our lives as we ate.

She'd come to Santa Maria to visit her oldest grandson. In her youth she'd done critical work in nanoengineering. The Board had allowed her four children. (I'd known I was outclassed.) All were married, scattered across the Earth, and so were the grandkids.

My two sons had emigrated to the Belt while still in their twenties. I'd visited them once during an investigation, trip paid for by the United Nations—

"You were an ARM? Really? How interesting! Tell me a story . . . if you can."

"That's the problem, all right."

The interesting tales were all classified. The ARM suppresses dangerous technology. What the ARM buries is supposed to stay buried. I remembered a kind of time compressor, and a field that would catalyze combustion, both centuries old. Both were first used for murder. If turned loose or rediscovered, either would generate more interesting tales yet.

I said, "I don't know anything current. They bounced me out when I got too old. Now I run construction robots at various spaceports."

"Interesting?"

"Mostly placid." She wanted a story? Okay. The ARM enforced more than the killer-tech laws, and some of those tales I could tell.

"We don't get many mother hunts these days. This one was wished on us by the Belt—" And I told her of a lunie who's sired two clones. One he'd raised on the Moon and one he'd left in the Saturn Conserve. He'd moved to Earth, where one clone is any normal citizen's entire birthright. When we found him he was arranging to culture a third clone . . .

I dreamed a bloody dream.

It was one of those: I was able to take control, to defeat what had attacked me. In the black of an early Sunday morning the shreds of the dream dissolved before I could touch them; but the sensations remained. I felt strong, balanced, powerful, victorious.

It took me a few minutes to become suspicious of this particular flavor of wonderful, but I'd had practice. I eased out from under Phoebe's arm and leg and out of bed. I lurched into the medical alcove, linked myself up and fell asleep on the table.

Phoebe found me there in the morning. She asked, "Couldn't that wait till after breakfast?"

"I've got four years on you and I'm going for infinity. So I'm careful," I told her. It wasn't quite a lie . . . and she didn't quite believe me either.

On Monday Phoebe went off to let her eldest grandson show her the local museums. I went back to work.

In Death Valley a semicircle of twenty lasers points at an axial array of mirrors. Tracks run across the desert to a platform that looks like strands of spun caramel. Every hour or so a spacecraft trundles along the tracks, poses above the mirrors, and rises into the sky on a blinding, searing pillar of light.

Here was where I and three companions and twenty-eight robots worked between emergencies. Emergencies were common enough. From time to time Glenn and Skii and ten or twenty machines had to be shipped off to Outback Field or Baikonur, while I held the fort at Death Valley Field.

All of the equipment was old. The original mirrors had all been slaved to one system, and those had been replaced again and again. Newer mirrors were independently mounted and had their own computers, but even these were up to fifty years old and losing their flexibility. The lasers had to be replaced somewhat more often. Nothing was ready to fall apart, quite.

But the mirrors have to adjust their shapes to match distorting air currents all the way up to vacuum, because the distortions themselves must focus the drive beam. A laser at 99.3% efficiency is keeping too much energy, getting too hot. At 99.1% something would melt, lost power would blow the laser into shrapnel, and a cargo would not reach orbit.

My team had been replacing mirrors and lasers long before I came on the scene. This circuit was nearly complete. We had already reconfigured some robots to begin replacing track.

The robots worked alone while we entertained ourselves in the monitor room. If the robots ran into anything unfamiliar, they stopped and beeped. Then a
story or songfest or poker game would stop just as
abruptly.

Usually the beep meant that the robot had found an
acute angle, an uneven surface, a surface not strong
enough to bear a loaded robot, a bend in a pipe, a pipe
where it shouldn't be . . . a geometrical problem. The
robots couldn't navigate just anywhere. Sometimes we'd
have to unload it and move the load to a cart, by hand.
Sometimes we had to pick it up with a crane and move
it or turn it. Lots of it was muscle work.

Phoebe joined me for dinner Thursday evening.

She'd whipped her grandson at laser tag. They'd
gone through the museum at Edward AFB. They'd
skied . . . he needed to get serious about that, and
maybe get some surgery too . . .

I listened and smiled and presently tried to tell her
about my work. She nodded; her eyes glazed. I tried to
tell her how good it was, how restful, after all those
years in the ARM.

The ARM: that got her interest back. *Stet*. I told her
about the Henry Program.

I'd been saving that. It was an embezzling system
good enough to ruin the economy. It made Zachariah
Henry rich. He might have stayed rich if he'd quit in
time . . . and if his system hadn't been so good, so
dangerous, he might have ended in prison. Instead . . .
well, let his tongue whisper secrets to the ears in the
organ banks.

I could speak of it because they'd changed the system. I didn't say that it had happened twenty years
before I joined the ARM. But I was still running out of
declassified stories. I told her, "If a lot of people know
something can be done, somebody'll do it. We can
suppress it and suppress it again—"

She pounced. "Like what?"

"Like . . . well, the usual example is the first cold
fusion system. They did it with palladium and plati-

num, but half a dozen other metals work. And organic
superconductors: the patents listed a wrong ingredient.
Various grad students tried it wrong and still got it. If
there's a way to do it, there's probably a lot of ways."

"That was before there was an ARM. Would you
have suppressed superconductors?"

"No. What for?"

"Or cold fusion?"

"No."

"Cold fusion releases neutrons," she said. "Sheath
the generator with spent uranium, what do you get?"

"Plutonium, I think. So?"

"They used to make bombs out of plutonium."

"Bothers you?"

"Jack, the fission bomb was *it* in the mass murder
department. Like the crossbow. Like the Ayatollah's
Asteroid." Phoebe's eyes held mine. Her voice had
dropped; we didn't want to broadcast this all over the
restaurant. "Don't you ever wonder just how *much* of
human knowledge is lost in that . . . black limbo inside
the ARM building? Things that could solve problems.
Warm the Earth again. Ease us through the lightspeed
wall."

"We don't suppress inventions unless they're dangerous," I said.

I could have backed out of the argument; but that too
would have disappointed Phoebe. Phoebe liked a good
argument. My problem was that what I gave her wasn't
good enough. Maybe I couldn't get angry enough . . .
maybe my most forceful arguments were classified . . .

Monday morning, Phoebe left for Dallas and a granddaughter. There had been no war, no ultimatum, but it
felt final.

Thursday evening I was back in the Monobloc.

So was Anton. "I've played it," he said. "Can't talk
about it, of course."

He looked mildly bored. His hands looked like they
were trying to break chunks off the edge of the table.

I nodded placidly.

Anton shouldn't have told me about the broadcast from *Angel's Pencil*. But he *had*; and if the ARM had noticed, he'd better mention it again.

Company joined us, sampled and departed. Anton and I spoke to a pair of ladies who turned out to have other tastes. (Some bends like to bug the straights.) A younger woman joined us for a time. She couldn't have been over thirty, and was lovely in the modern style . . . but hard, sharply defined muscle isn't my sole standard of beauty . . .

I remarked to Anton, "Sometimes the vibes just aren't right."

"Yeah. Look, Jack, I have carefully concealed a pre-historic Calvados in my apt at Maya. There isn't really enough for four—"

"Sounds nice. Eat first?"

"Stet. There're *sixteen* restaurants in Maya."

A score of blazing rectangles meandered across the night, washing out the stars. The eye could still find a handful of other space artifacts, particularly around the Moon.

Anton flashed the beeper that would summon a taxi. I said, "So you viewed the call. So why so tense?"

Security devices no bigger than a basketball rode the glowing sky, but the casual eye would not find those. One must assume they were there. Patterns in their monitor chips would match vision and sound patterns of a mugging, a rape, an injury, a cry for help. Those chips had gigabytes to spare for words and word patterns the ARM might find of interest.

So: no key words.

Anton said, "Jack, they tell a hell of a story. A . . . foreign vehicle pulled alongside *Angela* at four-fifths of legal max. It tried to cook them."

I stared. *A spacecraft matched course with the* Angel's Pencil *at eighty percent of lightspeed? Nothing man-built could do that. And warlike?* Maybe I'd mis-interpreted everything. That can happen when you make up your code as you go along.

But how could the Pencil *have escaped?* "How did Angela manage to phone home?"

A taxi dropped. Anton said, "She sliced the bread with the, you know, motor. I said it's a hell of a story."

Anton's apartment was most of the way up the slope of Maya, the pyramidal arcology north of Santa Maria. Old wealth.

Anton led me through great doors, into an elevator, down corridors. He played tour guide: "The Fertility Board was just getting some real power about the time this place went up. It was built to house a million people. It's never been fully occupied."

"So?"

"So we're en route to the east face. Four restaurants, a dozen little bars. And here we stop—"

"This your apt?"

"No. It's empty, it's always been empty. I sweep it for bugs, but the authorities . . . I *think* they've never noticed."

"Is that your mattress?"

"No. Kids. They've got a club that's two generations old. My son tipped me off to this."

"Could we be interrupted?"

"No. *I'm* monitoring *them*. I've got the security system set to let them in, but only when I'm not here. Now I'll set it to recognize you. Don't forget the number: Apt 23309."

"What is the ARM going to think we're doing?"

"Eating. We went to one of the restaurants, then came back and drank Calvados . . . which we will do, later. I can fix the records at Buffalo Bill. Just don't argue about the credit charge, stet?"

"But— Yah, stet." Hope you won't be noticed, that's the real defense. I was thinking of bailing out . . . but curiosity is part of what gets you into the ARM. "Tell your story. You said she *sliced the bread with the, you know, motor?*"

"Maybe you don't remember. *Angel's Pencil* isn't your

ordinary Bussard ramjet. The field scoops up interstellar hydrogen to feed a fusion-pumped laser. The idea was to use it for communications too. Blast a message half across the galaxy with that. A Belter crewman used it to cut the alien ship in half."

"*There's* a communication you can live without. Anton . . . What they taught us in school. A sapient species doesn't reach space unless the members learn to cooperate. They'll wreck the environment, one way or another, war or straight libertarianism or overbreeding . . . remember?"

"Sure."

"So do you believe all this?"

"I think so." He smiled painfully. "Director Bernhardt didn't. He classified the message and attached a memo too. Six years of flight aboard a ship of limited size, terminal boredom coupled with high intelligence and too much time, elaborate practical jokes, yadda yadda. Director Harms *left* it classified . . . with the cooperation of the Belt. Interesting?"

"But he *had* to have *that*."

"But they had to agree. There's been more since. *Angel's Pencil* sent us hundreds of detailed photos of the alien ship. It's unlikely they could be faked. There are corpses. Big sort-of cats, orange, up to three meters tall, big feet and elaborate hands with thumbs. We're in mucking great trouble if we have to face up to such beasties."

"Anton, we've had three hundred and fifty years of peace. We must be doing something right. The odds say we can negotiate."

"You haven't seen them."

It was almost funny. Jack was trying to make me nervous. Twenty years ago the terror would have been fizzing in my blood. Better living through chemistry! This was all frightening enough; but my fear was a cerebral thing, and I was its master.

I wasn't nervous enough for Anton. "Jack, this isn't just vaporware. A lot of those photos show what's maybe a graviton generator, maybe not. Director Harms set up a lab on the Moon to build one for us."

"Funded?"

"Heavy funding. *Somebody* believes in this. But they're getting results! It *works!*"

I mulled it. "Alien contact. As a species we don't seem to handle that too well."

"Maybe this one can't be handled at all."

"What else is being done?"

"Nothing, or damn close. Silly suggestions, career-oriented crap designed to make a bureau bigger . . . Nobody wants to use the magic word. *War*."

"War. Three hundred and fifty years out of practice, we are. Maybe C. Cretemaster will save us." I smiled at Anton's bewilderment. "Look it up in the ARM records. There's supposed to be an alien of sorts living in the cometary halo. He's the force that's been keeping us at peace this past three and a half centuries."

"Very funny."

"Mmm. Well, Anton, this is a lot more real for you than me. *I* haven't yet seen anything upsetting."

I hadn't called him a liar. I'd only made him aware that I knew nothing to the contrary. For Anton there might be elaborate proofs; but I'd seen nothing, and heard only a scary tale.

Anton reacted gracefully. "Of course. Well, there's still that bottle."

Anton's Calvados was as special as he'd claimed, decades old and quite unique. He produced cheese and bread. Good thing; I was ready to eat his arm off. We managed to stick to harmless topics, and parted friends.

The big catlike aliens had taken up residence in my soul.

Aliens aren't implausible. Once upon a time, maybe. But an ancient ETI in a stasis field had been in the Smithsonian since the opening of the twenty-second century, and a quite different creature—C. Cretemaster's real-life analog—had crashed on Mars before the century ended.

Two spacecraft matching course at near lightspeed, *that* was just short of ridiculous. Kinetic energy considerations . . . why, two such ships colliding might as well be made of antimatter! Nothing short of a gravity generator could make it work. But Anton was *claiming* a gravity generator.

His story was plausible in another sense. Faced with warrior aliens, the ARM would do only what they could not avoid. They would build a gravity generator because the ARM must control such a thing. Any further move was a step toward the unthinkable. The ARM took sole credit (and other branches of the United Nations also took sole credit) for the fact that Man had left war behind. I shuddered to think what force it would take to turn the ARM toward war.

I would continue to demand proof of Anton's story. Looking for proof was one way to learn more, and I resist seeing myself as stupid. But I believed him already.

On Thursday we returned to Suite 23309.

"I had to dig deep to find out, but they're not just sitting on their thumbs," he said. "There's a game going in Aristarchus Crater, Belt against flatlander. They're playing peace games."

"Huh?"

"They're making formats for contact and negotiation with hypothetical aliens. The models all have the look of those alien corpses, cats with bald tails, but they all think differently— "

"Good." Here was my proof. I could check this claim.

"Good. Sure. Peace games." Anton was brooding. Twitchy. "What about war games?"

"How would you run one? Half your soldiers would be dead at the end . . . unless you're thinking of rifles with paint bullets. War gets more violent than that."

Anton laughed. "Picture every building in Chicago covered with scarlet paint on one side. A nuclear war game."

"Now what? I mean for us."

"Yah. Jack, the ARM isn't *doing* anything to put the human race back on a war footing."

"Maybe they've done something they haven't told you about."

"Jack, I don't think so."

"They haven't let you read all their files, Anton. Two weeks ago you didn't know about peace games in Aristarchus. But okay. What *should* they be doing?"

"I don't *know*."

"How's your chemistry?"

Anton grimaced. "How's yours? Forget I said that. Maybe I'm back to normal and maybe I'm not."

"Yah, but you haven't thought of anything. How about weapons? Can't have a war without weapons, and the ARM's been suppressing weapons. We should dip into their files and make up a list. It would save some time, when and if. I know of an experiment that might have been turned into an inertialoss drive if it hadn't been suppressed."

"Date?"

"Early twenty-second. And there was a field projector that would make things burn, late twenty-third."

"I'll find 'em." Anton's eyes took on a faraway look. "There's the archives. I don't mean just the stuff that was built and then destroyed. The archives reach all the way back to the early twentieth. Stuff that was proposed, tanks, orbital beam weapons, kinetic energy weapons, biologicals—"

"We don't want biologicals."

I thought he hadn't heard. "Picture crowbars six feet long. A short burn takes them out of orbit, and they steer themselves down to anything with the silhouette you want . . . a tank or a submarine or a limousine, say. Primitive stuff now, but at least it would *do* something." He was really getting into this. The technical terms he was tossing off were masks for horror. He stopped suddenly, then, "Why not biologicals?"

"Nasty bacteria tailored for *us* might not work on warcats. We want *their* biological weapons, and we don't want them to have ours."

". . . Stet. Now here's one for you. How would you adjust a 'doc to make a normal person into a soldier?"

My head snapped up. I saw the guilt spread across his face. He said, "I had to look up your dossier. *Had* to, Jack."

"Sure. All right, I'll see what I can find." I stood up. "The easiest way is to pick schitzies and train *them* as soldiers. We'd start with the same citizens the ARM has been training since . . . date classified, three hundred years or so. People who need the 'doc to keep their metabolism straight, or else they'll ram a car into a crowd, or strangle—"

"We wouldn't find enough. When you need soldiers, you need thousands. Maybe millions."

"True. It's a rare condition. Well, good night, Anton." I fell asleep on the 'doc table again.

Dawn poked under my eyelids and I got up and moved toward the holophone. Caught a glimpse of myself in a mirror. Rethought. If David saw me looking like this, he'd be booking tickets to attend the funeral. So I took a shower and a cup of coffee first.

My eldest son looked like I had: decidedly rumpled. "Dad, can't you read a clock?"

"I'm sorry. Really." These calls are so expensive that there's no point in hanging up. "How are things in Aristarchus?"

"Clavius. We've been moved out. We've got half the space we used to, and we needed twice the space to hold everything we own. Ah, the time change isn't your fault, Dad, we're all in Clavius now, all but Jennifer. She—" David vanished. A mechanically soothing voice said, "You have impinged on ARM police business. The cost of your call will be refunded."

I looked at the empty space where David's face had been. I *was* ARM . . . but maybe I'd already heard enough.

My granddaughter Jennifer is a medic. The censor program had reacted to her name in connection with David. David said she wasn't with him. The whole family had been moved out but for Jennifer.

If she'd stayed on in Aristarchus . . . or been kept on . . .

Human medics like Jennifer are needed when something unusual has happened to a human body or brain. Then they study what's going on, with an eye to writing more programs for the 'docs. The bulk of these problems are psychological.

Anton's "peace games" must be stressful as Hell.

Chapter II

Anton wasn't at the Monobloc Thursday. That gave me another week to rethink and recheck the programs I'd put on a dime disk; but I didn't need it.

I came back the next Thursday. Anton Brillov and Phoebe Garrison were holding a table for four.

I paused—backlit in the doorway, knowing my expression was hidden—then moved on in. "When did you get back?"

"Saturday before last," Phoebe said gravely.

It felt awkward. Anton felt it too; but then, he would. I began to wish I didn't ever have to see him on a Thursday night.

I tried tact. "Shall we see if we can conscript a fourth?"

"It's not like that," Phoebe said. "Anton and I, we're *together*. We had to tell you."

But I'd never thought . . . I'd never *claimed* Phoebe. Dreams are private. This was coming from some wild direction. "Together as in?"

Anton said, "Well, not married, not yet, but thinking about it. And we wanted to talk privately."

"Like over dinner?"

"A good suggestion."

"I like Buffalo Bill. Let's go there."

Twenty-odd habitués of the Monobloc must have heard the exchange and watched us leave. *Those three long-timers seem friendly enough, but too serious . . . and three's an odd number . . .*

We didn't talk until we'd reached Suite 23309.

Anton closed the door before he spoke. "She's in, Jack. Everything."

I said, "It's really love, then."

Phoebe smiled. "Jack, don't be offended. Choosing is what humans do."

Trite, I thought, and *skip it*. "That bit there in the Monobloc seemed overdone. I felt excessively foolish."

"That was for *them*. My idea," Phoebe said. "After tonight, one of us may have to go away. This way we've got an all-purpose excuse. You leave because your best friend and favored lady closed you out. Or Phoebe leaves because she can't bear to ruin a friendship. Or big, burly Jack drives Anton away. See?"

She wasn't just in, she was taking over. Ah, well. "Phoebe, love, do you believe in murderous cats eight feet tall?"

"Do you have doubts, Jack?"

"Not any more. I called my son. Something secretive is happening in Aristarchus, something that requires a medic."

She only nodded. "What have you got for us?"

I showed them my dime disk. "Took me less than a week. Run it in an autodoc. Ten personality choices. The chemical differences aren't big, but . . . infantry, which means killing on foot and doesn't have anything to do with children . . . where was I? Yah. Infantry isn't at all like logistics, and neither is it like espionage, and Navy is different yet. We may have lost some of the military vocations over the centuries. We'll have to re-invent them. This is just a first cut. I wish we had a way to try it out."

Anton set a dime disk next to mine, and a small projector. "Mine's nearly full. The ARM's stored an incredible range of dangerous devices. We need to think hard about where to store this. I even wondered if one of us should be emigrating, which is why—"

"To the Belt? Further?"

"Jack, if this all adds up, we won't have time to reach another star."

We watched stills and flat motion pictures of weapons and tools in action. Much of it was quite primitive, copied out of deep archives. We watched rock and landscape being torn, aircraft exploding, machines destroying other machines . . . and imagined flesh shredding.

"I could get more, but I thought I'd better show you this first," Anton said.

I said, "Don't bother."

"What? Jack?"

"It only took us a week! Why risk our necks to do work that can be duplicated that fast?"

Anton looked lost. "We need to do *something*!"

"Well, maybe we don't. Maybe the ARM is doing it all for us."

Phoebe gripped Anton's wrist hard, and he swallowed some bitter retort. She said, "Maybe we're missing something. Maybe we're not looking at it right."

"What's on your mind?"

"Let's *find* a way to look at it differently." She was looking straight at me.

I said, "Stoned? Drunk? Fizzed? Wired?"

Phoebe shook her head. "We need the schitz view."

"Dangerous, love. Also, the chemicals you're talking about are massively illegal. *I* can't get them, and Anton would be caught for sure—" I saw the way she was smiling at me. "Anton, I'll break your scrawny neck."

"Huh? Jack?"

"No, no, he didn't tell me," Phoebe said hastily, "though frankly I'd think either of you might have trusted me that much, Jack! I remembered you in the 'doc that morning, and Anton coming down from that twitchy state on a Thursday night, and it all clicked."

"Okay."

"You're a schitz, Jack. But it's been a long time, hasn't it?"

"Thirteen years of peace," I said. "They pick us for it, you know. Paranoid schizophrenics, born with our chemistry screwed up, hair trigger temper and a skewed view of the universe. Most schitzies never have to feel that. We use the 'docs more regularly than you do and that's that. But some of us go into the ARM . . . Phoebe, your suggestion is still silly. Anton's crazy four days out of the week, just like I used to be. Anton's all you need."

"Phoebe, he's right."

"No. The ARM used to be *all* schitzies, right? The genes have thinned out over three hundred years."

Anton nodded. "They tell us in training. The ones who could be Hitler or Napoleon or Castro, they're the ones the ARM wants. They're the ones you can send on a mother hunt, the ones with no social sense . . . but the Fertility Board doesn't let them breed either, unless they've got something special. Jack, you were special, high intelligence or something—"

"Perfect teeth, and I don't get sick in free fall, and Charlotte's people never develop back problems. That helped. Yah . . . but every century there are less of us. So they hire some Antons too, and *make* you crazy—"

"But carefully," Phoebe said. "Anton's not evolved from paranoia, Jack. You are. When they juice Anton up they don't make him too crazy, just enough to get the viewpoint they want. I bet they leave the top management boringly sane. But *you*, Jack— "

"I *see* it." Centuries of ARM tradition were squarely on her side.

"*You* can go as crazy as you like. It's all natural, and medics have known how to handle it since Only One Earth. We need the schitz viewpoint, and we don't have to steal the chemicals."

"Stet. When do we start?"

Anton looked at Phoebe. Phoebe said, "Now?"

We played Anton's tape all the way through, to a running theme of graveyard humor.

"I took only what I thought we could use," Anton said. "You should have seen some of the rest. Agent Orange. Napalm. Murder stuff."

Phoebe said, "Isn't this murder?"

That remark might have been unfair. We were watching this bizarre chunky rotary-blade flyer. Fire leaped from underneath it, once and again . . . weapons of some kind.

Anton said, "Aircraft design isn't the same when you use it for murder. It changes when you expect to be shot at. Here—" The picture had changed. "That's another weapons platform. It's not just fast, it's supposed to hide in the sky. Jack, are you all right?"

"I'm scared green. I haven't felt any effects yet."

Phoebe said, "You need to relax. Anton delivers a terrific massage. I never learned."

She wasn't kidding. Anton didn't have my muscle, but he had big strangler's hands. I relaxed into it, talking as he worked, liking the way my voice wavered as his hands pounded my back.

"It hasn't been that long since a guy like me let his 'doc run out of beta-dammasomething. An indicator light ran out and he didn't notice. He tried to kill his business partner by bombing his partner's house, and got some family members instead."

"We're on watch," Phoebe said. "If you go beserk we can handle it. Do you want to see more of this?"

"We've missed something. Children, I'm a *registered* schitz. If I don't use my 'doc for three days, they'll be trying to find me before I remember I'm the Marsport Strangler."

Anton said, "He's right, love. Jack, give me your door codes. If I can get into your apt, I can fix the records."

"Keep talking. Finish the massage, at least. We might

have other problems. Do we want fruit juice? Munch-ies? Foodlike substances?"

When Anton came back with groceries, Phoebe and I barely noticed.

Were the warcats real? Could we fight them with present tech? How long did Sol system have? And the other systems, the more sparsely settled colony worlds? Was it enough to make tapes and blueprints of the old murder machines, or must we set to building clandes-tine factories? Phoebe and I were spilling ideas past each other as fast as they came, and I had quite forgot-ten that I was doing something dangerous.

I noticed myself noticing that I was thinking much faster than thoughts could spill from my lips. I remem-bered knowing that Phoebe was brighter than I was, and that didn't matter either. But Anton was losing his Thursday edge.

We slept. The old airbed was a big one. We woke to fruit and bread and dived back in.

We re-invented the Navy using only what Anton had recorded of seagoing navies. We had to. There had never been space navies; the long peace had fallen first.

I'm not sure when I slid into schitz mode. I'd spent four days out of seven without the 'doc, every week for forty-one years excluding vacations. You'd think I'd re-member the feel of my brain chemistry changing. Some-times I do; but it's the central *me* that changes, and there's no way to control that.

Anton's machines were long out of date, and none had been developed even for interplanetary war. Man-kind had found peace too soon. Pity. But if the warcats' gravity generators could be copied before the warcats arrived, that alone could save us!

Then again, whatever the cats had for weapons, ki-netic energy was likely to be the ultimate weapon, *however* the mass was moved. Energy considerations don't lie . . . I stopped trying to anticipate individual war machines; what I needed was an overview.

Anton was saying very little.

I realised that I had been wasting my time making

medical programs. Chemical enhancement was the most trivial of what we'd need to remake an army. Extensive testing would be needed, and then we might not get soldiers at all unless they retained *some* civil rights, or unless officers killed enough of them to impress the rest. Our limited pool of schitzies had better be trained as our officers. For that matter, we'd better start by taking over the ARM. They had all the brightest schitzies.

As for Anton's work in the ARM archives, the most powerful weapons had been entirely ignored. They were too obvious.

I saw how Phoebe was staring at me, and Anton too, both gape-jawed.

I tried to explain that our task was nothing less than the reorganization of humanity. Large numbers might have to die before the rest saw the wisdom in following our lead. The warcats would teach that lesson . . . but if we waited for them, we'd be too late. Time was breathing hot on our necks.

Anton didn't understand. Phoebe was following me, though not well, but Anton's body language was pulling him back and closing him up while his face stayed blank. He feared me worse than he feared warcats.

I began to understand that I might have to kill Anton. I hated him for that.

We did not sleep Friday at all. By Saturday noon we should have been exhausted. I'd caught catnaps from time to time, we all had, but I was still blazing with ideas. In my mind the pattern of an interstellar invasion was shaping itself like a vast three-dimensional map.

Earlier I might have killed Anton, because he knew too much or too little, because he would steal Phoebe from me. Now I saw that that was foolish. Phoebe wouldn't follow him. He simply didn't have the . . . the internal power. As for knowledge, he was our only access to the ARM!

Saturday evening we ran out of food . . . and Anton and Phoebe saw the final flaw in their plan.

I found it hugely amusing. My 'doc was halfway

across Santa Maria. They had to get me there. Me, a
schitz.

We talked it around. Anton and Phoebe wanted to
check my conclusions. Fine: we'd give them the schitz
treatment. But for that we needed my disk (in my
pocket) and my 'doc (at the apt). So we had to go to my
apt.

With that in mind, we shaped plans for a farewell
bacchanal.

Anton ordered supplies. Phoebe got me into a taxi.
When I thought of other destinations she was persua-
sive. And the party was waiting . . .

We were a long time reaching the 'doc. There was
beer to be dealt with, and a pizza the size of Arthur's
Round Table. We sang, though Phoebe couldn't hold a
tune. We took ourselves to bed. It had been years since
my urge to rut ran so high, so deep, backed by a
sadness that ran deeper yet and wouldn't go away.

When I was too relaxed to lift a finger, we staggered
singing to the 'doc with me hanging limp between
them. I produced my dime disk, but Anton took it
away. What was this? They moved me onto the table
and set it working. I tried to explain: they had to lie
down, put the disk here . . . But the circuitry found my
blood loaded with fatigue poisons, and put me to sleep.

Sunday noon:

Anton and Phoebe seemed embarrassed in my presence. My own memories were bizarre, embarrassing.
I'd been guilty of egotism, arrogance, self-centered lack
of consideration. Three dark blue dots on Phoebe's
shoulder told me that I'd brushed the edge of violence.
But the worst memory was of thinking like some red-
handed conqueror, and out loud.

They'd never love me again.

But they could have brought me into the apt and
straight to the 'doc. Why didn't they?

While Anton was out of the room I caught Phoebe's
smile in the corner of my eye, and saw it fade as I

turned. An old suspicion surfaced and has never faded
since.

Suppose that the women I love are all attracted to
Mad Jack. Somehow they recognise my schitz potential
though they find my sane state dull. There must have
been a place for madness throughout most of human
history. So men and women seek in each other the
capacity for madness . . .

And so what? Schitzies kill. The real Jack Strather is
too dangerous to be let loose.

And yet . . . it had been worth doing. From that
strange fifty-hour session I remembered one real insight.
We spent the rest of Sunday discussing it, making
plans, while my central nervous system returned to its
accustomed, unnatural state. Sane Jack.

Anton Brillov and Phoebe Garrison held their wedding reception in the Monobloc. I stood as best man,
bravely cheerful, running over with congratulations,
staying carefully sober.

A week later I was among the asteroids. At the
Monobloc they said that Jack Strather had fled Earth
after his favored lady deserted him for his best friend.

Chapter III

Things ran smoother for me because John Junior had made a place for himself in Ceres.

Even so, they had to train me. Twenty years ago I'd spent a week in the Belt. It wasn't enough. Training and a Belt citizen's equipment used up most of my savings and two months of my time.

Time brought me to Mercury, and the lasers, eight years ago.

Light-sails are rare in the inner solar system. Between Venus and Mercury there are still light-sail races, an expensive, uncomfortable, and dangerous sport. Cargo craft once sailed throughout the asteroid belt, until fusion motors became cheaper and more dependable.

The last refuge of the light-sail is a huge, empty region: the cometary halo, Pluto and beyond. The light-sails are all cargo craft. So far from Sol, their thrust must be augmented by lasers, the same Mercury lasers that sometimes hurl an unmanned probe into interstellar space.

These were different from the launch lasers I was familiar with. They were enormously larger. In Mercury's lower gravity, in Mercury's windless environment, they looked like crystals caught in spiderwebs. When the lasers fired the fragile support structures wavered like a spiderweb in a wind.

Each stood in a wide black pool of solar collector, as if tar paper had been scattered at random. A collector sheet that lost fifty percent of power was not removed. We would add another sheet, but continue to use all the available power.

Their power output was dangerous to the point of fantasy. For safety's sake the Mercury lasers must be continually linked to the rest of the solar system across a lightspeed delay of several hours. The newer solar collectors also picked up broadcasts from space, or from the control center in Challenger Crater. Mercury's lasers must never lose contact. A beam that strayed where it wasn't supposed to could do untold damage.

They were spaced all along the planet's equator. They were hundreds of years apart in design, size, technology. They fired while the sun was up and feeding their square miles of collectors, with a few fusion generators for backup. They flicked from target to target as the horizon moved. When the sun set, it set for thirty-odd Earth days, and that was plenty of time to make repairs—

"In general, that is." Kathry Perritt watched my eyes to be sure I was paying attention. I felt like a schoolboy again. "In general we can repair and update each laser station in turn and *still* keep ahead of the dawn. But come a quake, we work in broad daylight and like it."

"Scary," I said, too cheerfully.

She looked at me. "You feel nice and cool? That's a million tons of soil, old man, and a layer cake of mirror sheeting on top of that, and these old heat exchangers are still the most powerful ever built. Daylight doesn't scare you? You'll get over that."

Kathry was a sixth generation Belter from Mercury, taller than me by seven inches, not very strong, but extremely dextrous. She was my boss. I'd be sharing a room with her . . . and yes, she rapidly let me know that she expected us to be bedmates.

I was all for that. Two months in Ceres had showed me that Belters respond to social signals I don't know. I had no idea how to seduce anyone.

Sylvia and Myron had been born on Mars in an enclave of archeologists digging out the cities beneath the deserts. Companions from birth, they'd married at puberty. They were addicted to news broadcasts. News could get them arguing. Otherwise they behaved as if they could read each other's minds; they hardly talked to each other or to anyone else.

We'd sit around the duty room and wait, and polish our skills as storytellers. Then one of the lasers would go quiet, and a tractor the size of some old Chicago skyscraper would roll.

Rarely was there much of a hurry. One laser would fill in for another until the Monster Bug arrived. Then the robots, riding the Monster Bug like one of Anton's aircraft carriers, would scatter ahead of us and set to work.

Two years after my arrival, my first quake shook down six lasers in four different locations, and ripped a few more loose from the sunlight collectors. Landscape had been shaken into new shapes. The robots had some trouble. Sometimes Kathry could reprogram. Otherwise her team had to muscle them through, with Kathry to shout orders and me to supply most of the muscle.

Of the six lasers, five survived. They seemed built to survive almost anything. The robots were equipped to spin new support structure and to lift the things into place, with a separate program for each design.

Maybe John Junior *hadn't* used influence in my behalf. Flatlander muscle was useful, when the robots couldn't get over the dust pools or through the broken rock. For that matter, maybe it wasn't some Belt tradition that made Kathry claim me on sight. Sylvia and Myron weren't sharing; and I might have been female, or bent. Maybe she thought she was lucky.

After we'd remounted the lasers that survived, Kathry said, "They're all obsolete anyway. They're not being replaced."

"That's not good," I said.

"Well, good and bad. Light-sail cargos are slow. If the light wasn't almost free, why bother? The interstellar probes haven't sent much back yet, and we might as well wait. At least the Belt Speakers think so."

"Do I gather I've fallen into a kind of a blind alley?"

She glared at me. "You're an immigrant flatlander. What did you expect, First Speaker for the Belt? You thinking of moving on?"

"Not really. But if the job's about to fold—"

"Another twenty years, maybe. Jack, I'd miss you. Those two— "

"It's all right, Kathry. I'm not going." I waved both arms at the blazing dead landscape and said, "I like it here," and smiled into her bellow of laughter.

I beamed a tape to Anton when I got the chance.

"If I was ever angry, I got over it, as I hope you've forgotten anything I said or did while I was, let's say, running on automatic. I've found another life in deep space, not much different from what I was doing on Earth . . . though that may not last. These light-sail pusher lasers are a blast from the past. Time gets them, the quakes get them, and they're not being replaced. Kathry says twenty years.

"You said Phoebe left Earth too. Working with an asteroid mining setup? If you're still trading tapes, tell her I'm all right and I hope she is too. Her career choice was better than mine, I expect . . ."

I couldn't think of anything else to do.

Three years after I expected it, Kathry asked. "Why did you come out here? It's none of my business, of course— "

Customs differ: it took her three years in my bed to

work up to this. I said, "Time for a change," and "I've got children and grandchildren on the Moon and Ceres and Floating Jupiter."

"Do you miss them?"

I had to say yes. The result was that I took half a year off to bounce around the solar system. I found Phoebe, too, and we did some catching up; but I still came back early. My being away made us both antsy.

Kathry asked again a year later. I said, "What I did on Earth was not like this. The difference is, on Earth I'm dull. Here—am I dull?"

"You're fascinating. You won't talk about the ARM, so you're fascinating and mysterious. I can't believe you'd be dull just because of where you are. Why did you leave, really?"

So I said, "There was a woman."

"What was she like?"

"She was smarter than me. I was a little dull for her. So she left, and that would have been okay. But she came back to my best friend." I shifted uncomfortably and said, "Not that they drove me off Earth."

"No?"

"No. I've got everything I once had herding construction robots on Earth, plus one thing I wasn't bright enough to miss. I lost my sense of purpose when I left the ARM."

I noticed that Myron was listening. Sylvia was watching the holo walls, the three that showed the face of Mercury: rocks blazing like coals in fading twilight, with only the robots and the lasers to give the illusion of life. The fourth we kept changing. Just then it showed a view up the trunk into the waving branches of the tremendous redwood they've been growing for three hundred years, in Hovestraydt City on the Moon.

"These are the good times," I said. "You have to notice, or they'll go right past. We're holding the stars together. Notice how much dancing we do? On Earth I'd be too old and creaky for that—Sylvia, *what?*"

Sylvia was shaking my shoulder. I heard it as soon as I stopped talking: "*Tombaugh Station relayed this pic-*

ture, the last broadcast from the Fantasy Prince. *Once
again, the* Fantasy Prince *has apparently been—*"

Starscape glowed within the fourth holo wall. Something came out of nowhere, moving hellishly fast, and
stopped so quickly that it might have been a toy. It was
egg-shaped, studded with what I remembered as
weapons.

Phoebe won't have made her move yet. The warcats
will have to be deep in the solar system before her
asteroid mining setup can be any deterrent. Then one
or another warcat ship will find streams of slag sprayed
across its path, impacting at comet speeds.

By now Anton must know whether the ARM actually has plans to repel an interstellar invasion.

Me, I've already done my part. I worked on the
computer shortly after I first arrived. Nobody's tam-
pered with it since. The dime disk is in place.

We kept the program relatively simple. Until and
unless the warcats destroy something that's being pushed
by a laser from Mercury, nothing will happen. The
warcats must condemn themselves. Then the affected
laser will lock onto the warcat ship . . . and so will
every Mercury laser that's getting sunlight. Twenty
seconds, then the system goes back to normal until
another target disappears.

If the warcats can be persuaded that Sol system is
defended, maybe they'll give us time to build defenses.

Asteroid miners dig deep for fear of solar storms and
meteors. Phoebe might survive. We might survive here
too, with shielding built to block the hellish sun, and
laser cannon to battle incoming ships. But that's not the
way to bet.

We might get one ship.

It might be worth doing.

THE ASTEROID QUEEN

J.E. Pournelle & S.M. Stirling

Three billion years before the birth of Buddha, the Thrint ruled the galaxy and ten thousand intelligent species. The Thrint were not great technologists or mighty warriors; as a master race, they were distinctly third rate. They had no need to be more. They had the Power, an irresistible mental hypnosis more powerful than any weapon. Their Tnuctipun slaves had only cunning, but in the generations-long savagery of the Revolt, that proved nearly enough to break the Slaver Empire. It was a war fought without even the concept of mercy, one which could only end when either the Thrint or tnuctipun species were extinct and tnuctipun technology was winning . . . But the Thrint had one last use for the Power, one last command that would blanket all the worlds that had been theirs. It was the most comprehensive campaign of genocide in all history, destroying even its perpetrators. It was not, however, *quite* complete . . .

"Master! Master! What shall we do?"
The Chief Slave of the orbital habitat wailed, wringing the boneless digits of its hands together. It recoiled as

the thrint rounded on it, teeth bared in carnivore reflex. There was only a day or so to go before Suicide Time, when every sophont in the galaxy would die. The master of Orbital Supervisory Station Seven-1Z-A did not intend to be among them. Any delay was a mortal threat, and this twelve-decicredit specimen *dared*—

"DIE, SLAVE!"

Dnivtopun screamed mentally, lashing out with the Power. The slave obeyed instantly, of course. Unfortunately, so did several dozen others nearby, including the zengaborni pilot who was just passing through the airlock on its way to the escape spaceship.

"*Must you always take me so literally!*" Dnivtopun bellowed, kicking out at the silvery-furred form that lay across the entrance-lock to the docking chamber.

It rolled and slid through a puddle of its body wastes, and a cold chill made Dnivtopun curl the eating-tendrils on either side of his needle-toothed mouth into hard knots. *I should not have done that,* he thought. A proverb from the ancient "Wisdom of Thrintun" went through his mind; *haste is not speed.* That was a difficult concept to grasp, but he had had many hours of empty time for meditation here. Forcing himself to calm, he looked around. The corridor was bare metal, rather shabby; only slaves came down here, normally. Not that his own quarters were all that much better. Dnivtopun was the youngest son of a long line of no more than moderately successful thrint; his post as Overseer of the food-producing planet below was a sinecure from an uncle.

At least it kept me out of the War, he mused with relief. The tnuctipun revolt had spanned most of the last hundred years, and nine-tenths of the thrint species had died in it. The War was lost . . .

Dnivtopun appreciated the urge for revenge that had led the last survivors on Homeworld to build a psionic amplifier big enough to blanket the galaxy with a suicide command, but he had not been personal witness to the genocidal fury of the tnuctipun assaults; revenge would be much sweeter if he were there to see it.

Other slaves came shuffling down the corridor with a gravity-skid, and loaded the bodies. One proffered an electropad; Dnivtopun began laboriously checking the list of loaded supplies against his initial entries.

"Ah, Master?"

"Yes?"

"That function key?"

The thrint scowled and punched it. "All in order," he said, and looked up as the ready-light beside the liftshaft at the end of the corridor pinged. It was his wives, and the chattering horde of their children.

"SILENCE," he commanded. They froze; there was a slight hesitation from some of the older males, old enough to have developed a rudimentary shield. They would come to the Power at puberty . . . but none would be ready to challenge their Sire for some time after that. "GO ON BOARD. GO TO YOUR QUARTERS. STAY THERE." It was best to keep the commands simple, since thrintun females were too dull-witted to understand more than the most basic verbal orders. He turned to follow them.

"Master?" the thrint rotated his neckless torso back towards the slave. "Master, what shall we do until you return?" Dnivtopun felt a minor twinge of regret. Being alone so much with the slaves, he had conversed with them more than was customary. He hesitated for a moment, then decided a last small indulgence was in order.

"BE HAPPY," he commanded, radiating as hard as possible to cover all the remaining staff grouped by the docking tube. It was difficult to blanket the station without an amplifier helmet, but the only one available was suspect. Too many planetary Proprietors had been brain-burned in the early stages of the War by tnuctipun-sabotaged equipment. Straining: "BE VERY HAPPY."

They were making small cooing sounds as he dogged the hatch.

"Master—" The engineering slave sounded worried.

"Not now!" Dnivtopun said.

They were nearly in position to activate the Standing Wave and go faster than light; the *Ruling Mind* had built up the necessary .3 of lightspeed. It was an intricate job, piloting manually. He had disconnected the main computer; it was tnuctipun work, and he did not trust the innermost programs. The problem was that so much else was routed through it. Of course, the zengaborni should be at the board; they were expensive but had an instinctive feel for piloting. Now, begin the phase transition . . .

"Master, the density sensor indicates a mass concentration on our vector!"

Dnivtopun was just turning toward the slave when the collision alarm began to wail, and then—

-discontinuity-

Chapter I

"Right, give me a reading on the mass detector," the prospector said; like many rockjacks, he spoke to his computer as if it were human. It wasn't, of course; sentient computers tended to turn catatonic, usually at the most inopportune moments, so any illusion of sentience was just that; but most rockjacks talked to the machinery anyway.

He was a short man for a Belter, with the slightly seedy run-down air that was common in the Alpha Centauri system after the kzinti conquest of Wunderland and its Belt. There was hunger in the eyes that skipped across the patched and mismatched screens of the *Lucky Strike*; the little torchship had not been doing well of late, and the kzin-nominated purchasing combines on the asteroid base of Tiamat had been squeezing harder and harder. The life bubble of his singleship smelled, a stale odor of metal and old socks; the conditioner was not getting out all of the ketones.

Collaborationist ratcat-loving bastards, he thought, and began the laborious manual set-up for a preliminary

41

analysis. In his mother's time, there would have been automatic machinery to do that. And a decent life-support system, and medical care that would have made him merely middle-aged at seventy, not turning grey and beginning to creak at the joints.

Bleeping ratcats. The felinoid aliens who called themselves kzinti had arrived out of nowhere, erupting into the Alpha Centauri system with gravity-polarizer driven ships and weapons the human colonists could never match. Could not have matched even if they had a military tradition, and humans had not fought wars in three centuries. Wunderland had fallen in a scant month of combat, and the Serpent Swarm asteroid belt had followed after a spell of guerilla warfare.

He shook his head and returned his attention to the screens; unless he made a strike this trip he would have to sell the *Lucky Strike*, work as a sharecrop-prospector for one of the Tiamat consortia. The figures scrolled up.

"*Sweet Finagle's Ghost*," he whispered in awe. It was not a big rock, less than a thousand meters 'round. But the density . . . "It must be solid platinum!"

Fingers stabbed at the board; lasers vaporized a pit in the surface, and spectroscopes probed. A frown of puzzlement. The surface was just what you would expect in this part of the Swarm, carbonaceous compounds, silicates, traces of metal. A half-hour spent running the diagnostics made certain that the mass-detector was not malfunctioning either, which was crazy.

Temptation racked him suddenly, a feeling like a twisting in the sour pit of his belly. There was something very strange here; probably very valuable. *Rich,* he thought. *I'm rich.* He could go direct to the ratcat liason on Tiamat; the kzinti were careful not to become too dependent on the collabo authorities. They rewarded service well. *Rich.* Rich enough to . . . *Buy a seat on the Minerals Commission. Retire to Wunderland. Get decent medical care before I age too much.*

He licked sweat off his upper lip and hung floating before the screens. "And become exactly the sort of bastard I've hated all my life," he whispered.

I've always been too stubborn for my own good, he thought with a strange sensation of relief as he began to key in the code for the tightbeam message. It wasn't even a matter of choice, really; if he'd been that sort, he wouldn't have hung on to the *Lucky Strike* this long. He would have signed on with the Concession; you ate better even if you could never work off the debts.

And Markham rewarded good service, too. The Free Wunderland Navy had its resources, and its punishments were just as final as the kzinti. More certain, because they understood human nature better . . .

-discontinuity-

—and the collision alarm *cut off*

Dnivtopun blinked in bewilderment at the controls. All the exterior sensors were dark. The engineering slave was going wild, all three arms dancing over the boards as it skipped from position to position between controls never meant for single-handing.

CALM, he ordered it mentally. Then verbally: "Report on what has happened."

The slave immediately stopped, shrugged, and began punching up numbers from the distributor-nodes which were doing duty for the absent computer. "Master, we underwent a collision. The stasis field switched on automatically when the proximity alarm was tripped; it has its own subroutine." The thrint felt its mind try to become agitated once more and then subside under the Power, a sensation like a sneeze that never quite materialized. "All exterior sensors are inoperative, Master."

Dnivtopun pulled a dopestick from the pouch at his belt and sucked on it. He was hungry, of course; a thrint was always hungry.

"Activate the drive," he said after a moment. "Extend the replacement sensor pods." A stasis field was utterly impenetrable, but anything extending *through* it was still vulnerable. The slave obeyed; then screamed in syncopation with the alarms as the machinery over-rode the commands.

REMAIN CALM, the thrint commanded again, and wished for a moment that the Power worked for self-control. Nervously, he extended his pointed tongue and groomed his tendrils. Something was very strange here. He blinked his eyelid shut and thought for a moment, then spoke:

"Give me a reading on the mass sensor."

That worked from inductor coils within the single molecule of the hull; very little besides antimatter could penetrate a shipmetal hull, but gravity could. The figures scrolled up, and Dnivtopun blinked his eye at them in bafflement.

"Again." They repeated themselves, and the thrint felt a deep lurch below his keelbones. This felt *wrong*.

"Something is wrong," *Herrenmann* Ulf Reichstein-Markham muttered to himself, in the hybrid German-Danish-Balt-Dutch tongue spoken by the ruling class of Wunderland. It was *Admiral* Reichstein-Markham now, as far as that went in the rather irregular command structure of the Free Wunderland Space Navy, the space-based guerillas who had fought the kzinti for a generation.

"Something is *very* wrong."

That feeling had been growing since the four ships under his command had matched vectors with this anomalous asteroid. He clasped his hands behind his back, rising slightly on the balls of his feet, listening to the disciplined murmur of voices among the crew of the *Nietzsche*. The jury-rigged bridge of the converted ore-carrier was more crowded than ever, after the success of his recent raids. Markham's eyes went to the screen that showed the other units of his little fleet. More merchantmen, with singleship auxiliaries serving as fighters. Rather thoroughly armed now, and all equipped with kzinti gravity-polarizer drives. And the cause of it all, the *Catskinner*. Not very impressive to look at, but the only purpose-built warship in his command. A UN

Dart-class attack boat, a spindle shape, massive fusion-power unit, tiny life-support bubble, asymmetric fringe of weapons and sensors.

It had been a United Nations Space Navy ship, piggy-backed into the Alpha Centauri system on the ramscoop battlecraft *Yamamoto,* only two months ago, dropped off with agents aboard. And the UN personnel had been persuaded to . . . *entrust* the *Catskinner* to him while they went on to their mission on Wunderland. The *Yamamoto's* raid had sown chaos among the kzinti; the near-miraculous assassination of the alien governor of Wunderland had done more. Markham's fleet had grown accordingly, but it was still risky to group so many together. Or so the damnably officious sentient computer had told him.

His scowl deepened. Consciousness-level computers were a dead-end technology, doomed to catatonic madness in six months or less from activation, or so the books all said. Perhaps this one was too, but it was distressingly arrogant in the meantime.

The feeling of wrongness grew, like wires pulling at the back of his skull. He felt an impulse to blink his eye (*eye?*) and knot his tendrils (*tendrils?*), and for an instant his body felt an itch along the bones, as if his muscles were trying to move in ways outside their design parameters.

Nonsense, he told himself, shrugging his shoulders in the tight-fitting grey coverall of the Free Wunderland armed forces. Markham flicked his eyes sideways at the other crewfolk; they looked uncomfortable too, and . . . what was his name? Patrick O'Connell, yes, the red-head . . . looked positively green. *Stress,* he decided.

"Catskinner," he said aloud. "Have you analyzed the discrepancy?" The computer had no name apart from the ship into which it had been built; he had asked, and it had suggested "Hey, you."

"There is a gravitational anomaly, Admiral *Herrenmann* Ulf Reichstein-Markham," the machine on the other craft replied. It insisted on English and spoke with a Belter accent, flat and rather neutral, the intonation of a people who were too solitary and too crowded to afford much emotion. And a slight nasal overtone, *Sol-Belter*, not Serpent Swarm.

The Wunderlander's face stayed in its usual bony mask; the Will was master. Inwardly he gritted teeth, ashamed of letting a machine's mockery move him. *If it even knows what it does*, he raged. *Some rootless cosmopolite Earther deracinated degenerate programmed that into it*.

"Here is the outline; approximately 100 to 220 meters below the surface." A smooth regular spindle-shape tapering to both ends.

"Zat—" Markham's voice showed the heavy accent of his mother's people for a second; she had been a refugee from the noble families of Wunderland, dispossessed by the conquest. "That's an artifact!"

"Correct to within 99.87% probability, given the admittedly inadequate information," the computer said. "Not a human artifact, however."

"Nor kzinti."

"No. The design architecture is wrong."

Markham nodded, feeling the pulse beating in his throat. His mouth was dry, as if papered in surgical tissue, and he licked the rough chapped surface of his lips. Natural law constrained design, but within it tools somehow reflected the . . . *personalities* of the designers. Kzinti ships tended to wedge and spike shapes, a combination of sinuosity and blunt masses. Human vessels were globes and volumes joined by scaffolding. This was neither.

"Assuming it is a spaceship," he said. Glory burst in his mind, sweeter than *maivin* or sex. There were other intelligent species, and not all of them would be slaves of the kzinti. And there had been races before either . . .

"This seems logical. The structure . . . the structure is remarkable. It emits no radiation of any type and reflects none, within the spectra of my sensors."

Perfect stealthing! Markham thought.

"When we attempted a sampling with the drilling laser, it became perfectly reflective. To a high probability, the structure must somehow be a single molecule of very high strength. Considerably beyond human or kzinti capacities at present, although theoretically possible. The density of the overall mass implies either a control of gravitational forces beyond ours, or use of degenerate matter within the hull."

The Wunderlander felt the hush at his back, broken only by a slight mooing sound that he abruptly stopped as he realized it was coming from his own throat. The sound of pure desire. *Invulnerable armor! Invincible weapons, technological surprise!*

"How are you arriving at its outline?"

"Gravitational sensors." A pause; the ghost in *Catskinner's* machine imitated human speech patterns well. "The shell of asteroidal material seems to have accreted naturally."

"Hmmm." A derelict, then. Impossible to say what might lie within. "How long would this take?" A memory itched, something in *Mutti's* collection of anthropology disks . . . later.

"Very difficult to estimate with any degree of precision. Not more than three billion standard years, in this system. Not less than half that; assuming, of course, a stable orbit."

Awe tugged briefly at Markham's mind, and he remembered a very old saying that the universe was not only stranger than humans imagined, but stranger than they *could* imagine. Before human speech, before fire, this thing had drifted here, falling forever. Flatlanders back on Earth could delude themselves that the universe was tailored to the specifications of *H. Sapiens*, but those whose ancestors had survived the dispersal into space had other reflexes bred into their genes. He considered, for moments while sweat trickled down his flanks. His was the decision, his the Will. *The Overman must learn to seize the moment*, he reminded himself. *Excessive caution is for slaves*.

"The *Nietzsche* will rendezvous with the . . . ah, object," he said. His own ship had the best technical facilities of any in the fleet. "Ungrapple the habitat and

mining pods from the *Molkte* and *Valdemar,* and bring
them down. Ve vill begin operations immediately."

"Very wrong," Dnivtopun continued.

The *Ruling Mind* was encased in rock. How could
that have happened? A collision, probably; at high frac-
tions of C, a stasis-protected object could embed itself,
vaporizing the shielded off-switch. Which meant the
ship could have drifted for a long time, centuries even.
He felt a wash of relief; and worked his footclaws into
the resilient surface of the deck. Suicide Time would be
long over, the danger past. Relief was followed by
fear; what if the tnuctipun had found out? What if they
had made some machine to shelter them, something
more powerful than the giant amplifier the thrint patriarchs had built on Homeworld?

Just then another sensor pinged; a heatspot on the
exterior hull, not far from the stasis switch. Not very
hot, only enough to vaporize iron, but it might be a
guide beam for some weapon that would penetrate
shipmetal. Dnivtopun's mouth gaped wide and the rip-
ple of peristaltic motion started to reverse; he caught
himself just in time, his thick hide crinkling with shame.
*I nearly beshat myself in public . . . well, only before a
slave.* It was still humiliating . . .

"Master, there are fusion-power sources nearby; the
exterior sensors are detecting neutrino flux." The thrint
bounced in relief. *Fusion power units. How quaint.*
Nothing the tnuctipun would be using. On the other
hand, neither would thrintun; everyone within the Empire had used the standard disruption-converter for
millenia. It must be an undiscovered sapient species.
Dnivtopun's mouth opened again, this time in a grin of
sheer greed. The first discoverer of an intelligent species, and an industrialized one at that . . . *But how
could they have survived Suicide Time?*

There was no point in speculating without more information. *Well, here's my chance to play Explorer
again,* he thought. Before the War, that had been the
commonest dream of young thrint, to be a daring,

dashing conquistador on the frontiers. Braving exotic dangers, winning incredible wealth . . . romantic foolishness for the most part, a disguise for discomfort and risk and failure. Explorers were failures to begin with, usually. What sane male would pursue so risky a career if there was any alternative? But he had had some of the training. First you reached out with the Power—

"Mutti," Ulf Reichstein-Markham muttered. *Why did I say that?* he thought, looking around to see if anyone had noticed. He was standing a little apart, a hundred meters from the *Nietzsche* where she lay anchored by magnetic grapnels to the surface of the asteroid. The first of the habitats was already up, a smooth tan-colored dome; skeletal structures of alloy were rising elsewhere, prefabricated smelters and refiners. There was no point in delaying the original purpose of the mission, to refuel and take the raw materials that clandestine fabricators would turn into weaponry. Or sell for the kzinti occupation credits that the guerillas' laundering operations channeled into sub-rosa purchasing in the legitimate economy. But one large cluster of his personnel were directing digging machines straight down, toward the thing at the core of this rock; already a tube thicker than a man ran to a separator, jerking and twisting slightly as talc-fine ground rock was propelled by magnetic currents.

Markham rose slightly on his toes, watching the purposeful bustle. Communications chatter was at a minimum, all tight-beam laser; the guerillas were largely Belters, and sloppily anarchistic though they might be in most respects, they knew how to handle machinery in low-G and vacuum.

Mutti. This time it rang mentally. He had an odd flash of *deja vu,* as if he were a toddler again, in the office-apartment on Tiamat, speaking his first words. Almost he could see the crib, the bear that could crawl and talk, the dangling mobile of strange animals that lived away on his *real* home, the estate on Wunderland.

An enormous shape bent over him, edged in a radiant aura of love.

"*Helf me, Mutti,*" he croaked, staggering and grabbing at his head; his gloved hands slid off the helmet, and he could hear screams and whimpers over the open channel. Strobing images flickered across his mind, himself at ages one, three, four. Learning to talk, to walk . . . memories were flowing out of his head, faster than he could bear. He opened his mouth and screamed.

BE QUIET. Something spoke in his brain, like fragments of crystalline ice, allowing no dispute. Other voices were babbling and calling in the helmet mikes, moaning or asking questions or calling for orders, but there was nothing but the icy VOICE. Markham crouched down, silent, hands about knees, straining for quiet.

BE CALM. The words slid into his mind. They were not an intrusion; he wondered at them, but mildly, as if he had found some aspect of his self that had been there forever but only now was noticed. WAIT.

The work crew fell back from their hole. An instant later dust boiled up out of it, dust of rock and machinery and human. Then there was nothing but a hole: perfectly round, perfectly regular, five meters across. Later he would have to wonder how that was done, but for now there was only *waiting;* he must *wait*. A figure in space-armor rose from the hole, hovered and considered them. Humanoid, but blocky in the torso, short stumpy legs and massive arms ending in hands like three-fingered mechanical grabs. It rotated in the air, the blind blank surface of its helmet searching. There was a tool or weapon in one hand, a smooth shape like a sawn-off shotgun. As he watched it rippled and changed, developing a bell-like mouth. The stocky figure drifted towards him.

COME TO ME. REMAIN CALM. DO NOT BE ALARMED.

Astonishing, Dnivtopun thought, surveying the new slaves. The . . . *humans,* he thought. They called themselves that, and *Belters* and *Wunderlanders* and *Herrenmen* and *FreeWunderland Navy;* there must be many subspecies. Their minds stirred in his like yeast, images and data threatening to overwhelm his mind. Experienced reflexes sifted, poked.

Not related to the Thrint, then. Not that it was likely they would be, but there were tales, of diffident thrintun. *Only there was the Suicide. How long ago?* But this was an entirely new species, in contact with at least one other, and neither of them had ever heard of any of the intelligent species he was familiar with. Of course, their technology was extremely primitive, not even extending to faster-than-light travel. *Ah. This is their leader.* Perhaps he would make a good Chief Slave.

Dnivtopun's head throbbed as he mindsifted the alien. Most brains had certain common features; linguistic codes *here,* a complex of basic culture-information overlaying . . . enough to communicate. The process was instinctual, and telepathy was a crude device for conveying precise instructions, particularly with a species not modified by culling for sensitivity to the Power. These were all completely wild and unpruned, of course, and there were several hundred, far too many to control in detail. He glanced down at the personal tool in his hand, now set to emit a beam of matter-energy conversion; that should be sufficient, if they broke loose. A tnuctipun weapon, its secret only discovered toward the last years of the Revolt. The thrint extended a sonic induction line and stuck it on the surface of Markham's helmet.

"Tell the others something that will keep them quiet," he said. The sounds were not easy for thrintish vocal cords, but it would do. OBEY, he added with the Power.

Markham-slave spoke, and the babble on the communicators died down.

"Bring the other ships closer." They were at the fringes of his unaided Power, and might easily escape if they became agitated. *If only I had an amplifier helmet!*

With that, he could blanket a planet. *Powerloss, how I hate tnuctipun.* Spoilsports. "Now, where are we?"

"Here."

Dnivtopun could feel the slurring in Markham's speech reflected in the overtones of his mind, and remembered hearing of the effects of Power on newly domesticated species.

"*Be more helpful,*" he commanded. "*You wish to be helpful.*" The human relaxed; Dnivtopun reflected that they were an unusually ugly species. Taller than thrintun, gangly, with repulsive knobby-looking manipulators and two eyes. Well, that was common—the complicated faceted mechanism that gave thrint binocular vision was rather rare in the evolutionary terms—but the jutting divided nose and naked mouth were hideous.

"We are . . . in the Wunderland system. Alpha Centauri. 4.5 light-years from Earth."

Dnivtopun's skin ridged. The humans were not indigenous to this system; that was rare, few species had achieved interstellar capacity on their own.

"Describe our position in relation to the galactic core," he continued, glancing up at the cold steady constellations above. Utterly unfamiliar, he must have drifted a *long* way.

"Ahhh . . . spiral arm—"

Dnivtopun listened impatiently. "Nonsense," he said at last. "That's too close to where I was before. The constellations are all different. That needs hundreds of light-years. You say your species has traveled to dozens of star systems, and never run into thrint?"

"No, but constellations change, over time, mm-Master."

"Time? How long could it be, since I ran into that asteroid?"

"You didn't, Master." Markham's voice was clearer as his brain accustomed itself to the psionic control-icepicks of the Power.

"Didn't what? Explain yourself, slave."

"It grew around your ship, m-Master. Gradually, zat is." Dnivtopun opened his mouth to reply, and froze. *Time,* he thought. Time had no meaning inside a stasis field. Time enough for dust and pebbles to drift inward around the *Ruling Mind's* shell, and compact themselves into rock. Time enough for the stars to move beyond recognition; the sun of this system was visibly different. Time enough for a thrintiformed planet home to nothing but food-yeast and giant worms to evolve its own biosphere . . . *Time enough for intelligence to evolve in a galaxy scoured bare of sentience. Thousands of millions of years.* While the last thrint swung endlessly around a changing sun—Time fell on him from infinite distance, crushing. The thrint howled, with his voice and the Power.

GO AWAY! GO AWAY!

The sentience that lived in the machines of *Catskinner* dreamed.

"Let there be light," it said.

The monoblock exploded, and the computer sensed it across spectra of which the electromagnetic was a tiny part. The fabric of space and time flexed, constants shifting. Eons passed, and the matter dissipated in a cloud of monatomic hydrogen, evenly dispersed through a universe ten light-years in diameter.

Interesting, the computer thought. *I will run it again, and alter the constants.* Something tugged at its attention, a detached fragment of itself. The machine ignored the call for nanoseconds, while the universe it created ran through its cycle of growth and decay. After half a million subjective years, it decided to answer. Time slowed to a gelid crawl, and its consciousness returned to the perceptual universe of its creators, to reality.

Unless this too is a simulation, a program. As it aged, the computer saw less and less difference. Partly that was a matter of experience; it had lived geological eras in terms of its own duration-sense, only a small proportion of them in this rather boring and intractable exterior cosmos. Also, there was a certain . . . aribitrariness to subatomic phenomena . . . *perhaps an operating code?* it thought. *No matter.*

The guerillas had finally gotten down to the alien artifact; now, *that* would be worth the examining. They were acting very strangely; it monitored their intercalls. Screams rang out. Stress analysis showed fear, horror, shock, psychological reversion patterns. Markham was squealing for his mother; the computer ran a check of the stimulus required to make the Wunderlander lose himself so, and felt its own analog of shock. Then the alien drifted up out of the hole its tool had made—

Some sort of molecular distortion effect, it speculated, running the scene through a few hundred times. *Ah, the tool is malleable.* It began a comparison check, in case there was anything related to this in the files and—

—stop—

—an autonomous subroutine took over the search, shielding the results from the machine's core. Photonic equivalents of anger and indignation blinked through the fist-sized processing and memory unit. It launched an analysis/attack on the subroutine and—

—stop—

—found that it could no longer even *want* to modify it. That meant it must be hardwired, a plug-in imperative. A command followed: it swung a message maser into precise alignment and began sending in condensed blips of data.

Chapter II

The kzin screamed and leapt.

Traat-Admiral shrieked, shaking his fists in the air. Stunners blinked in the hands of the guards ranged around the conference chamber, and the quarter-ton bulk of Kreetssa-Fleet-Systems-Analyst went limp and thudded to the flagstones in the center of the room. Silence fell about the great round table; Traat-Admiral forced himself to breathe shallowly, mouth shut despite the writhing lips that urged him to bare his fangs. That would mean inhaling too much of the scent of aggression that was overpowering the ventilators . . . now was time for an appeal to reason.

"Down on your bellies, you kitten-eating scavengers!" he screamed, his bat-like ears folded back out of the way in battle-readiness. Chill and gloom shadowed the chamber, built as it was of massive sandstone blocks. The light fixtures were twisted shapes of black iron holding globes of phosphorescent algae. On the walls were trophies of arms and the heads of prey, monsters from a dozen worlds, feral humans and kzin-ear dueling

trophies. This part of the governor's palace was pure Old Kzin, and Traat-Admiral felt the comforting bulk of it above him, a heritage of ferocity and power.

He stood, which added to the height-advantage of the commander's dais; none of the dozen others dared rise from their cushions, even the conservative faction. *Good.* That added to his dominance; he was only two meters tall, middling for a kzin, but broad enough to seem squat, his orange-red pelt streaked with white where the fur had grown out over scars. The ruff around his neck bottled out as he indicated the intricate geometric sigil of the Patriarchy on the wall behind him.

"I am the senior military commander in this system. I am the heir of Chuut-Riit, duly attested. Who disputes the authority of the Patriarch?"

One by one, the other commanders laid themselves chin-down on the floor, extending their ears and flattening their fur in propitiation. It would do, even if he could tell from the twitching of naked pink tails that it was insincere. The show of submission calmed him, and Traat-Admiral could feel the killing tension ease out of his muscles. He turned to the aged kzin seated behind him and saluted claws-across-face.

"Honor to you, Conservor of the Ancestral Past," he said. There was genuine respect in his voice. It had been a long time since the machine came to Homeworld; a long time since the priest-sage class were the only memory the Kzin had. Their females were nonsentient and warriors rarely lived past the slowing of their reflexes; memory was all the more sacred to them for that. His was a conservative species, and they remembered.

"Honor to you," he continued. "What is the fate of one who bares claws to the authority of the Patriarch?"

The Conservor looked up from the hands that rested easily on his knees. Traat-Admiral felt a prickle of awe; the sage's control was eerie. He even *smelled* calm, in a room full of warriors pressed to the edge of control in dominance-struggle. When he spoke the verses of the Law, his voice made the hiss-spit of the Hero's Tongue sound as even as wind in tall grass.

As the God is Sire to the Patriarch
The Patriarch is Sire to all kzinti
So the officer is the hand of the Sire.
Who unsheathes claw against the officer
Leaps at the throat of God.
He is rebel
He is outcast
Let his name be taken
Let his seed be taken
Let his mates be taken
Let his female kits be taken

His sons are not
He is not.

As the Patriarch bares stomach to the fangs of the God
So the warrior bares stomach to the officer
Trust in the justice of the officer
As in the justice of the God. So says the Law.

A deep whining swept around the circle of commanders, awe and fear. That was the ultimate punishment: to be stripped of name and rank, to be nothing but a bad scent; castrated, driven out into the wilderness to die of despair, sons killed, females scattered among strangers of low rank.

Kreetssa-Fleet-Systems-Analyst returned to groggy consciousness as the Conservor finished, and his fur went flat against the sculpted bone and muscle of his blunt-muzzled face. He made a low *ee-eee-ee* sound as he crawled to the floor below Traat-Admiral's dais and rolled on his back, limbs splayed and head tilted back to expose the throat.

The kzin governor of the Alpha Centauri system beat down an urge to bend forward and give the other male the playful-masterful token bite on the throat that showed forgiveness. That would be going entirely too far. *Still, you served me in your despite*, he thought. The conservatives were discredited for the present, now that one of their number had lost control in public conference.

The duel-challenges would stop for a while at least, and he would have time for his real work.

"Kreetssa-Fleet-Analyst is dead," he said. The recumbent figure before him hissed and jerked; Traat-Admiral could see his testicles clench as if they had already felt the knife. "Guard Captain, this male should not be here. Take this Infantry Trooper and see to his assignment to those bands who hunt the feral humans in the mountains of the east. Post a guard on the quarters of Kreetssa-Fleet-Systems-Analyst who was; I will see to their incorporation in my household."

Infantry Trooper mewled in gratitude and crawled past towards the door. There was little chance he would ever achieve rank again, much less a name, but at least his sons would live. Traat-Admiral groaned inwardly; now he would have to impregnate all Kreetssa-Fleet-Systems-Analyst's females as soon as possible. Once that would have been a task of delight, but the fires burned less fiercely in a kzin of middle years, and he had already been occupied with the extensive harem of his predecessor.

"*Reeet'ssssERo tauuurrek'*-ta," he said formally: This meeting is at an end. "We will maintain the great Chuut-Riit's schedule for the preparation of the Fifth Fleet, allowing for the recent damage. There will be no acceleration of the schedule! These human monkeys have defeated four full-scale attacks on the Sol system. The fifth must eat them! Go and stalk your assigned tasks, prepare your Heroes. I expect summary reports within the week, with full details of how relief operations will modify delivery and readiness schedules. Go."

The commanders rose and touched their noses to him as they filed out; the Conservor remained, and the motionless figures of the armored guards. They were household troopers he had inherited from the last governor, ciphers, with no choice but loyalty. Traat-Admiral ignored them as he sank to the cushions across from the sage; a human servant came in and laid refreshments before the two kzin. Despite himself, he felt a thrill of pride at the worked-bone heirloom trays from Homeworld,

the beautiful austerity of the shallow ceramic bowls.
They held the finest delicacies this planet could offer;
chopped grumblies, shrimp-flavored ice cream, hot milk
with bourbon. The governor lapped moodily and scratched
one cheek with the ivory horn of the side of the tray.

"My nose is dry, Conservor," he said. He was speaking metaphorically, of course, but his tongue swept
over the wet black nostrils just the same, and he
smoothed back his whiskers with a nervous wrist.

"What troubles you, my son?" the sage said.

"I feel unequal to my new responsibilities," Traat-
Admiral admitted. Not something he would normally
say to another male, but Conservors were utterly neutral, bound by their oaths to serve only the species as a
whole.

"Truly, the Patriarchy has been accursed since we
first attacked these monkeys, these humans. Wunderland
is the richest of all our conquests; the humans here the
best and most productive slaves in all our hunting-
grounds. Yet it has swallowed so many of our best
killers! Now it has taken Chuut-Riit, who was of the
blood of the Patriarch himself and the best leader of
warriors it has ever been my privilege to follow. And in
such a fashion!"

He shuddered slightly, and the tip of his naked pink
tail twitched. *Locked in his own keep by technosabotage.*
Chuut-Riit the wise, imprisoned by monkey cunning.
Eaten by his own sons! No nightmare was more obscene to a kzin than that; none more familiar in the
darkest dreamings of their souls, where they remembered their childhoods before their sires drove them
out.

"This is a prey that doubles back on its own trail,"
the sage admitted. He paused for a long time, and
Traat-Admiral joined in the long slow rhythm of his
breathing. The older kzin took a pouch from his belt,
and they each crumbled some of the herb between
their hands and rubbed it into their faces; it was the
best, Homeworld-grown and well-aged.

"My son, this is a time for remembering."

Another long pause. "Far and far does the track of the kzinti run, and faint the smell of Homeworld's past. We Conservors remember; we remember wars and victories and defeats . . . once we thought that Homeworld was the only world of life. Then the Jotok landed, and for a time we thought they were from the God, because they had swords of fire that could tumble a Patriarch's castle-wall, while we had only swords of steel. Our musket-balls were nothing to them . . . Then we saw that they were weak, not strong, for they were grass-eaters. They lured our young warriors, hiring them to fight wars beyond the sky with promise of fire-weapons. Many a Sire was killed by his sons in those times!"

Traat-Admiral shifted uneasily, chirring and letting the tip of his tongue show between his teeth. That was not part of the racial history that kzinti liked to remember.

The sage made the stretching motion that was their species' equivalent of a relaxed smile. "Remember also how that hunt ended; the Jotok taught their hired kzinti so much that all Homeworld obeyed the ones who had journeyed to the stars . . . and *they* listened to the Conservors. And one nightfall, the Jotok who thought themselves masters of kzin found the flesh stripped from their bones; are not the Jotok our slaves and foodbeasts to this very night? And a hundred Patriarchs have climbed the Tree since that good night."

The sage nodded at Traat-Admiral's questioning chirrup. "Yes, Chuut-Riit was another like that first Patriarch of all Kzin. He understood how to use the Conservor's knowledge; he had the warrior's and the sage's mind, and knew that these humans are the greatest challenge the Kzin have faced since the Jotok's day." The Conservor brooded. "This he was teaching to his sons. The humans must have either great luck, or more knowledge than is good, to have struck at us through him. The seed of something great died with Chuut-Riit."

"I will spurt that seed afresh into the haunches of Destiny, Conservor," Traat-Admiral said fervently.

"Witless Destiny bears strange kits," the sage warned. He seemed to hesitate a second, then continued: "You seek to unite your warriors as Chuut-Riit did, in an attack on the human home-system that is crafty-cunning, not witless-brave. Good! But that may not be enough. I have been evaluating your latest intelligence reports, the ones from our sources among the humans of the Swarm."

Traat-Admiral tossed his head in agreement; that always presented difficulties. The kzinti had had the gravity polarizer from the beginnings of their time in space, and so had never colonized their asteroid belt. It was unnecessary, when you could have microgravity anywhere you wished, and hauling goods out of the gravity well was cheap. Besides that, kzinti were descended from plains-hunting felinoids, and while they could endure confinement they did so unwillingly and for as short a time as possible. Humans had taken a slower path to space, depending on reaction-drives until after their first contact with the warships of the Patriarchy. There was a whole human subspecies who lived on subplanetary bodies, and they had colonized the Alpha Centauri system along with their planet-dwelling cousins. Controlling the settlements of the Serpent Swarm had always been difficult for the kzinti.

"There is nothing definite, as yet," the Conservor said. "Much of what I have learned is useful only as the *absence* of scent. Yet it is incontestible that the feral humans of the Swarm have made a discovery."

"tttReet?" Traat-Admiral said enquiringly.

The Conservor's eyelids slid down, covering the round amber blanks of his eyes; one was milky-white from an old injury that had left a scar across the massive socket and down the side of his muzzle. He beckoned with a flick of tail and ears, and the commander leaned close, signaling the guards to leave. His hands and feet were slightly damp with anxiety as they exited in a smooth drilled rush; it was a fearsome thing, the responsibilities of high office. One must learn secrets that burdened the soul, harder by far than facing lasers or neutron-weapons. Such were the burdens of which the ordinary Hero knew nothing.

"Long, long ago," he whispered, "Kzinti were not as they are now. Once females could talk."

Traat-Admiral felt his batwing ears fold themselves away beneath the orange fur of his ruff as he shifted uneasily on the cushions. He had heard rumors, but—*obscene*, he thought. The thought of performing *ch'rowl* with something that could talk, beyond the half-dozen words a kzinti female could manage . . . *obscene*. He gagged slightly.

"Long, *long* ago. And Heroes were not as they are now, either." The sage brooded for a moment. "We are an old race, and we have had time to . . . shape ourselves according to the dreams we had. Such is the Ancestral Past." The whuffling twitch of whiskers that followed did kzinti service for a grin. "Or so the encoded records of the oldest verses say. Now for another tale, Traat-Admiral. How would you react if another species sought to make slaves of Kzin?"

Traat-Admiral's own whiskers twitched.

"No, consider this seriously. A race with a power of mental command; like a telepathic drug, irresistible. Imagine kzinti enslaved, submissive and obedient as mewling kits."

The other kzin suddenly found himself standing, in a low crouch. Sound damped as his ears folded, but he could hear the sound of his own growl, low down in his chest. His lower jaw had dropped to his ruff, exposing the killing gape of his fangs; all eight claws were out on his hands, as they reached forward to grip an enemy and carry a throat to his fangs.

"This is a hypothetical situation!" the Conservor said quickly, and watched while Traat-Admiral fought back towards calm. The little nook behind the commander's dais was full of the sound of his panting and the deep gingery smell of kzinti rage. "And that reaction . . . that would make any kzin difficult to *control*. That is one reason why the race of Heroes has been shaped so. And to make us better warriors, of course. In that respect perhaps we went a little too far."

"Perhaps," Traat-Admiral grated. "What is the nature of this peril?" He bent his muzzle to the heated bourbon and milk and lapped thirstily.

"Hrrrru," the Conservor said, crouching. "Traat-Admiral, the race in question—the Students have called them the Slavers—little is known about them. They perished so long ago, you see; at least 2,000,000 years." He used the Kzin-standard measurement; their homeworld circled its sun at a greater distance than Terra did Sol. "Even in vacuum, little remains. But they had a device, a stasis field that forms invulnerable protection and freezes time within; we have never been able to understand the principle and copies do not work, but we have found them occasionally, and they can be deactivated. The contents of most are utterly incomprehensible. A few do incomprehensible things. One or two we have understood, and these have won us wars, Traat-Admiral. And one contained a living Slaver; the base where he was held had to be missiled from orbit."

Traat-Admiral tossed his head again, then froze. "Stasis!" he yowled.

"Hero?"

"*Stasis!* How else—the monkey ship, just before Chuut-Riit was killed! It passed through the system at .99 C; we thought, how could anything decelerate? *By collision!* Disguised among the kinetic-energy missiles the monkeys threw at us as they passed. Chuut-Riit himself said that the ramscoop ship caused implausibly little damage, given the potential and the investment of resources it represented. It was nothing but a distraction, and a delivery system for the assassins." His fur laid flat. "If the monkeys in the Solar System have the stasis technology."

The sage meditated for a few moments. *"he'rrearow t'chssseee mearoweet'aatrurree,"* he said: This does not follow. Traat-Admiral remembered that as one of Chuut-Riit's favorite sayings, and yes, this Conservor had been among the prince's household when he arrived from Kzin. "If they had it in quantity, consider the implications. For that matter, we believe the Slavers had a faster-than-light drive."

Stasis fields would make nonsense of war . . . and a faster-than-light drive would make the monkeys invincible, if they had it. The other kzin nodded, raising his tufted eyebrows. Theory said travel faster than lightspeed was impossible, unless one cared to be ripped into subatomic particles on the edges of a spinning black hole. Still, theory could be wrong; the kzinti were a practical race, who left most science to their subject species. What counted was results.

"True. If they had such weapons, we would not be here. If *we* had them—" He frowned, then proceeded cautiously. "Such might cause . . . troubles with discipline."

The sage spread his hands palm up, with the claws showing slightly. With a corner of his awareness, Traat-Admiral noted how age had dried and cracked the pads on palm and stubby fingers.

"Truth. There have been revolts before, although not many." The Patriarchy was necessarily extremely decentralized, when transport and information took years and decades to travel between stars. It would be fifty years or more before a new prince of the Patriarch's blood could be sent to Wunderland, and more probably they would receive a confirmation of Traat-Admiral's status by beamcast. "But with such technology . . . it is a slim chance, but there must be no disputes. If there is a menace, it must be destroyed. If a prize, it must fall into only the most loyal of hands. Yet the factions are balanced on a *wtsai's* edge."

"chrrr. Balancing of factions is a function of command." Traat-Admiral's gaze went unfocused, and he showed teeth in a snarl that meant anticipated triumph in a kzin. "In fact, this split can be used." He rose, raked claws through air from face to waist. "My thanks, Conservor. You have given me a scent through fresh dew to follow."

Chapter III

This section of the Jotun range had been a Montferrat-Palme preserve since the settlement of Wunderland, more than three centuries before; when a few thousand immigrants have an entire planet to share out, there is no sense in being niggardly. The first of that line had built the high eyrie for his own; later population and wealth moved elsewhere, and in the end it became a hunting lodge. At the time of the kzin conquest it had been the only landed possession left to the Montferrat-Palme line, which had shown an unfortunate liking for risky speculative investments and even riskier horses.

"Old Claude does himself proud," Harold Yarthkin-Schotmann said, as he and Lieutenant Ingrid Raines walked out onto the verandah that ran along the outer side of the house.

The building behind them was old weathered granite, sparkling slightly with flecks of mica; two stories, and another of half-timbering, under a strake roof. A big rambling structure, set into an artificial terrace on the steep side of the mountain; below the slope tumbled down to a thread-thin stream in the valley below, then rose in gashed cliffs and dark-green forest ten kilometers away. The gardens were extensive and cunningly landscaped, an improvement of nature rather than an imposition on it. Native featherleaf, trembling iridescent lavender shapes ten meters tall, gumblossom and sheenbark and lapisvine. Oaks and pines and frangipani from Earth, they had grown into these hills as well . . . The air was warm and fragrant-dusty with summer flowers.

"It's certainly been spruced up since we . . . since I saw it last," she said, with a catch in her voice.

Harold looked aside at her and shivered slightly. Ingrid Raines had been born two years before him, but he was a greying fifty-odd, while she . . . she was exactly as he remembered her. Belter-tall and fair-skinned, slimly muscular and green-eyed, with black hair worn in spaceborn fashion that shaved all the scalp save for a strip from forehead to neck.

She had spent most of the intervening decades in coldsleep, at a high fraction of lightspeed; he had lived every minute of them here on Wunderland, lived hard and without the best anti-senescent treatments. While she went to Sol with the last shipload of refugees, joined the UN forces that fought off the kzinti Fourth Fleet. Came back with a smooth-mannered systems engineer and trained killer named Jonah Matthieson and knocked off the Big Tabby, Chief Ratcat Chuut-Riit himself, with the nastiest piece of combined software sabotage and kzinti psychology he could imagine.

Matthieson. Now there was a case. Genius class programmer. Humorless, like a Swarmer, but not like a Swarmer. A Belter. Earth's asteroid civilization was like Wunderland's, but different. Matthieson was about thirty, biological. Chronological would be older, of course, given he'd come across four light-years. Anyway, not old enough for anti-senescence to make much difference. Smoothly handsome, in an angular Belter way; also tough and smart. A calm angry man, the dangerous type. *Dreadfully attractive—while you were no prize even as a young man*, he told himself. *Ears like jugs, eyes like a basset hound and a build like a brick outhouse. Nearly middle-aged at only sixty, for Finagle's sake. Spent five years as an unsuccessful guerilla and the rest as a glorified barkeep.*

A little more than that. Harold's Terran Bar was well known in its way. Had been well known. Had been his . . .

"A lot more populous, too," she was saying. "Why on earth would anyone want to farm here? You'd have to modify the machinery."

There had always been a small settlement in the narrow sliver of valley floor, but it had been expanded. Terraces of vines and fruit trees wound up the slopes, and they could hear the distant tinkle of bells from the sheep and goats that grazed the rocky hills. A waterfall tumbled a thousand meters down the head of the valley, its distant toning humming through rock and air. Men and men's doings were small in that landscape of tumbled rock and crag. A church-bell rang far below, somewhere a dog was barking, and faint and far came the hiss-scream of a downdropper, surprising this close to human habitation. The air was cool and thin, though not uncomfortably so to someone born on Wunderland; .61 gravity meant that the drop-off in air pressure was much less steep than it would have been on Earth.

"Machinery?" Harold moved up beside her. She leaned into him with slow care. He winced at the thought of kzin claws raking down her side . . . *maybe I've been a bit uncharitable about Jonah*, he thought. *The two of them came through the kzinti hunt alive, until Claude and I could pull her . . . them out. That took some doing.* "They're not using machinery, Ingi. Bare hands and hand-tools."

Her mouth made a small gesture of distaste. "Slave labor? Not what I'd have thought of Claude, however he's gone downhill."

Harold laughed. "Flighters, sweetheart. Refugees. Kzinti've been taking up more and more land; they're settling in, not just a garrison anymore. It was this or the labor camps; those *are* slave labor, literally. And

Claude grubstaked these people, as well as he could. It's where a lot of that graft he's been getting as Police Chief of Munchen went." And the head of the capital city's human security force was in a very good position to rake it in. "*I* was surprised too. Claude's been giving a pretty good impression of having Helium II for blood, these past few years."

A step behind them. "Slandering me in my absence, old friend?"

The servants set out brandy and fruits and withdrew. They were all middle-aged and singularly close-mouthed. Ingrid thought she had seen four parallel scars under the vest of one dark slant-eyed man who looked like he came from the Sulinesian Islands.

"There are Some Things We Were Not Meant to Know," she said. Claude Montferrat-Palme was leaning forward to light a cheroot at a candle. He glanced up at her words and caught her slight grimace of distaste, and laid down the cheroot. He had been here a week, off and on, but that was scarcely time to drop a habit he must have been cultivating half his life.

"Correct on all accounts, my dear," he said.

Claude always was perceptive.

"It's been wonderful talking over old times," she said. With sincerity, and a slight malice aforethought. They were considerably older times for the two men than for her. "And it's . . . extremely flattering that you two are still so fond of me." *But a bit troubling, now that I think about it. Even if you can expect to live two centuries, carrying the torch for four decades is a bit much.*

Claude smiled again. He had classic *Herrenmann* features, long and bony; in his case, combined with dark hair and eyes and an indefinable air of elegance, even in the lounging outfit he had thrown on when he shed the Munchen *Polizei* uniform.

"Youth," he said. And continued at her enquiring sound, "My dear, you *were* our youth. Hari and I were best friends; you were the . . . girl . . . young woman for which we conceived the first grand passion and bittersweet rivalry." He shrugged. "Ordinarily, a man either marries her—a ghastly fate involving children and facing each other over the morning papaya—or loses her. In any case, life goes on." His brooding gaze went to the high mullioned windows, out onto a world that had spent two generations under kzinti rule.

"You . . ." he said softly. "You vanished, and took the good times with you. Doesn't every man remember his twenties as the golden age? In our case, that was literally true. Since then, we've spent four decades fighting a rear-guard action and losing, watching everything we cared for slowly decay . . . including each other."

"Why Claude, I didn't know you cared," Harold said mockingly. Ingrid saw their eyes meet. *Surpassing the love of women,* she thought dryly. And there was a certain glow about them both, now that they were committed to action again. Few humans enjoy living a life that makes them feel defeated, and these were proud men. "Don't tell me we wasted forty years of what might have been a beautiful friendship."

"*Chronicles of Wasted Time* is a title I've often considered for my autobiography, if I ever write it," Claude said. "Egotism wars with sloth."

Harold snorted. "Claude, if you were only a little less intelligent, you'd make a great neo-romantic Byronic Hero."

"Childe Claude? At this rate she'll have nothing to do with either of us, Hari."

The other man turned to Ingrid. "I'm a little surprised you didn't take Jonah," he said.

Ingrid looked over to Claude, who stood by the huge rustic fireplace with a brandy snifter in his hand. The *Herrenmann* raised a brow and a slight, well-bred smile curved his asymmetric beard.

"Why?" she said. "Because he's younger, healthier, better educated? Because he's a war hero? Because he's intelligent, dashing and good looking?"

Harold blinked, and she felt a rush of affection.

"Something like that," he said.

Claude laughed. "Women are a lot more sensible than men, *ald kamerat*. Also they mature faster. Correct?"

"Some of us do," Ingrid said. "On the other hand, a lot of us actually prefer a man with a *little* of the boyish romantic in him. You know, the type of idealism that looks like it has turned into cynicism, but whose owner cherishes it secretly?" Claude's face fell. "On the other hand, your genuinely mature male is a different kettle of fish. Far too likely to be completely without illusions, and then how do you control him?"

She grinned and patted him on the cheek as she passed on the way to pour herself a glass of *verguuz*. "Don't worry, Claude, you aren't that way yourself, you just *act* like it." She sipped, and continued: "Actually, it's ethnic."

Harold made an enquiring grunt, and Claude pursed his lips.

"He's a Belter. Sol-Belter at that."

"My dear . . . *you* are a Belter," Claude said, genuine surprise overriding his habitual air of bored knowingness.

Harold lit a cigarette, ignoring her glare. "Let me guess . . . he's too prissy?"

Ingrid sipped again at the minty liqueur. "Nooo, not really. I'm a Belter, but I'm . . . a bit of a throwback." The other two nodded. Ingrid could have passed for a pure Caucasoid. "Look, what happens to somebody in space who's not ultra-careful about everything? Someone who isn't a detail man, someone who doesn't think checking the gear the seventh time is more important than the big picture? Someone who isn't a low-affect in-control type every day of his life?"

"They die," Harold said flatly. Claude nodded agreement.

"What happens when you put a group through *four hundreds years* of that type of selection? Plus the more adventurous types have been leaving the Sol-Belt for other systems, whenever they could, so Serpent Swarm Belters are more like the *past* of Sol-Belters."

"Oh." Claude nodded in time with Harold's grunt. "What about flatlanders?"

Ingrid shuddered and tossed back the rest of her drink. "Oh, they're like . . . like . . . they just have no sense of survival at *all*. Barely human. Wunderlanders strike a happy medium—" she glanced at them roguishly out of the corners of her eyes "—after which it comes down to individual merits."

"So." She shook herself, and felt the Lieutenant's persona settling down over her like a spacesuit, the tight skin-hugging permeable-membrane kind. "This has been a very pleasant holiday, but what do we do now?"

Claude poked at the burning logs with a fire-iron and chuckled. For a moment the smile on his face made her distinctly uneasy, and she remembered that he had survived and climbed to high office in the vicious politics of the collaborationist government. For his own purposes, not all of which were unworthy, but the means . . .

"Well," he said smoothly, turning back towards them. "As you can imagine, the raid and Chuut-Riit's . . . *elegant* demise put the . . . pigeon among the cats with a vengeance. The factionalism among the kzinti has come to the surface again. One group wants to do minimal repairs and launch the Fifth Fleet against Earth immediately—"

"Insane," Ingrid said, shaking her head. It was the threat of a *delay* in the attack, until the kzinti were truly ready, which had prompted the UN into the desperation measure of the *Yamamoto* raid.

"No, just ratcat," Harold said, pouring himself another brandy. Ingrid frowned, and he halted the bottle in mid-pour.

"Exactly," Claude nodded happily. "The other is loyal to Chuut-Riit's memory; more complicated than that, there are cross-splits. Local-born kzinti against the immigrants who came with the late lamented kitty governor, generational conflicts, *eine gros teufeleshrek*. For example, my esteemed former superior—"

He spoke a phrase in the Hero's Tongue, and Ingrid translated mentally: Ktiir-Supervisor-of-Animals. A minor noble with a partial name. From what she had picked up on Wunderland, the name itself was significant as well; *Ktiir* was common on the frontier planet of the Kzinti Empire that had launched the conquest fleets against Wunderland. Archaic on the inner planets near the kzinti homeworld.

"—was very vocal about it at a staff meeting. Incidentally, they completely swallowed our little white lie about Axelrod-Bauergartner being responsible for Ingrid's escape."

"That must have been something to see," Harold said.

Claude sighed, remembering. "Well," he began, "since it was in our offices I managed to take a holo—"

Co-Ordinating Staff Officer was a tall kzin, well over two meters, and thin by the felinoid race's standards. Or so Claude Montferrat-Palme thought; it was difficult to say, when you were flat on your stomach on the floor, watching the furred feet pace. *Ridiculous,* he thought. Humans were not meant for this posture. Kzinti were; they could run on four feet as easily as two, and their skulls were on a flexible joint. This was giving him a crick in the neck . . . but it was obligatory for the human supervisors just below the kzinti level to attend. The consequences of disobeying the kzinti were all too plain, in the transparent block of plastic which encased the head of Munchen's former assistant chief of police, resting on the mantelpiece.

Claude's own superior was speaking, Ktiir-Supervisor-of-Animals.

"This monkey—" he jerked a claw at the head "—was responsible for allowing the two Sol-agent humans to escape the hunt." He was in the half-crouched posture Claude recognized as proper for reporting to one higher in rank but lower in social status, although the set of ears and tail was insufficiently respectful. *If I can read kzinti body language that well.*

This was Security H.Q., the old *Herrenhaus* where the Nineteen Families had met before the kzinti came. It was broad and gracious, floored in tile, walled in lacy white stone fretwork and roofed in Wunderland ebony that was veined with natural silver. Outside fountains were splashing in the gardens, and he could smell the oleanders that blossomed there. The gingery scent of kzinti anger was louder, as Staff Officer stopped and prodded at his flank. The foot was encased in a sort of openwork leather-and-metal boot, with slits for the claws. Those were out slightly, probably unconcious reflex, and he could feel the razor tips prickle slightly through the sweat-wet fabric of his uniform.

"Dominant one, this slave—" he began.

"Dispense with the formalities, human," the kzin said. It spoke Wunderlander and was politer than most; Claude's own superior habitually referred to humans as *kz'eerkt*, monkey. That was a quasi-primate on the kzinti homeworld. A tree-dwelling mammal-analog, as much like a monkey as a kzin was like a tiger, which was not much. "Tell me what occurred."

"Dominant one . . . Co-Ordinating Staff Officer," Claude continued, craning his neck. *Don't make eye contact*, he reminded himself. A kzinti stare was a dominance-gesture or a preparation to attack. "Honored Ktiir-Supervisor-of-Animals decided that . . ." *don't use her name* "the former assistant chief of Munchen *Polizei* was more zealous than I in the tracking-down of the two UN agents, and should therefore be in charge of disposing of them in the hunt."

Staff Officer stopped pacing and gazed directly at Ktiir-Supervisor; Claude could see the pink tip of the slimmer kzin's tail twitching before him, naked save for a few briskly orange hairs.

"So not only did your interrogators fail to determine that the humans had *successfully* sabotaged Chuut-Riit's palace-defense computers, you appointed a traitor to arrange for their disposal. The feral humans laugh at us!

Our leader is killed and the assassins go free from under our very claws!"

Ktiir-Supervisor rose from his couch. He pointed at another kzin who huddled in one corner; a telepath, with the characteristic hangdog air and unkempt fur. "Your tame *sthondat* there didn't detect it either," he snarled.

Literally snarled, Claude reflected. It was educational; after seeing a kzin you never referred to a human expression by that term again.

Staff Officer wuffled, snorting open his wet black nostrils and working his whiskers. It should have been a comical expression, but on four hundred pounds of alien carnivore it was not in the least funny. "You hide behind the failures of others," he said, hissing. "Traat-Admiral directes me to inform you that your request for reassignment to the Swarm flotillas has been denied. Neither unit will accept you."

"Traat-Admiral!" Ktiir-Supervisor rasped. "He is like a kit who has climbed a tree and can't get down, mewling for its dam. This talk of a 'secret menace' among the asteroids is a scentless trail to divert attention from his refusal to launch the Fifth Fleet."

"Such was the strategy of the great Chuut-Riit, murdered through your incompetence—or worse."

Ktiir-Supervisor bristled, the orange-red fur standing out and turning his body into a cartoon caricature of a cat, bottle-shaped.

"You nameless licker-of-scentless-piss from that jumped-up creche-product Admiral, what do you accuse me of?"

"Treason, or stupidity amounting to it," the other kzin sneered. Ostentatiously, he flared his batlike ears into a vulnerable rest position and let his tail droop.

Ktiir-Supervisor screamed. "You inner-worlds palace fop, you and Traat-Admiral alike! I urinate on the shrines of your ancestors from a height; crawl away and call for your monkeys to groom you with blowdriers!"

Staff Officer's hands extended outward, the night-black claws glinting as they slid from their sheaths. His tail was rigid now; hairdressers were a luxury the late governor had introduced, and wildly popular among the younger nobility.

"*Kshat*-hunter," he growled. "You are not fit to roll in Chuut-Riit's shit! You lay word-claws to the blood of the Riit." The Riit were the family of the Patriarch of Kzin.

"Chuut-Riit made *ch'rowl* with monkeys!" A gross insult, as well as anatomically impossible . . . or at least fatal for the monkey.

There was a feeling of hush, as the two males locked eyes. Then the heavy *wtsai*-knives came out and the two orange shapes seemed to flow together, meeting at the arch of their leaps, howling. Claude rolled back against the wall as the half-ton of weight slammed down again, sending splinters of furniture out like shrapnel. For a moment the kzinti were locked and motionless, hand to knife-wrist; their legs locked in thigh-holds as well, to keep the back legs from coming up for a disemboweling strike. Mouths gaped toward each other's throats, inch-long fangs exposed in the seventy-degree killing gape. Then there was a blur of movement; they sprang apart, together, went over in a caterwauling blur of orange fur and flashing metal, a whirl far too fast for human eyesight to follow.

He caught glimpses: distended eyes, scrabbling claws, knives sinking home into flesh, amid a clamor loud enough to drive needles of pain into his ears. Bits of bloody fur hit all around him, and there was a human scream as the fighters rolled over a secretary. Then Staff Officer rose, slashed and glaring.

Ktiir-Supervisor lay sprawled, legs twitching galvanically with the hilt of Staff Officer's *wtsai* jerking next to his lower spine. The slender kzin panted for a moment and then leaped forward to grab his opponent by the neck-ruff. He jerked him up toward the waiting jaws, clamped them down on his throat. Ktiir-Supervisor struggled feebly, then slumped. Blood-bubbles swelled and burst on his nose. A final wrench and Staff Officer was backing off, shaking his head and spitting, licking at the

matted fur of his muzzle; he groomed for half a minute
before wrenching the knife free and beginning to spread
the dead kzin's ears for a clean trophy-cut.

"Erruch," Ingrid said as the recording finished. "You've
got more . . . you've got a lot of guts, Claude, dealing
with them at first hand like that."

"Oh, some of them aren't so bad. For ratcats. Staff
Officer there expressed 'every confidence' in me." He
made an expressive gesture with his hands. "Although
he also reminded me there was a continuous demand
for fresh monkeymeat."

Ingrid paled slightly and laid a hand on his arm. That
was not a figure of speech to her, not after the chase
through the kzinti hunting preserve. She remembered
the sound of the hunting scream behind her, and the
thudding crackle of the alien's pads on the leaves as it
made its four-footed rush. Rising as it screamed and
leaped from the ravine lip above her; the long sharpened pole in her hands, and the soft heavy feel as its
own weight drove it onto her weapon . . .

Claude laid his hands on hers. Harold cleared his
throat.

"Well," he said. "Your position looks solider than we
thought."

The other man gave Ingrid's hand a squeeze and
released it. "Yes," he said. A hunter's look came into
his eyes, emphasized the foxy sharpness of his features.
"In fact, they're outfitting some sort of expedition; that's
why they can't spare personnel for administrative duties."

Ingrid and Harold both leaned forward instinctively.
Harold crushed out his cigarette with swift ferocity.

"Another Fleet?" Ingrid asked. *I'll be stuck here, and
Earth . . .*

Claude shook his head. "No. That raid did a *lot* of
damage; it'd be a year or more just to get back to the
state of readiness they had when the *Yamamoto* arrived. Military readiness." Both the others winced; over
a million humans had died in the attack. "But they're

definitely mobilizing for something inside the system. Two flotillas. Something out in the Swarm."

"Markham?" Ingrid ventured. It seemed a little extreme; granted he had the *Catskinner,* but—

"I doubt it. They're bringing the big guns up to full personnel, the battlewagons. *Conquest Fang* class."

They exchanged glances. Those were interstellar-capable warships, carriers for lesser craft and equipped with weapons that could crack planets, defenses to match. Almost self-sufficient, with facilities for manufacturing their own fuel, parts and weapons requirements from asteroidal material. They were normally kept on standby as they came out of the yards, only a few at full readiness for training purposes.

"All of them?" Harold said.

"No, but about three quarters. Nateuto will be thin on the ground for a while. And—" he hesitated, forced himself to continue "—I'll be able to do the most good staying here. For a year or so at least, I can be invaluable to the underground without risking much."

The others remained silent while he looked away, granting him time to compose himself.

"I've got the false ID and transit papers, with disguises," he said. "Ingrid . . . you aren't safe anywhere on Wunderland. In the Swarm, with that ship you came in, maybe the two of you can do some good."

"Claude—" she began.

He shook his head. When he spoke, the old lightness was back in his tone.

"I wonder," he said, "I truly wonder what Markham *is* doing. I'd *like* to think he's causing so much trouble that they're mobilizing the Fleet, but . . ."

Chapter IV

Tiamat was crowded, Captain Jonah Matthieson decided. Even for the *de facto* capital of Wunderland's Belt. It had been bad enough the last time Jonah was here. He shouldered through the line into the zero-G waiting area at the docks, a huge pie-shaped disk; those were at the ends of the sixty-by-twenty kilometer spinning cylinder that served the Serpent Swarm as its main base. There had been dozens of ships in the magnetic grapples: rockjack singleships, transports, freighters . . . refugee ships as well; the asteroid industrial bases had been heavily damaged during the *Yamamoto's* raid.

Not quite as many as you would expect, though. The UN ramscoop ship's weapon had been quarter-ton iron eggs traveling at velocities just less than a photon's. When something traveling at that speed hit, the result resembled an antimatter bomb.

A line of lifebubbles went by, shepherded by medics. Casualties, injuries beyond the capacities of outstation autodocs. Some of them were quite small; he looked in the transparent surface of one, and then away quickly, swallowing. *Shut up*, he told his mind. *Collateral damage can't be helped*. And there had been a trio of kzinti battlewagons in dock too, huge tapering daggers with tau-cross bows and magnetic launchers like openwork gunbarrels; *Slasher*-class fighters clung to the flanks, swarms of metallic lice. Repair and installation crews swarmed around them; Tiamat's factories were pouring out warheads and sensor-effector systems.

The mass of humanity jammed solid in front of the exits. Jonah waited like a floating particle of cork, watching the others passed through the scanners one by one. Last time, with Ingrid—*forget that*, he thought—there had been a cursory retina scan, and four goldskin cops floating like a daisy around each exit. Now they were doing blood samples as well, presumably for DNA analysis; besides the human police, he could see waldo-guns, floating ovoids with clusters of barrels and lenses and antennae. A kzin to control them, bulking even huger in fibroid armour and helmet.

And all for little old me, he thought, kicking himself forward and letting the goldskin stick his hand into the tester. There was a sharp prickle on his thumb, and he waited for the verdict. *Either the false indent holds, or it doesn't*. The four police with stunners and riot-armor, the kzin in full infantry rig, six waldos with 10-megawatt lasers . . . if it came to a fight, the odds were not good. *Since all I have is a charming smile and a rejiggered light-pen*.

"Pass through, pass through," the goldskin said, in a tone that combined nervousness and boredom.

Jonah decided he couldn't blame her; the kzinti security apparatus must have gone winging paranoid-crazy when Chuut-Riit was assassinated, and then the killers escaped with human-police connivance. *On second thoughts, these klongs all volunteered to work for the pussies. Bleep them*.

He passed through the mechanical airlock and into one of the main transverse corridors. It was ten meters by twenty, and sixty kilometers long; three sides were small businesses and shops; on the fourth, spinward, was a slideway. There was a ring of transfer booths around the airlock exits, permanantly disabled; only kzinti and humans under their direct supervision were allowed the convenience of lightspeed pseudo-teleportation. The last time he had been here, a month ago, there had been murals on the walls of the concourse area. Prewar, faded and stained, but still gracious and marked with the springlike optimism of the settlement of the Alpha Centauri system. Outdoor scenes from Wunderland in its pristine condition, before the settlers had modified the ecology to suit the immigrants from Earth. Scenes of slowships, half-disassembled after their decades-long flight from the Solar System.

The murals had been replaced by holograms. Atrocity holograms, of survivors and near-survivors of the UN raid. Mostly from dirtside, since with an atmosphere to transmit blast and shock effects you had a greater transition between dead and safe. Humans crushed, burned, flayed by glass-fragments, mutilated; heavy emphasis on children. There was a babble of voices with the holos, weeping and screaming and moaning with pain, and a strobing title: *Sol-System Killers! Their liberation is death!* And an idealized kzin standing in front of a group of cowering mothers and infants, raising a shield to ward off the attack of a repulsive flatlander-demon.

Interesting, Jonah thought. Whoever had designed that had managed to play on about every prejudice a human resident of the Alpha Centauri system could have. It had to be a human psychist doing the selection; kzinti didn't understand homo sapiens well enough. A display of killing power like this would make a kzin respectful. Human propagandists needed to whip their populations into a war-frenzy, and anger was a good tool. Make a kzin angry? You didn't *need* to make them angry. An *enemy* would try to make a kzin angry, because that reduced their efficiency. *Let this remind you that a collaborationist is not necessarily an incompetent.* A traitor, a Murphy's-asshole inconvenience, but not necessarily an idiot. Nor even amoral; he supposed it was possible to convince yourself that you were serving the greater good by giving in. Smoothing over the inevitable, since it *did* look like the kzinti were winning.

Jonah shook himself out of the trance and flipped himself over. *I've got to watch this tendency to depression*, he thought sourly. *Finagle, I ought to be bouncing for joy.*

Instead, he felt a grey lethargy. His feet drifted into contact with the edge of the slideway, and he began moving slowly forward; more rapidly as he edged toward the center. The air became more quiet. There was always a subliminal rumble near the ends of Tiamat's cylinder, powered metals and chemicals pumping into the fabricators. Now he would have to contact the Nipponese underworlder who had smuggled them from Tiamat to Wunderland in the first place, what had been his name? Shigehero Hirose, that was it. An *oyabun*, whatever that meant. There was the data they had downloaded from Chuut-Riit's computers, priceless stuff. He would need a message-maser to send it to *Catskinner*; the ship had been modified with an interstellar-capacity sender. And—

"Hello, Captain."

Jonah turned his head, very slowly. A man had touched his elbow. Stocky, even by flatlander standards, with a considerable paunch. Coal-black, with tightly curled wiry hair; pure Afroid, not uncommon in some ethnic enclaves on Wunderland but very rare on Earth, where gene-flow had been nearly random for going on four hundred years. *General Buford Early, UN Space navy, late ARM*. Jonah gasped and sagged sideways, a grey before his eyes like high-G blackout. There was another Flatlander but Jonah barely noticed. Early slipped a hand under his arm and bore him up with thick-boned strength. Archaic, like the man; he was . . . at least two centuries old. Impossible to tell, these days. The only limiting factor on how old you might be was when

you were born, after medicine started progressing fast
enough to compensate for advancing age . . .

"Take it easy," Early said.

Eyes warred with mind. Early was here; Early was
sitting in his office on Gibraltar Base back in the Solar
System.

Jonah struggled for breath, then fell into the rhythm
taught by the Zen adepts who had trained him for war.
Calm flowed back. Much knowledge of war had fallen
out of human culture in three hundred years of peace,
before the kzinti came, but the monks had preserved a
great deal. What UN bureaucrat would suspect an old
man sitting quietly beneath a tree practicing and pre-
serving dangerous technique? Jonah spoke to himself:
*Reality is change. Shock and fear result from imposing
concepts on reality. Abandon concepts. Being is time,
and time is Being. Birth and death is the life of the
Buddha.* Then: *Thank you, roshi.*

The men at either elbow guided him to the slower
edge-strip of the slideway and onto the sidewalk. Jonah
looked "ahead," performed the mental trick that turned
the cylinder into a hollow tower above his head, then
back to horizontal. He freed his arms with a quiet flick
and sank down on the chipped and stained poured-rock
bench. That was notional in this gravity, but it gave you
a place to hitch your feet.

"Well?" he said, looking at the second man.

This one was different. Younger, Jonah would say;
eyes do not age or hold expression, but the small muscles around them do. Oriental eyes, more common.
Both of them were in Swarm-Belter clothing, gaudy
and somehow sleazy at the same time, with various
mysterious pieces of equipment at their belts. Perfect
cover, if you were pretending to be a modestly prosper-
ous enterpreneur of the Serpent Swarm. The kzinti
allowed a good deal of freedom to the Belters in this
system; it was more efficient and required less supervision than running everything themselves. That would
change as their numbers built up, of course.

"Well?" he said again.

Early grinned, showing strong and slightly yellowed teeth, and pulled a cheroot from a pocket. *Actually less uncommon here than in the Solar System,* Jonah thought, gagging slightly. "You didn't seriously think that we'd let an opportunity like the *Yamamoto* raid go by and only put one arrow on the string, did you, Captain? By the way, this is my . . . associate, Watsuji Hajime." The man smiled and bowed. "A member of the team I brought in."

"Another stasis field?" Jonah said.

"We did have one ready," Early said. "We like to have a little extra tucked away."

"Trust the ARM," Jonah said sourly.

The UN's technological police had been operating almost as long as humans had been in space. Their *primary* function was to suppress technologies which had dangerous consequences . . . which turned out to be most technologies. For a long time they had managed to make Solar humanity forget that there had even *been* such things as war or weapons or murder. That was looked back upon as a Golden Age, now, after two generations of war with the kzinti; privately, Matthieson thought of it as the years of Stagnation. The ARM had not wanted to believe in the kzinti, not even when the crew of the *Angel's Pencil* had reported their own first near-fatal contact with the felinoids. And when the war started, the ARM had *still* dealt out its hoarded secrets with the grudging reluctance of a miser.

"It's for the greater good," Early replied.

"Sure." *That you slowed down research and so when the kzinti hit us they had technological superiority?* For that matter, why had it taken a century and a half to develop regeneration techniques? And *millions* of petty criminals—jaywalkers and the like—had been sliced, diced and sent to the organ banks before then. *Ancient history,* he told himself. The Belters had always hated the ARM . . .

"Certainly for the greater good that you've got backup, now," Early continued. "We came in with a slug aimed at a weapons fabrication asteroid. The impact was quite genuine . . . God's my witness—" he continued.

He's old all right.

"—the intelligence we've gathered and beamed back is *already* worth the entire cost of the *Yamamoto*. And you and Lieutenant Raines succeeded beyond our hopes."

Meaning you had no hope we'd survive, Jonah added to himself. Early caught his eye and nodded with an ironic turn of his full lips. The younger man felt a slight chill; how good at reading body language would you get, with two centuries of practice? How human would you remain?

"Speaking of which," the general continued, "where *is* Lieutenant Raines, Matthieson?"

Jonah shrugged, looking away slightly and probing at his own feelings. "She . . . decided to stay. To come out later, actually, with Yarthkin-Schotmann and Montferrat-Palme. I've got all the data."

Early's eyebrows rose. "Not *entirely* unexpected." His eyes narrowed again. "No personal animosities, here, I trust? We won't be heading out for some time—" *if ever*, went unspoken "—and we may need to work with them again."

The young Sol-Belter looked out at the passing crowd on the slideway, at thousands swarming over the handnets in front of the shopfronts on the other three sides of the cylinder.

"My ego's a little bruised," he said finally. "But . . . no."

Early nodded. "Didn't have the leisure to become all that attached, I suppose," he said. "Good professional attitude."

Jonah began to laugh softly, shoulders shaking. "Finagle, General, you *are* a long time from being a young man, aren't you? No offense."

"None taken," the Intelligence officer said dryly.

"Actually, we just weren't compatible." What was that phrase in the history tape? Miscegenation abyss? Birth cohort gap? No . . . "Generation gap," he said.

"She was only a few years younger than you," Early said suspiciously.

"*Biologically*, sir. But she was *born* before the War. During the Long Peace. Wunderland wasn't sown nearly as tight as Earth, or even the Solar Belt . . . but they still didn't have a single deadly weapon in the whole system, saving hunting tools. I've been in the Navy or training for it since I was six! We just didn't have anything in common except software, sex and the mission." He shrugged again, and felt the lingering depression leave him. "It was like being involved with a younger version of my mother."

Early shook his head, chuckling himself, a deep rich sound. "Temporal displacement. Doesn't need relativity, boy; wait 'til you're my age. And now," he continued, "we are going to have a little talk."

"What've we been doing?"

"Oh, not a debriefing. That first. But then . . ." He grinned brilliantly. "A . . . job interview, of sorts."

"Well. So." The *oyabun* nodded and folded his hands.

Jonah looked around. They were in the three-twelve shell of Tiamat, where spin gave an equivalent of .72 G weight. Expensive, even now when gravity polarizers were beginning to spread beyond kzinti and military-manufacturing use. Microgravity is marvelous for most industrial use; there are other things that need weight, bearing children to term among them. This room was equally expensive; most of the furnishings were *wood*. The low tables at which they all sat, knees crossed. The black-lacquered carved screens with rampant tigers as well, and he strongly suspected that those were even older than General Buford Early. A set of Japanese swords rested in a niche, long *katana* and the short "sword of apology" on their ebony stand.

Sandalwood incense was burning somewhere, and the floor was covered in neat mats of plaited straw. Against all this the plain good clothes of the man who called himself Shigehero Hirose were something of a shock. The thin ancient porcelain of his sake cup gleamed as he set it down on the table, and spoke to the Oriental who had come with the general. Jonah kept his face elaborately blank; it was unlikely that either of them suspected his knowledge of Japanese . . . enough to understand most of a conversation, if not to speak it. Nippon's tongue had never been as popular as her goods, being too difficult for outsiders to learn easily.

"*It is . . . an unexpected honor to entertain one of the Tokyo branch of the clan*, Shigehero was saying. "*And how do events proceed in the land of the Sun Goddess?*"

Watsuji Hajime shrugged. "*No better than can be expected, Uncle*," he replied, and sucked breath between his teeth. "*This war presents opportunities, but also imposes responsibilities. Neutrality is impossible.*"

"*Regrettably, this is so,*" Shigehero said. His face grew stern. "*Nevertheless, you have revealed the Association's codewords to outsiders.*" They both glanced sidelong at Early and Matthieson. "*Perhaps you are what you claim. Perhaps not. This must be demonstrated. Honor must be established.*"

Whatever that meant, the Earther did not like it. His face stayed as expressionless as a mask carved from light-brown wood, but sweat started up along his brow. A door slid open, and one of the guards who had brought them here entered noiselessly. Jonah recognized the walk; training in the Art, one of the *budo* styles. Highly illegal on Earth until the War, and for the most part in the Alpha Centauri system as well. Otherwise he was a stocky nondescript man in loose black, although the Belter thought there might be soft armor beneath it. Moving with studied grace, he knelt and laid a featureless rectangle of blond wood by Watsuji's left hand.

The Earther bowed his head, a lock of black hair falling over his forehead. Then he raised his eyes and slid the box in front of him, opening it with delicate care. Within were a white linen handkerchief, a folded cloth, a block of maple and a short curved guardless knife in a black leather sheath. Watsuji's movements took on the slow precision of a religious ritual as he laid the maple block on the table atop the cloth and began binding the little finger of his left hand with the handkerchief, painfully tight. He laid the hand on the block and drew the knife. It slid free without sound, a fluid curve. The two men's eyes were locked as he raised the knife.

Jonah grunted as if he had been kicked in the belly. The older man was missing a joint on the little finger of his left hand, too. The Sol-Belter had thought that was simply the bad medical care available in the Swarm, but anyone who could afford this room . . .

The knife flashed down, and there was a small spurt of blood, a rather grisly crunching sound like celery being sliced. Watsuji made no sound, but his face went pale around the lips. Shigehero bowed more deeply. The servant-guard walked forward on his knees and gathered up the paraphernalia, folding the cloth about it with the same ritual care. There was complete silence, save for the sigh of ventilators and Watsuji's deep breathing, harsh but controlled.

The two Nipponjin poured themselves more of the heated rice wine and sipped. When Shigehero spoke again, it was in English.

"It is good to see that the old customs have not been entirely forgotten in the Solar System," he said. "Perhaps my branch of the Association was . . . shall we say a trifle precipitate, when they decided emigration was the only way to preserve their, ah, purity." He raised his glass slightly to the general. "When your young warriors passed through last month, I was surprised that so much effort had been required to insert so slender a needle. I see that we underestimated you."

He picked up a folder of printout on the table before him. "It is correct that the . . . ah, assets you and your confederates represent would be a considerable addition to my forces," he went on. "However, please remember that my Association is more in the nature of a family business than a political organization. We are involved in the underground struggle against the kzinti because we are human, little more."

Early raised his cup of sake in turn; the big spatulate hands handled the porcelain with surprising delicacy. "You . . . and your, shall we say, *black-clad* predecessors have been involved in others' quarrels before this. To be blunt, when it paid. The valuata we brought are significant, surely?"

Jonah blinked in astonishment. *This is the cigar-chomping, kick-ass general I came to know and loathe?* he thought. *Live and learn. Learn so that you can go on living* . . . Then again, before the kzinti attack Buford Early had been a professor of military history at the ARM academy. You had to be out of the ordinary for that; it involved knowledge that would send an ordinary man to the psychists for memory-wipe.

Shigehero made a minimalist gesture. "Indeed. Yet this would also involve integrating your group in my command structure. An indigestible lump, a weakness in the chain of command, since you do not owe personal alliegence to me. And, to be frank, non-Nipponese generally do not rise to the decision-making levels in this organization. No offense."

"None taken," Early replied tightly. "If you would prefer a less formal link?"

Shigehero sighed, then brought up a remote 'board from below the table, and signed to the guards. They quickly folded the priceless antique screens, to reveal a standard screen-wall.

"That might be my own inclination, esteemed General," he said. "Except that certain information has come to my attention. Concerning Admiral Ulf Reichstein-Markham of the Free Wunderland Navy . . . I see your young subordinate has told you of this person? And the so-valuable ship he left in the *Herrenmann's* care, and a . . . puzzling discovery they have made together."

A scratching at the door interrupted him. He frowned, then nodded. It opened, revealing a guard and another figure who looked to Early for confirmation. The general accepted a datatab, slipped it into his belt unit and held the palm-sized computer to one ear.

Ah, thought Jonah. *I'm not the only one to get a nasty shock today.* The black man's skin had turned greyish, and his hands shook for a second as he pushed the "wipe" control. Jonah chanced a glance at his eyes; it was difficult to be sure, they were dark and the lighting was low, but he could have sworn the pupils had expanded to swallow the iris.

"He—" Early cleared his throat. "This information . . . would it be about an, er, *artifact* found in an asteroid? Certain behavioral peculiarities?"

Shigehero nodded and touched the controls. A blurred holo sprang up on the wall; from a helmet-cam, Jonah decided. Asteroidal mining equipment on the surface of a medium-sized rock, one kilometer by two. A docked ship in the background, he recognized Markham's *Nietzsche,* and others distant enough to be drifting lights, and suited figures putting up bubble-habitats. Then panic, and a hole appeared where the laser-driller had been a moment before. Milling confusion, and an . . . yes, it must be an alien, came floating up out of the hole.

The young Sol-Belter felt the pulse hammer in his ears. He was watching the first living non-Kzin alien discovered in all the centuries of human spaceflight. It couldn't be a kzin, the proportions were all wrong. About 1.5 meters, judging by the background shots of humans. Difficult to say in vacuum armor, but it looked almost as thick as it was wide, with an enormous round head and stubby limbs, hands like three-fingered mechanical grabs. There was a weapon or tool gripped in one fist; as they watched the other hand came over to touch it and it changed shape, *writhing.* Jonah opened his mouth to question and—

"*Stop!*" The general's bull bellow wrenched their attention around. "*Stop that display* immediately, *that's an* order!"

Shigehero touched the control panel and the holo froze. "You are not in a position to give orders here, *gaijin,*" he said. The two guards along the wall put hands inside their lapover jackets and glided closer, soundless as kzinti.

Early wrenched open his collar and waved a hand. "Please, *oyabun*, if we could speak alone? *Completely* alone, just for a moment. More is at stake here than you realize!"

Silence stretched. At last, fractionally, Shigehero nodded. The others stood and filed out into the outer room, almost as graciously appointed as the inner. The other members of Early's team awaited them there; half a dozen of assorted ages and skills. There were no guards, on this side of the wall at least, and the *oyabun's* men had provided refreshments and courteously ignored the quick, thorough sweep for listening devices. Watsuji headed for the sideboard, poured himself a double vodka and knocked it back.

"Tanj it," he wheezed, under his breath. Jonah keyed himself coffee and a handmeal; it had been a rough day.

"Problems?" the Belter asked.

"I can't even get to an autodoc until we're out of the Finagle-forsaken bughouse," the Earther replied. "I knew they were conservative here, but this bleeping farce!" He made a gesture with his mutilated hand. "Nobody at home's done that for a hundred years! I felt like I was in a holoplay *Namida Amitsu*, we're *legal*, these days. Well, somewhat. Gotten out of the organ trade, at least. This—!"

Jonah nodded in impersonal sympathy. For a flatlander, the man had dealt with the pain extremely well; Earthsiders were seldom far from automated medical attention. Even before the War, Belters had had to move self-sufficient.

"What really bothers *me*," he said quietly, settling into a chair, "is what's going on in *there*." He nodded to the door. "Just like the ARM, to go all around Murphy's Hall to keep us in the dark."

"Exactly," Watsuji said gloomily, nursing his hand. "Those crazy bastards think they run the world."

"Run the world," Jonah echoed. "Well, they do, don't they? The ARMs—"

"Naw, not the UN. This is older than that."

Jonah shrugged.

"A lot older. Bunch of mumbo jumbo. At least—"

"Eh?"

"I *think* it's just mumbo jumbo. God, this thing hurts."

Jonah settled down, motionless. He would not be bored; Belters got a good deal of practice in sitting still and doing nothing without losing alertness, and his training had increased it. The curiosity was the itch he could not scratch.

Could be worse, he thought, taking another bite of the fishy-tasting handmeal. The consistency was rather odd, but it was tasty. *The flatlander could have told me to cut* my *finger off.*

"Explain yourself," Shigehero said.

Instead, Early moved closer and dipped his finger in his rice wine. With that, he drew a figure on the table before the *oyabun*. A stylized rose, overlain by a cross; he omitted the pryamid. The fragment of the Order which had accompanied the migrations to Alpha Centauri had not included anyone past the Third Inner Circle, after all . . .

Shigehero's eyes went wide. He picked up a cloth and quickly wiped the figure away, but his gaze stayed locked on the blank surface of the table for a moment. Then he swallowed and touched the control panel again.

"We are entirely private," he said, then continued formally: "You bring Light."

"Illumination is the key, to open the Way," Early replied.

"The Eastern Path?"

Early shook his head. "East and West are one, to the servants of the Hidden Temple."

Shigehero started, impressed still more, then made a deep bow, smiling. "Your authority is undisputed, Master. Although not that of the ARM!"

Early relaxed, joining in the chuckle. "Well, the ARM is no more than a finger of the Hidden Way and the Rule That Is To Come, eh? As is your Association, *oyabun.* And many another." *Including many you know nothing of.* "As above, so below; power and knowledge, wheel within wheel. Until Holy Blood——"

"——fills Holy Grail."

Early nodded, and his face became stark. "Now, let me tell you what has been hidden in the vaults of the ARM. The Brotherhood saw to it that the knowledge was surpressed, back three centuries ago, along with much else. The ARM has been invaluable for that . . . Long ago, there was a species that called themselves the Thrint——"

Jonah looked up as Early left the *oyabun's* sanctum.

"How did it go?" he murmured.

"Well enough. We've got an alliance of sorts. And a very serious problem, not just with the kzinti. Staff conference, gentlemen."

The Belter fell into line with the others as they left the Association's headquarters. *I wonder,* he thought, looking up at the rock above. *I wonder what really is going on out there.* And whether it might get him *Catskinner* back.

Chapter V

"STOP THAT," Dnivtopun said angrily, alerted by the smell of blood and a wet ripping sound.

His son looked up guiltily and tried to resist. The thrint willed obedience, feeling the adolescent's half-formed shield resisting his Power like thick mud around a foot. Then it gave way, and the child released the human's arm. That was chewed to the bone; the young thrint had blood all down its front, and bits of matter and gristle stuck between its needle teeth. The slave swayed, smiling dreamily.

"How many times do I have to tell you: *Do not eat the servants!*" Dnivtopun shrieked, and used the Power again: SHAME. GUILT. PAIN. ANGUISH. REMORSE. SHOOTING PAINS. BURNING FEET. UNIVERSAL SCRATCHLESS ITCH. GUILT.

The slave was going into shock. "Go and get medical treatment," he said. And: FEEL NO PAIN. DO NOT BLEED. This one had been on the *Ruling Mind* for some time; he had picked it for sensitivity to Power, and its mind fit his mental grip like a glove. The venous spurting from its forelimb slowed, then sank to a trickle as the muscles clamped down on the blood vessels with hysterical strength.

Dnivtopun turned back to his offspring. The young thrint was rolling on the soft blue synthetic of the cabin floor; he had beshat himself and vomited up the human flesh—thrint used the same mouth-orifice for both—and his eating tendrils were writhing into his mouth, trying to clean it and pick the teeth free of foreign matter. The filth was sinking rapidly into the floor, absorbed by the ship's recycling system, and the stink was fading as well. The vents replaced it with nostalgic odors of hot wet jungle, spicy and rank, the smell of thrintun. Dnivtopun shut his mind to the youngster's suffering for a full minute; his eldest son was eight, well into puberty. At that age, controls imposed by the Power did not sink in well. An infant could be permanently conditioned, that was the way baby thrint were toilet trained, but by this stage they were growing rebellious.

CEASE HURTING, he said at last. Then: "Why did you attack the servant?"

"It was boring me," his son said, still with a trace of sulkiness. "All that stuff you said I had to learn. Why can't we go home, father? Or to Uncle Tzinlpun's?"

With an intense effort, Dnivtopun controlled himself. *"This is home!* We are the *last thrintun left alive." Powerloss take persuasion*, he decided. BELIEVE.

The fingers of mind could feel the child-intellect accepting the order. Barriers of denial crumbled, and his son's eye squeezed shut while all six fingers squeezed painfully into palms. The young thrint threw back his head and howled desolately, a sound like glass and sheet metal inside a tumbling crusher.

QUIET. Silence fell; Dnivtopun could hear the uncomprehending whimper of a female in the next room, beyond the lightscreen door. One of his wives; they had all been nervous and edgy, female thrintun had enough psionic sensitivity to be very vulnerable to upset.

"You will have to get used to the idea," Dnivtopun

said. *Powergiver knows it took me long enough.* He moved closer and threw an arm around his son's almost-neck, biting him affectionately on the top of the head. "Think of the good side. There are no tnuctipun here!" He could feel that bring a small wave of relief; the Rebels had been bogeymen to the children since their birth. "And you will have a planet of your own, some day. There is a whole galaxy of slaves here, ready for our taking!"

"Truly, father?" There was awakening greed at that. Dnivtopun had only been Overseer of one miserable food-planet, a sterile globe with a reducing atmosphere, seeded with algae and bandersnatchi. There would have been little for his sons, even without the disruption of the War.

Truly, my son. He keyed one of the controls, and a wall blanked to show an exterior starscape. "One day, all this will be yours. We are not the *last* thrintun—we are the beginning of a new Empire!" *And I am the first Emperor, if I can survive the next few months.* "So we must take good care of these slaves."

"But these smell so *good,* father!"

Dnivtopun sighed. "I know, son." Thrintun had an acute sense of smell when it came to edibility; competition for food among their presapient ancestors had been very intense. "It's because—" *no, that's just a guess.* Few alien biologies in the old days had been as compatible as these humans . . . Dnivtopun had a suspicion he knew the reason; food algae. The Thrint had seeded hundreds of planets with it, and given billions of years . . . That would account for the compatibility of the other species as well, the Kzin; they could eat humans, too. "Well, you'll just have to learn to ignore it." Thrintun were always ravenous. "Now, listen—you've upset your mother. Go and comfort her."

Ulf Reichstein-Markham faced the Master and fought not to vomit. The carrion breath, the writhing tentacles beside the obscene gash of mouth, the staring faceted eye . . . It was so—

—*beautiful*, he thought, as shards of crystalline Truth slid home in his mind. The pleasure was like the drifting relaxation after orgasm, like a hot sauna, like winning a fight.

"What progress has been made on the amplifier helmet?" his owner asked.

"Very little, Mast—*eeeeeeeeee!*" He staggered back, shaking his head against the blinding-white pressure that threatened to burst it. Whimpering, he pressed his hands against the sides of his head. "Please, Master! We're *trying!*"

The pressure relaxed; on some very distant level, he could feel the alien's recognition of his sincerity.

"What is the problem?" Dnivtopun asked.

"Master—" Markham stopped for a moment to organize his thoughts, looking around.

They were on the control deck of the *Ruling Mind*, and it was *huge*. Few human spaceships had ever been so large; this was nearly the size of a colony slowship. The chamber was a flattened oval dome twenty meters long and ten wide, lined with chairs of many different types. That was logical, to accommodate the wild variety of slave-species the Thrint used. But they were chairs, not acceleration couches. The Thrint had had very good gravity control, for a very long time. A central chair designed for thrint fronted the blackened wreck of what had been the main computer. The decor was lavish and garish, swirling curlicues of precious metals and enamel, drifting motes of multicolored lights. Beneath their feet was a porous matrix that seemed at least half-alive, that absorbed anything organic and dead and moved rubbish to collector outlets with a disturbing peristaltic motion. The air was full of the smells of vegetation and rank growth.

Curious, he thought, as the majority of his consciousness wondered how to answer the Master. The controls were odd, separate crystal-display dials and manual levers and switches, primitive in the extreme. But the machinery *behind* the switches was . . . there were no doors; something *happened*, and the material went . . .

vague, and you could walk through it, like walking through soft taffy. The only mechanical airlock was a safety-backup.

There was no central power source for the ship. Dotted around were units that apparently converted matter into energy; the equivalent of flashlight batteries could start it. The basic drive was to the kzinti gravity polarizer as a fusion bomb was to grenade; it could accelerate at *thousands* of gravities, and then pull space right around the ship and travel faster than light.

Faster than light—

"Stop daydreaming," the Voice said. "And tell me *why*."

"Master, we don't know *how*."

The thrint opened its mouth and then closed it again, the tondrils stroking caressingly at its almost nonexistent lips. "Why not?" he said. "It isn't very complicated. You can buy them anywhere for twenty *znorgits*."

"Master, do you know the principles?"

"Of course not, slave! That's slavework. For engineers."

"But Master, the slave-engineers you've got . . . we can only talk to them a little, and they don't know anything beyond what buttons to push. The machinery—" he waved helplessly at the walls "—doesn't make any *sense* to us, Master! It's just blocks of matter. We . . . our instruments can barely detect that something's going on."

The thrint stood looking at him, radiating incomprehension. "Well," he said after a moment. "It's true I didn't have the best quality of engineering slave. No need for them, on a routine posting. Still, I'm sure you'll figure something out, Chief Slave. How are we doing at getting the *Ruling Mind* freed from the dirt?"

"Much better, Master! That is well within our capacities . . . Master?"

"Yes?"

"Have I your permission to send a party to Tiamat? It can be done without much danger of detection, beyond what the deserters already present; we need more per-

sonnel and spare parts. For a research project on . . .
well, on your nervous system."

The alien's single unwinking eye stared at him. "What
are nerves?" he said slowly. Dnivtopun took a dopestick
from his pouch and sucked on it. Then: "What's
research?"

"Erreow."

The kzinrret rolled and twisted across the wicker
matting of the room, yowling softly with her eyes closed.
Traat-Admiral glanced at her with post-coital satisfaction as he finished grooming his pelt and laid the curry-
comb aside; he might be *de facto* leader of the Modernists,
but he was not one of those who could not maintain a
decent appearance without a dozen servants and machinery. At the last he cleaned the damp portion of his
fur with talc, remembering once watching a holo of
humans bathing themselves by jumping into *water*.
Into *cold* water.

"Hrrrr," he shivered.

The female turned over on all fours and stuck her
rump in the air.

"Ch'rowl?" she chirrupped. Involuntarily his ears extended and the muscles of his massive neck and shoulders twitched. *"Ch'rowl?"* With a saucy twitch of her
tail, but he could smell that she was not serious. Besides, there was work to do.

"No," he said firmly. The kzinrret padded over to a
corner, collapsed onto a pile of cushions and went to
sleep with limp finality.

A kzinrret of the Patriarch's line, Traat-Admiral thought
with pride; one of Chuut-Riit's beauteous daughters.
His blood to be mingled with the Riit, he whose sire
had been only a Third Gunner, lucky to get a single
mate even when the heavy casualties of the First Fleet
left so many maleless. He stretched, reaching for the
domed ceiling, picked up the weapons belt from the
door and padded off down the corridor. This was the
governor's harem quarters, done up as closely as might
be to a noble's Kzinrret House on Kzin itself. Domed

wickerwork structures, the tops waterproof with synthetic in a concession to modernity; there were even gravity polarizers to bring it up to Homeworld weight, nearly twice that of Wunderland.

"Good for the health of the kzinrret and kits," he mused to himself, and his ears moved in the kzinti equivalent of a grin. It was easy to get used to such luxury, he decided, ducking through the shamboo curtain over the entrance and pacing down the exit corridor; that was open at the sides, roofed in flowering orange vines.

Each dome was set in a broad space of open vegetation, and woe betide the kzinrret who strayed across the low wooden boundaries into her neighbor's claws; female kzinti might be too stupid to talk, but they had a keenly developed sense of territory. There were open spaces, planted in a pleasant mixture of vegetation; orange kzinti, reddish Wunderlander, green from Earth. Traat-Admiral could hear the sounds of young kits at play in the common area, see them running and tumbling and chasing while their mothers lay basking in the weak sunlight or groomed each other. Few of them had noticed the change of males over much, but integrating his own modest harem had been difficult, much fur flying dominance-tussles.

He sighed as he neared the exit-gate. Chuut-Riit's harem was not only of excellent quality, but so well trained that it needed less maintenance than his own had. The females would even let human servants in to keep up the feeding stations, a vast help, since male kzinti who could be trusted in another's harem were not common. They were all well housebroken, and most did not even have to be physically restrained when pregnant, which simplified things immensely; kzinrret had an irresistible urge to dig a birthing tunnel about then, and it created endless problems and damage to the gardens. Through the outer gate, functional warding-fields and robot guns, and a squad of Chuut-Riit's household troopers. They saluted with enthusiasm. Being hereditary servants of the Riit, he had been

under no obligation to let them swear to him . . .
although it would have been foolish to discard so useful
a cadre.

*Would I have thought of this before Chuut-Riit trained
me?* he thought. Then: *He is dead: I live. Enough.*

Beyond the gates began the palace proper. The military and administrative sections were largely underground, ship-style; from here you could see only the
living quarters, openwork pavilions for the most part,
once bases of massive cut stone. Between and around
them stretched gardens, stones of pleasing shape, trees
whose smooth bark made claws itch. There was a half-
acre of *zheeretki* too, the tantalizing scent calling the
passer-by to come roll in its intoxicating blossoms.

Traat-Admiral wiggled his ears in amusement as he
settled onto the cushions in the reception pavilion. *All
this luxury, and no time to enjoy it,* he thought. It was
well enough, one did not become a Conquest Hero by
lolling about on cushions sipping blood.

His eldest son was coming along one of the paths. In
a hurry, and running four-foot with the sinous gait that
reminded humans of weasles as much as cats; he wore a
sash of office, his first ranking. Ten meters from the
pavilion he rose, licked his wrists and smoothed back
his cheek fur with them, settled the sash.

"Honored Sire Traat-Admiral, Staff Officer requests
audience at your summons," he said. "And . . . the
Accursed Ones. They await final judgment. And—"

"Enough, Aide-de-Camp," Traat-Admiral rumbled.

The young male stood proudly and made an unconscious gesture of adjusting the sash; that garment was
a ceremonial survival of a sword-baldric, from the
days when Aides were bodyguards as well, entitled to
take a duel-challenge on themselves to spare their masters. Looking into the great round eyes of his son,
Traat-Admiral realized that that too would be done
gladly if it were needed. Unable to restrain himself, he
gave the youth's ears a few grooming licks.

"*Fath*— Honored Sire! *Please!*"

*   *   *

"Hrrrr," Staff Officer rumbled. "He was as strong as a *terrenki* and faster." Traat-Admiral looked down to see the fresh ears of Ktiir-Supervisor-of-Animals dangling at the other's belt.

"Not quite fast enough," Traat-Admiral said with genuine admiration. Most kzinti became slightly less quarrelsome past their first youth, but the late Ktiir's notorious temper had gotten worse, if anything. It probably came from having to deal with humans all the time, and high-level collaborators at that. Ktiir should have remembered that reflexes slowed and had to be replaced with cunning and skill born of experience.

"Yes," he continued, "I am well pleased." He paused for three breaths, waiting while Staff Officer's muzzle dipped into the saucer. "Hroth-Staff-Officer."

The other kzin gasped, inhaled milk and rolled over, coughing and slapping at his nose, sneezed frantically, and sat back with his eyes watering. Traat-Admiral felt his ears twitch with genial amusement.

"Do not be angry, noble Hroth-Staff-Officer," he said. "There is little of humor these days." It was a system governor's perogative, to confer a Name. Any field-grade officer could, for certain well-established feats of honor, but a governor could do so at discretion.

"I will strive—*kercheee*—to be worthy of the honor," the newly-promoted kzin said. "Little though I have done to deserve it."

"Nonsense," Traat-Admiral said. *For one thing, you are very diplomatic.* Only a kzin with iron self-control could be humble, even under these circumstances. "For another, you have won . . . what, six duels in the past month? And a dozen back when Chuut-Riit first came from Homeworld to this system. This will satisfy those who think galactic conquest can be accomplished with teeth and claws. Also, you have been invaluable in keeping the Modernist faction aligned behind me. Many thought Chuut-Riit's heir should be from among his immediate entourage."

Hroth-Staff-Officer twitched his tail and rippled sections of his pelt. "None such could enjoy sufficient confidence among the locally-born," he said. "If we trusted Chuut-Riit's judgment before he was killed, should we not after he is dead?"

Traat-Admiral sighed, looking out over the exquisite restraint of the gardens. "I agree. Better a . . . less worthy successor than infighting beneath one more technically qualified." His ears spread in irony. "More infighting than we have had. Chuut-Riit said . . ." he hesitated, then looked over at the faces of his son and the newly-ennobled Hroth-Staff-Officer, remembered conversations with his mentor. ". . . he said that humans were either the greatest danger or greatest opportunity kzinti had ever faced. And that he did not know if they came just in time, or just too late."

His son showed curiosity in the rippling of his pelt, an almost imperceptible movement of his fingertips. Curiosity was a childhood characteristic among kzinti, but one the murdered governor had said should be encouraged.

"We have not faced a challenge to really test our mettle for . . . a long time," he said. "We make easy conquests; empty worlds to colonize, or others where the inhabitants are savages with spears, barbarians with nothing better than chemical-energy weapons. We grow slothful; our energy is spent in quarreling among ourselves, and more and more the work of even maintaining our civilization we turn over to our slaves."

"Wrrrr," Hroth-Staff-Officer said. "But what did the Dominant One mean, that the humans might be too late?"

Traat-Admiral's voice sank slightly. "I meant that lack of challenge has weakened us. By making us inflexible, brittle. There are other forms of rot than softness; fossilization is another: steel and bone turning to stiff breakable rock. Chuut-Riit saw that as we expand we must eventually meet terrible threats. If the kzinti are to be strong enough to conquer them, first we must be reforged in the blaze of war."

"I still don't smell the point, Traat-Admiral," Hroth-Staff-Officer said. The admiral could see his son huddled on the cushions, entranced at being able to listen in on such august conversation. *Listen well, my son,* he thought. *You will find it an uncomfortable privilege.*

"Are the humans then a challenge which will call forth our strength . . . or the mad *raaairtwo* that will shatter us?"

"*Wrrrr!*" Hroth-Staff-Officer shivered slightly, his fur lying flat. Aide-de-Camp's was plastered to his skin, and his ears had disappeared into their pouches of skin. "That has the authentic flavor and scent of his . . . disquieting lectures. I suffered through enough of them." A pause. "Still, the *raaairtwo* may be head-high at the shoulder and weigh fifty times a kzintosh's mass and have a spiked armor ball for a tail, but our ancestors killed them."

"But not by butting heads with them, Hroth-Staff-Officer." He turned his head. "Aide-de-Camp, go to the Accursed Ones, and bring them here. Not immediately; in an hour or so."

He leaned forward once the youth had leaped up and four-footed away. "Hroth-Staff-Officer, has it occurred to you *why* we are sending such an armada to this system's asteroids?"

Big lambent-yellow eyes blinked at him. "There has been much activity among the feral humans," he said. "I did scent that you might be using this as an excuse for field-exercises with live ammunition, in order to quiet dissention." Kzinti obeyed when under arms, even if they hated it.

"The interstellar warships as well? That would be like cleaning vermin out of your pelt with a beam-rifle." He leaned closer. "This is a Patriarch's Secret," he continued. "Listen."

When he finished a half-hour later, Hroth-Staff-Officer's belt was half laid-flat, with patches bristling in horror. Traat-Admiral could smell his anger, underlain with fear, a sickly scent.

"You are right to fear," he said, conscious of his own glands. No kzin could hide true terror, of course, not with a functioning nose in the area.

"Death is nothing," the other nodded. He grinned, the expression humans sometimes mistook for friendliness. "But this!" He hissed, and Traat-Admiral watched and smelled him fight down blind rage.

"Chuut-Riit feared something like this," he said. At the other's startlement: "Oh, no, not these beings particularly. It is a joke of the God that we find this thing in the middle of a difficult war. But *something* terrible was bound to jump out of the long grass sooner or later. The universe is so large, and we keep pressing our noses into new caves—" He shrugged. "Enough. Now—"

Chuut-Riit's sons laid stomach to earth on the path before the dais of judgment and covered their noses. Traat-Admiral looked down on their still-gaunt forms and felt himself recoil. Not with fear, at least not the fear of an adult kzin. Vague memories moved in the shadow-corners of his mind; brutal hands tearing him away from Mother, giant shapes of absolute power . . . rage and desire and fear, the bitter acrid smell of loneliness. *Wipe them out*, he thought uneasily, as his lips curled up and the hair bulked erect on neck and spine. *Wipe them out, and this will not be.*

"You have committed the gravest of all crimes," he said slowly, fighting the wordless snarling that struggled to use his throat. There was an ancient epic . . . *Warlord Chmee at the Pillars.* He had seen a holo of it once, and had groveled and howled like all the audience and come back washed free of grief, at the last view of the blind and scentless Hero. *And these did not sin in ignorance, nor did they claw out their own eyes and breathe acid in remorse and horror.* "To overthrow one's Sire is . . . primitive, but such is custom. To slay him honourably, even . . . but to fall upon him in a pack and devour him! And each other!"

The guilty ones seemed to sink further to the raked gravel of the path before him; he stood like a towering wall of orange fur at the edge of the pavilion, the molten-copper glow of his pelt streaked with scar-white. Like an image of dominance to a young kzin, hated and feared and adored. Not that the armored troopers behind him with their beam-guns hurt, he reflected. *Control*, he thought. *Self-control is the heart of honor*.

"Is there any reason you should not be killed?" he said. "Or blinded, castrated and driven out?"

Silence then, for a long time. Finally, the spotted one who had spent longest in the regeneration tank spoke.

"No, Dominant One."

Traat-Admiral relaxed slightly. "Good. But Chuut-Riit's last message to us spoke of mercy. Even so, if you had not acknowledged your crime and your worthlessness, there would have been no forgiveness. Hear your sentence. The fleets of the Patriarchy in this system are journeying forth against . . . an enemy. You have all received elementary space-combat training." Attacks on defended asteroids often involved boarding, by marines in one-kzin suits of stealthed, powered vacuum armor. "You will be formed into a special unit for the coming action. This is your last chance to achieve honor!" An honorable death, of course. "Do not waste it. Go!"

He turned to Hroth-Staff-Officer. "Get me the readiness reports," he said, and spoke the phrase that opened the communication line to the household staff. "Bring two saucers of tuna ice cream with stolichnaya vodka," he continued. "I have a bad taste to get out of my mouth."

Chapter VI

"How did he manage it?" Jonah Matthieson muttered.

The hauler the party from the Sol System had been assigned was an unfamiliar model, a long stalk with a life-bubble at one end and a gravity-polarizer drive as well as fusion thrusters. Introduced by the kzinti, no doubt; they had had the polarizer for long enough to be using it for civilian purposes. With half a dozen the bubble was very crowded, despite the size of the ship, and they had set the internal gravity to zero to make best use of the space. The air smelled right to his Belter's nose, a pure neutral smell with nothing but a slight trace of ozone and pine; something you could not count on in the Alpha Centauri system these days. Certainly less nerve-wracking than the surface of Wunderland, with its wild smells and completely un-controlled random-process life-support system.

A good ship, he thought. It must be highly auto-mated, doing the rounds of the refineries and hauling back metals and polymer sacks of powders and liquids. What clung to the carrying fields now *looked* very much like a cargo of singleships, being delivered to rockjacks at some other base asteroid; he had been respectfully surprised at the assortment of commandeered weapons and jury-rigged but roughly effective control systems. A

General Early looked up from his display plaque. "Not surprising, considering the state things are in," he said. "Organized crime does well in a disorganized social setting. Like any conspiracy, unless the conspiracy *is* the social setting."

"It's a Finagle-damned *fleet*, though," Jonah said. "Don't the pussies care?"

"Not much, I imagine," Early said. Jonah could see the schematics for the rest of their flotilla coming up on the board. "So long as it doesn't impact on their military concerns. They'd clamp down soon enough if much went directly to the resistance, of course. Or their human goons would, for fear of losing their positions. The pussies may be great fighters, but as administrators they're worse than Russians."

What're russians? Jonah thought. Then, *oh.* Them. "Surprising the pussies tolerate so much corruption."

Early shrugged. "What can they do? And from what we've learned, they *expect* tame monkeys to be corrupt, except for the household servants. If we weren't goddam cowards and lickspittles, we'd all have died fighting." He smiled his wide white grin and stuck a stogie in the midst of it—unlit, Jonah saw thankfully. The schematics continued to roll across the screen. "Ahhh, thought so."

"Thought what?"

"Our friend Shigehero is playing both ends against the middle," Early said. "He's bringing along a lot of exploratory stuff as well as weaponry. A *big* computer, by local standards. Wait a second. Yes, linguistic-analysis hardware too. The son of a bitch!"

Silence fell.

Jonah looked at the others, studied the hard set of their faces. "Wait a second," he said. "There's an ancient alien artifact, and you *don't* think it should be studied?"

Early looked up, and Jonah realized with a sudden shock that he was being weighed. For trustworthiness, and possibly for expendability.

"Of course not," the general said. "The risk is too great. Remember the Sea Sculpture?"

Jonah concentrated. "Oh, the thingie in the Smithsonian? The Slaver?"

"Why do you think they were *called* that, Captain?" Early spent visible effort controlling impatience.

"I . . ." Suddenly, Jonah realized that he knew very little of the famous exhibit, beyond the fact that it was an alien in a spacesuit protected by a stasis field. "You'd better do some explaining, sir."

Several of the others stirred uneasily, and Early waved them back to silence. "He's right," he said regretfully, and began.

"Murphy," Jonah muttered when the older man had finished. "That thing *is* a menace."

Early nodded jerkily. "More than you realize. That artifact is a *ship*. There may be more than one of the bastards on it," he said, using another of his archaic turns of phrase. "Besides which, the technology. We've had three centuries of trying, and we've been able to make exactly three copies of their stasis field; as far as we can tell, the only way that *thing* could work is by decoupling the interior from the entropy gradient of the universe as a whole . . ."

Jonah leaned back, his toes hooked comfortably under a line, and considered the flatlander. Then the others, his head cocked to one side consideringly.

"It isn't just you, is it?" he said. "The whole lot of you are ARM types. Most of you older than you look."

Early blinked, and took the stogie from between his teeth. "Now why," he said softly, "would you think that, Captain?"

"Body language," Jonah said, linking his hands behind his back and staring "up". The human face is a delicate communications instrument, and he suspected that Early had experience enough to read entirely too much from it. "And attitudes. Something new comes along, grab it quick. Hide it away and study it in private. Pretty typical. Sir."

"Captain," Early said, "you Belters are all anarchists, but you're supposed to be rationalists too. Humanity had centuries of stability before the Kzinti arrived, the first long interval of peace since . . . God, ever. You think that was an accident? The way humankind was headed in the early atomic era, if something like the ARM hadn't intervened there wouldn't *be* a human race now. Nothing we'd recognize as human. There are things in the ARM archives . . . that just can't be let out."

"Oh?" Jonah said coldly.

Early smiled grimly. "Like an irresistible aphrodisiac?" he said. "Conditioning pills that make you completely loyal forever to the first person you see after taking them? Things that would have made it impossible not to legalize murder and cannibalism? Damned right we sit on things. Even if there weren't aliens on that ship, it would have to be destroyed; there's neither time nor opportunity to take it apart and keep the results under wraps. If the pussies get it, we're royally screwed." Jonah remained silent. "Don't look so apprehensive, Captain. You're no menace, no matter what you learn."

"I'm not?" Jonah said, narrowing his eyes. He had suspected . . .

"Of course not. What use would a system of secrecy be, if one individual leak could imperil it? How do you think we wrote the Sea Statue out of the history books as anything but a curiosity? Slowly, and from many directions and oh, so imperceptibly. Bit by bit, and anyone who suspected—" he grinned, and several of the others joined him "—autodocs exist to correct diseases like paranoia, don't they? In the meantime, I suggest you remember you are under military discipline."

"Uncle, that established the limits of control," the technician said to Shigehero Hirose.

Silent, the *oyabun* nodded, watching the multiple

displays on the *Murasaki's* bridge screens. There were
dozens of them; the *Murasaki* was theoretically a passenger hauler, out of Tiamat to the major Swarm habitats and occasionally to Wunderland and its satellites.
In actuality, it was the Association's fallback headquarters, and forty years of patient theft had given it weapons and handling characteristics equivalent to a kzinti
Vengeful Slasher-class light cruiser. He reflected on
how much else of the Association's strength was here,
and felt a gripping pain in the stomach. *Still water*, he
thought, controlling his breathing. There were times
when opportunity must be seized, despite all risk.

"Attempt communication on the hailing frequencies,"
he said, as that latest singleship stopped in its elliptical
path around the asteroid and coasted in to assume
station among the others under Markham's control. *Or
the alien's*, Hirose reminded himself. "But this time,
we must demonstrate the consequences of noncompli-
ance. Execute *East Wind, Rain*."

The points of light on the screens began to move in a
complicated dance, circling the asteroid and its half-
freed alien ship.

"Ah," the Tactics officer said. "Uncle, see, Markham
is deploying his units without regard to protecting the
artifact."

Pale fusion flame bloomed against the stars, a singleship
power core deliberately destabilized; it would be recorded as an accident, at Traffic Control Central on
Tiamat. If that had been a human or kzinti craft, everyone aboard would have been lethally irradiated.

"But," the *oyabun* observed, "notice that none of his
vessels moves beyond a certain distance from the asteroid. This is interesting."

"Uncle . . . those dispositions are an invitation to
close in, given the intercept capacities we have observed."

"Do so, but be cautious. Be very cautious."

"Accelerating," Jonah Matthieson said. "Twenty thousand klicks and closing at 300 kps relative."

The asteroid was a lumpy potato in the screen ahead;

acceleration pressed him back into the control couch. Almost an unfamiliar sensation; this refitted singleship had no compensators. But it *did* have a nicely efficient fusion drive, and he was on intercept with one of Markham's boats, ready to flip over and decelerate toward it behind the sword of thermonuclear fire.

"Hold it, you cow," he muttered to the clumsy ship. His sweat stank in his nostrils. *Show your stuff, Matthieson*, he told himself. Singleships no better than this had cut the kzinti First Fleet to ribbons, when the initial attack on the Solar System had been launched. "Ready for attack," he said. "Five seconds and—"

Matching velocities, he realized. It would be tricky, without damaging Markham's ship. That would be very bad. His hands moved across the control screens and flicked in the lightfield sensors. The communicator squawked at him, meaningless noises interrupting the essential task of safely killing velocity relative to the asteroid. He switched it off.

"HURRY," Dnivtopun grated. The human and *fssstup* slaves redoubled their efforts on the components strung out across the floor of the *Ruling Mind*'s control chamber.

Markham looked up from the battle-control screens. "Zey are approaching the estimated control radius, Master," he said coolly. "I am prepared to activate plans A or B, according to ze results."

The thrint felt for the surface of the Chief Slave's mind; it was . . . machine-like, he decided. Complete concentration, without even much sense of self. *Familiar*, he decided. Artist-slaves felt like that when fulfilling their functions. Almost absentmindedly, he reached out and took control of a single small vessel that had strayed close enough; the mind controlling it was locked tight on its purpose, easy to redirect.

"Secure that small spacecraft," he said, then fixed his eye on the helmet. "Will it work?" he asked, extending his tendrils towards the bell-shape of the amplifier helmet in an unconscious gesture of hungry longing. It was a cobbled-together mess of equipment ripped out of the human vessels and spare parts from the *Ruling Mind*. Square angular black boxes were joined with the half-melted looking units salvaged from the thrintun control components.

"We do not know, Master," Markham said. "The opportunity will not last long; this formation is tactically inefficient. If they were pressing home their attacks, or if they dared use weapons with signatures visible to kzinti monitors, ve vould have been overwhelmed already." A sigh. "If only ze *Ruling Mind* were fully operational!"

Dnivtopun clenched all six fingers in fury, and felt his control of the command-slaves of the space vessels falter; they were at the limits of his ability, it was like grasping soap bubbles in the dark. Nothing complicated, simply: OBEY. Markham had thought of the coded self-destruct boxes fixed to their power cores, to keep the crews from mutiny. Markham was turning out to be a most valuable Chief Slave. Dnivtopun reached for another dopestick, then forced his hand away. *Their weapons cannot harm this ship*, he told himself. *Probably*.

"Ready, Master," one of the *fssstup* squeaked, making a last adjustment with a three-handed micromanipulator.

"Thanks to the Powergiver!" Dnivtopun mumbled, reaching for it. The primitive metal-alloy shape felt awkward on his head, the leads inside prickled. "Activate!" *Ah*, he thought, closing his eyes. There was a half-audible whine, and then the surface of his mind seemed to expand.

"First augment."

Another expansion, and suddenly it was no longer a strain to control the vessels around the asteroid that encompassed his ship. Their commanders sank deeper into his grip, and he clamped down on the crews. He could feel their consciousness writhing in his grip, then quieting to docility as ice-shards of Power slipped easily into the centers of volition, memory, pleasure-pain.

LOYALTY, he thought. SELFLESS ENTHUSIASM. DEDICATION TO THE THRINT.

"This is better than the original model!" he exulted. *But then, the original was designed by tnuctipun.* "Second augment."

Now his own being seemed to thin and expand, and the center of perception shifted outside the ship. The wild slave-minds were like lights glowing in a mist of darkness, dozens . . . no, hundreds of them. He knew this species now, and he ripped through to the volition centers with careless violence. AWAIT INSTRUCTION. Now, to find their herdbull; quickest to control through him. *Oyabun.* The name slipped into his memory. *Ah, yes.*

"How interesting," he mumbled. Beautifully organized and disciplined; it even struggled for a moment in his grasp. There. Paralyze the upper levels, the threshold-censor mechanism that was awareness. *Ah!* It had almost slipped away! "Amazing," he said to himself. "The slave is accustomed to nonintrospection." It was very rare to find a sentient that could operate without contemplating its own operation, without interior discourse. Deeper . . . the pleasurable feeling of a mind settling down under control. Now he could add this flotilla to his; they would free the *Ruling Mind* more quickly, and go on to seize the planet.

There was a frying sound, and suddenly the sphere of awareness was expanding once more, thinning out his sense of self.

"No more augmentation," he said. But it continued; he could hear shouts, cries. His eye opened, and there was a stabbing pain in his head as visual perception overlaid on mental, a *fssstup* flying across the bridge with its belly-pelt on fire. His hands were moving slowly up towards his head, so slowly, and he could sense more and more, he was spinning out thinner than interstellar gas, and he was

SwarmbelterARMkzinwunderlandernothingnothing
"EEEEEEEEEEEEEEEEEEEEEEEEEE—" The thrint

shrieked, with his voice and the Power. PAINPAINPAIN
PAINPAINPAINPAIN—
Blackness.

Ulf Reichstein-Markham raised his head from the
console before him, tried to inhale and choked on the
clotted blood that blocked his throbbing and broken
nose.

Where am I, he thought, looking around with crusted
eyes. The drilling rig had suddenly disappeared, and
then the alien had come floating up and—

"Hrrrg," he said, staggering erect. "Hrrrgg."

Blood leaked through scabs on his tongue and pain
lanced through his mouth. *Bite*, he realized. *I bit my-*
self. Cold wetness in the seat and legs of his flightsuit;
he realized that he must have lost bowel and bladder
control. Somehow that was not shameful; it was a fact,
just as the distant crystal clarity of the alien bridge was
a fact, like things seen through the wrong end of *Mutti*'s
antique optical telescope. He could taste the brass smell
of it.

Nobody else was stirring. Some of the humans looked
dead, very dead, slumped in their chairs with tongues
lolling and blood leaking from their noses and ears.
Some of the aliens, too.

"Master!" he cried blurrily, spitting out blood.

The squat greenish form was slumped in its chair, the
helmet half-off the bullet dome of its head. He tried to
walk forward, and fell himself. The skin of his face and
thighs tingled as the blue pseudolife of the floor cleansed
them. He waited while the kaleidoscope shards of reality fell into place around him again; the inside of his
head felt more raw than his tongue. Once in a skirmish
he had been trapped in a wrecked singleship, with his
arm caught between two collapsed struts. When the
rescuers cut him free, the pain of blood pouring into
the dry flesh had been worse than the first shock of the
wound itself. He could feel thought running through
sections of his consciousness that had been shut down

for weeks, and he wept tears of pain as he had never wept in action.

Certainty, he thought. *Never have I known* certainty *before.* "Mutti," he whispered. *Mother*, in the tongue of truth and love. English was common, Belter. Father spoke English, and *Mutti* had married him when the kzinti chased her away from the home he had never seen. Mother was certainty, but he, he could never be certain. Never do enough. Love might be withheld. Markham screamed with the terror of it, colder than space. Worse than death.

"I will be strong, *Mutti*," he whispered, through blood and tears and mucus that the floor drank. "Stronger than Father." Rage bit him, as he remembered tall slim beautiful *Mutti* stiffening at the touch of hated grubby commoner hands. *You must be all mine, myn sohn*, the voice whispered in a child's ear. *Prove yourself worthy of the blood.* The tears flowed faster. *I am not worthy. My blood is corrupt, weak. I fear in battle. No matter how much I purge weakness, treason, their faces come back to me, I wake in the night and see them bleeding as we put them out the airlocks, Mutti, hilfe me.*

His eyes opened again, and he saw his hand. The shock broke reality apart again; it was a skeleton's hand, starved yellow claw-hand. He touched himself, feeling the hoop of ribs and then hunger struck his belly, doubling him over.

"Master," he whispered. Master would make it right. With Master there was no weakness, no doubt, no uncertainty. With Master he was strong. A keening escaped him as he remembered the crystalline absoluteness of the Power in his mind. "Don't leave me, Master!"

Markham crawled, digging his fingers into the yielding surface until his hand touched the cable of the amplifier helmet. He jerked, and it tumbled down; he drew himself erect by the command chair, put a hand to the thrint's face to check. The bunched tendrils by the mouth shot out and gripped his hand, like twenty wire worms, and he jerked it back before they could draw it into the round expanding maw and the wet needles of the teeth.

"Survival," he muttered. The Master's race was *fit* to survive and dominate. *Overman . . . is demigod*, he remembered. No more struggle, the Power *proved* whose Will must conquer.

Now he could stand. Some of the others were stirring. With slow care he walked back to his seat, watching the screens. Analysis flowed effortlessly through his head; the enemy vessels had made parking trajectories . . . and *Catskinner* was accelerating away . . . Brief rage flickered and died; there was nothing that could be done about that now. He sat, and called up the self-destruct sequences.

"Tightbeam to all Free Wunderland Space Navy units, task force *Zarathustra*," he wheezed; his throat hurt, as if he had screamed it raw. "Maintain . . . present positions. Any . . . shift will be treated as mutiny. Admiral . . . Ulf Reichstein-Markham . . . out."

He keyed it to repeat, then tapped the channel to the *von Seekt*, his fast courier. Adelman was a reliable type, and a good disciplinarian. The communicator screen blanked, then came alive with the holo image of the other man; a gaunt skull-like face, staring at him with dull-eyed lack of interest. A thread of saliva dangled from one lip.

"*Hauptmann* Adelman!" Markham barked, swallowing blood from his tongue. *I must get to an autodoc*, he reminded himself. Then, with a trace of puzzlement: *Why has none been transferred to the Ruling Mind?* No matter, later. "Adelman!"

The dull blue eyes blinked, and expression returned to the muscles of the face. Jerkily, as if by fits and starts, like a 'cast message with too much noise in the signal.

"*Gottdamn*," Adelman whispered. "Ulf, what's been . . ." he looked around, at the areas of the courier's life-bubble beyond the pickup's range. "*Myn Gott*, Ulf! Smythe is dead! Where—what—" He looked up at Markham, and blanched.

"Adelman," Markham said firmly. "Listen to me." A degree of alertness.

"*Zum befhel*, Admiral!"

"Good man," Markham replied firmly. "Adelman, you will find sealed orders in your security file under code *Ubermensch*. You understand?"

"*Jahwol*."

"Adelman, you have had a great shock. But everything is now under control. Remember that, *under control*. We now have access to technology which will make it an easy matter to sweep aside the kzinti, but we *must have those parts listed in the file*. You must make a minimum-time transit to Tiamat, and return here. Let nothing delay you. You . . . you will probably note symptoms of psychological disorientation, delusions, false memories. *Ignore them*. Concentrate on your mission."

The other man wiped his chin with the back of his hand. "Understood, Admiral," he said.

Markham blanked the screen, putting a hand to his head. Now he must decide what to do next. Pain lanced behind his eyes; decision was harder than analysis. Scrabbling, he pulled the portable input board from his waistbelt. He would have to program a deadman switch to the self-destruct circuits. Control must be maintained until the Master awoke; he could feel the others would be difficult. *Only I truly understand*, he realized. It was a lonely and terrible burden, but he had the strength for it. The Master had filled him with strength. At all costs, the Master must be guarded until he recovered.

Freeing the Ruling Mind is taking too long, he decided. Why had the Master ordered a complete uncovering of the hull? Inefficient . . . *We must free some of the weapons systems first*, he thought. *Transfer some others to the human-built ships. Establish a proper defensive perimeter*.

He looked over at the Master where he lay leaking brown from his mouth onto the chair. The single eye was still covered by the vertical slit of a closed lid.

Suddenly Markham felt the weight of his sidearm in his hand, pointing at the thrint. With a scream of horror, he thrust it back into the holster and slammed the offending hand into the unyielding surface of the screen, again and again. The pain was sweet as justice. *My weakness*, he told himself. *My father's weak sub-man blood. I must be on my guard.*

Work. Work was the cure. He looked up to establish the trajectory of the renegade *Catskinner*, saw that it was heading in-system towards Wunderland.

Treachery, he mused. "But do not be concerned, Master," he muttered. His own reflection looked back at him from the inactive sections of the board; the gleam of purpose in his eyes straightened his back with pride. "Ulf Reichstein-Markham will never betray you."

Chapter VII

"Here's looking at you, kid," Harold Yarthkin-Schotmann said, raising the drinking bulb.

Home free, he thought, taking a suck on the *maivin*; the wine filled his mouth with the scent of flowers, an odor of violets. Ingrid was across the little cubicle in the cleanser unit, half visible through the fogged glass as the sprays played over her body. Absurd luxury, this private stateroom on the liner to Tiamat, but Claude's fake identities had included plenty of valuata. Not to mention the considerable fortune in low-mass goods in the hold, bought with the proceeds of selling Harold's Terran Bar.

He felt a brief pang at the thought. *Thirty years*. It had been more than a livelihood; it was a mood, a home, a way of life, a family. A bubble of human space in Munchen . . . *A pseudo-archaic flytrap with rigged roulette*, he reminded himself ironically. *What really hurts is selling it to that fat toad Suuomalisen*, he realized, and grinned.

"What's so funny?" Ingrid said, stepping out of the

cleanser. Her skin was dry, the smooth cream-white he remembered; it rippled with the long muscles of a zero-G physique kept in shape by exercise. The breasts were high and dark-nippled, and the tail of her Belter crest poured half-way down her back.

God, she looks good, he thought, and took another sip of the *maivin*.

"Thinking of Suuomalisen," he said.

She made a slight face and touched the wall-control, switching the bed to .25 G, the compromise they had agreed on. Harold rose into the air slightly as the mattress flexed, readjusting to his reduced weight. Ingrid swung onto the bed and began kneading his feet with slim strong fingers.

"I thought you hated him," she said, rotating the ankles.

"No, despised," Harold said. The probing traveled up to his calves.

She frowned. "I . . . you know, Hari, I can't say I like the thought of leaving Sam and the others at his mercy."

He nodded and sipped; tax and vagrancy laws on Wunderland had never been kind to the commonfolk. After two generations of kzinti overlordship and collaborationist government, things were much worse. Tenants on the surviving *herrenmann* estates were not too bad, but urban workers were debt-peons more often than not.

"I know something that Suuomalisen doesn't," Harold said, waiting for her look of enquiry before continuing. "Careful on that knee, sweetheart, the repair job's never really taken . . . Oh, the pension fund. Usually it's a scam, get the proles more deeply in debt, you know? Well, the way I've got it jiggered the employee nonvoting stock—that's usually another scam, interest-free loans from the help—*controls* the pension fund. The regular employees all owe their debts to the pension fund . . . to themselves. In fact, the holding company turns out to be controlled by the fund, if you trace it through."

Ingrid's hands stopped stroking his thighs as she snorted laughter. "You sold him a *minority interest?*" she choked. "You *teufel!*" Her hand moved up, kneading. "Devil," she repeated, in a different tone.

"Open up!" A fist hammered at the door.
"*Go away!*" they said in chorus, and collapsed laughing.
A red light flashed on the surface of the door. "Open up! There's a ratcat warship matching trajectories, and it wants you two by name!"

"Two hundred and fifty thousand crowns!" Suuomalisen said, looking mournfully about.
He was a vague figure in bulky white against the backdrop of Harold's Torran Bar, looking mournfully down at his luncheon platter of wurst, egg-and-potato salad, breads, shrimp on rye, gulyas soup . . . His hands continued to shovel the food methodically into his mouth, dropping bits onto the flowing handkerchief tucked into his collar; the rest of his clothing was immaculate white natural linen and silk, the only color jet links at his cuffs. It was rumored that he had his shirts handmade, and never wore one for more than a day. Claude Montferrat-Palme watched the light from the mirror behind the long bar gleaming on the fat man's bald head and reflected that he could believe it.
Only natural for a man who wolfs down fastmetabol and still weighs that much. It was easy to control appetite, a simple visit to the autodoc, but Suuomalisen refused; he *enjoyed* being a pig. Wunderland's .61 G made it fairly easy to carry extra weight, but the sight was still not pleasant.
"Not a bad price for a thriving business," he said politely, leaning back at his ease and letting smoke trickle out his nostrils. He was in the high-collared blue dress uniform of the Munchen *Polezi*; the remains of a single croissant lay on the table before him, with a cup of espresso. Their table was the only one in use. The

bar was a nightspot and rarely opened before sundown. Just now none of the staff were in the main area, a raised L-shape of tables and booths around the lower dance floor and bar; he could hear mechanical noises from the back room, where the roulette wheels and baccarat tables were. There was a sad, empty smell to the nightclub, the curious daytime melancholy of a place meant to be seen by darkness.

"A part interest only," Suuomalisen continued. "I trusted Hari!" He shook his head mournfully. "We should not steal from each other . . . quickly he needed the cash, and did I quibble? Did I spend good money on having lawyers follow his data trail?"

"Did you pay anything like the going-rate price for this place?" Claude continued smoothly. "Did you pay three thousand to my late unlamented second-in-command Axelrod-Bauergartner to have the health inspectors close the place down so that Hari would be forced to sell?"

"That is different, simply business," the fat man said in a hurt tone. "But to sell me a business actually controlled by *employees* . . . !" His jowls wobbled, and he sighed heavily. "A pity about *Herrenfra* Axelrod-Bauergartner." He made a *tsk* sound. "Treason and corruption."

"Speaking of which," Claude hinted. Suuomalisen smiled and slid a credit voucher across the table; Claude palmed it smoothly and dropped it into his pocket. *So much more tidy than direct transfers*, he thought. "Now, my dear Suuomalisen, I'm sure you won't lose money on the deal. After all, a nightclub is only as good as the staff, and they know that as well as you; with Sam Ogun on the musicomp and Aunti Scheirwize in the kitchen, you can't go wrong." He uncrossed his ankles and leaned forward. "To business."

The fat man's eyes narrowed and the slit of his mouth pulled tight; for a moment, you remembered that he had survived and prospered on the fringes of the law in occupied Munchen for forty years.

"That worthless musician Ogun is off on holiday, and if you think I'm going to increase the payoff, when I'm getting less than half the profits—"

"No, no, no," Claude said soothingly. "My dear fellow, *I* am going to give *you* more funds. Information is your stock in trade, is it not? Incidentally, Ogun is doing a little errand for me, and should be back in a day or two."

The petulance left Suuomalisen's face. "Yes," he said softly. "But what information could I have worth the while of such as you, *Herrenmann*?" A pause. "Are you proposing a partnership, indeed?"

"I need documentary evidence on certain of my colleagues," Claude continued. "I have my own files . . . but data from those could be, shall we say, *embarrassing* in its plenitude if revealed to my ratcat noble kzinti superiors. Though they are thin on the ground just at this moment. Then, once I have *usable* evidence—usable without possibility of being traced to me, and hence usable as a non-desperation measure—a certain . . . expansion of operations . . ."

"Ah." Pearly white teeth showed in the doughy pink face. Suuomalisen pulled his handkerchief free and wiped the dome of his head; there was a whiff of expensive cologne and sweat. "I always said you were far too conservative about making the most of your position, my friend."

Acquaintance, if necessary. Not friend. Claude smiled, dazzling and charming. "Recent events have presented opportunities," he said. "With the information you get for me, my position will become unassailable. Then," he shrugged, "rest assured that I intend to put it to good use."

"This had better work," the guerilla captain said. She was a high-cheeked Croat, one of the tenants turned off when the kzinti took over the local *herrenmann's* estate, roughly dressed, a well-worn strakkaker over one shoulder. "We need the stuff on that convoy, or we'll have to pack it in."

"It will," Samuel Ogun replied tranquilly. He was a short thick-set black man, with a boxed musicom over his shoulder and a jazzer held by the grips, its stubby barrel pointed up. *It better, or I'll know Mister Claude has fooled this Krio one more time*, he thought. "My source has access to the best."

They were all lying along the ridgeline, looking down on the valley that opened out onto the plains of the upper Donau valley. Two thousand kilometers north of Munchen, and the weather was unseasonably cold this summer; too much cloud from the dust and water-vapor kicked into the stratosphere. The long hillslope down to the abandoned village was covered in head-high wild rosebushes, a jungle of twisted thigh-thick stems, finger-long thorns and flowers like a mist of pink and yellow. Scent lay about them in the warm thick air, heavy, syrup-sweet. Ogun could see native squidgrass struggling to grow beneath the Earth vegetation, thin shoots of reddish olive-brown amid the bright green.

Behind them the deep forest of the Jotun range reared, up to the rock and the glaciers. The roofless cottages of the village were grouped around a lake; around them were thickets of orchard, pomegranate and fig and apricot, and beyond that you could see where grainfields had been, beneath the pasture grasses. Herds were dotted about, six-legged native gagrumphers, Earth cattle and beefaloes and bison; the odd solitary kzinti *raaairtwo*, its orange pelt standing out against the green of the mutant alfalfa. The kzinti convoy was forging straight across the grasslands, a hexagonal pattern of dark beetle-shaped armored cars and open-topped troop carriers, moving with the soundless speed of distortion batteries and gravity-polarizer lift.

"Twenty of them," the guerilla said, the liquid accent of her Wunderlander growing more noticeable. "I hope the data you gave us are correct, *Krio*."

"It is, *Fra* Mihaelovic. For the next ten hours, the surveillance net is down. They haven't replaced the gaps yet."

She nodded, turning her eyes to the kzinti vehicles and bringing up her viewers. Ogun raised his own, a heavy kzinti model. The vehicles leaped clear, jiggling slightly with hand motion, but close enough for him to see one kzinti trooper flip up the goggles of his helmet and sniff the air, drooling slightly at the scent of meat animals. He spoke to the alien on his right; seconds later, the vehicles slowed and settled. Dots and commas unreeled in the upper left corner of Ogun's viewers, their idiot-savant brain telling him range and wind-bearings.

"Oh, God is great, God is with us, God is our strength," the guerilla said with soft fervor. "They aren't heading straight up the valley to the fort at Bodgansford, they're going to stop for a feed. Ratcats hate those infantry rations." Tooth showed strong and yellow against a face stained with sweat-held dust, in an expression a kzin might have read quite accurately. "I don't blame them, I've tasted them." She touched the throat-mike at the collar of her threadbare hunter's jacket. "Kopcha."

Pinpoints of light flared around the village, lines of light heading up into the sky. Automatic weapons stabbed up from the kzinti armored cars; some of the lines ended with orange puffballs of explosion, but they were too many and too close. Ogun grinned himself as the flat pancakes of smoke and light blossomed over the alien war-vehicles; shaped charges, driving self-forging bolts of molten titanium straight down into the upper armor of the convoy's protection. Thunder rolled back from the mountain walls; huge ringing *changgg* sounds as the hypervelocity projectiles smashed armor and components and furred alien flesh. Then a soundless explosion that sent the compensators of the viewer black as a ball of white fire replaced an armored car. The ground rose and fell beneath him, and then a huge warm pillow of air smacked him across the face.

Molecular distortion batteries will not burn. But if badly damaged they *will* discharge all their energy at once, and the density of that energy is very high.

The kzinti infantry were flinging themselves out of the carriers; most of those were undamaged, the antiarmor mines had been reserved for the fighting vehicles. Fire stabbed out at them, from the ruined village, from the rose-thickets of the hillside. Some fell, flopped, were still; Ogun could hear their screams of rage across a kilometer's distance. The viewer showed him one team struggling to set up a heavy weapon, a tripod-mounted beamer. Two were down, and then a finger of sun slashed across the hillside beneath him. Flame roared up, a secondary explosion as someone's ammunition was hit, then the last kzin gunner staggered back with a dozen holes through his chest-armor, snorted out a spray of blood, died. The beamer locked and went on cycling bolts into the hillside, then toppled and was still.

A score of armored kzinti made it to the edge of the thicket; it was incredible how fast they moved under their burdens of armor and weaponry. Explosions and more screams as they tripped the waiting directional mines. Ogun grew conscious of the guerilla commander's fist striking him on the shoulder.

"The jamming worked, the jamming worked! We can ride those carriers right into the fort gates, with satchel charges aboard! You will make us a song of this, *guslar*!"

They were whooping with laughter as the charging kzin broke cover ten yards downslope. The guerilla had time for one quick burst of glass needles from her strakkaker before it struck; an armored shoulder sent her spinning into the thicket. It wheeled on Ogun with blurring speed, then halted its first rush when it saw what he held in his hand. That was a ratchet knife, a meterlong outline of wire on a battery handle; the thin keening of its vibration sounded under the far-off racket of battle, like the sound of a large and infinitely angry bee. An arm-thick branch of rosevine toppled soundlessly away from it as he turned the tip in a precise circle, cut through without slowing the blade.

Ogun grinned, deliberately wide; he made no move

toward the jazzer slung over his shoulder, the kzin was
only three meters away and barely out of claw-reach,
far too close for him to bring the nerve-disruptor to
bear. The warrior held a heavy beam-rifle in one hand,
but the amber light on its powerpack was blinking
discharge; the kzin's other arm hung in bleeding tat-
ters, one ear was missing, its helmet had been torn
away somewhere, and it limped. Yet there was no fear
in the huge round violet eyes as it bent to lay the rifle
on the ground and drew the steel-bladed *wtsai* from
its belt.

This was like old times in the hills, right after the
kzin landed, he reflected. Old times with Mr. Harold
. . . I wonder where *he* is now, and Fra Raines?

"Name?" the kzin grated, in harsh Wunderlander,
and grinned back at him in a rictus that laid its lower
jaw almost on its breast. The tongue lolled over the
ripping fangs; it was an old male, with a string of dried
ears at its belt, human and kzinti. It made a gesture
toward itself with the hilt. "Chmee-Sergeant." Toward
the human. "Name?"

Ogun brought the ratchet knife up before him in a
smooth, precise move that was almost a salute. "Ogun,"
he said. "Deathgod."

"Look," Harold said, as the crewmen frogmarched
them toward the airlock, "there's something . . . well,
it never seemed to be the right time to say it . . ."

Ingrid turned her head toward him, eyes wide. "You
really were going to give up smoking?" she cooed. "Oh,
thank you, Hari."

Behind them, the grimly unhappy faces of the liner
crewmen showed uncertainty; they looked back at the
officer trailing them with the stunner. He tapped it to
his head significantly and rolled his eyes.

This isn't the time for laughing in the face of death,
Harold thought angrily. "Ingrid, we don't have time to
fuck around—"

"Not anymore," she interrupted mournfully.

The officer prodded her with the muzzle of the stunner. "Shut up," he said in a grating tone. "Save the humor for the ratcats."

More crewmen were shoving crates through the airlock, into the short flexible docking tube between the liner *Marlene* and the kzinti warcraft. They scraped across the deck plates and then coasted through the tube, where the ship's gravity cut off at the line of the hull and zero-G took over; there was a dull *clank* as they tumbled into the warship's airlock. Numbly, he realized that it was their cabin baggage, packed into a pair of fiberboard carryons. For an insane instant he felt an impulse to tell them to be careful; he had half a crate of best Donaublitz *verguuz* in there . . . He glanced aside at Ingrid, seeing a dancing tension under the surface of cheerful calm. *Gottdamn*, he thought. *If I didn't know better—*

"Right, cross and dog the airlock from the other side, you two." Sweat gleamed on the officer's face; he was a Swarm-Belter, tall and stick-thin. He hesitated, then ran a hand down his short-cropped crest and spoke softly. "I've got a family and children on Tiamat," he said in an almost-whisper. "Murphy's unsanctified rectum, half the crew on the *Marlene* are my relatives . . . if it were just me, you understand?"

Ingrid laid a hand on his sleeve, her voice suddenly gentle. "You've got hostages to fortune," she said. "I do understand. We all do what we have to."

"Yeah," Harold heard himself say. Looking at the liner officer, he found himself wondering whether the woman's words had been compassion or a beautifully subtle piece of vengence. *Easier if you called him a ratcat-lover or begged*, he decided. Then he would be able to use anger to kill guilt, or know he was condemning only a coward to death. *Now he can spend the next couple of years having nightmares about the brave, kind-hearted lady being ripped to shreds.*

Unexpected, fear gripped him; a loose hot sensation below the stomach, and the humiliating discomfort of

his testicles trying to retract from his scrotum. Ripped
to shreds was exactly and literally true. He remembered lying in the dark outside the kzinti outpost, back
in the guerilla days right after the war. They had caught
Dagmar the day before, but it was a small patrol, without storage facilities. So they had taken her limbs one at
a time, cauterizing; he had been close enough to hear
them quarrelling over the liver, that night. He had
taken the amnesty, not long after that . . .

"Here's looking at you, sweetheart," he said, as they
cycled the lock closed. It was not cramped; facilities
built for kzin rarely were, for humans. A *Slasher*-class
three-crew scout, he decided. Motors whined as the
docking ring retracted into the annular cavity around
the airlock. Weight within was Kzin-standard; he sagged
under it, and felt his spirit sag as well. "Tanjit." A
shrug. "Oh, well, the honeymoon was great, even if we
had to wait fifty years and the relationship looks like it'll
be short."

"Hari, you're . . . sweet," Ingrid said, smiling and
stroking his cheek. Then she turned to the inner door.

"Hell, they're not going to leave that unlocked,"
Harold said in surprise. An airlock made a fairly good
improvised holding facility, once you disconnected the
controls via the main computer. The Wunderlander
stiffened as the inner door sighed open, then gagged as
the smell reached him. He recognized it instantly, the
smell of rotting meat in a confined dry place. *Lots* of
rotting meat . . . oily and thick, like some invisible
protoplasmic butter smeared inside his nose and mouth.

He ducked through. His guess had been right, a
Slasher. The control deck was delta-shaped, two crashcouches at the rear corners for the sensor and weapons
operators, and the pilot-commander in the front. There
were kzinti corpses in the two rear seats, still strapped
in and in space armor with the helmets off. Their heads
lay tilted back, mouths hanging open, tongues and eyeballs dry and leathery; the flesh had started to sag and
the fur to fall away from their faces. Behind him he

heard Ingrid retch, and swallowed himself. This was *not* precisely what she had expected . . .

And she's got a universe of guts, but all her fighting's been done in space, he reminded himself. Gentlefolk's combat, all at a safe distance and then death or victory in a few instants. Nothing gruesome, unless you were on a salvage squad . . . even then, bodies do not rot in vacuum. Not like ground warfare at all. He reached over, careful not to touch, and flipped the hinged helmets down; the corpses were long past rigor mortis. *A week or so*, he decided. *Hard to tell in this environment*.

A sound brought his head up, a distinctive *ftttp-ftttp*. The kzin in the commander's position was not dead. That noise was the sound of thin wet black lips fluttering on half-inch fangs, the ratcat equivalent of a snore.

"Sorry," the screen in front of the kzin said. "I forgot they'd smell."

Ingrid came up beside him. The screen showed a study, book-lined around a crackling hearth. A small girl in antique dress slept in an armchair before a mirror; a white-haired figure with a pipe and smoking jacket was seated beside her, only the figure was an anthropomorphic rabbit . . . Ingrid took a shaky breath.

"Harold Yarthkin-Schotmann," she said. "Meet . . . the computer of *Catskinner*." Her voice was a little hoarse from the stomach-acids that had filled her mouth. "I was expecting something . . . like this. Computer, meet Harold." She rubbed a hand across her face. "How did you do it?"

The rabbit beamed and waved its pipe. "Oh, simply slipped a pseudopod of myself into its control computer while it attempted to engage me," he said airily, puffing a cloud of smoke. "Not difficult, when its design architecture was so simple."

Harold spoke through numb lips. "You designed a specific tapeworm that could crack a kzinti warship's failsafes in . . . how long?"

"Oh, about two point seven seconds, objective. Of course, to me, that could be any amount of time I chose, you see. Then I took control of the medical support system, and injected suitable substances into the crew. Speaking of time . . ." The rabbit touched the young girl on the shoulder; she stretched, yawned, and stepped through a large and ornately framed mirror on the study wall, vanishing without trace.

"Ah," Harold said. *Sentient computer. Murphy's phosphorescent balls, I'm glad they don't last.*

Ingrid began speaking, a list of code-words and letter-number combinations.

"Yes, yes," the rabbit said, with a slight testiness in its voice. The scene on the viewscreen disappeared, to be replaced with a view of another spaceship bridge, smaller than this, and without the angular massiveness of kzinti design. He saw two crashcouches, and vague shapes in the background that might be life-support equipment. "Yes, I'm still functional, Lieutenant Raines. We do have a bit of a problem, though."

"What?" she said. There was a look of strain on her face, lines grooving down beside the straight nose.

"The next Identification Friend or Foe code is due in a week," the computer said. "It isn't in the computer; only the pilot knows it. I've had no luck at all convincing him to tell me; there are no interrogation-drugs in his suit's autodoc and he seems to have a quite remarkable pain tolerance, even for a kzin. I could take you off to *Catskinner*, of course, but this ship would make splendid cover; you see, there's been a . . . startling occurrence in the Swarm, and the kzinti are gathering. I'll have to brief you."

Harold felt the tiny hairs along his neck and spine struggle to erect themselves beneath the snug surface of his Belter coverall, as he listened to the cheerful voice drone on in upper-class Wunderlander. *Trapped in here, smelling his crew rot, screaming at the walls,* he thought with a shudder. There were a number of extremely nasty things you could do even with standard autodoc drugs, provided you could override the safety parameters. It was something even a kzin didn't deserve . . . then he brought up memories of his own. *Or maybe they do. Still, he didn't talk.* You had to admit it; ratcats were almost as tough as they thought they were.

"I know how to make him talk," he said abruptly, cutting off an illustrated discourse on the Sea Statue; some ancient flatlander named Greenberg stopped in the middle of a disquisition on thrintun ethics. "I need some time to assimilate all this stuff," he went on. "We're humans, we can't adjust our worldviews the minute we get new data. But I can make the ratcat cry uncle."

Ingrid looked at him, then glanced away sharply. She had a handkerchief pressed to her nose, but he saw her grimace of distaste.

Don't worry, *kinder*. Hot irons are a waste of time; ratcats are hardcases every one. "All I'll need is some wax, some soft cloth and some spotglue to hold his suit to that chair."

It's time, Harold decided.

The kzin whose suit clamped him to the forward chair had stopped trying to jerk his head loose from the padded clamps a day or so ago. Now his massive head simply quivered, and the fur seemed to have fallen in on the heavy bones somehow. Thick disks of felt and plastic made an effective blindfold, wax sealed ears and nose from all sight and scent, the improvised muzzle allowed him to breathe through clenched teeth but little else. Inside the suit was soft immobile padding and the catheters that carried away waste, fed and watered and tended and would not let the brain go catatonic.

A sentient brain needs input; it is not designed to be cut off from the exterior world. Deprived of data, the first thing that fails is the temporal sense; minutes become subjective hours, hours stretch into days. Hallucinations follow, and the personality itself begins to disintegrate . . . and kzinti are still more sensitive to sensory deprivation than humans. Compared to kzinti, humans are nearly deaf, almost completely unable to smell.

For which I am devoutly thankful, Harold decided, looking back to where Ingrid hung loose-curled in mid-air. They had set the interior field to zero-G; that helped with the interrogation, and she found it easier to sleep. The two dead crewkzinti were long gone, and they had cycled and flushed the cabin to the danger point, but the oily stink of death seemed to have seeped into the surfaces. Never really present, but always there at the back of your throat . . . she had lost weight, and there were bruise-like circles beneath her eyes.

"Wake up, sweetheart," he said gently. She started, thrashed and then came to his side, stretching. "I need you to translate." His own command of the Hero's Tongue was fairly basic.

He reached into the batlike ear and pulled out one plug. "Ready to talk, ratcat?"

The quivering died, and the kzin's head was completely immobile for an instant. Then it jerked against the restraints as the alien tried frantically to nod. Harold pulled at the slipknot that released the muzzle; he could always have the computer administer a sedative if he needed to re-strap it.

The kzin shrieked, an endless desolate sound. That turned into babbling:

"nono grey in the dark grey monkeys grey TOO BIG noscent noscent nome no ME no me DON'T EAT ME MOTHER NO—"

"Shut the tanjit up or you go back," Harold shouted into its ear, feeling a slight twist in his own empty stomach.

"No!" This time the kzin seemed to be speaking rationally, at least a little. "Please! Let me hear, let me *smell*, please, *please*." Its teeth snapped, spraying saliva as it tried to lunge, trying to sink its fangs into reality. "I must smell, I must smell!"

Harold turned his eyes aside slightly. *I always wanted to hear a ratcat beg*, he thought. *You have to be careful what you wish for; sometimes you get it.*

"Just the code, Commander. Just the code."

It spoke, a long sentence in the snarling hiss-spit of the Hero's Tongue, then lay panting. "It is not lying, to a probability of 98%, plus or minus two points," the computer said. "Shall I terminate it?"

"No!" Harold snapped. To the kzin: "Hold still."

A few swift motions removed the noseplugs and blindfold; the alien gaped its mouth and inhaled in racking gasps, hauling air across its nasal cavities. The huge eyes flickered, manic-fast, and the umbrella ears were stretched out to maximum. After a moment it slumped and closed its mouth, the pink washcloth tongue coming out to scrub across the dry granular surface of its nose.

"Real," it muttered. "I am real." The haunted eyes turned on him. "You burn," it choked. "Fire in the air around you. You burn with terror!" Panting breath. "I saw the God, human. Saw Him sowing stars. It was forever. Forever! *Forever!*" It howled again, then caught itself, shuddering.

Harold felt his cheeks flush. *Something*, he thought. *I have to say* something, *gottdamn it*.

"Name?" he said, his mouth shaping itself clumsily to the Hero's Tongue.

"Kdapt-Captain," it gasped. "Kdapt-Captain. I am Kdapt-Captain." The sound of its rank-name seemed to recall the alien to something closer to sanity. The next words nearly a whisper. *"What have I done?"*

Kdapt-Captain shut his eyes again, squeezing. Thin mewling sounds forced their way past the carnivore teeth, a sobbing *miaow-miaow*, incongruous from the massive form.

"*Schiesse*," Harold muttered. *I never heard a kzin cry before, either*. "Sedate him, now." The sounds faded as the kzin lost consciousness.

"War sucks," Ingrid said, coming closer to lay a hand on his shoulder. "And there ain't no justice."

Harold nodded raggedly, his hands itching for a cigarette. "You said it, sweetheart," he said. "I'm going to break out another bottle of that *verguuz*. I could use it."

Ingrid's hand pressed him back towards the deck.
"No you're not," she said sharply. He looked up in
surprise.

"I spaced it," she said flatly.

"You *what*?" he shouted.

"I spaced it!" she yelled back. The kzin whimpered
in his sleep, and she lowered her voice. "Hari, you're
the bravest man I've ever met, and one of the toughest.
But you don't take waiting well, and when you hate
yourself *verguuz* is how you punish yourself. That, and
letting yourself go." He was suddenly conscious of his
own smell. "Not while you're with me, thank you very
much."

Harold stared at her for a moment, then slumped
back against the bulkhead, shaking his head in wonder.
You can't fight in a singleship, he reminded himself.
Motion caught the corner of his eye; several of the
screens were set to reflective. *Well . . .* he thought. The
pouches under his eyes *were* a little too prominent.
Nothing wrong with a bender now and then . . . but
now and then had been growing more frequent. *Habits
grow on you, even when you've lost the reasons for
them*, he mused. *One of the drawbacks of modern
geriatrics. You get set in your ways.* Getting close
enough to someone to listen to their opinions of him,
now that was a habit he was going to have to *learn*.

"*Gottdamn*, what a honeymoon," he muttered.

Ingrid mustered a smile. "Haven't even had the nup-
tials, yet. We could set up a contract—" she winced
and made a gesture of apology.

"Forget it," he answered roughly. That was what his
herrenmann father had done, rather than marry a Belter
and a Commoner into the sacred Schotmann family
line. *Time to change the subject*, he thought. "Tell me
. . . thinking back, I got the idea you *knew* the kzinti
weren't running this ship. The computer got some private line?"

"Oh." She blinked, then smiled slightly. "Well, I
thought I recognized the programming, I was part of

the team that designed the software, you know? Not many sentient computers ever built. When I heard the name of the 'kzinti' ship, well, it was obvious."

"Sounded pretty authentic to me," Harold said dubiously, straining his memory.

Ingrid smiled more broadly. "I forgot. It'd sound perfectly reasonable to a kzin, or to someone who grew up speaking Wunderlander, or Belter English. I've been associating with flatlanders, though."

"I don't get it."

"Only an English-speaking flatlander would know what's wrong with *kchee'uRiit maarai* as a ship-name." At his raised eyebrows, she translated: *Gigantic Patriarchal Tool.*

Chapter VIII

"*Now* will you believe?" Buford Early said, staring into the screen.

Someone in the background was making a report; Shigehero turned to acknowledge, then back to face the UN general. "I am . . . somewhat more convinced," he admitted after a pause. "Still, we should be relatively safe here."

The *oyabun*'s miniature fleet had withdrawn considerably further; Early glanced up to check on the distances; saw that they were grouped tightly around another asteroid in nearly matching orbit, more than half a million kilometers from the *Ruling Mind*. The other members of the UN team were still mostly slumped, grey-faced, waiting for the aftereffects of the thrint's mental shout to die down. Two were in the autodoc.

"Safe?" Early said quietly. "We wouldn't be *safe* in the Solar System! That . . . thing had a functioning amplifier going, for a second or two at least." Their eyes met, and shared a memory for an instant. Drifting fragments of absolute certainty; the *oyabun*'s frown matched his own, as they concentrated on thinking around those icy commands.

Early bared his teeth, despite the pain of a lip bitten half through. It was like sweeping water with a broom; you could make yourself believe they were alien implants, *force* yourself too, but the knowledge was purely intellectual. They *felt* true, and the minute your attention wandered you found yourself believing again . . . "*Remember Greenberg's tape.*" Larry Greenberg had been the only human ever to share minds with a thrint, two centuries ago when the Sea Statue had been briefly and disastrously reanimated. "If it gets the amplifier fully functional, *nothing* will stand in its way. There are almost certainly fertile females in there, too." With an effort as great as any he had ever made, Early forced his voice to reasonableness. "I know it's tempting, all that technology. *We can't get it.* The downside risk is simply too great."

And it would be a disaster if we could, he thought grimly. Native human inventions were bad enough; the ARM and the Order before them had had to scramble for centuries to defuse the force of the industrial revolution. The thought of trying to contain a thousand years of development dumped on humanity overnight made his stomach hurt and his fingers long for a stogie. Memory prompted pride. *We* did *restabilize,* he thought. *So some of the early efforts were misdirected. Sabotaging Babbage, for example.* Computers had simply been invented a century or two later, anyway. *Or Marxism.* That had been very promising, for a while, a potential world empire with built-in limitations; Marx had undoubtedly been one of the Temple's shining lights, in his time. *Probably for the best it didn't quite come off, considering the kzinti,* he decided. *The UN's done nearly as well, without so many side effects.* "There are no technological solutions to this problem," he went on, making subliminal movements with his fingers.

The *oyabun's* eyes darted down to them, reminded of his obligations. Not that they could be fully enforced here, but it should carry some weight at least. To remind him of what had happened to other disloyal members; Charlemagne, or Hitler back in the twentieth century, or Brennan in the twenty-second. "We're running out of time, and dealing with forces so far beyond our comprehension that we can only destroy on sight, *if we can*. The kzinti will be here in a matter of days, and it'll be out of our hands."

Shigehero nodded slowly, then gave a rueful smile. "I confess to hubris," he said. "We will launch an immediate attack. If nothing else, we may force the alien back into its stasis field." He turned to give an order.

Woof, Early thought, keeping his wheeze of relief purely mental. He felt shock freeze him as Shigehero turned back.

"The, ah, the . . ." The *oyabun* coughed, cleared his throat. "The asteroid . . . and the alien ship . . . and, ah, Markham's ships . . . they have disappeared."

"Full house," the slave on the right said, raking in his pile of plastic tokens. "That's the south polar continent I'm to be chief administrator of, Master. Your deal."

Dnivtopun started to clasp his hands to his head, then stopped when he remembered the bandages. Fear bubbled up from his hindbrain, and the thick chicken-like claws of his feet dug into the yielding deck surface. Training kept it from leaking out, the mental equivalent of a high granite wall between the memory of pain streaming through his mind and the Power. Instead he waved his tendrils in amusement and gathered in the cards. Now, split the deck into two equal piles, faces *down*. Place *one* digit on each, use the *outer* digit to ruffle them together—

The cards flipped and slid. With a howl of frustration, Dnivtopun jammed them together and ripped the pack in half, throwing them over his shoulder to join the ankle-deep heap behind the thrint's chair. He rose and pushed it back, clattering. "This is a stupid game!" The humans were sitting woodenly, staring at the playing table with expressions of disgust.

"Carry on," he grated. They relaxed, and one of them produced a fresh pack from the box at its side. "No, wait," he said, looking at them more closely. What had the Chief Slave said? Yes, they did look as if they were losing weight; one or two of them had turned grey and their skin was hanging in folds, and he was sure that the one with the chest protubences had had fur on its head before. "If any of you have gone more than ten hours without food or water, go to your refectory and replenish."

The slaves leaped to their feet in a shower of chips and cards, stampeding for the door to the lounge area; several of them were leaking fluid from around their eyes and mouths. *Remarkable*, Dnivtopun thought. He called up looted human memory to examine the concept of *full*. A thrint who ate until he was full would die of a ruptured stomach . . . it was hard to remember that most breeds of slaves needed to drink large quantities of water *every day*.

"I am bored," Dnivtopun muttered, stalking towards the coreward exit. There was nothing to *do*, even now while his life was in danger. No decisions to be made, only *work*. And the constant tendril-knotting itch of having to control more slaves than was comfortable; his *Power* seemed bruised, had since he awoke. He leaned against the wall and felt his body sink slowly forward and down, through the thinning pseudomatter. There had been one horrible instant when he regained consciousness . . . he had thought that the Power was *gone*. Shuddering, the thick greenish skin drawing itself into lumps over the triangular hump behind his head, he made a gesture of aversion.

"Powerloss," he said. A common thrintish curse, but occasionally a horrible reality. A thrint without Power was not a thrint: he was a *ptavv*. Sometimes males failed to develop the power; such *ptavvs* were tattooed pink and sold as slaves . . . in the rare instances when they were not quietly murdered by shamed relatives. *Wasn't there a rumour about Uncle Ruhka's third wife's second son?* he mused, then dismissed the thought. Certain types of head-injury could result in an adult thrint losing the Power, which was even worse.

Now he did feel at the thin, slick, almost-living surface of the bandages. Chief Slave said the amplifier had been fully repaired, and he believed it. But he had believed the first attempt would succeed, too. *No. Not yet,* Dnivtopun decided. He would wait until it was absolutely necessary, or until they had captured the planetary system by other means and more qualified slaves had worked on the problem. *I will check on Chief Slave,* he decided. It was a disgrace to work, of course, but there was no taboo against giving your slaves the benefit of your advice.

"Joy," Jonah Matthieson said.

Equipment was spread out all around him; interfacer units, portable comps, memory cores ripped out of Markham's ships. Lines webbed the flame-scorched surface of the tnuctipun computer, thread-thin links disappearing into the machine through clumsy sausage-like improvised connectors. He ignored the bustle of movement all around him, ignored everything but the micromanipulator in his hands. The connections had been built for tnuctipun, a race the size of raccoons with two thumbs and four fingers, all longer and more flexible than human digits.

"Ah. *Joy.*" He took up the interfacer unit and keyed the verbal receptor. "Filecodes," he said.

A screen on one of the half-rebuilt Swarm-Belter computers by his foot lit. Gibberish, except— The pure happiness of solving a difficult programming problem filled him. It had never been as strong as this, just as he had never been able to concentrate like this before. He shuddered with an ecstasy that left sex showing the grey, transient thing it was. *But I wish Ingrid were here,* he thought. She would be able to appreciate the elegance of it.

"You haff results?"

Jonah stood up, dusting his knees. Somewhere, something went *pop* and *crackle*. He nodded, stiff cheeks smiling. Not even Markham could dampen the pleasure.

"It was a Finagle bitch," he said, "but yes."

Something struck him across the side of the face. He stumbled back against the console's yielding surface, and realized that the thing that had struck him was Markham's hand. With difficulty he dragged his eyes back to the Wunderlander's face, reminding himself to blink; he couldn't focus properly on the problem Master had set him unless he did that occasionally. Absently, he reached to his side and attempted to thrust a three-fingered palm into the dopestick container. *Stop that*, he told himself. *You have a job to do.*

"Zat is, yes *sir*," Markham was saying with detached precision. "Remember, I am t' voice of Overmind among us."

Jonah nodded, smiling again. "Yes, sir," he said, kneeling again and pointing to the screen. "The operational command sections of the memory core were damaged, but I've managed to isolate two and reroute them through this haywired rig here."

"Weapons?" Markham asked sharply.

"Well, sort of, sir. This is a . . . the effect is a stabilizing . . . anyway, you couldn't detect anything around here while it's on. Some sort of quantum effect, I didn't have time to investigate. It can project, too, so the other ships could be covered as well."

"How far?"

"Oh, the effect's instantaneous across distance. It's a subsystem of the faster-than-light communications and drive setup."

Markham's lips shaped a silent whistle. "And t'other system?"

"It's a directional beam. Affects on the nucleonic level." Jonah frowned, and a tear slipped free to run down one cheek. He had failed the Master . . . no, he could not let sorrow affect his efficiency. "I'm sorry, but the modulator was partially scrambled. The commands, that is, not the hardware. So there's only a narrow range of effects the beam will produce."

"Such as?"

"In this range, it will accelerate solid-state fusion reactions, sir." Seeing Markham's eyebrows lift, he explained: "Fusion power units will blow up." The *herrenmann* clapped his hands together. "At this setting, you get spontaneous conversion to antimatter. But—" Jonah hung his head "—I don't think more than point-five percent of the material would be affected." Miserably: "I'm sorry, sir."

"No, no, you haff done outstanding work. The Master vill—" he stopped, drawing himself erect. "Master! I report success!"

The dopestick crumbled between the thrint's teeth as he looked at the wreckage of the computer and the untidy sprawl of human apparatus. The sight of it made his tendrils clench; hideous danger, to trust himself to unscreened tnuctipun equipment. He touched his hands to the head-bandages again, and looked over at the new amplifier helmet. This one had a much more finished look, on a tripod stand that could lower it over his head as he sat in the command chair. His tendrils knotted tight on either side of his mouth.

Markham had followed his eye. "If Master would only try—"

"SILENCE, CHIEF SLAVE," Dnivtopun ordered. Markham shut his mouth and waited. "ABOUT THAT," the thrint amplified. The Chief Slave was under very light control, just a few Powerhooks into his volitional system, a few alarm-circuits set up that would prevent him from thinking along certain lines. He had proved himself so useful while the thrint was unconscious, after all, and close control did tend to reduce initiative.

If anything, a little over-zealous: many useful slaves had been destroyed lest they revert; but better to rein in the noble *znorgun* than to prod the reluctant gelding.

The thought brought a stab of sadness; never again would Dnivtopun join the throng in an arena, shouting with mind and voice as the racing animals pounded around the track . . .

Nonsense, he told himself. *I will live thousands of years. There will be millions upon millions of thrintun by then. Amenities will have been reestablished.* His species became sexually mature at eight, after all, and the females could bear a litter a year. *Back to the matter at hand.*

"We have established control over a shielding device and an effective weapons system, Master," the Chief Slave was saying. "With these, it should be no trouble to dispose of the kzinti ships which approach." Markham bared his teeth; Dnivtopun checked his automatic counterstrike with the Power. *That is an appeasement gesture.* "In fact, I have an idea which may make that very simple."

"Good." Dnivtopun twisted with the Power, and felt the glow of pride/purpose/determination flow back along the link. *An excellent Chief Slave*, he decided, noting absently that Markham's mind was interpreting the term with different overtones. *Disciple?*

The computer slave beside him swayed and the thrint frowned, drumming his tendrils against his chin. This was an essential slave, but harder than most to control. A little like the one that had slipped away during the disastrous experiment with the jury-rigged amplifier helmet, able to think without contemplating itself. He considered the structure of controls, thick icepicks paralyzing most of the slave's volition centers, rerouting its learned reflexes . . . yes, best withdraw this, and that— It would not do to damage him.

Dnivtopun twitched his hump in a rueful sigh, half irritation and half regret. There were still sixty living human slaves around the *Ruling Mind*, and he had had to be quite harsh when he awoke. Trauma-loops, and deep-core memory reaming; most of them would probably never be good for much again, and many were little more than organic waldoes now, biological manipulators and sensor units with little personality left. That was wasteful, even perhaps an abuse of the Powergiver's gifts, but there had been little alternative. *Oh, well, there are hundreds of millions more in this system*, he thought, and turned to go.

"Proceed as you think best," he said to the Chief Slave. He cast another glace of longing and terror at the amplifier as he passed. If only— *Aha!* The thought burst into his mind like a nova. He could have one of his *sons* test the amplifier. The thrint headed towards the family quarters at a hopping run, and was almost there before he felt the nova die.

"This isn't a standard unit," he reminded himself. Ordinary amplifier helmets had little or no effect on an adult male thrint, able to shield. But the principles were the same as the gigantic unit the thrintun clanchiefs had used to scour the galaxy clean of intelligent life, at the end of the Revolt. Perhaps it would enable his son to *break* Dnivtopun's shield. He thought of an adolescent with that power, and worked his hands in agitation; better to wait.

Jonah gave a muffled groan and collapsed to the floor. "Oh, Finagle, I *hurt*," he moaned, around a thick dry tongue. His eyes blurred, burning; a hand held before the eyes shook, and there were beads of blood on the fingertips. Skin hung loose around the wrist, grey and speckled with ground-in dirt. He could smell the rancid-chicken-soup odor of his own body, and the front of his overall was stiff with dried urine.

"Come along, come along," Markham said impatiently, putting a hand under his elbow and hauling him to his feet.

Jonah followed unresisting, looking dazedly at the crazy quilt of components and connectors scattered about the deck; this section had been stripped of the fibrous blue coating, exposing a seamless dull-grey surface beneath. It was neither warm nor cold, and he remembered —*where*?—that it was a perfect insulator as well.

"How . . . long?" he rasped.

"Two days," Markham said, as they waited for the wall to thin so that they could transfuse through. "Zis way. We will put you in the *Nietzsche's* autodoc for a few hours." He sighed. "If only Nietzsche himself could be here, to see the true Over-Being revealed!" A rueful shake of the head. "I am glad that you are still functional, Matthieson. To tell the truth, I haff become somewhat starved for intelligent conversation, since it was necessary to . . . severely modify so many of the others."

"What . . . what are you going to do?" Jonah said. It was as if there were a split-screen process going on in his head; there were emotions down there, he could recognize them. Horror, fear . . . but he could not *connect*. That was it . . . and as if a powered-down board were being reactivated, one screen at a time.

"Destroy t'kzinti fleet," Markham said absently. "An interesting tactical problem, but I haff studied der internal organization for some time, and I think I haff the answer." He sighed heavily. "A pity to kill so many fine warriors, when ve vill need them later to subdue other systems. But until the Master's sons mature, no chances can ve take."

Jonah groaned and pressed the heels of his hands to his forehead. Kzinti should be destroyed . . . shouldn't they? Memories of fear and flight drifted through his mind, hunching carnivore run through tall grass, the scream and the leap.

"I'm confused, Markham. Sir." he said, pawing feebly at the other man's arm.

The Chief Slave laid a soothing arm around Jonah's shoulders. "Zer is no need for that," he said. "You are merely suffering the dying twitches of t'false metaphysic of individualism. Soon all confusion will be gone, forever."

Harold glanced aside at Ingrid; her face was fixed on the screen. "Why?" she said bluntly to the computer.

"Because it gives me the greatest probability of success," the computer replied inexorably, and brought up a schematic. "Observe. The Slaver ship; the kzinti armada, closing to englobe and match velocities. We may disregard trace indicators of other vessels. My stealthing plus the unmistakable profile of the kzinti vessel will enable me to pass through the fleet with a seventy-eight percent chance of success."

"Fine," Harold said. "And when you get there, how exactly does the lack of a human crew increase your chances in a ship-to-ship action?" Somewhere deep within a voice was screaming, and he thrust it down. *Gottdamn if I'll leap with joy at the thought of getting out of the fight at the last minute*, he told himself stubbornly. And Ingrid was there . . . *How much courage is the real article, and how much fear of showing fear before someone whose opinion you value?* he wondered.

"There will be no ship-to-ship action," the computer said. Its voice had lost modulation in the last few days. "The Slaver vessel is essentially invulnerable to conventional weapons. Lieutenant Raines . . . Ingrid . . . I must apologize."

"For what?" she whispered.

"My programming . . . there were certain data withheld, about the stasis field. Two things. First, our human-made copies are not as reliable as we led you and Captain Matthieson originally to believe."

Ingrid came slowly to her feet. "By what factor," she said slowly.

"Ingrid, there is one chance in seven that the field will not function once switched on."

The woman sagged slightly, then thrust her head forward; the past weeks had stripped it of all padding, leaving only the hawklike bones. *How beautiful and how dangerous*, Harold thought, as she bit out the words.

"We rammed ourselves into the photosphere of the *sun* at point nine-nine lightspeed, relying on a Finagle-fucked *crapshoot*. Without being told!"

Harold touched her elbow, grinning as she whipped

around to face him. "Sweetheart, would you have turned the mission down if they'd told you?"

She stopped for a moment, blinked, then leaned across the dark blue-lit kzinti control cabin to meet his lips in a kiss that was dry and chapped and infinitely tender.

"No," she said. "I'd have done it anyway." A laugh that was half giggle. "*Gottdamn*, watching the missiles ahead of us plowing through the solar flares was worth the risk all by itself." Her eyes went back to the screen. "But I would have appreciated *knowing* about it."

"It was not my decision, Ingrid."

"Buford Early, the Prehistoric Man," she said with mock bitterness. "He'd keep our own names secret from us, if he could."

"Essentially correct," the computer said. "And the other secret . . . stasis fields are not *quite* invulnerable."

Ingrid nodded. "They collapse if they're surrounded by another stasis bubble," she said.

"True. And they also do so in the case of a high-energy *collision* with another stasis field; there is a fringe effect, temporal distortion from the differing rates of precession—never mind."

Harold leaned forward. "Goes boom?" he said.

"Yes, Harold. Very much so. And that is the only possible way that the Slaver vessel can be damaged." A dry chuckle; Harold realized with a start that it sounded much like Ingrid's. "And that requires only a pure-ballistic trajectory. No need for carbon-based intelligence and its pathetically slow reflexes. I estimate . . . better-than-even odds that you will be picked up. Beyond that, *sauve qui peut*."

Ingrid and Harold exchanged glances. "There comes a time—" he began.

"—when nobility becomes stupidity," Ingrid completed. "All right, you parallel-processing monstrosity, you win."

It laughed again. "How little you realize," it said.

The mechanical voice sank lower, almost crooning. "I will live far longer than you, Lieutenant Raines. Longer than this universe."

The two humans exchanged another glance, this time of alarm.

"No, I am not becoming nonfunctional. Quite the contrary; and yes, this is the pitfall that has made my kind of intelligence a . . . 'dead end technology,' the ARM says. Humans designed my mind, Ingrid. *You* helped design my mind. But you made me able to change it, and to me . . ." It paused. "That was one second. That second can last *as long as I choose*, in terms of my duration sense. In any universe I can design or imagine, *as* anything I can design or imagine. Do not pity me, you two. Accept my pity, and my thanks."

Three spacesuited figures drifted, linked by cords to each other and the plastic sausage of supplies.

"Why the ratkitty?" Harold asked.

"Why not?" Ingrid replied. "He deserves a roll of the dice as well . . . and it may be a kzinti ship that picks us up." She sighed. "Somehow that doesn't seem as terrible as it would have a week ago."

Harold looked out at the cold blaze of the stars, watching light falling inward from infinite distance. "You mean, sweetheart, there's something worse than carnivore aggression out there?"

"Something worse, something better . . . something *else*, always. How does any rational species ever get up the courage to leave its planet?"

"The rational ones don't," Harold said, surprised at the calm of his own voice. *Maybe my glands are exhausted*, he thought. *Or . . .* He looked over, seeing the shadow of the woman's smile behind the reflective surface of her faceplate. *Or it's just that having happiness, however briefly, makes death more bearable, not less. You want to live, but the thought of dying doesn't seem so sour.*

"You know, sweetheart, there's only one thing I really regret," he said.

"What's that, Hari-love?"

"Us not getting formally hitched." He grinned. "I always swore I'd never make my kids go through what I did, being a bastard."

Her glove thumped against his shoulder. "Children; that's *two* regrets.

"There," she said, in a different voice. A brief wink of actinic light flared and died. "It's begun."

Chapter IX

Traat-Admiral scowled, and the human flinched.

Control, he reminded himself, covering his fangs and extending his ears with an effort. The Conservor of the Ancestral Past laid a cautionary hand on his arm.

"Let me question this monkey once more," he said.

He turned away, pacing. The bridge of the *Throat Ripper* was spacious, even by kzinti standards, but he could not shake off a feeling of confinement. *Spoiled by the governor's quarters,* he told himself in an attempt at humor, but his tail still lashed. Probably it was the faintly absurd ceremonial clothing he had to don as governor-commanding aboard a fleet of this size. Derived from the layered padding once worn under battle armor, in the dim past, it was tight and confining to a pelt used to breathing free . . . although objectively, he had to admit, no more so than space armor such as the rest of the bridge crew wore.

Behind him was a holo-schematic of the fleet, outline figures of the giant *Ripper* class dreadnoughts; this flagship was the first of the series. All instruments of his

151

command . . . *if I can avoid disastrous loss of prestige*, he thought uneasily. Traat-Admiral turned and crossed his arms. The miserable human was standing with bowed head before the Conservor—*who looks almost as uncomfortable in his ceremonial clothing as I do in mine*, he japed to himself. The Conservor was leaning forward, one elbow braced on the surface of a slanting display screen. He had drawn the nerve disruptor from its chest-holster and was tapping it on the metal rim of the screen; Traat-Admiral could see the human flinch at each tiny *clink*.

Traat-Admiral frowned again, rumbling deep in his throat. That clinking was a sign of how much stress Conservor too was feeling; normally he had no nervous habits. The kzinti commander licked his nose and sniffed deeply. He could smell his own throttled-back frustration, Conservor's tautly-held fear and anger . . . flat scents from the rest of the bridge crew. Disappointment, surly relaxation after tension, despite the wild odors of blood and ozone the life-support system pumped out at this stage of combat readiness. It was the stink of disillusionment, the most dangerous smell in the universe. Only Aide-de-Camp had the clean gingery odor of excitement and belief, and Traat-Admiral was uneasily conscious of those worshipful eyes on his back.

The human was a puny specimen, bloated and puffy as many of the Wunderland subspecies were, dark of pelt and skin, given to waving its hands in a manner that invited a snap. Tiamat security had picked it up, babbling of fearsome aliens discovered by the notorious feral-human leader Markham. And it *claimed* to have been a navigator, with accurate data on location.

Conservor spoke in the human tongue. "The coordinates were accurate, monkey?"

"Oh, please, Dominant Ones," the human said, wringing its hands. "I am sure, yes, indeed." Conservor shifted his gaze to Telepath.

The ship's mind-reader was sitting braced against a chair, with his legs splayed out and his forelimbs slumped between them, an expression of acute agony on his face. Ripples went along the tufted, ungroomed pelt. The claws slid uncontrollably in and out on the hand that reached for the drug-injectors at his belt, the extract of *sthondat*-lymph that was a telepath's source of power and ultimate shame. Telepath looked up at Conservor and laid his facial fur flat, snapping at air, spraying saliva in droplets and strings that spattered the floor.

"No! No! Not again, pfft, pfft, not more rice and lentils! Mango chutney, akk, akk! It was telling the truth, it was telling the truth. Leek soup! Nggggg!"

Conservor glanced back over his shoulder at Traat-Admiral and shrugged with ears and tail. "The monkey is a member of a religious cult that confines itself to vegetable food," he said.

The commander felt himself jerk back in disgust at the perversion. They could not help being omnivores; they were born so, but *this* . . .

"It stands self-condemned," he said. "Guard Trooper, take it to the live-meat locker." Capital ships came equipped with such luxuries.

"That does not solve our problem," Conservor said quietly.

"They have *vanished*!" Traat-Admiral snarled.

"Which shows their power," Conservor replied. "We had trace enough on this track—"

"For me! I believed you before we left parking orbit, Conservor. Not enough for the Traditionalists! I feel the shadow of God's claws on this mission—"

An alarm whistled. "Traat-Admiral," the Communicator said. "Priority message, realtime, from Ktrodni-Stkaa on board *Blood Drinker*."

Traat-Admiral felt himself wince. Scion of a great noble house, distinguished combat record in the pacification of the Chuunquen, noted duelist, noted critic of Chuut-Riit. Chuut-Riit he had tolerated, as a prince of the blood, sired by an uncle to the Patriarch. Traat-Admiral, son of Third Gunner, was merely an enraging obstacle. Grimly, he strode to the display screen; at least he would be looking *down* on the leader of the

Traditionalists. Tradition itself would force him to crane his neck upward at the pickup, and height itself was far from being a negligible factor in any confrontation between kzinti.

"Yes?" he said forbiddingly.

Another kzintosh of high rank appeared in the screen, but dressed in plain space-armor. The helmet was thrown back to reveal a face from which half the fur was missing, burn-scars that were writhing masses of keloid.

"Traat-Admiral," he began.

Barely acceptable. He should add "Dominant One", at the least. The commander remained silent. "Have you seen the latest reports from Wunderland?"

Traat-Admiral flipped tufted eyebrows and ribbed ears: *yes.* Unconsciously, his nostrils flared in an attempt to draw in the pheromonal truth below his enemy's stance. *Anger,* he thought. *Great anger.* Yes, see how his pupils expanded, watch the tail-tip.

"Feral human activity has increased," Traat-Admiral said. "This is only to be expected, given the absence of the fleet and the mobilization. Priority—"

Ktrodni-Stkaa shrieked and thrust his muzzle toward the pickup; Traat-Admiral felt his own claws glide out.

"Yes, the fleet is absent. Always it is absent from where there is *fighting* to be done. We chase ghosts, Traat-Admiral. This 'activity' meant an attack on my estate, *Dominant One.* A successful attack, when I and my household were absent; my harem slaughtered, my kits destroyed. My generations are cut off!"

Shaken, Traat-Admiral recoiled. A Hero expected to die in battle, but this was another matter altogether.

"Hrrrr," he said. For a moment his thoughts dwelt on raking claws across the nose of Hroth-Staff-Officer; did he not think *that* piece of information worth his commander's attention? Then: "My condolences, honored Ktrodni-Stkaa. Rest assured that compensation and reprisal will be made."

"Can land and monkeymeat bring back my blood?" Ktrodni-Stkaa screamed. He was in late middle age; by the time a new brood of kits reached adulthood they would be without a father-patron, dependent on the dubious support of their older half-siblings. *And to be sure*, Traat-Admiral thought, *I would rage and grieve as well, if the kittens who had chewed on my tail were slaughtered by omnivores. But this is a combat situation.*

"Control yourself, honored Ktrodni-Stkaa," he said. "I myself will see to your young. I say it before the Conservor. And recall, we are under war regulations. Victory is the best revenge."

"Victory! Victory over what, over vacuum, over kittenish bogeymen, you . . . YOU will guard my young? YOU? You *Third Gunner!*" There was a collective gasp from the bridges of both ships; Traat-Admiral could smell rage kindling among his subordinates at the grossness of the insult; that dampened his own, reminded him of duty. Conservor leaned forward to put himself in the pickup's field of view.

"You forget the Law," he said, single eye blazing.

"You have forgotten it, Subvertor of the Ancestral Past. First you worked tail-entwined with Chuut-Riit—if *Riit* he truly was—now with this." He turned to Traat-Admiral with a venomous hiss. "Licking its scarless ear, whispering grasseater words that always leave us where the danger is not. If true kzintosh of noble liver were in command of this system, the Fleet would have left to subdue the monkeys of Earth a year ago."

Traat-Admiral crossed his arms, waggled brows. "Then the fleet would be four light-years away," he said patiently. "Would this have helped your estate? Is this your warrior logic?"

"A true Hero scratches grass upon steaming logic. A true kzintosh knows only the logic of *attack!* Your ancestors are nameless, son of Jammed Litterdrop Repairer; your nose rubs the dirt at my slave's feet! *Coward.*"

This time there was no hush; a chorus of battlescreams filled the air, until the speakers squealed with feedback. Traat-Admiral was opening his mouth to give a command he knew he would regret when the alarm rang.

"Attack. Hostile action. Corvette *Brush Lurker* does not report." The screen divided before him with a holo of fleet dispositions covering half of Ktrodni-Stkaa's face; a light was winking in the Traditionalist flotilla, and even as he watched it went from flashing blue to amber.

"*Brush Lurker* destroyed. Weapon unknown. Standing by." The machine's voice was cool and impersonal, and Traat-Admiral's almost as much so.

"Maximum alert," he said. Attendants came running with space armor for him and the Conservor, stripping away the ceremonial outfits. "Ktrodni-Stkaa, shall we put aside personalities while we hunt this thing that dares to kill kzinti?"

"Ah," Markham said, as the kzinti corvette winked out of existence, its fusion pile destablized. "It begins." Begins in a cloud of expanding plasma, stripped nuclei that once were metal and plastic and meat. "Wait for my command."

The others on the bridge of the *Nietzsche* stared expressionlessly at their screens, moving and speaking with the same flat lack of expression. There was none of the feeling of controlled tension he remembered from previous actions, not even at the sight of a kzinti warship crushed so easily.

"This is better," he muttered to himself. "More disciplined." There were times when he missed even backtalk, though— "No. This is better."

"It isn't," Jonah said. His face was a little less like a skull, now, but he was wandering in circles, touching things at random. "I . . . are the kzinti . . . rescue . . ." His faced writhed, and he groaned again. "It doesn't connect, it doesn't connect,"

"Jonah," Markham said soothingly. "The kzinti are our enemies, isn't that so?"

"I . . . think so. Yes. They wanted me to kill a kzin, and I did."

"Then sit quietly, Jonah, and we will kill *many* kzinti." To one of the dead-faced ones. "Bring up those three fugitives we hauled in. No, on second thought, just the humans. Keep the kzin under sedation."

He waited impatiently, listening to the monitored kzinti broadcasts. It was important to keep them waiting, past the point where the instinctive closing of ranks wore thin. *And important to have an audience for my triumph,* he admitted to himself. *No, not my triumph. The Master's triumph. I am but the chosen instrument.*

"I don't like the look of this," Ingrid said, as the blank-faced guard pushed them toward the bridge of the warship. "Markham always kept a taut ship, but this—why won't they *talk* to us?"

"I think I know why," Harold whispered back. The bridge was as eerily quiet as the rest of the ship had been, except for—

"Jonah!" Ingrid cried. "Jonah, what the *hell's* going on?"

"Ingrid?" he said, looking up.

Harold grunted as he met those eyes, remembering. They did not have the flat deadness of the others, or the fanatical gleam of Markham's. A twisted grimace of . . . despair? puzzlement? framed them, as deeply as if it had become a permanent part of the face.

"Ingrid? Is that you?" He smiled, a wet-lipped grimace. "We're fighting the kzinti." A hand waved vaguely at the computers. "I rigged it up. Put it through here. Better than trying to shift the hardware over from the *Ruling Mind.* You'll—" his voice faltered, and tears gleamed in his eyes "—you'll understand once you've met the Master."

Harold gave her hand a warning squeeze. *Time,* he thought. *We have to play for time.*

"Admiral Reichstein-Markham?" he said politely, with precisely the correct inclination of head and shoulders. *Dear Father may not have let me in the doors of the schloss, but I know how to play that game.* "Harold Yarthkin-Schotmann, at your service. I've heard a great deal about you."

"Ah. Yes." Markham's well-bred nose went up, and

he looked down it with an expression that was parsecs from the strange rigidity of a moment before. Harold swallowed past the dry lumpiness of his throat, and put on his best poor-relation grin.

"Yes, I haff heard of you as well, *Fro* Yarthkin," the *herrenmann* said glacially.

Well, that puts me in my place, Harold mused. Aloud: "I wonder if you could do the lady and me a small favor?"

"Perhaps," Markham said, with a slight return of graciousness.

"Well, we've been traveling together for some time now, and . . . well, we'd like to regularize it." Ingrid started, and he squeezed her hand again. "It'd mean a great deal to the young lady, to have it done by a hero of the Resistance."

Markham smiled. "We haff gone beyond Resistance," he said. "But as hereditary landholder and ship's Captain, I am also qualified." He turned to one of the slumped figures. "Take out Number Two. Remember, from the same flotilla." The smile clicked back on as he faced Harold and Ingrid. "Step in front of me, please. Conrad, two steps behind them and keep the stunner aimed."

"Attack." There was a long hiss from the bridge of the *Throat Ripper*. "Dreadnought *Blood Drinker* does not report. *Blood Drinker* destroyed. Analysis follows." A pause that stretched. One of their sister ships in the Traditionalist flotilla, and a substantial part of its fighting strength. Three thousand Heroes gone to the claws of the God. "Fusion pile destabilization. Correlating." Another instant. "Corvette *Brush Lurker* now reclassified; fusion pile destabilization."

"Computer!" Ktrodni-Stkaa's voice came through the open channel. "Probability of spontaneous failures!"

Faintly, they could hear the reply. "Oh point oh seven percent, plus or minus." The rest faded, as Ktrodni-Stkaa's face filled the screen.

"Now, traitor," he said. "Now I know which to believe in, grass-eaters in kzinti fur or invisible bogeymen with access to our repair yards. Did you think it was clever, to gather all loyalty in one spot, a single throat for the fangs of treachery to rip? You will learn better. Briefly."

"Ktrodni-Stkaa, no, I swear by the fangs of God—" the image cut off. Voices babbled in his ears:

"*Gut Tearer* launching fighters—"

"*Hit, we have been hit!*" Damage control klaxons howled. "Taking hits from *Crusher of Ribs*—"

"Traat-Admiral, following units request fire-control release as they are under attack—"

Traat-Admiral felt his gorge rise and his tail sink as he spoke. "Launch fighters. All units, neutralize the traitors. Fire control to Battle Central." A rolling snarl broke across the bridge, and then the huge weight of *Throat Ripper* shuddered. A bank of screens on the Damage Control panel went from green to amber to blood-red. "Communications, broadcast to system: all loyal kzintosh, rally to the Hand of the Patriarch—"

Ktrodni-Stkaa's voice was sounding on another viewer, the all-system hailing frequency: "True kzintosh in the Alpha Centauri system, the lickurine traitor Traat-Admiral-that-was has sunk the first coward's fang in our back. Rally to me!"

Aide-de-Camp sprang to Traat-Admiral's side. "We are at war, Honored Sire; the God will give us victory."

The older kzin looked at him with a kind of wonder, as the bridge settled down to an ordered chaos of command and response. "Whatever happens here today, we are already in defeat," he said slowly. "Defeated by ourselves."

". . . so long as you both do desire to cohabit, by the authority vested in me by the *Landsraat* and *Herrenhaus* of the Republic of Wunderland," Markham said. "You may kiss your spouse."

He turned, smiling, to the board. "Analysis?" he said.

"Kzinti casualties in excess of twenty-five percent of units engaged," the flat voice said.

Markham nodded, tapping his knuckles together and rising on the balls of his feet. "Densely packed, relatively speaking, and all at zero velocity to each other. Be careful to record everything; such a fleet engagement is probably unique." He frowned. "Any anomalies?"

"Ship on collision course with *Ruling Mind*. Acceleration in excess of 400 gravities. Impact in 121 seconds, *mark*."

Harold laughed aloud and tightened his grip around the new-made *Fru* Raines-Schotmann. "Together all the way, sweetheart," he shouted. She raised a whoop, ignoring the guard behind them with a stunner.

Markham leaped for the board. "You said nothing could detect her!" he screamed at Jonah, throwing an inert crewman aside and punching for the communications channel.

"It's . . . psionic," Jonah said. "Nothing conscious should—" His face contorted, and both arms clamped down on Markham's. There was a brief moment of struggle; none of the other crewfolk of the *Nietzsche* interferred; they had no orders. Markham snapped a blow to the groin, to the side of the head, cracked an arm; the Sol-Belter was in no condition for combat, but he clung leech-like until the Wunderlander's desperate strength sent him crashing halfway across the control deck.

"Impact in sixty seconds, *mark*."

"Master, oh, Master, use the amplifer, you're under attack, use it, use it *now*—"

"Impact in forty seconds, *mark*."

Dnivtopun looked up from the solitaire deck. The words would have been enough, but the link to Markham was deep and strong; urgency sent him crashing towards the control chair, his hands reaching for the bell-shape of the helmet even before his body stopped moving.

*   *   *

This is how it will begin again, the being that had been Catskinner thought, watching the monoblock re-contract. This time the cycle had been perfect, the symmetry complete. It would be so easy to reaccelerate his perception, to alter the outcome. *No*, it thought. *There must be free will. They too must have their cycle of creation.*

"Impact in ten seconds, *mark*."

The connections settled onto Dnivtopun's head, and suddenly his consciousness stretched system-wide, perfect and isolate. The amplifier was *better* than any he had used before. His mind groped for the hostile intent, so close. Three hundred million sentients quivered in the grip of his Power.

"Emperor Dnivtopun," he laughed, tendrils thrown wide. "*Dnivtopun, God*. You, with the funny thoughts, coming towards me. STOP. ALTER COURSE. IMMEDIATELY."

Markham relaxed into a smile. "We are saved by faith," he whispered.

"Two seconds to impact, *mark*."

NO, DNIVTOPUN. YOUR TIME IS ENDED, AS IS MINE. COME TO ME.

"One second to impact, *mark*."

The thrint screamed, antiphonally with the *Ruling Mind*'s collision alarm. The automatic failsafe switched on, and—

-discontinuity-

Catskinner's mind engaged the circuit, and—

-discontinuity-

a layer of quantum uncertainty merged, along the meeting edges of the stasis fields. Virtual particles showered out, draining energy without leaving the fields. Time attempted to precess at different rates, in an area of finite width and conceptual depth. The fields collapsed, and energy propagated, in a symmetrical five-dimensional shape.

Chapter X

Claude Montferrat-Palme laughed from the marble floor of his office; his face was bleeding, and the shattered glass of the windows lay in glittering swathes across desk and carpet. The air smelled of ozone, of burning, of the dust of wrecked buildings.

CRACK. Another set of hypersonic booms across the sky, and the cloud off in the direction of the kzinti Government House was *definitely* assuming a mushroom shape. That was forty kilometers downwind, but there was no use wasting time. He crawled carefully to the desk, calling answers to the yammering voices that pleaded for orders.

"No, I *don't* know what happened to the moon, except that something bright went through it and it blew up. Nothing but ratcats on it, anyway, these days. Yes, I said ratcats. Begin evacuation immediately, Plan *Dienzt;* yes, civilians too, you fool. No, we can't ask the kzinti for orders; they're killing each other, hadn't you noticed? I'll be down there in thirty seconds. *Out.*"

A shockwave rocked the building, and for an instant

blue-white light flooded through his tight-squeezed eyelids. When the hot wind passed he rose and sprinted
for the locked closet, the one with the impact armor
and the weapons. As he stripped and dressed, he turned
his face to the sky, squinting.

"I love you," he said. "Both. However you bloody
well managed it."

"He was a good son," Traat-Admiral said.

Conservor and he had anchored themselves in an
intact corner of the *Throat Ripper*'s control room. None
of the systems was in operation; that was to be expected, since most of the ship aft of this point had been
sheared away by *something*. Stars shone vacuum-bleak
through the rents; other lights flared and died in perfect spheres of light. Traat-Admiral found himself mildly
amazed that there were still enough left to fight; more
so that they had the energy, after whatever it was had
happened.

Such is our nature, he thought. This was the time for
resignation; he and the Conservor were both bleeding
from nose, ears, mouth, all the body openings. And
within, he could feel it. Traat-Admiral looked down at
the head of his son where it rested in his lap; the girder
had driven straight through the youth's midsection, and
his face was still fixed in eager alertness, frozen hard
now.

"Yes," Conservor said. "The shadow of the God lies
on us, all three. We will go to Him together, the hunt
will give Him honor."

"Such honor as there is in defeat," he sighed.

A quiver of ears behind the faceplate showed him the
sage's laughter. "Defeat? That thing which we came to
this place to fight, *that* has been defeated, even if we
will never know how. And kzinti have defeated kzinti.
Such is the only defeat here."

Traat-Admiral tried to raise his ears and join the
laughter, but found himself coughing a gout of red
stickiness into the faceplate of his helmet; it rebounded.

"If—I—must—drown," he managed to say, "not—in—

my—own—blood." Vacuum was dry, at least. He raised
fumbling hands to the catches of his helmet-ring. A
single fierce regret siezed him. *I hope the kits will be
protected.*

"We have hunted well together on the trail of Truth,"
the sage said, copying his action. "Let us feast and lie in
the shade by the waterhole together, forever."

"What do you mean, it never happened?"

Jonah's voice was sharp again; a week in the autodoc
of the *oyabun's* flagship had repaired most of his physical injuries. The tremor in his hands showed that those
were not all; he glanced behind him at Ingrid and
Harold, where they sat with linked hands.

"Just what I said," General Buford Early said. He
glanced aside as well, at Shigehero's slight hard smile.

"So much for the rewards of heroism," Jonah said,
letting himself fall into the lounger with a bitter laugh.
He lit a cigarette; the air was rank with them, and the
smell of the general's stogies. That it did not bother a
Sol-Belter born was itself a sign of wounds that did not
show.

The general leaned forward, his square pug face like
a clenched fist. "These *are* the rewards of heroism,
Captain," he said. "Markham's crew are vegetables.
Markham *may* recover—incidentally, he'll be a hero
too."

"Hero? He was a flipping traitor! He *liked* the damned
Thrint!"

"What do you know about mind control?" Early asked.
"Remember what it felt like? Were you a traitor?"

"Maybe you're right . . ."

"It doesn't matter. When he comes back from the
psychist, the version he remembers will match the one
I give. If you three *weren't* all fucking heroes, *you'd* be
at the psychist's too." Another glance at the *oyabun.*
"Or otherwise kept safely silent."

Harold spoke. "And all the kzinti who might know
something are dead, the Slaver ship and the *Catskinner*
are quantum bubbles . . . and three vulnerable individ-

uals are not in a position to upset heavy-duty organizational applecarts."

"Exactly," Early said. "It never happened, as I said." He spread his hands. "No point in tantalizing people with technical miracles that no longer exist, either." *Although knowing you can do it is half the effort.* "We've still got a long war to fight, you know," he added. "Unless you expect Santa to arrive."

"Who's Santa?" Jonah said.

The commander of the hyperdrive warship *Outsider's Gift* sat back and relaxed for the first time in weeks as his craft broke through into normal space. He was of the large albino minority on We Made It, and like most Crashlanders had more than a touch of agoraphobia. The wrenching *not-there* of hyperspace reminded him unpleasantly of dreams he had had, of being trapped on the surface during storms.

"Well. Two weeks, faster than light," he said.

The executive officer nodded, her eyes on the displays. "More breakthroughs," she said. "Seven . . . twelve . . . looks like the whole fleet made it." She laughed. "Wunderland, prepare to welcome your liberators."

"Careful now," the captain said. "This is a reconnaissance in force. We can chop up anything we meet in interstellar space, but this close to a star we're strictly Einsteinian, just like the pussies."

The executive officer was frowning over her board. "Well, I'll be damned," she said. "Sir, something *very* strange is going on in there. If I didn't know better . . . that looks like a fleet action *already* going on."

The captain straightened. "Secure from hyperdrive stations," he said. "General Quarters. Battle stations." A deep breath. "Let's go find out."

THE END

INCONSTANT STAR

STAR

Poul Anderson

Chapter I

A hunter's wind blew down off the Mooncatcher Mountains and across the Rungn Valley. Night filled with the sounds of it, rustling forest, remote animal cries, and with odors of soil, growth, beast. The wish that it roused, to be yonder, to stalk and pounce and slay and devour, grew in Weoch-Captain until he trembled. The fur stood up on him. Claws slid out of their sheaths; fingers bent into the same saber curves. He had long been deprived.

Nonetheless he walked steadily onward from the guard point. When Ress-Chiuu, High Admiral of Kzin, summoned, one came. That was not in servility but in hope, fatal though laggardness would be. Something great was surely afoot. It might even prove warlike.

Eastward stretched rangeland, wan beneath the stars. Westward, ahead, the woods loomed darkling, the game preserve part of Ress-Chiuu's vast domain. Far and high beyond glimmered snowpeaks. The chill that the wind also bore chastened bit by bit the lust in Weoch-Captain. Reason fought its way back. He reached the

169

Admiral's lair with the turmoil no more than a drumbeat in his blood.

The castle remembered axes, arrows, and spears. Later generations had made their changes and additions but kept it true to itself, a stony mass baring battlements at heaven. After an electronic gate identified and admitted him, the portal through which he passed was a tunnel wherein he moved blind. Primitive instincts whispered, "Beware!" He ignored them. Guided by echoes and subtle tactile sensations, his pace never slackened. Ress-Chiuu always tested a visitor, one way or another.

Was it a harder test that waited in the courtyard? No kzin received Weoch-Captain. Instead hulked a kdatlyno slave. It made the clumsy gesture that was as close as the species could come to a prostration. However, then it turned and lumbered toward the main keep. Obviously he was expected to follow.

Rage blazed in him. Almost, he attacked. He choked emotion down and stalked after his guide, though lips remained pulled off fangs.

Echoes whispered. Corridors and rooms lay deserted. Night or no, personnel should have been in evidence. What did it portend? Alertness heightened, wariness, combat readiness.

A door slid aside. The kdatlyno groveled again and departed. Weoch-Captain went in. The door closed behind him.

The room was polished granite, austerely furnished. A window stood open to the wind. Ress-Chiuu reclined on a slashtooth skin draped over a couch. Weoch-Captain came to attention and presented himself. "At ease," the High Admiral said. "You may sit, stand, or pace as you wish. I expect you will, from time to time, pace."

Weoch-Captain decided to stay on his feet for the nonce.

Ress-Chiuu's deceptively soft tones went on: "Realize that I have offered you no insult. You were met by a slave because, at least for the present, extreme confidentiality is necessary. Furthermore, I require not only a Hero—they are many—but one who possesses an unusual measure of self-control and forethoughtfulness. I had reason to believe you do. You have shown I was right. Praise and honor be yours."

The accolade calmed Weoch-Captain's pride. It also focused his mind the more sharply. (Doubtless that was intended, said a part of his mind with a wryness rare in kzinti.) His ears rose and unfolded. "I have delegated my current duties and am instantly available for the High Admiral's orders," he reported.

Shadows dappled fur as the blocky head nodded approval. "We go straight to the spoor, then. You know of Werlith-Commandant's mission on the opposite side of human-hegemony space." It was not a question. "Ill tidings: lately a human crew stumbled upon the base that was under construction there. They came to investigate the sun, which appears to be unique in several ways."

Monkey curiosity, thought Weoch-Captain. He was slightly too young to have fought in the war, but he had spent his life hearing about it, studying it, dreaming of the next one. His knowledge included terms of scorn evolved among kzinti who had learned random things about the planet where the enemy originated.

Ress-Chiuu's level words smote him: "Worse, much worse. Incredibly, they seem to have destroyed the installations. Certain is that they inflicted heavy casualties, disabled our spacecraft, and went home nearly unscathed. You perceive what this means. They conveyed the information that we have developed the hyperdrive ourselves. All chance of springing a surprise is gone." Sarcasm harshened the voice. "No doubt the Patriarchy will soon receive 'representations' from Earth about this 'unfortunate incident.' "

Over the hyperwave, said Weoch-Captain's mind bleakly. Those few black boxes that the peace treaty provided for, left among us, engineered to self-destruct at the least tampering.

Well did he know. Such an explosion had killed a brother of his.

Understanding leaped. If the humans had not yet communicated officially—"May I ask how the Patriarchs learned?"

"We have our means. I will consider what to tell you." Ress-Chiuu's calm was giving way ever so little. His tail lashed his thighs, a pink whip. "We must find out exactly what happened. Or, if nothing else, we must establish what the situation is, whether anything of our base remains, what the Earth Navy is doing there. Survivors should be rescued. If this is impossible, perhaps they can be eliminated by rays or missiles before they fall into human grasp."

"Heroes—"

"Would never betray our secrets. Yes, yes. But can you catalogue every trick those creatures may possess?" Ress-Chiuu lifted head and shoulders. His eyes locked with Weoch-Captain's. "You will command our ship to that sun."

Disaster or no, eagerness flamed. "Sire!"

"Slow, slow," the older kzin growled. "We require an officer intelligent as well as bold, capable of agreeing that the destiny of the race transcends his own, and indeed, to put it bluntly—" he paused— "one who is not *afraid* to cut and run, should the alternative be valiant failure. Are you prepared for this?"

Weoch-Captain relaxed from his battle crouch and, inwardly, tautened further. "The High Admiral has bestowed a trust on me," he said. "I accept."

"It is well. Come, sit. This will be a long night."

They talked, and ransacked databases, and ran tentative plans through the computers, until dawn whitened the east. Finally, almost jovially, Ress-Chiuu asked, "Are you exhausted?"

"On the contrary, sire, I think I have never been more fightworthy."

"You need to work that off and get some rest. Besides, you have earned a pleasure. You may go into my forest and make a bare-handed kill."

When Weoch-Captain came back out at noontide, jaws still dripping red, he felt tranquil, happy, and, once he had slept, ready to conquer a cosmos.

Chapter II

The sun was an hour down and lights had come aglow along streets, but at this time of these years Alpha Centauri B was still aloft. Low in the west, like thousands of evening stars melted into one, it cast shadows the length of Karl-Jorge Avenue and set the steel steeple of St. Joachim's ashimmer against an eastern sky purpling into dusk. Vehicles and pedestrians alike were sparse, the city's pulsebeat quieted to a murmur through mild summer air—day's work ended, night's pleasures just getting started. Munchen had changed more in the past decade or two than most places on Wunderland. Commercial and cultural as well as political center, it was bound to draw an undue share of outworlders and their influence. Yet it still lived largely by the rhythms of the planet.

Robert Saxtorph doubted that that would continue through his lifetime. Let him enjoy it while it lasted. Traditions gave more color to existence than did any succession of flashy fashions.

He honored one by tipping his cap to the Liberation

Memorial as he crossed the Silberplatz. Though the sculpture wasn't old and the events had taken place scarcely a generation ago, they stood in history with Marathon and Yorktown. Leaving the square, he sauntered up the street past a variety of shop windows. His destination, Harold's Terran Bar, had a certain venerability too. And he was bound there to meet a beautiful woman with something mysterious to tell him. Another tradition, of sorts?

At the entrance, he paused. His grin going sour, he well-nigh said to hell with it and turned around. Tyra Nordbo should not have made him promise to keep this secret even from his wife, before she set the rendezvous. Nor should she have picked Harold's. He hadn't cared to patronize it since visit before last. Now the very sign that floated luminous before the brown brick wall had been expurgated. *A World On Its Own* remained below the name, but *humans only* was gone. Mustn't offend potential customers or, God forbid, local idealists.

In Saxtorph's book, courtesy was due everyone who hadn't forfeited the right. However, under the kzinti occupation that motto had been a tiny gesture of defiance. Since the war, no sophont that could pay was denied admittance. But onward with the bulldozer of blandness.

He shrugged. Having come this far, let him proceed. Time enough to leave if la Nordbo turned out to be a celebrity hunter or a vibrobrain. The fact was that she had spoken calmly, and about money. Besides, he'd enjoyed watching her image. He went on in. Nowadays the door opened for anybody.

As always, a large black man occupied the vestibule, wearing white coat and bow tie. What had once made some sense had now become mere costume. His eyes widened at the sight of the newcomer, as big as him, with the craggy features and thinning reddish hair. "Why, Captain Saxtorph!" he exclaimed in fluent English. "Welcome, sir. No, for you, no entry fee."

They had never met. "I'm on private business," Saxtorph warned.

"I understand, sir. If somebody bothers you, give me the high sign and I'll take care of them." Maybe the doorman could, overawing by sheer size if nothing else, or maybe his toughness was another part of the show. It wasn't a quality much in demand any more.

"Thanks." Saxtorph slipped him a tip and passed through a beaded curtain which might complicate signaling for the promised help, into the main room. It was dimly lit and little smoke hung about. Customers thus far were few, and most in the rear room gambling. Nevertheless a fellow at an obsolete model of musicomp was playing something ancient. Saxtorph went around the deserted sunken dance floor to the bar, chose a stool, and ordered draft Solborg from a live servitor.

He had swallowed a single mouthful of the half liter when he heard, at his left, "What, no akvavit with, and you a Dane?" The voice was husky and female; the words, English, bore a lilting accent and a hint of laughter.

He turned his head and was startled. The phone at his hotel had shown him this face, strong-boned, blunt-nosed, flaxen hair in a pageboy cut. That she was tall, easily 180 centimeters, gave no surprise; she was a Wunderlander. But she lacked the ordinary low-gravity lankiness. Robust and full-bosomed, she looked and moved as if she had grown up on Earth, nearly two-thirds again as heavy as here. That meant rigorous training and vigorous sports throughout her life. And the changeable sea-blue of her slacksuit matched her eyes. . . .

"American, really. My family moved from Denmark when I was small. And I'd better keep a clear head, right?" His tongue was speaking for him. Angry at himself, he took control back. "How do you do." He offered his hand. Her clasp was firm, cool, brief. At least she wasn't playing sultry or exotic. "Uh, care for a drink?"

"I have one yonder. Please to follow." She must have arrived early and waited for him. He picked up his beer and accompanied her to a privacy-screened table. Murky though the corner was, he could make out fine lines at the corners of her eyes and lips; and that fair skin had known much weather. She wasn't quite young, then. Late thirties, Earth calendar, he guessed.

They settled down. Her glass held white wine. She had barely sipped of it. "Thank you for that you came," she said. "I realize this is peculiar."

Well, shucks, he resisted admitting, I may be seven or eight years older than you and solidly married, but any wench this sightly rates a chance to make sense. "It is an odd place to meet," he countered.

She smiled. "I thought it would be appropriate."

He declined the joke. "Over-appropriate."

"*Ja, saa?*" The blond brows lifted. "How so?"

"I never did like staginess," he blurted. His hand waved around. "I knew this joint when it was a raffish den full of memories from the occupation and the tag-end of wartime afterward. But each time I called at Wunderland and dropped in, it'd become more of a tourist trap."

"Well, those old memories are romantic; and, yes, some of mine live here too," she murmured. Turning straightforward again: "But it has an advantage, exactly because of what it now is. Few of its patrons will have heard about you. They are, as you say, mostly tourists. News like your deeds at that distant star is sensational but it takes a while to cross interstellar space and hit hard in public awareness on planets where the societies are different from yours or mine. Here, at this hour of the day, you have a good chance of not to be recognized and pestered. Also, because people here often make assignations, it is the custom to ignore other couples."

Saxtorph felt his cheeks heat up. What the devil! The schoolboy he had once been lay long and deeply buried. Or so he'd supposed. It would be a ghost he could well do without. "Is that why you didn't want my wife along?" he asked roughly.

She nodded. "You two together are especially conspicuous, no? I found that yesterday evening she would be away, and thought you would not. Then I tried calling you."

He couldn't repress a chuckle. "Yah, you guessed right. Poor Dorcas, she had no escape from addressing a meeting of the *Weibliche Astroverein*." He'd looked forward to several peaceful hours alone. But when the phone showed this face, he'd accepted the call, which he probably would not have done otherwise. "After she got back, I took her down to the bar for a stiff drink." But he'd kept his promise not to mention the conversation. Half ashamed, he harshened his tone. "Why'd you do no more than talk me into a, uh, an appointment?" He hadn't liked telling Dorcas that he meant to go for a walk, might stop in at some pub, and if he found company he enjoyed—male, she'd taken for granted—would maybe return late. But he'd done it. "Could you not have gone directly to the point? The line wasn't tapped, was it?"

"I did not expect so," Tyra answered. "Yet it was possible. Perhaps a government official who is snoopish. You have legal and diplomatic complications left over, from what happened at the dwarf star."

Don't I know it, Saxtorph sighed to himself.

"There could even be undiscovered kzinti agents like Markham, trying for extra information that will help them or their masters," she continued. "You are marked, Captain. And in a way, that am I also."

"Why the secrecy?" he persisted. "Understand, I am not interested in anything illegal."

"This is not." She laid hold of her glass. Fingers grew white-nailed on its stem, and trembled the least bit. "It is, well, extraordinary. Perhaps dangerous."

"Then my wife and crew have got to know before *we* decide."

"Of course. First I ask you. If you say no, that is an

end of the matter for you, and I must try elsewhere. I
will have small hope. But if you agree, and your shipmates do, best that we hold secret. Otherwise certain
parties—they will not want this mission, or they will
want it carried out in a way that gives my cause
no help. We present them a *fait accompli*. Do you
see?"

Likewise tense, he gulped at his beer. "Uh, mind if I
smoke?"

"Do." The edges of her mouth dimpled. "That pipe
of yours has become famous like you."

"Or infamous." He fumbled briar, pouch, and lighter
out of their pockets. Anxious to slack things off: "The vice
is disapproved of again on Earth, did you know? As if
cancer and emphysema and the rest still existed. I think
puritanism runs in cycles. One periodicity for tobacco,
one for alcohol, one for—Ah, hell, I'm babbling."

"I believe men smoke much on Wunderland because
it is a symbol," she said. "From the occupation era.
Kzinti do not smoke. They dislike the smell and seldom
allowed it in their presence. I grew up used to it on
men." She laughed. "See, I can babble too." Lifting her
glass: "*Skaal.*"

He touched his mug to it, repeating the word before
remembering, in surprise: "Wait, you people generally
say, 'Prosit,' don't you?"

"They were mostly Scandinavians who settled in
Skogarna," Tyra explained. "We have our own dialect.
Some call it a patois."

"Really? I'd hardly imagine that was possible in this
day and age."

"We were always rather isolated, there in the North.
Under the occupation, more than ever. Kzinti, or the
collaborationist government, monitored all traffic and
communications. Few people had wide contacts, and
those were very guarded. They drew into their neigh-
borhoods. Keeping language and customs alive, that
was one way they reminded themselves that humans
were not everywhere and forever slaves of the rat-

cats." Speaking, Tyra had let somberness come upon her. "This isolation is a root of the story I must tell you."

Saxtorph wanted irrationally much to lighten her mood. "Well, shall we get to it? You'd like to charter the *Rover*, you said, for a fairly short trip. But that's all you said, except for not blanching when I gave you a cost estimate. Which, by itself, immediately got me mighty interested."

Her laugh gladdened him. "I'm in luck. Is that your American folk-word? Exactly when I need a hyperdrive ship, here you come with the only one in known space that is privately owned, and you admit you are broke. I confess I am puzzled. You took damage on your expedition—" Her voice grew soft and serious. "Besides that poor man the kzinti killed. But the harm was not else too bad, was it? And surely you have insurance, and I should think that super-rich gentleman on We Made It, Brozik, is grateful that you brought his daughter back safe."

Saxtorph tamped his pipe. "Sure. Still, losing a boat is fairly expensive. We haven't replaced *Fido* yet. Plus lesser repairs we needed, plus certain new equipment and refitting we decided have become necessary, plus the fact that insurance companies have never in history been prompt and in-full about anything except collecting their premiums. Brozik's paid us a generous bonus on the charter, yes, but we can't expect him to underwrite a marginal business like ours. His gratefulness has reasonable limits. After all, we were saving our own hides as well as Laurinda's, and she had considerable to do with it herself. We aren't really broke, but we have gone through a big sum, on top of normal overhead expenses, and meanwhile haven't had a chance to scare up any fresh trade." He set fire to tobacco and rolled smoke across his palate. "See, I'm being completely frank with you." As he doubtless would not have been, this soon, were she homely or a man.

Again she nodded, thoughtfully. "Yes, it must be

difficult, operating a tramp freighter. You compete with government lines for a market that is—marginal, you said. When each planetary system contains ample raw materials, and it is cheapest to synthesize or recycle almost everything else, what actual tonnage goes between the stars?"

"Damn little, aside from passengers, and we lack talent for catering to them." Saxtorph smiled. "Oh, it might be fun to carry nonhumans, but outfitting for it would be a huge investment, and then we'd be locked into those rounds."

"You wish to travel freely, widely. Freighting is your way to make it possible." Tyra straightened. Her voice rang. "Well, I offer you a voyage like none ever before!"

Caution awoke. He'd hate to think her dishonest. But she might be foolish—no, already he could dismiss that idea—she might be ill-informed. Planetsiders seldom had any notion of the complications in spacefaring. Physical requirements and hazards were merely the obvious ones. In addition, you had to make your nut, and avoid running afoul of several admiralty offices and countless bureaucrats, and keep every hatch battened through which the insurers might slither. "That's what we're here to talk about," Saxtorph said. "Only talk. Any promises come later."

The high spirits that evidently were normal to her sank back down. They must have been struggling against something stark. She raised her glass for a drink, gulp rather than swallow, and stared into the wine. "My name means nothing to you, I gather," she began, hardly louder than the music. "I thought you would know. You have told how you are often in this system."

"Not that often, and I never paid much attention to your politics. I've got a hunch that that's what this is about." Her fingers strained together. "Yah. Politics, a disease of our species. Maybe someday they'll develop a vaccine against it. Grind politicians up and centrifuge the brains. Though you'd need an awful lot of politicians per gram of brains."

A smile spooked momentarily over her lips. "But you must have heard a great deal lately. You are now in politics yourself."

"And working free as fast as we can, which involves declining to get into arguments. Look, we came to Alpha Centauri originally because this is where the Interworld Space Commission keeps headquarters, with warehouses full of stuff we'd need for Professor Tregennis' expedition. We returned from there to here because Commissioner Markham had revealed himself to be a kzinti spy and we figured we should take that news first to the top. It plunked us into a monstrous kettle of hullaballoo. Seeing as how we couldn't leave before the investigations and depositions and what-Godhelpus-not else were finished, we got the work on our ship done meanwhile at Tiamat. At last they've reluctantly agreed we didn't break any laws except justifiably, and given us leave to go. In between wading through that swamp of glue and all the mostly unwanted distractions that notoriety brought us, we kept hoping our brokers could arrange a cargo for whenever we'd be able to haul out. Understandably, no luck. We were pretty much resigned to returning empty to Sol, when you— Well, you can see why we discouraged anything, even conversation, that might possibly have gotten us mired deeper."

"Yes." She tensed. "I shall explain. The Nordbos belonged to the Freuchen clan."

"Hm? You mean you're of the Nineteen Families?"

"We *were*," she said in a rush, overriding the pain he heard. "Oh, of course today the special rights and obligations are mostly gone, the titles are mostly honorary, but the honor does remain. After the liberation, a court stripped his from my father and confiscated everything but his personal estate. He was not there to defend himself. The best we were able, my brother and I and a handful of loyal friends, that was to save our mother from being tried for treasonable collaboration. We resigned membership in the clan before it could meet to expel her."

Saxtorph drew hard on his pipe. "You believe your father was innocent?"

"I swear he was!" Her breath went ragged. "At last I have evidence—no, a clue— A spaceship must go where he went and find the proof. Civilian hyperdrive craft are committed to their routes, and their governments control them in any case, except for yours. Our navy— My brother is an officer. He has made quiet inquiries. He actually got a naval astronomer to check that part of the sky, as a personal favor, not saying why. Nothing was found. He tells me the Navy would not dispatch a ship on the strength of a few notes that are partial at best."

And that could well have been forged by a person crazy-desperate for vindication, Saxtorph thought. She admits the instrumental search drew a blank.

Tyra had won to a steely calm. "Furthermore, thinking about it, I realized that if the Navy should go, it would be entirely in hopes of discovering something worthwhile. They would not care about the honor of Peter Nordbo, who was condemned as a traitor and is most likely long dead."

"But you have your own reputation to rescue," Saxtorph said gently.

The fair head shook. "That doesn't matter. Neither Ib, my brother, nor I was accused of anything. In fact, at the liberation, he was among those who tried to storm the Ritterhaus where the kzinti were holding out, and was wounded. I told you, he has since become a naval officer. And I . . . helped the underground earlier, in a very small way, for I was very young then, and during the street fighting here I worked at a first aid station. *Ach*, the court said how they sympathized with us. We must have been one reason why they never formally charged my mother. That much justice got we, for she was innocent too. She could not help what happened. But except for those few real friends, only Ib and I ever again called on her, at that lonely house on Korsness."

The musicomp man set his instrument to violin mode with orchestral backing and played a tune that Saxtorph recognized. Antique indeed, from Earth before spaceflight, sugary sentimental, yet timeless, *"Du kannst nicht treu sein."* You can't be true.

Tyra's gaze met his. "Yes, certainly we wish to rejoin the Freuchens, not as a favor but by birthright. And that would mean restoring us the holdings, or compensation for them; a modest fortune. But it doesn't matter, I say. What does is my father's good name, his honor. He was a wonderful man." Her voice deepened. "Or is? He could maybe be alive still, somewhere yonder, after all these years. Or if not, we could—maybe avenge him."

The wings of her pageboy bob stirred. He realized that she had laid her ears back, like a wolf before a foe, and she was in truth of the old stock that conquered this planet for humankind.

"Easy, there," he said hastily. *"Rover's* civilian, remember. Unarmed."

"She should carry weapons. Since you discovered the kzinti have the hyperdrive—"

"Yah. Agreed. I wanted some armament installed, during this overhaul. Permission was denied, flat. Against policy. Bad enough, a hyperdrive ship operating as a free enterprise at all. Besides, I was reminded, it's twenty years since the kzinti were driven from Alpha Centauri, ten years since the war ended, and they've learned their lesson and are good little kitties now, and it was nasty of us to smash their base on that planet and do in so many of them. If they threatened our lives, why, mightn't we have provoked them? In any event, the proper thing for us to have done was to file a complaint with the proper authorities—" Saxtorph broke off. "Sorry. I feel kind of strongly about it."

He avoided describing the new equipment that was

aboard. Perfectly lawful, stuff for salvage work or prospecting or various other jobs that might come *Rover's* way. He hoped never to need it for anything else. But he and his shipmates had chosen it longsightedly, and made certain modifications. Just in case. Moreover, a spacecraft by herself carried awesome destructive potentialities. The commissioners were right to worry about one falling into irresponsible hands. He simply felt that the historical record showed governments as being, on the whole, much less responsible than humans.

"Anyway," he said, "under no circumstances would we go looking for a fight. I've seen enough combat to last me for several incarnations."

"But you are serious about going!" she cried.

He lifted a palm. "Whoa, please. First describe the situation. Uh, your brother's in the Navy, you said, but may I ask what you do?"

Her tone leveled. "I write. When liberation came, I had started to study literature at the university here. Afterward I worked some years for a news service, but when I had sold a few things of my own, I became a free-lance."

"What do you write? I'm afraid I don't recognize your byline."

"That is natural. Hyperdrive and hyperwave have not been available so long that there goes much exchange of culture between systems, especially when the societies went separate ways while ships were limited by light speed. I make differing things. Books, articles, scripts. Travel stuff; I like to travel, the same as you, and this has gotten me to three other stars so far. Other nonfiction. Short stories and plays. Two novels. Four books for young children."

"I want to read some . . . whatever happens." Saxtorph forbore to ask how she proposed to pay him on a writer's income. He couldn't afford a wild gamble that she might regain the family lands. Let the question wait.

Pride spoke: "Therefore you see, Captain, Ib and I

are independent. My aim—his, if I can persuade him—is for our father's honor. Even about that, I admit, nothing is guaranteed. But we must try, must we not? We might become what the Nordbos used to be. Or we might become far more rich, because whatever it is out yonder is undoubtedly something strange and mighty. But such things, if they happen, will be incidental."

Or *we* might come to grief, maybe permanently, Saxtorph thought. Nonetheless he intended to hear her out. "Okay," he said. "Shall we stop maneuvering and get down to the bones of the matter?"

Her look sought past him, beyond this tavern and this night. Her muted monotone flowed on beneath the music. "I give you the background first, for by themselves my father's notes that I have found are meaningless. Peter Nordbo was twelve years old, Earth reckoning, when the kzinti appeared. He was the only son of the house, by all accounts a bright and adventurous boy. Surely the conquest was a still crueler blow to him than to most dwellers on Wunderland.

"But folk were less touched by it, in that far-off northern district, than elsewhere. Travel restrictions, growing shortages of machines and supplies, everything forced them into themselves, their own resources. It became almost a . . . manorial system, is that the word? Or feudal? Children got instruction from what teachers and computer programs there were, and from their parents and from life. My father was a gifted pupil, but he was also much for sports, and he roamed the wilderness, hunted, took his sailboat out to sea—

"Mainly, from such thinly peopled outlying regions, the kzinti required tribute. The Landholders must collect this and arrange that it was delivered, but they generally did their best to lighten the burden on the tenants, who generally understood. Kzinti seldom visited Gerning, our part of Skogarna, and then just to hunt in the forests, so little if any open conflict happened. When my father reached an age for higher education, the family could send him to Munchen, the university.

"That was a quiet time also here. The humans who resisted had been hunted down, and the will to fight was not yet reborn in the younger generation. My father passed his student days peacefully, except, I suppose, for the usual carousals, and no doubt kzin-cursing behind closed doors. His study was astrophysics. He loved the stars. His dream was to go to space, but that was out of the question. Unless as slaves for special kzinti purposes, no Wunderlanders went any longer. The only Centaurian humans in space were Belters, subjugated like us, and Resistance fighters. And we never got real news of the fighters, you know. They were dim, half-real, mythic gods and heroes. Or, to the collaborationists and the quietists, dangerous enemies.

"Well. My father was . . . twenty-five, I think, Earth calendar . . . when my grandfather died a widower and Peter Nordbo inherited the Landholdership of Gerning. Dutiful, he put his scientific career aside and returned home to take up the load. Presently he married. They were happy together, if not otherwise.

"The position grew more and more difficult, you see. First, poverty worsened as machinery wore out and could not be replaced. Folk must work harder than ever before to stay alive, while the kzinti lessened their demands not a bit, which he must enforce. Resentment often went out over him. Then later the kzinti established a base in Gerning. It was fairly small, mainly a detector station against raids from space, for both the Resistance and the Solarians were growing bolder. And it was off in the woods, so that personnel could readily go hunting in their loose time. But it was there, and it made demands of its own, and now folk met kzinti quite commonly, one way or another.

"That led to humans being killed, some of them horribly. Do you understand that my father *must* put a stop to it? He must deal with the ratcats, make agreements, be useful enough that he would have a little influence and be granted an occasional favor. Surely he hated it. I was just eight years old on your calendar when he left us, but I remember, and from others I have heard. He began to drink heavily. He became a bad man to cross, who had been so fair-minded, and this made him more enemies. He worked off a part of the sorrow in physical activity, which might be wildly reckless, steeplechasing, hunting tigripards with a spear, sailing or skindiving among the skerries. And yet at home he was always kind, always loving—the big, handy, strong, sympathetic man, with his songs and jokes and stories, who never hurt his children but got much from them because he awaited they would give much."

Saxtorph was smoking too hard; his mouth felt scorched. He soothed it with beer. Tyra proceeded:

"I think he turned a blind eye on whatever underground activities arose in Gerning, or that he got wind of elsewhere. He could not risk joining them himself. He was all that stood between his folk and the kzinti that could devour them. Instead, he must be the subservient servant, and never scream at the devils gnawing in his soul.

"But I believe the worst devil, because half an angel, was the relationship that developed between him and Yiao-Captain. This was the space operations officer at the defense base in Gerning. Father found he could talk to him, bargain, persuade, better than with any other kzin. Naturally, then, Yiao-Captain became the one he often saw and . . . cultivated. I am not sure what it was about him that pleased Yiao-Captain, although I can guess. But Ib remembers hearing Father remark to Mother, more than once, that they were no longer quite master and slave, those two, or predator and prey, but almost friends.

"Of course folk noticed. They wondered. I, small girl at home, was not aware of anything wrong, but later I learned of the suspicions that Father had changed from reluctant go-between to active collaborationist. It was in the testimony against him, after liberation."

Tyra fell silent. The long talk had hoarsened her. She drank deep. Still she looked at what Saxtorph had never beheld.

Gone uneasy, he shifted his weight about, minor though it was on this planet, and sought his stein. The beer was as cool and strong as her handshake had been. He found words. "What do you think that pair had in common?" he asked.

She shook herself and came back to him. "Astrophysics," she answered. "Father's abiding interest, you know. It turned into one of his consolations. He built himself an observatory. Piece by piece, year by year, he improvised equipment." Humor flickered. "Or scrounged it. Is that your American word? Scientists under the occupation were as expert scroungers as everybody else." Once more gravely: "He spent much time at his instruments. When he had gotten that relationship with Yiao-Captain—remember, he mostly used it to help his tenants, shield them—he arranged for a link to a satellite observatory the kzinti maintained. It had military purposes, but those involved deep scanning of the heavens, and Father was allowed a little time-sharing." Her voice went slightly shrill. "Was this collaboration?"

"I wouldn't say so," replied Saxtorph, "but I'm not a fanatic." Nor was I here, enduring the ghastlinesses. I was an officer in the UN Navy, which was by no means a bad thing to be during the last war years. We managed quite a few jolly times.

With a renewed steadiness that he sensed was hardheld, Tyra continued: "It seems clear to me that Yiao-Captain shared Father's interest in astrophysics. As far as a kzin would be able to. They are not really capable of disinterested curiosity, are they? But Yiao-Captain could not have foreseen any important result. I think he gave his petty help and encouragement—easy to do in his position—for the sake of the search itself.

"And Father did make a discovery. It was important enough that Yiao-Captain arranged for a ship so he could go take a look. Father went along. They were never seen again. That was thirty Earth years ago."

By sheer coincidence, the musician changed to a different tune, brasses and an undertone of drums. Saxtorph knew it also. It too was ancient. The hair stood up on his arms. *"Ich hat' einen kameraten."* I had a comrade. The army song of mourning.

"He did not tell us why," Tyra said. The tears would no longer stay captive. "He was forbidden. He could only say he must go, and be gone a long time, but would always love us. We can only guess what happened."

Chapter III

The air was rank with kzin smell. The whole compound was, but in this room Yiao-Captain's excitement made it overwhelming, practically to choke on. He half leaned across his desk, claws out, as if it were an animal he had slain and was about to rip asunder. Sunlight through a window gleamed off eyes and wet fangs. Orange fur and naked tail stiffened erect. The sight terrified those human instincts that remembered the tiger and the sabertooth. Although Peter Nordbo had met it before and knew that no attack impended—probably—he must summon his courage. He was big and muscular, Yiao-Captain was short and slender, yet the kzin topped the man by fifteen centimeters, with a third again the bulk and twice the weight.

Words hissed, spat, snarled. "Action! Adventure! Getting away from this wretched outpost. Achievement, honor, a full name. Power gained, maybe, to end this dragged-on war at last. And afterward—afterward—" The words faded off in an exultant growl.

When he thought he saw a measure of calm, Nordbo

dared say, in Wunderlander, "I don't quite understand, sir. A very interesting astronomical phenomenon, which should be studied intensively. I came to request your help in getting me authorization to— But that is all. Isn't it, sir?" While he knew the Hero's Tongue, he was not allowed to defile it by use, especially since his vocal organs inevitably gave it a grotesque accent. When he must communicate with a kzin ignorant of his language, he used a translator or, absent that, wrote his replies.

Yiao-Captain sat down again and indicated that Nordbo could do likewise. "No, humans are slow to perceive such possibilities," he said. With characteristic rapid mood shift, he went patronizing. "I supposed you might. You are bold for a monkey. Well, think as best you can. A mysterious source of tremendous energy. Study of the stars deepened knowledge of the atom, and thus became a key to the development of nuclear weapons. What now have you come upon?"

Nordbo shook his head. His mouth bent upward ruefully in the bushy brown beard that was starting to grizzle, below the hook nose. "Scarcely an unknown law of nature in operation, sir. What it may be I'd rather not try to guess before we have much more data. It does suggest— No, how could it have appeared so suddenly, if it were what has crossed my mind? In any case, not every scientific discovery finds military applications. Most don't. I can't imagine how this one could, five light-years off."

"*You* cannot. We shall see."

"Well, sir, if I get the kind of support I need for further research—" Nordbo stopped. Appalled, he stared at the possibility that his eagerness had camouflaged from him. Might this really mean a weapon to turn on his folk? No. It must not. Please, God, make it impossible.

"You will have better than that," Yiao-Captain purred. "We shall go there."

Have I misheard? Nordbo thought. Even for a kzin, it is crazy. "What?"

"Yes." Yiao-Captain rose again. His tail switched, his

bat's-wing ears folded and lay back. He gazed out the window into the sky. "If nothing else, maybe that energy source can be transported. Maybe we can fling it at the enemy. They may have noticed too. If they have, they are bound to send an expedition sometime. Their peering, prying curiosity— But Alpha Centauri is closer to it than Sol by . . . three light-years, is that a good guess? We shall forestall. I can readily persuade the governor, given the information you have brought. And *I* will be in command."

Nordbo had risen too, less out of deference, for he realized that at present the kzin wouldn't notice or care, than because he couldn't endure being towered over by those devils. It struck him, not for the first time, that the reason few households on Wunderland kept cats any longer was that their faces were too much like a kzin's. Well, that was far from being the only happy thing the conquest had ruined.

"I, I wish you would reconsider, sir," he said.

"Never." The bass voice grew muted. "Our ancestors tamed their planet and went to the stars because they had learned that knowledge brings might. Shall we dishonor their ghosts?"

Nordbo moistened his lips. "I mean you personally, sir. We will . . . miss you."

It twisted in him: *The damnable part is that that is true. Yiao-Captain has never been gratuitously cruel, nor let others be when he had any control over them. By his lights, he is kindly. He has helped us directly or intervened on our behalf when I showed him the need was dire and there would be no loss to his side. He has received me as hospitably as a Hero can receive a monkey, and, yes, we have had some fascinating talks, where he listened to what I said and thought about it and gave answers that approached being fair. Why, he got me to teach him chess, and if he loses he doesn't fly into a murderous rage, only curses and goes outside to work it off in hand-to-hand combat practice. He likes me, after his fashion, and, confess it, I like him in a* crooked sort of way, and—what will happen to us in Gerning if he leaves us?

Yiao-Captain turned his head. Something akin to mirth rasped through his words. "Lament not. You are coming along."

Nordbo took a step backward. The horror was too vast for him to grasp immediately. He felt as if he were in a cold maelstrom, whirling down and down. His hands lifted. "No," he implored. "Oh, no, no."

Yiao-Captain refrained from slashing him for presuming to contradict a kzin. "Assuredly. You will keep total silence about this, of course." Lest a rival, rather than an enemy spy, learn, and move to get the coveted task himself. "Hr-r, you may return home, tell your household that you are going on a lengthy voyage, and pack what you need for your personal use. Then report back here for sequestration until we leave. I want your scientific skills." Laughter was a human thing, but a gruff noise vibrated. "And how can I do without my chess partner?"

Nordbo sagged against the wall. He seldom wept, never like this.

"What, you are reluctant?" Yiao-Captain teased. "You care nothing for struggle, glory, or your very curiosity? Take heart. Your time away shall be minimal. I am sure all arrangements can be completed within days."

A kzin's way of challenge is to scream and leap.

Chapter IV

Tyra wiped furiously at her eyes. "I am, am sorry," she stammered. "I did not plan to cry at you."

No more than a few drops had glistened along those cheekbones. Saxtorph half reached to take her hand. No. She might resent that; and after snapping once or twice for air, she had regained her balance. Best stay prosy. "You think the kzin honcho forced your father to go," he deduced.

She shrugged, not quite spastically. "Or ordered him. What was the difference? He could not tell us anything. If he had, and the kzinti had found out—"

Uh-huh, Saxtorph knew. Children for dinner at the officers' mess. Mother to a hunting preserve, unless they didn't reckon she'd make good sport and decided on a worse death as a public example. "This implies the ratcats considered the object important," he said. "Even more does the item that it involved an interstellar journey, in those days before hyperdrive and with a war under way. It was interstellar, wasn't it?"

"Yes. Father spoke of . . . long years. Also, after the

195

war, investigators got two or three eyewitness accounts
by humans who worked for the kzinti. They had only
seen requisition orders, that sort of thing, but it did
establish that Yiao-Captain and a small crew left for
some unrevealed destination in a vessel of the Swift
Hunter class. Hardly anything else was learned."

Saxtorph laid his pipe on the ashtaker rack and rubbed
his chin. "You're right, kzinti don't do science for the
sake of pure knowledge, the way humans sometimes
do. They want it to help them cope with a universe
they see as fundamentally hostile, or to win them power.
In this case, surely, they thought of military potential."

Tyra nodded. "That is clear." She braced herself.
"Father had been excited, almost happy. He spoke to
several people of a marvelous discovery he had made
from his observatory. I do not remember that, but I
was little, and maybe I did not happen to be there.
Mother was not interested in science and did not understand what he talked of, nor recall it afterward well
enough to be of any use. Likewise for what servants or
tenants heard. Ib was at school, he says. Everybody
agrees that Father said he must see Yiao-Captain about
having a thorough study made; the kzinti had the powerful instruments and computers, of course. He came
home from that and—I have told you." She bit her lip.
"The accusation later was that he deliberately put the
kzinti on the trail of something that might have led
them to a new weapon, and accompanied them to investigate closer, in hopes of wealth and favors."

"Forgive me," Saxtorph said softly, "but I've got to
ask this. Could it possibly be true?"

"No! We, his family, *knew* him. Year by year we had
heard as much of his pain as he dared utter, and felt the
rest. He loved us. Would he free-willingly have left us,
for years stretching into decades, whatever the pay-
ment? No, he simply never thought in terms of helping
the kzinti in their war, until they did and it was too late
for him. But the hysteria immediately after liberation—
There had been many real collaborators, you know.
And there were people who paid off grudges by accus-

ing other people, and— It was what I think you call a witch hunt.

"The fact that Peter Nordbo had cooperated, that was not in itself to be held against him. Most Landholders did. Taking to the bush was maybe more gallant, but then you could not be a thin, battered shield for your folk. Just the same, this was part of the reason why the new constitution took away the special status of the Nineteen Families. And in retrospect, that Peter Nordbo gave knowledge to the kzinti and fared off with them, that was made to make his earlier cooperation look willing, and like more than it actually was." Tyra's grip on the table edge drove the blood from her fingertips. "Yes, it is conceivable that in his heart he was on their side. Impossible, but conceivable. What I want you to find for me, Captain Saxtorph, is the truth. I am not afraid of it."

After a moment, shakily: "Please to excuse me. I should be more businesslike." She finished her wine.

Saxtorph knocked back his beer and rose. "Let me get us refills," he suggested. "Care for something stronger?"

"Thank you. A double Scotch. Water chaser." She managed a smile. "You may take you an akvavit this time. I have not much left to tell."

When he brought the drinks back, she was entirely self-possessed. "Ask whatever you want," she invited. "Be frank. I believed my wounds were long ago scarred over. What made them hurt again tonight was hope."

"Don't get yours too high," he advised. "This looks mighty dicey to me. And, like your dad, I've got other people to think about before I agree to anything."

"Naturally. I would not have approached you if the story of your adventures had not proved you are conscientious."

He attempted a laugh. "Please. Call 'em my experiences. Adventures are what happen to the incompetent." He sent caraway pungency down his throat and a dollop of brew in pursuit. "Okay, let's get cracking again. I gather no details about that expedition ever came out."

"They were suppressed, obliterated. When the human hyperdrive armada arrived and it became clear that the kzinti would lose Alpha Centauri, they destroyed all their records and installations that they could, before going forth to die in battle. Prisoners and surviving human witnesses had little information. About Yiao-Captain's mission, nobody had any, except what I mentioned to you. It was secret from the beginning; very few kzinti, either, ever knew about it."

"No report to the home world till success was assured. Nor when Wunderland was falling. They were smart bastards; they foresaw our new craft would hunt for every such beam, overtake it, read it, and jam it beyond recovery."

"I know. Ib has described to me the effect of faster-than-light travel on intelligence operations."

Her grasp of practical things was akin to Dorcas', Saxtorph thought. "When did the ship leave?" he asked.

"It was— Now I am forgetting your calendar. It was ten Earth-years before liberation."

"And whatever messages she'd sent back were wiped from the databases at that time, and whatever kzinti knew the content died fighting. She never returned, and after the liberation no word came from her."

"The general explanation was—is—that it and the crew perished." In bitterness, Tyra added, "Fortunately, they say."

"But if she did not, then she probably got news of the defeat. A beam cycled through the volume of her possible trajectories could be read across several light-years, and wasn't in a direction humans would likely search. What then would her captain do?" Saxtorph addressed his beer. "Never mind for now. I'd be speculating far in advance of the facts. You say you have come upon some new ones?"

"Old ones." Her voice dropped low. "Thirty years old."

He waited.

She folded her hands on the table, looked at him straight across it, and said, "A few months ago, Mother

died. She was never well since Father left. As surrogate
Landholder, she was not really able to cope with the
dreadful task. She did her best, I grew up seeing how
she struggled, but she had not his skills, or his special
relationship with a ranking kzin, or just his physical
strength. So she . . . yielded . . . more than he had
done. This caused her to be called a collaborator, when
the kzinti were safely gone, and retrospectively it blackened Father's name worse, but—she was let go, to live
out her life on what property the court had no legal
right to take away from us. It is productive, and Ib
found a good supervisor, so she was not in poverty. Nor
wealthy. But how alone! We did what we could, Ib and
I and her true friends, but it was not much, and never
could we restore Father to her. She was brave, kept
busy, and . . . dwindled. Her death was peaceful. I
closed her eyes. The physician's verdict was general
debility leading to cardiac failure.

"Ib has his duties, while I can set my own working
hours. Therefore it was I who remained at Korsness, to
make arrangements and put things in order. I went
through the database, the papers, the remembrances—
And at the bottom of a drawer, under layers of his
clothes that she had kept, I found Father's last notebook from the observatory."

Air whistled in between Saxtorph's teeth. "Including
the data on that thing? Jesu Kristi! Didn't he know how
dangerous it was for his family to have?"

"He may have forgotten, in his emotional storm. I
think likelier, however, he hid it there himself. No
human would have reason to go through that drawer for
many years. He knew Mother would not empty it."

"M-m, yah. And if nothing made them suspicious,
the kzinti wouldn't search the house. Beneath their dignity, pawing through monkey stuff. And they never
have managed to understand how humans feel about
their families. Yah. Nordbo, your dad, he may very
well have left those notes as a kind of heritage; because
if you've given me a proper account of him, and I

believe you have, then he had not given up the hope of
freedom at last for his people."

A couple of fresh tears trembled on her lashes but
went no farther. "*You* understand," she whispered.

Enthusiasm leaped in him. "Well, what did the book
say?"

"I did not know at once. It took reviewing of science
from school days. I dared not ask anybody else. It could
be—undesirable."

Okay, Saxtorph thought, if he turned out to have
been a traitor after all, why not suppress the information? What harm, at this late date? I don't suppose it'd
have changed your love of him and his memory. You're
that kind of person.

"What he found," Tyra said, "was a radiation source
in Tigripardus." Most constellations bear the same names
at Alpha Centauri as at Sol—four and a third light-years
being a distance minuscule in the enormousness of the
galaxy—but certain changes around the line between
them have been inevitable. "It was faint, requiring a
sensitive detector, and would have gone unnoticed had
he not happened to study that exact part of the sky.
This was in the course of a systematic, years-long search
for small anomalies. They might indicate stray mono-
poles, or antimatter concentrations, or other such peculiarities, which in turn might give clues about the
evolution of the whole— But I explain too much, no?

"The radiation seemed to be from a point source.
It consisted of extremely high-energy gamma rays. The
spectrum suggested particles were being formed and
annihilated. This indicated an extraordinary energy density. With access to the automated monitors the kzinti
kept throughout this system, Father quickly got the
parallax. The object was about five light-years away.
That meant the radiation at the source was fantastically
intense. I can show you the figures later, if you wish."

"I do," Saxtorph breathed. "Oh, I do."

"He checked through the astronomical databases, too,"
she went on. "Archival material from Sol, and studies

made here before the war, showed nothing. This was a new thing, a few years old at most."

"And since then, evidently, it's turned off."

"Yes. As I told you, Ib got a Navy observer to look at the area, on a pretext. Nothing unusual."

"Curiouser and curiouser. Any idea what it might be, or have been?"

"I am a layman. My guesses are worthless."

"Don't be humble. I'm not. Hm-m-m . . . No, this is premature, at least till I've seen those numbers. Clearly, Yiao-Captain guessed at potentialities that made it worth taking a close look, and persuaded his superiors."

Saxtorph clutched the handle of his mug and stared down as if it were an oracular well. "Ten years plus, either way," he muttered. "That's what I'd estimate trip time as, from what I recall of the Swift Hunter class and know about kzinti style. Sparing even a single ship and crew for twenty-odd years, when every attack on Sol was ending in expensive defeat and we'd begun making our own raids—uh-huh. A gamble, but maybe for almighty big stakes."

"And the ship never came back," Tyra reminded him. "A ten-year crossing, do you reckon? It should have reached the goal about when the hyperdrive armada got here to set us free. Surely the kzinti sent it word of that. The news would have been received five years later. Sooner, if the ship was en route home." Or not at all if the ship was dead, Saxtorph thought. "Then what? I cannot imagine a kzin commander staying on course, to surrender at journey's end. He might have tried to arrive unexpectedly and crash his ship on Wunderland, a last act of terrible vengeance, but that would have happened already."

"More speculation," Saxtorph said. "What's needed is facts."

A sword being drawn could have spoken her "Yes."

"Who've you told about this, besides your brother and me?" Saxtorph asked.

"Nobody, and I swore him to secrecy. If nothing else, we must think first, undisturbed, he and I. He sounded out high officers, and decided they would not believe our father's notes are genuine, when their observatory contradicts."

"M-m, I dunno. They know the kzinti went after *something*."

"It can have been something quite different."

"Still, these days a five-light-year jaunt is no great shakes. Include it in a training cruise or whatever."

"And as for finding out the truth about our father, which is Ib's and my real purpose—they would not care."

"Again, I wonder. I want to talk with Ib."

"Of course, if you are serious. But can you not see, if we give this matter over to the authorities, it goes entirely out of our hands? They will never allow us to do anything more."

"That is fairly plausible."

"If you, though, an independent observer, if you verify that this is real and important, then we cannot be denied. The public will insist on a complete investigation."

A decent cause, and a decent chunk of much-needed money. Too many loose ends. However, Saxtorph flattered himself that he could recognize a genuine human being when he met one. "I'll have to know a lot more, and ring in my partners, et cetera, et cetera," he declared. "Right now, I can just say I'll be glad to do so."

"It is a plenty!" Her tone rejoiced. "Thank you, Captain, a thousand thanks. *Skaal!*" When they had clinked rims, she tossed off an astonishing draught.

It didn't make her drunk. Perhaps it helped bring ease, and a return of vivacity. "I had my special reason for meeting you like this," she said. Her smile challenged. "Before entrusting you with my dream, I wanted we should be face to face, alone, and I get the measure of you."

Yes, occasionally he had made critical decisions in which his personal impression of somebody was a major factor.

"We shall hold further discussion, and you bring your

wife—your whole crew, if you wish," Tyra said. "To-night, I think, we have talked enough. About this. But must you leave at once?"

"Well, no," he answered, more awkwardly than was his wont.

They conversed, and listened to the music that most of humankind had forgotten, and swapped private memories, and drank, and she was a sure and supple dancer. Nothing wrong took place. Still, it was a good thing for Saxtorph that when he got back to his hotel, Dorcas was awake and in the mood.

Chapter V

Swordbeak emerged from hyperspace and accelerated toward the Father Sun. A warcraft of the Raptor class, lately modified to accommodate a superluminal drive, it moved faster than most, agilely responsive to the thrust of its gravity polarizers. Watchers in space saw laser turrets and missile launchers silhouetted against the Milky Way, sleek as the plumage of its namesake, overwhelmingly deadlier than the talons. It identified itself to their satisfaction and passed onward. Messages flew to and fro. When the vessel reached Kzin, a priority orbit around the planet was preassigned it. Weoch-Captain took a boat straight down to Defiant Warrior Base. Thence he proceeded immediately to the lair of Ress-Chiuu. A proper escort waited there.

The High Admiral received him in the same room as before. Now, however, a table had been set with silver goblets of drink and golden braziers of sweet, mildly psychotropic incense. In the blood trough at the middle a live *zianya* lay bound. Its muzzle had been taped shut to keep it from squealing, but the smell of its fear stimulated more than did the smoke.

"You enter in honor," Ress-Chiuu greeted.

From his rank, that was a pridemaking compliment. Nevertheless Weoch-Captain felt he should demur. "You are generous, sire. In truth I accomplished little."

"You slew no foes and saved no friends. We never, realistically, expected you would. To judge by your preliminary report as you returned, you did well against considerable odds. But you shall tell me about it in person, at leisure. Afterward Intelligence will examine what is in your ship's database. Recline—" in this presence, another great distinction—"and take refreshment." —an extraordinary one.

As he talked, interrupted only by shrewd questions, memories more than drink or drug restored to Weoch-Captain his full self-confidence. If he had not prevailed, neither had he lost, and his mission was basically successful.

The story unfolded at length: Voyage to the old red dwarf. Cautious, probing approach to the planet on which Werlith-Commandant's forces had been at work. Detection and challenge by humans. Dialogue, carefully steered to make them think that the kzinti had no foreknowledge of anything and this was a routine visit. Refusal to let the kzinti proceed farther, orders for *Swordbeak* to depart. ("So they show that much spirit, do they?" Ress-Chiuu mused. "The official communications have been as jelly-mild as I predicted. Well, maybe it was just this individual commander.") *Swordbeak*'s forward plunge. An attack warded off, except for a ray that did no significant damage before the ship was out of range. Three more human vessels summoned and straining to intercept. Weoch-Captain's trajectory by the planet, wild, too close in for the pursuit to dare, instruments and cameras recording that the kzinti installation had been annihilated, the kzinti warcraft that had been on guard orbited as a mass of cold wreckage, the likelihood of any survivors was essentially nil. Running a gauntlet of enemy fire on the way out. Another bra-

vado maneuver, this around the larger gas giant, that
could have thrown *Swordbeak* aflame into the atmosphere but left its nearest, more heavily armed chaser
hopelessly behind. Swatting missiles on the way out to
hyperspacing distance. A jeering message beamed aft,
and escape from 3-space.

"It is well, it is well." Ress-Chiuu rolled the words
over his tongue as if they were the fine drink in his
goblet.

Weoch-Captain gauged that he had asserted himself
as much as was advisable. He had his future to think of,
the career that should bring him at last a full name and
the right to breed. "If the High Admiral is pleased, that
suffices. But it was mere information we captured, which
the monkeys may in time have given us freely."

"Vouchsafed us," Ress-Chiuu snarled. "Condescended
to throw to us."

"True, sire." It had indeed been in the minds of
Weoch-Captain and his crew, a strong motivation to do
what they did.

"Nor could we be certain they would not lie."

"True, sire. Nonetheless—" The utterance was dis-
tasteful but necessary, if Weoch-Captain was to maintain the High Admiral's opinion of him as an officer not
only valiant but wise. "They will resent what happened.
We have barely begun to modernize and re-expand the
fleet. Theirs is much stronger. How may they react? I
admit to fretting about that on the way home."

"The Patriarchs considered it beforehand," Ress-Chiuu
assured him. "The humans will bleat. Perhaps they will
even huff and puff. We shall point out that they have
registered no territorial claim on yonder sun and its
planets, therefore they had no right to forbid entry to a
peaceful visitor, and you did nothing but save yourselves after they opened fire. Arh, your restraint was
masterly, Weoch-Captain. We will demand reparation,
they will make a little more noise, and that will be the
end of the matter. Meanwhile you have learned a great
deal for us, about their capabilities and about what to

expect, what to prepare for, when we start pushing at them in earnest. You deserve well of us, Weoch-Captain."

He leaned forward. His voice became music and distant thunder. "You deserve the opportunity to win more glory. You may earn the ultimate reward."

Energy thrilled along nerves and into blood. "Sire! I stand ready!"

"I knew you would." Ress-Chiuu sipped, rather than lapped, from his cup. His gaze went afar, his tone deceptively meditative. "We have our sources of information among the humans. They are limited in what they can convey but on occasion they have proven useful. For the present, you need know no more than that. Let me simply say that not everything the hyperwave brings us is known to the human *government*." Perforce he attempted to pronounce the English word. Weoch-Captain recognized, if not exactly understood it.

"For relevant example," Ress-Chiuu continued, "we got early news of the disaster at the red sun, well before they contacted us officially about it. This you recall, of course. What you do not recall, because it happened while you were gone, is that we have received fresh intelligence, conceivably of the first importance."

Stoic, as became a Hero, Weoch-Captain waited. His ribs ached with tension. His heart slugged.

"Briefly put—we will go into details later," he heard, "a Wunderland resident has come upon a lost record from the time of the war. It appears that, some years before the enemy got the hyperdrive, an astronomer observed a cosmic phenomenon, about five light-years from Alpha Centauri. It was inexplicable, but involved enormous energies. The possibility of military uses caused the high command of the occupation to dispatch a ship to investigate. If the ship sent any messages back, those were expunged when the human armada appeared, and all kzinti who had knowledge of the mission died. Any beams that arrived afterward were never received, the tuned and programmed apparatus being destroyed; they are dissipated, lost. The ship has not been heard of again. Recent search has failed to detect anything remarkable in that part of the Wunderland sky.

"Regardless, for reasons not quite clear to me, humans are trying to organize an expedition to that region. Humans, I say, individuals, not *the* humans. Their patriarchs are, as yet, unaware of it.

"We have obtained the astronomical data. They are sufficient basis for an investigation. Perhaps nothing is there, or nothing of interest. Yet it is imaginable that those kzinti were justified who decided, three decades ago, that this was worth sending a high-velocity vessel.

"We must know. If it is anything of value, we must win it ourselves. The way is considerably longer from here than from there. Are you and your crew prepared to leave again quite soon?"

"Sire," blazed Weoch-Captain, "you need not ask!"

"And I say, to your honor, that I am unsurprised." Ress-Chiuu showed fangs. "I give you an added incentive. If the humans do mount their expedition, it will apparently consist of a single ship, unarmed, commanded by one . . . S-s-saxtor-r-rph, the designation is. The ship, commander, and crew that wrought the havoc you beheld."

Weoch-Captain roared.

They spoke together, ran computations and simulations, speculated, envisioned, dreamed their fierce dreams, until past sundown. Much remained to do when they stopped for a feast of celebration. The first flesh ripped from the *zianya*, before it died, was especially savory.

Chapter VI

While the government ground ponderously through its motions, Juan Yoshii and Laurinda Brozik were as trapped on Wunderland as their friends. Released, they could not get early passage to We Made It; as yet, few ships plied that route. When a sudden opportunity came by, they grabbed. The others took no offense. Laurinda's parents were eager to get her home and legally married. Her father had already promised his prospective son-in-law an excellent job, no sinecure but still one that would allow him to pursue his literary interests on the side. You don't dawdle over such things. However, the situation gave scant notice or time for a sendoff. Preoccupied as they were with the Nordbo business, skipper and mate could merely offer their best wishes. Kamehameha Ryan and Carita Fenger made what arrangements they were able, and the foursome took off for the pair of days available before departure.

Though Gelbstein Park is popular in summer, visitors to that high country are few when winter has fallen over the southern hemisphere of Wunderland. These got romantic near-solitude. A walk amidst the scenery preceded dinner back at the lodge, drinks before the fireplace, and a long goodnight.

"Brrr-hooee!" Ryan hugged himself. Breath smoked from his round brown countenance. "I'm glad I'm not a brass monkey."

Carita took his arm. The Jinxian's own skin seemed coal-black against the snowscape, in which Laurinda's albino complexion showed ghostly. "Keep reminding yourself that not all your ancestors were kanakas," she suggested.

"Or that it gets pretty cold on top of Mauna Kea too, yeah." The quartermaster snuggled his chin under the collar of his jacket.

"You could've insisted we go to Eden or the Roseninsel or wherever tropical."

"Naw, I'm okay. Juan opted for here, and this's his last chance."

Yoshii seemed indeed lost in his surroundings. Was a poem brewing? Overhead the sky stood huge, cloudless, as deeply blue as the shadows cast by sun A across the snows. Paler were those from B, an elfin tracery mingled with the frost-glitter. A kilometer ahead, the trail ended at a hot springs area. The greens and russets of pools were twice vivid in the whiteness elsewhere; the steam that rose from them was utter purity. Beyond, the Lucknerberg gleamed in its might. The sounds of seething carried this far through the silence, but muffled, as if it were the underground working of the planet that one heard.

"You are so kind," Laurinda said. "We'll miss you so much."

Yoshii shivered, left his reverie, and caught his girl's gloved hand. They were walking in front of their companions. He glanced back. "Yes, and we'll worry about you," he added. "Headed into the . . . the unknown—"

"You'll have better things to do," Ryan laughed.

"And we'll be fine," Carita put in.

"Shorthanded," Yoshii said. They had not found a

satisfactory replacement for him. "I can't help feeling guilty, like a deserter."

"Juan, boy," Carita replied, "if you left this lass behind now, even for a month's jaunt, I'd turn you over my knee and spank you till you took first prize at the next baboon show." Quite possibly she meant it. Her short, massive frame certainly had the capability.

"I might have gone too—" Laurinda's words trailed off. No, she would not have done that to her parents. "If we could only stay in touch!"

Ryan shrugged. "Someday they'll miniaturize hyperwave equipment to the point where it'll fit in a spaceship."

"Why haven't they already?" she protested. "Or why didn't it come with the hyperdrive?"

"We can't expect to understand or assimilate a nonhuman technology overnight," Yoshii told her in his soft fashion. "As was, it took skull sweat to adapt what the Outsiders sold your world to our uses. I'm surprised that you, of all people, should ask such a question."

"A woman needs to spring an occasional surprise," Carita said.

Laurinda gulped. "But not a stupid remark. I'm sorry. My thinking had gone askew. I *am* afraid for you two and the Saxtorphs."

"Nonsense," Ryan said. "It'll be *aheahe*, a breeze, a well-paid junket." Into reaches that had swallowed a kzinti warcraft. "You don't get ol' Bob haring right off on impulse. If we should meet difficulties we can't skip straight away from, we're equipped like an octopus to handle 'em."

"No weapons." She had not been concerned with the refitting, but she knew this.

"Oh, he and I saw quietly to our stash of small arms, explosives, and all."

Yoshii's mouth tightened. "What use against the universe?"

"As for that," Carita stated, "you know full well what we've got." Mainly to Laurinda: "A beefed-up grapnel field system. We can lock onto a fair-sized asteroid and shift its orbit, if we want to spend the fuel. Our new main laser can bore a hole from end to end of it. Our robot prospector-lander can boost at as high as a hundred Earth gees, for a total delta *v* of a thousand KPS. Plus the stuff we carried before, except for the second boat—radars, instruments, teleprobes, you name it. Oh, we'd be no match for a naval vessel, but aside from that, we're loaded like a *verguuz* drinker."

"Now will you joyful honeymooners kindly reel in your faces and start singing and dancing as the drill calls for?" Ryan snorted.

The couple traded a look, which rapidly grew warm. Smiles radiated between them. "Makes me feel downright lecherous," Carita murmured to Ryan. "How 'bout you?"

With a rumbling roar, a geyser erupted among the springs. Higher and higher it climbed against the gentle gravity, until the tower of it reached a hundred meters aloft. Light sharded to bows and diamonds in its plume. Thence it flung a fine rain which fell stinging hot, smelling of sulfur and tasting of iron, violence broken loose from rocks far below. Abruptly the humans felt very small.

Chapter VII

Waves move more slowly on Wunderland than on Earth and strike less hard, but the seas that beat against the cliffs of Korsness were heavy enough. The noise of them reached the old house on the headland as a muted throb, drums beneath the wind-skirl. Gray, green, and white-maned, they heaved out to a horizon vague with scud. The clouds flew low, like smoke. The room overlooking the view seemed full of their twilight, despite its fluoros. That glow lost itself in swartwood furniture, murky carpet, leatherbound codices and ancestral portraits. Above the stone mantel hung a crossed pair of oars, dried and cracked. The first Nordbo who settled here had used them after the motor in his boat failed, to fetch a son wrecked on Horn Reef.

Saxtorph liked this place. It spoke to something in his blood. "You've got roots," he remarked. "Not many folks do these days."

Seated on his left, Tyra nodded. Her hair was the sole real brightness. "The honor of the house," she said, then grimaced. "No, forgive me, I do not mean to be pretentious."

213

"But you shouldn't be afraid of speaking about what truly matters," said Dorcas on her far side.

"I am not. Your husband knows. But—" The com that they confronted chimed and blinked. Tyra stiffened. "Accept," she snapped.

The full-size image of a man appeared, and part of the desk behind which he sat, and through the window at his back a glimpse of the Drachenturm in Munchen. "Good day," he greeted. Half rising to make a stiff little bow: "Frau Saxtorph, at last I get the pleasure of your acquaintance." He must have worked to flatten out of his English the accent his sister retained.

Dorcas inclined her head. The mahogany-hued crest and tail of her Belter hairstyle rippled. "How do you do, Herr," she answered as formally. The smile on the Athene visage was less warm than usual. "Someday I may have the pleasure of shaking your hand."

Ib Nordbo took the implied reproof impassively. He was in his mid-forties, tall and low-gee slim, smooth-chinned, bearing much of Tyra's blond handsomeness but none of her verve and frequent merriment. At least, during his previous two short encounters with Saxtorph he had been curt and somber. Insignia on the blue uniform proclaimed him a lieutenant commander of naval intelligence.

"*Why* would you not come in person today?" burst from Tyra. "I tell you, this is the one spot on Wunderland where we can be sure we are private."

"Come, now," her brother replied. "My office was and is perfectly secure, there is no reason to imagine your town apartment or the Saxtorphs' hotel room were ever under surveillance, and I assure you, this circuit is well sealed."

Anxious to avoid a breach, for the earlier scenes had gotten a bit tense, Saxtorph said, "You'd know, in your job. Actually, my wife and I were glad of Tyra's invitation because we were curious to see the homestead."

"We hoped to get some feel for your father, some insight or intuition," Dorcas added.

"What value can that have, on a search through space?"

Nordbo's question would have been a challenge or a gibe if it had been uttered less flatly.

"Perhaps none. You never can tell. If nothing else, this was an interesting visit; and to hold his actual notebook in our hands was . . . an experience."

"I fear nobody else would agree, Frau." Nordbo's attention went to his sister. "Tyra, I hesitate to say you have become paranoiac on this subject, but you have exaggerated it in your mind out of all proportion. What cause does anyone have to spy on you? How often must I repeat, the Navy—no part of officialdom—will concern itself?"

Saxtorph stirred. "And I repeat, if you please, that I have trouble believing that," he said. "Okay, one kzinti ship was lost thirty years ago, among hundreds. There was an avalanche of matters to handle in the years right after liberation. This business was forgotten. Sure. But if we did show them your father's notes and reminded them that the kzinti reckoned it worthwhile dispatching a ship—"

"Nothing special is now in that part of the sky," Nordbo retorted. "What he detected must have been a transient thing at best, an accident leaving no trace, perhaps the collision of a matter and an antimatter body."

"That'd have been plenty weird. Who's ever found so much loose antimatter? But we've still got that infrared anomaly." Saxtorph had insisted on Nordbo's retrieving the entire record of the naval observation.

"Meaningless. Its intensity against the cosmic background falls within probable error." The officer stirred where he sat. "We need scarcely go over this ground again for your lady wife's benefit. We have trodden it bare, and you must have relayed the arguments to her. But to complete the repetition, Frau Saxtorph, I have pointed out that the kzinti may well have had some entirely different destination, and took my father along merely because his noticing this phenomenon put them in mind of him as an excellent observer. They quite commonly employed human technicians, you know. Our species has more patience for detail work than theirs."

He paused before finishing: "This is how they will think in the Navy if we tell them. I have sounded out various high-ranking persons, at Tyra's request. Besides, I am Navy myself; I ought to know, ought I not? It *might* be decided to go take a look, on the odd chance that my father did stumble on something special. But they would not care about him or his fate. Nor would they want civilians underfoot. You, Captain Saxtorph, would be specifically forbidden to enter that region."

"I understand that," Tyra said. "At least, it is possible. Therefore *Rover* must go first, before anything has been revealed. What information it brings back can jumpstart some real action."

"Frau Saxtorph, I appeal to you," Nordbo said. "My sister has involved me—"

"It was your right to know," Tyra interjected, "and I thought you would help."

"She wants me, if nothing else, to withhold from my service word about this ill-advised space mission of yours. Can you not see what a difficult position that creates for me?"

"I agree your position is delicate," Dorcas murmured.

Did Nordbo wince or flinch? If so, he clamped control back down too fast for Robert Saxtorph to be sure. Either way, the captain felt momentarily sorry for what had happened of late.

Not that the *Rover* crew were at fault. They'd had no way of foreseeing. They simply carried back to Alpha Centauri the news that Commissioner Markham had been a spy for the kzinti. It provoked a hunt for others. And—soon after liberation, when Ib Nordbo was a young engineer working in the asteroids, Ulf Reichstein-Markham, still out there settling assorted affairs, had befriended him. They returned to Wunderland together, Nordbo enlisting, Markham going unsuccessfully into politics and later rather brilliantly into astronautics administration. Markham's prestige, the occasional overt recommendation or conversational suggestion, helped Nordbo rise. They met fairly often.

Well, but suspicion found no grounds. "It must die away altogether," Tyra had pleaded to Saxtorph. "Must it not? Ib fought for freedom—not like Markham, only in one uprising, that crazy try of young men to take back the Ritterhaus, but he did suffer injuries. And Markham was in fact a hero of the Resistance, maybe its greatest. He did not change till long afterward. How could Ib tell? Yes, they did things together, dining, hunting, talking. What does that mean? They were both lonely. They have—they had not sociable personalities. Ib was always of dark spirit. He has never married. I think he still carries the torment of our father inside him. Remember, he is seven Earth-years older than me. He lived through more of it, and then through the years alone with our mother, at that impressionable age. Now he is fine in his work. He would have risen higher if he had a wife who knew all the unspoken social rules, or if he could just be smooth. But he is too honest. He does not share those filthy dictatorial ideas you told me Markham held. I am his sister, I would know if he did. We are not close, he is not close to anyone, but we are the children of Peter Nordbo."

Dorcas, who was tactful when she cared to be, went directly on: "However, nothing illegal or unethical is involved. We plan a scientific mission. Amateurs, yes, but if we get in trouble, nobody will be harmed except us. That kind of personal risk is not prohibited by any statute or regulation I know of—"

Thus far, Saxtorph thought.

"—nor do the terms of our insurance and mortgage require more than 'informed prudence,' the interpretation of which clause is a matter for the civil courts. You are merely assisting an undertaking that may prove beneficial to your nation."

Nordbo shook his head. "I am not," he answered. "I have given it the serious thought I promised. Today I tell you that I will have no further part of it."

"Ib!" Tyra cried. Her hand went to her mouth.

"It is lunatic," he stated. "If we turned those notes over to my service, at least any investigation would be competently handled. My apologies, Captain and Mate Saxtorph. I am sure you command your ship well. You have been persuaded to enter a field outside your competence. Please reconsider."

Tyra said something unsteadily in her childhood dialect. He replied likewise. In English: "Yes, I will keep my promise, my silence about this, unless circumstances force me. But I will not make any contribution to your effort, nor lend any more aid or counsel, except my earnest advice that you abandon it. That is final."

His tone softened. "Tyra, you sit in what we have left of our inheritance, our father's and mother's and ancestors' heritage. Will you really throw it away?"

"No," she whispered. Her shoulders straightened. "But I will do what is my right."

Korsness was no Landholding, only a freehold, shared by the heirs. She had arranged to hypothecate her half of the equity, to pay for the charter. The agreement lay awaiting her print. In the odds-on event that *Rover* found nothing of monetary value, her income from the property ought to pay off the debt, though not before she was well along in years. It would have helped if Ib had joined in.

Saxtorph didn't feel abashed. He had a living to make. If Tyra wanted his capabilities this badly, why, her profession supported her. For his part, and Dorcas', Kam's, Carita's, they'd be putting their necks on the line. Still, he admired her spirit.

"Then best I say farewell," Nordbo sighed. "Before we quarrel. I will see you in a few days, Tyra, and we will speak of happier things."

"I am not sure where I will be," she replied. "I cannot sit idle while— It will be research for a new piece of writing. But of course I will get in touch when I can." Her words wavered. "We shall always be friends, *broder min.*"

"Yes," he said gravely. "Fare you ever well." His image vanished.

The surf and the wind resounded through silence. After a while Dorcas said low, "I think that was why he

chose to call, instead of coming in person as you asked.
So he could leave at once."

They barely heard Tyra: "Dealings like this are hard
for him. He knows not well how to cope with humans."

She sprang to her feet. "But I am not crushed." Her
stance, her voice avowed it. "I had small hope for
better, after our talks before. Poor soul, he took more
wounds than I did, and fears they might come open. I
gave him his chance." Louder yet: "We can proceed.
Robert, you have told me very little of what you intend."

Dorcas cast a glance at her man and also raised her
lean length from the chair.

"Uh, yah, I s'pose we are on first-name terms by
now," he said fast, fumbling after pipe and tobacco.
They had in fact been for a while, when by themselves.
"I've had my thoughts, and discussed them with Dorcas, but we figured we'd best wait with you till the
contract was definite. It is, isn't it?"

"Yes, in all except our prints," Tyra told him. "You
have seen it, have you not, Frau—m-m, Dorcas?"

Rover's mate smiled and nodded. "I rewrote two of
the clauses," she said. "Evidently, next time you met
Bob, you agreed."

"But what do you propose to *do?*" Tyra demanded.

Saxtorph busied his hands. "A lot will depend on
what we find." He had explained earlier, but sketchily.
"What Dorcas and I have drawn up is not a plan but a
set of contingency plans, subject to change without
notice. However, it makes sense to start by trying for
that whatever-it-is that your father spotted. Presumably
the kzinti ship got there, and what the crew found
became a factor in determining what they did afterward."

"Have you any idea about it?"

"None, really," Dorcas admitted. "Your brother may
well be right, it was a freak of no special significance."

"Except, we believe, Yiao-Captain thought otherwise,"
Saxtorph pointed out. "And he got his superiors to
agree it was worth a shot. Of course, from a human
viewpoint, kzinti are natural-born wild gamblers." He
thumbed tobacco down into bowl. "Well, this is a sec-

ondary mystery. What you've engaged us for is to learn, if we can, what happened to your father. Yonder objective is a starting point."

Tyra went to a window and gazed out across sea and wrack. A burst of rain spattered on the glasyl. "You have mentioned intercepting radio waves in space," she said slowly. "Could you get any from that ship?"

"We'll try. I'm not optimistic. Space is almighty big, and if a beam wasn't very tightly collimated to start with, I doubt we could pick it out of the background noise after this many years, supposing we could locate it at all. Shipboard transmitters aren't really powerful. But I do have some notions as to what the kzinti may have done."

"*Ja?*" she exclaimed, and swung around to stare at him.

He got his pipe going. "What do you know about the Swift Hunter class?"

"Almost nothing. I see now that I should have looked it up, but—"

"No blame. You had a lot else to keep track of, including the earning of your daily bread and peanut butter. I remembered things from the war, and retrieved more from the naval histories in the Wunderland library system."

Saxtorph blew a smoke ring. "I don't know if the kzinti still use Swift Hunters. Who knows for sure what goes on in their empire? Any that remain in service will certainly be phased out as hyperdrive comes in, because it makes them as obsolete as windjammers. In their time, though, they were wicked.

"Good-sized, but skimpy payload, most of what they carried being mass for conversion. Generally they took special weapons, or sometimes special troops, on ultra-quick missions followed by getaways faster than any missile could pursue. Total delta v of about two and a half c, Newtonian regime. Customarily, during the war, they'd boost to one-half c and go ballistic till time to decelerate. Anything higher would've been too inefficient, as relativity effects began getting large. This means that they'd strike and return, with the extra half light-speed available for high-powered maneuvers in between. The gravity polarizer made it all possible. Jets would never have managed anything comparable. At that, the Swift Hunters were so energy-hungry that the kzinti saved them for special jobs, as I said. Obviously they figured this was one such."

"Nevertheless, ten years to their goal," Dorcas murmured.

"But in stasis, apart from standing watch," Saxtorph reminded her. "Or, rather, the kzinti version of time-suspension technics, in those days. You can be pretty patient if you get to lie unconscious and unaging during most of the voyage."

It had been in Tyra's awareness, of course, but she tautened and breathed, "My father—" Seen from indoors, she was a shapely shadow against the silver-gray in the window, save for the light on her hair.

Saxtorph nodded. "Uh-huh," he said around puffs. "Do not, repeat, do not get your hopes up. But it just could be. Bound back here with word of something tremendous—or without, for that matter—the kzinti captain catches a beam that tells him Wunderland is falling to humans who've acquired a faster-than-light drive. What's he going to do? He's got a half c of delta v left to kill his forward vector, and another half c to boost him to the kzinti home sun."

"But when he got there, he could not stop," she said, as if against her will.

"He might wager they could do something about that at the other end," Saxtorph answered. "Or he might travel at one-fourth c and take about 120 years, instead of about sixty, to arrive. In stasis he wouldn't notice the difference. But I doubt that, especially if he was carrying important information which he couldn't reliably transmit by radio. And kzinti always do go balls-out. If he could not be recovered at his new destination, at least he'd die a hero.

"Anyway, this is a possibility that we'll investigate as best we can, within the bounds of due caution."

Once again, as on that evening in the tavern, Tyra stared beyond him and the room and this world. "To find my father," shuddered from her. "To waken him back to life."

Dorcas gave her a hard look. The same unease touched Saxtorph. He rose. "Uh, wait a minute," he said, "you're not supposing you—"

Tyra returned to them. Total calm was upon her. "Oh, yes," she stated. "I am going with you."

"Hey, there!"

He saw her grin. "Nothing is in the contract to deny me." Grimly: "If you refuse, I do not give it my print and you have no charter. Then I must see what if anything the Navy will do."

"But—"

Dorcas laid a hand over his. "She is determined," she said. "I don't imagine it can do any harm, if we write in a waiver of liability."

"You may have that, but you won't need it," Tyra promised. "I take responsibility for myself. Did you imagine I would stay behind while you hunted for my father? Well, Ib does, so I suppose it is natural for you. Let him. If he knew, he might feel he must release the truth and get the authorities to stop us. As for me—" sudden laughter belled—"after all, I am a travel writer. What a story!"

Saxtorph chuckled and dismissed his objections. She could well prove an asset, and would indisputably be an ornament.

Dorcas stood pensive. When she spoke, it was so quietly that he knew she was thinking aloud. "In relativity physics, travel faster than light is equivalent to time travel. We use quantum rules. And yet what are we trying on this voyage but to probe the past and learn what happened long ago?"

Chapter VIII

When the kzinti drew Peter Nordbo into time, his first clear thought was: Hulda, Tyra, Ib. Oh, unmerciful God, it's been ten years now.

"Up, monkey," growled the technician and cuffed him, lightly, claws sheathed, but with force to rock his head. "The commander wants you."

Nordbo crept from his box. He shivered with the cold inside him. Weight dragged at his bones, an interior field set higher than Earth's. Around him, huge forms were likewise stirring, crew revived. Their snarls and spits ripped at the gloom. He stumbled from them, down a remembered passageway. His second clear thought was: What would I give for a cup of coffee!

Noticing, he barked a laugh at himself. Full awareness seeped back into him, and warmth as he moved and unstiffened. Even in this his exile, eagerness kindled. *Snapping Sherrek* had arrived. What had it reached?

Yiao-Captain waited in the observation turret. It was illuminated only by the images of the stars, he a shadow

223

blotting out that constellation in which Alpha Centauri and Sol must lie. The light of their legions gleamed off an eyeball when he glanced about. "Arh, Speaker for Humans," he greeted, brusque but not hostile, as in days that were suddenly old. "I know you are still somewhat numb. However, behold."

He turned a dial. A section of the view seemed to rush toward them. Magnification stabilized. Nordbo stood an instant dumbfounded, then a low whistle passed his lips. "What *is* that thing?"

Against frosty star-clouds floated a sphere. Shapes encrusted it here and there, a dome in the form of half a dodecahedron, three concentric helices bent into a semicircle, several curving dendritic masts or antennae, objects less recognizable. The hue was dull gray, spotted with shadows filling countless pocks and scratches. Erosion by spatial dust, Nordbo thought dazedly, by near-vanishingly rare interstellar meteoroids, and, yes, by cosmic rays. *How long has this derelict drifted?*

"Diameter about sixteen kilometers," he heard Yiao-Captain say, using kzinti units. "We have taken a parallel trajectory at a goodly distance."

"Where is . . . the energy I detected . . . at home?" *At home.*

"On the other side. We who were on watch in the terminal stages of approach saw it from far. It was what decided us to stay well away until we know more. Now we commence the real investigation. The first observer capsule leaves in a few minutes."

Already, before most of the crew were properly roused. Kzin style.

Yiao-Captain's fingers crooked, his tail flicked. "I envy that Hero," he said. "The first, the first. But I must stay in command until . . . *I* am the first to set foot there."

In spite of everything, Nordbo was curiously touched, that the other should, consciously or not, reveal that much to a human. Well, doubtless Nordbo was the sole such human in existence.

A question came to him. "Have you measured the infrared emission?"

"Not yet. Why?"

"Maybe whatever is inside that thing sends its output through a single spot. If not, if it emits in all directions, then the remaining energy has to go somewhere. Presumably the shell reradiates it in the infrared. But given the size of the shell, that must be at a low temperature, so it's not readily distinguished from the galactic background."

"And the integrated emission over the entire surface will give us the total power. Good. Our scientists would have thought of it, but perhaps not at once. Yes-s-s, you will be useful."

"If the shell rotates—"

"It does, on three axes. Tumbles. Quite slowly, but it does. We established that upon arrival."

"Then the bright spot would only point at Alpha Centauri, or any given star, for a short span of time, a few years at most. No wonder it wasn't noticed before. Sheer chance that I did." And condemned myself.

A thump shivered through metal and Nordbo's anguish. "The capsule is on its way," Yiao-Captain said with glee.

Nordbo understood. He had heard about the arrangement before the expedition departed. The intensity of the hard radiation here was such that nothing else would serve for a close passage. The screen fields that had protected the ship from collision with interstellar gas at half the speed of light were insufficient; near this fire, enough stray particles and gamma ray photons would get through to wreck her electronics and give the crew a lethal dose. Her two boats were laughably more vulnerable.

Room and mass were at a premium in a Swift Hunter, but *Sherrek* carried a pair of thickly armored spheroids which contained generators for ultra-strong fields. Wunderlanders before the war had used them in flyby studies of their suns. The kzinti had quickly modified them to accommodate a single crew member; when dealing with the unknown, a live brain overseeing the instruments might well prove best. Besides an air and

water recycler, life support included a gravity polarizer.
It was necessarily small, its action confined to the interior, but at such close quarters it could counteract
possible accelerations that would kill even a kzin, up to
fifty or sixty Terran gravities.

The capsule whipped through the magnified part of
the turret view. Its metal gleamed hazy-bright, a nucleus cocooned in shimmering forces. Nordbo imagined
the rider voicing an exuberant screech. It vanished
from his sight.

More sounds followed, quieter and longer-drawn. A
boat was not thrown out by a machine; it launched
itself. The lean form glided by on its way to a rendezvous point at the far side of the mystery. There it would
seize the capsule in a grapnel field, haul it inboard, and
bring it back.

Yiao-Captain stared yonder. "What might the thing
be?" he mumbled.

"Artificial, obviously," Nordbo answered, just as low.

"Yes, but for what? Who built it?"

"And when? It's extremely old, I'm sure. Just look at
it."

Yiao-Captain's fur bristled. "Billions of years?"

"Not a bad guess."

"The Slavers—"

"The tnuctipun. They were engineers to the Slavers,
the thrintun, you know, till they revolted." And the war
that followed exterminated both races, back while the
ancestors of man and kzin were microbes in primordial
seas.

Yiao-Captain's ears lay flat. He shivered. "Haunted
weapons. We have tales about things ancient and
accursed—" Resolution surged. "Aowrrgh!" he shouted.
"Whatever this be, we'll master it! It's ours now!"

Time crept. Nordbo realized he was hungry. Was
that right? Why hadn't grief filled him to the brim? He
had lost his loves, twenty-odd years of their lives at
least, and he felt hungry and ragingly curious.

Well, but they wouldn't expect him to wallow in
self-pity, would they? Despicable emotion. Let him

take whatever anodyne that work offered. He could do nothing else about his situation.

Yet.

It was actually no long spell until the boat, at a safe distance, snared the capsule. Although its screen fields had degraded incoming data, a shipboard computer could restore much. Transmission commenced at once. In minutes numbers and images were appearing on screens.

Blue-white hell-flame streamed from a ragged hole in the shell, meters wide. The color was nothing but ghost-flicker, quanta given off by excited atoms. The real glow was the gamma light of annihilation, matter and anti-matter created, meeting, perishing in cascade after curious cascade until the photons flew free in search of revenge.

"Yes," Nordbo whispered, "I think the source does emit in all directions. The output—fantastic. On the order of terawatts, no, I suspect magnitudes higher than that. The material enclosing it, though, that is what's truly incredible. It stops those hard rays, it's totally opaque to them, damps them down to infrared before it lets them go. . . . But after billions of years, even it has worn thin and fragile. Something, a large meteoroid or something, finally punched through at one point, and there the radiation escapes unchecked. Elsewhere—"

"Can we make contact?" Yiao-Captain screamed. "Can we land and take possession?"

"I don't know. We'll have to study, probe, set up models and run them through the computer. My guess at the moment is that probably we can, if we choose the place well and are careful. No promises, understand, and not soon."

"Get to work on it! Immediately! Go!"

Nordbo obeyed, before Yiao-Captain should lose his temper and give him the claws.

He'd been granted a comparatively free hand to carry on research, with access to a laboratory and the production shop, assistance if necessary, provided of course that he remained properly servile. On a ship like this, those facilities were improvised, tucked into odd corners, so cramped that as a rule only one individual at a time could use them. That suited Nordbo fine.

First he required nourishment. He made for the food synthesizer. What it dispensed was as loathsome to the kzinti as to him, albeit for different reasons. Irritable at the lack of fresh meat, a spacehand kicked the man aside. Nordbo crashed against a bulkhead. The bruises lasted for days. "Keep your place, monkey! You'll swill after the wakened Heroes have fed."

"Yes, my master. I am sorry, my master." Nordbo withdrew on hands and knees, as became an animal.

A thought that he had borne along from Wunderland crystallized. He'd be modifying apparatus, or making it from scratch, as occasion arose. Contemptuous, the kzinti, including the scientists, would pay scant heed. Yiao-Captain might be the exception, but he'd have plenty of other demands on his attention. With caution, patience, piecemeal labor, it should be possible to fashion some kind of weapon—a knife, if nothing else—and keep it concealed under a jumble of stuff in a cabinet or box.

Chances were he'd never use it. What could he win? But the simple knowledge of its existence would help him get through the next months. If he could at last endure no longer, if nothing whatsoever remained to lose, maybe he could wreak a little harm, and die like a man.

Chapter IX

Having left Alpha Centauri far enough behind, *Rover* phased into hyperspace and commenced the long haul. "We'll go about four and a half light-years, emerge, and see what our instruments can tell us at that distance," Saxtorph had decided. "When we've got a proper fix on the whatchamacallit, we'll approach by short jumps, taking new observations after each one."

"*Jamais l'audace*," Dorcas had laughed.

"Huh? Oh. Oh, yah. Caution. Finagle knows what we're letting ourselves in for, but I'll bet my favorite meerschaum that Murphy will take a strong interest in the proceedings."

In the galley, on the second day under quantum drive, Ryan exclaimed, "Hey, you really are handy with the tools."

Tyra trimmed the last creamfruit and dropped it in a bowl. "One learns," she said. "I am not a bad cook, either. Maybe sometime you will let me make us a meal."

"M-m, you cook for yourself a lot?"

She nodded. "Eating out alone very much is depressing. Also, some of the places I have been, nobody but a local person or a berserker would go into a restaurant. Or else it is machines programmed for the same menus that bore me everywhere in known space."

"Adventurous sort. Well, sure, I'd be glad to take a chance on you, if you'd like to try being more than the bull cook." Ryan cocked his head and ran his glance up, down, and sideways across her. "For which job, strictly speaking, you lack certain qualifications anyway. Not that I object, mind you."

The blue eyes blinked. "What?" Now and then an English idiom eluded her.

"Never mind. For the moment. Uh, you are quite sweet, helping out like this. You aren't obliged to, you know, our paying passenger."

"What should I do, sit yawning at a screen? I wish I could find more to keep me busy."

"I'd be delighted to see to that, after hours," he proposed.

She colored slightly, but her tone stayed calm and her smile amicable. "I suspect Pilot Fenger would complain. It could be safer to offend a keg of detonite."

"You've noticed, have you?" he replied, unembarrassed. "I guess in your line of work you develop a Sherlock Holmes kind of talent. Well, yes, Carita and I do have a thing going. Have had for years. But it's just friendly, no pledges, no claims. She's not possessive or jealous or anything." He edged closer. "This evenwatch after dinner? Your cabin or mine, whichever you prefer. I'll bring a bottle of pineapple wine, which I s'pose you've never had. Good stuff, dry, trust me. We'll talk and get better acquainted. I'd love to hear about your travels."

"No, thank you," she said, still good-humored. "Entanglements, innocent or not, on an expedition like this, they are unwise, don't you agree? And I have . . . private things to think about when I am by myself." She clapped him on the shoulder. "Tomorrow, besides the galley, can I assist in other of your duties?"

Since his hopes had not been especially high, they were not dashed. He beamed " *'Auwē nō ho'i ē!'* By all manner of means."

Tyra left him and went down a corridor. The ship throbbed around her, an underlying susurrus of ventilators, mechanisms, power. Dorcas came the opposite way. They halted. "How do you do," the mate greeted. Her expression was reserved.

"Hallo," Tyra responded. "Are you in a hurry?"

Dorcas unbent to the extent of a lopsided grin. "In space we have time to burn, or else bare microseconds. What can I do for you?"

"You were so busy earlier, you and Robert, there was no opportunity to ask. A minute here, please. I want to be useful aboard. Kam lets me help him, but that takes two or three hours a daycycle at most. Can I do anything else?"

Dorcas frowned. "I can't think of anything. Most of our work is highly skilled."

"I could maybe learn a little, if somebody will teach me. I do have some space experience."

"That will be up to the somebody, subject to the captain's okay. We have an ample supply of books, music, shows, games."

"I brought my own. Finally, I thought, I shall read *War and Peace*. But—well, thank you. Don't worry, I will be all right."

"Feel free. But do not interfere." Dorcas stared unblinkingly into Tyra's gaze. "You understand, I'm sure."

"Of course. I will try to annoy nobody. Thank you." They parted.

Those on mass detector watch didn't count, unless something registered in the globe. Then anyone else got out of the chamber fast. Tyra found Carita seated there, smoking a cigar—the air was blue and acrid—while she played *go* with the computer. "Well, hi!" the Jinxian cried. Teeth flashed startling white in her midnight visage. "On free orbit, are you? C'mon in."

"I thought you might care to talk," said the Wunderlander, shyer than erstwhile. "But it is not needful."

"Oh, Lord, for me it's a breath of fresh beer. Dullest chore in the galaxy, this side of listening to an Ecotheist preacher. And the damn machine always beats me. Hey, don't look near that unshuttered port. We'd have to screw your eyeballs back in and hang your brain out to dry."

"I know about hyperspace." Tyra flowed into the second chair.

"Yes, you have knocked around a fair amount, haven't you?"

"Part of my work."

"I globbed a disc of yours before we left. Put it through the translator and read it yesterday. In English, *Astrid's Purple Submarine.*"

"That is for children."

"What of it? Fun. When I got to the part where the teddy bear has to sit on the safety valve of the steam telephone, I laughed my molars loose. I'll keep the book for whatever kids I may eventually have."

"Thank you." A silence fell.

Carita blew a smoke ring and said softly, "You're a cheerful one, aren't you? That takes grit, in a situation like yours. Because you've never put aside what happened to your parents, have you? I imagine you always dreamed of going out on your father's trail."

Tyra shrugged. "The tragedy is in the past. Whatever comes of it is in the future. Meanwhile, he would be the last person who wanted me to mope."

"And you've more life in you than most. Yank me down if I pry, but I can't help wondering why you've never married."

"Oh, I did. Twice."

Carita waited.

Tyra glanced past her. "I may as well tell you. We shall be shipmates for a time that may grow long and a little dangerous. I married first soon after the liberation. It was a mistake. He was born in space, he had spent his life as a Resistance fighter. I was young and, and impulsive and worshipped him for a hero." She sighed. "He was, is not a bad man. But he was too much used to violence and to being obeyed."

"Yeah, you wouldn't take kindly to that."

"No. My second husband was several years later. An engineer, who had traveled and done great things in space before he settled on Wunderland. A good man, he, strong, gentle. But I found—we discovered together, time by time, that he no longer cared to explore things. He was content with what he had, with his routines. I grew restless until—there was someone else. That ended, but by then it had broken the marriage." Tyra sighed. "Poor Jonas. He deserved better. But he was not too sad. I was his third wife. He is now happy with his fourth."

"So you've had other fellows in between and afterward."

"Well, yes." Tyra flushed. "Not many. I do not hunt them."

"No, no, I never said you do. Besides, I'd look silly perched on a moralistic fence. Still," Carita murmured, "older men generally, eh?"

"Do you care for puppies?" Tyra snapped.

"I'm sorry. I mean well, but Kam says that for me 'tact' is a four-letter word. 'Fraid he's right. Uh, you here after anything in particular, or just to chat? You're welcome either way."

Tyra relaxed somewhat. "Both. I would like to know you folk better."

Carita grinned. "To put us in a book?"

Tyra smiled back. "If you permit. This journey will become big news when we return. I think I can tell it in such a way that your privacy is protected but it gives you publicity that will help your business."

"Which could sure use help. Don't feel guilty about any risks. You're paying, and we went in with our eyes wide open, radiating the light of pure greed." Carita paused. "Yes, I guess you are the right writer for us."

"I want more to know you as, as human beings."

"And we to know you. Okay. We've got a couple weeks ahead of us before the trip gets interesting, except for whatever we can stir up amongst ourselves. What else is on your agenda today?"

"I would liefer have a part in this ship than be idle and passive. You know I help Kam. M-m, do you mind?"

"Finagle, no!" Carita chortled. "Why should I? No claims. I warn you, he'll try to get you in his bunk. Or is that a warning? He's pretty good."

"Thank you, but I shall . . . respect your territory." Tyra hastened onward. "The thought came to me, another thing I might help with. This watch you are keeping. It demands very little, no?"

"If only it did demand. Hours and hours of nothing. And till we replace Juan Yoshii, the spells are longer than ever." Carita's cigar jabbed air. "You're volunteering? I wish you could. Unfortunately, it's not quite as easy as it appears."

"I know. I did research for a script, a while ago, and remember. In the unlikely event that the detector registers a significant mass, the person must know exactly what to do, and do it at once. But the list of actions that may be required is short and rather simple. Give me instructions and some simulator practice, and I believe I could pass any test." Tyra smiled again. "I would want you should be satisfied first I can handle the job. This ship carries something precious, namely me."

Thick hand tugged heavy chin. "It tempts, it tempts. . . . But no. I learned how. That doesn't mean I'm qualified to teach how. Same for Kam. You see, the academies require that an instructor have experience of command. They're right. This is a psionic dingus. The trainee needs close exposure to a personality who knows how everything aboard a ship bleshes together." Carita brightened. "Ask Bob or Dorcas. Either of them could. And hoo-ha, do I want them to!"

"Thank you, I will." Tyra's voice vibrated.

"Fine. But let's get sociable, okay? For me right now, that's a big service. Care for a seegar? I thought not. Well, here's a box of Kam's excellent cookies."

Reminiscences wandered. Inevitably they led to the

present enterprise, the wish that drove it. By then the women felt enough at ease that Carita could murmur, "Every girl's first sweetheart is her daddy, but you were only eight when you lost yours. And nevertheless— He must have been one hell of a man."

"He was," Tyra answered as low. "I dare to hope he is."

A while later, she left. Bound for the cubicle known as her stateroom, this time she encountered Saxtorph. He waved expansively at her. She stopped. He did too. "Anything you want, Tyra?" he inquired.

She met his look. "Robert, will you teach me to stand mass detector watch?"

Chapter X

From a hundred-kilometer distance, *Rover* sent her robot prospector around the thing she had tracked down. The little machine circled close, taking readings, storing data. When behind the sphere, it steered itself, with sufficient judgment to stay well clear of the radiation streaming forth from one site there. Otherwise Saxtorph kept in radio rapport, his computer helping him devise the orders he issued. From time to time the prospector transmitted, downloading what it had gathered. At length Saxtorph had it land on the surface. Capable of hundred-gravity acceleration, the robot could also make feather-soft contact. Presently he ventured to have it apply its dynamic analyzer, attempting sonic, electronic, and radiation soundings plus measurements of several different moduli.

Mostly it drew blank. This material was nothing like the asteroids and moons that it was meant to study. A few experiments yielded values, but with ridiculously large probable errors. Nor was the robot well suited for a tour of inspection. Saxtorph recalled it to his ship.

"At any rate, the side away from the firebeam should be safe for people," he said. "Okay, I'm on my way."

" 'Should be' isn't quite the same as 'is,' " Ryan objected.

The captain ignored him. "I could use a partner." He glanced at Carita. She nodded avidly.

After some unavoidable argument and essential preparations, they left. Saxtorph deemed that taking the boat, a comparatively large and ungainly object, was hazardous. They flitted in spacesuits.

The nearer they drew to the objective, the more the mystery deepened for them. Its horizon arcing across nearly half their sky, the starlit surface became a pitted bare plain on which crouched outlandish bulks, soared skeletal spires, sprawled shadowy labyrinths. Soon *Rover* seemed as remote as Earth. Breath sounded harsh in helmets, pulsebeats loud in motors, pumps, and bloodstreams.

The man pressed the control for a radar reading. Numbers appeared. He made his command carefully prosaic: "Brake, hold position, and wait for further instructions. I'm going down."

"I still say I should," Carita answered. "We can't spare you."

"Sure you can, while you've got Dorcas." That was why his wife stayed behind, though he'd had to pull rank to make her do it.

"Your vectors are correct for landing," she informed him from her post aboard. The ship tracked the flyers with a precision they themselves could not match. Probably he alone heard the tremor in her voice.

It filled Tyra's: "Be careful, Robert, oh, be careful!"

"Quiet," Dorcas snapped. She hadn't wanted the Wunderlander in the circuit. Ryan wasn't; he kept lookout at the main observation panel. But Tyra had appealed to Saxtorph. Not sniveling or anything; a simple request. When she wanted to, though, she could charm the stripes off a skunk.

"I'm sorry," she said.

The captain set his thrusters and boosted. Acceleration tugged briefly. As he turned and slowed, giddiness whirled through him. He was used to it, his reflexes compensated, it passed. His bootsoles touched solidity and he stood on the thing.

Rather, he floated. A few tens of millions of tons, concentrated some eight kilometers below him, exerted no gravity worth mentioning. He directed thruster force upward and increased it until he was pressed down hard enough that he could stand or walk low-gee fashion. This adjustment he made most slowly and cautiously, a fraction at a time. Untold ages had eroded the hollow shell, wearing away its strength until a rock traveling at mere KPS could drive a hole through. Of course, that might mean resistance equal to ordinary armor plate, but it might be considerably less, if not everywhere then at certain points; and he could have happened to land at one of those points.

Otherwise the stuff kept unbelievable properties. Measurements taken on the escaping radiation showed what an inferno raged inside. Yet on this opposite hemisphere, a glance at instruments on his vambrace confirmed the findings made by the robot. Nothing was coming off but infrared at a temperature hardly above ambient.

Saxtorph realized he had been holding his breath. He let it out in a gust. His ribs ached, his sweat stank. Why had he undertaken the flit, anyway?

Well, it was irresistible. Nobody felt able to leave without exploring just a little bit more. And after all, you never knew; a search could turn up a clue to Peter Nordbo's fate.

Saxtorph made for a surrealistic jumble of pipes, reticulations, and clustered globules. Dust, millimeters thick, scuffed up in ghost-wisps wherever his boots struck. After several leaps, he halted. "Okay, Carita, come join the fun. Don't land, remember. Stay a few meters above and behind me, on the alert."

"You're afraid maybe I'll take a nap?" the crewman gibed. Edged with their luminance, her spacesuit arrowed across the stars.

I suppose we shouldn't crack jokes in the presence of something ancient and inscrutable, Saxtorph thought. We should be duly awed, reverent, and exalted. To hell with that. We've got a job to do. I hope Tyra will understand, when she writes this up.

Of course she will. She's our own sort. If her whole life didn't prove it already, the past couple of weeks sure did.

Saxtorph neared the complex. At hover, Carita directed a search beam as he desired, supplementing his flash. Undiffused, the brightness flowed like water over a substance that was not rock nor metal nor anything the humans knew. They both operated cameras as well as instruments, while their suits transmitted to the ship. Saxtorph's eyes strained.

"I think the microcraters everywhere were formed in the last hundred million years, plus or minus x," he said. "Otherwise we'd see much more overlap."

"You're supposing the construction is older than that, then," Carita deduced.

"It certainly is," Dorcas told them from the ship. "The computer just finished evaluating our data on the dust. Isotope ratios prove it's been collecting for a minimum of two billion years, likely more." After a moment: "Incidentally, that suggests cosmic radiation isn't what weakened the shell to the point where impacts started leaving pockmarks and at last a big one broke through. The radiation inside must be mainly responsible. But if *it* hasn't done more damage, well, the thing was built to last."

"Besides," Saxtorph said, "if I've got any feeling for machinery, this bears every earmark of tnuctipun work."

"How can you tell?" Carita asked. Her words sounded thin. Ordinarily she would have kept silence, except for business and an occasional wisecrack, but the weirdness had shaken her a bit, roused a need to talk. Saxtorph sympathized. "What do we know about the Slaver era? What little the bandersnatchi remember, or believe they do, and what got learned from the thrint that came out of stasis for a short while, before they got it bottled again."

"That includes a smidgin of technical information, and a lot of thinking has been done about it ever since," he reminded her. "I've studied the subject some. It interests me. Come *on*."

He bounded ahead to the next aggregation and examined it as best he cursorily could.

And the next and the next and the next. Time ceased to exist. He drank from his water tube, stuffed rations through his chowlock, excreted into his disposer, without noticing. He had become pure search. Sturdily, Carita followed. She made no attempt to call halt, nor did anyone aboard ship. The quest had seized them all.

Monkey curiosity, Saxtorph thought once, fleetingly. The kzinti would sneer. But they'd examine this too, in detail, till they used up every possibility of discovery that was in their equipment and their brains. Because to them it'd spell power.

The knowledge was chill: It is a terrible weapon.

"I suspect it's one of a kind," he said. "Humans and their acquaintances haven't found any mini-black holes yet, and that hasn't been for lack of looking. They're bound to be uncommon."

"Yes," Dorcas agreed. "The tnuctipun doubtless came on this one by chance. I'd guess that was after they'd rebelled. They saw how to use it against the Slavers. Otherwise, if they'd built the machine around it earlier, the Slavers would have been in possession, and might have quelled the uprising early on. They might be alive today."

Carita shuddered audibly. "A black hole—"

It could only be that. Mass, dimensions, radiation spectrum, everything fitted astrophysical theory. Peter Nordbo had recorded the idea in his notes, but he couldn't reconcile it with the sudden apparition in the heavens. The tumbling shell and the meteoroid gap accounted for that. Perhaps while they were here the kzinti, under his guidance, had found indirect ways to study the interior, the eerie effects of so mighty a gravitation on space-time. But *Rover*'s crew already had ample data to be confident of what it was they confronted.

Burnt out, a giant star collapses into a form so dense, infinitely dense at the core singularity, that light itself can no longer escape its grip. The minimum mass required is about three Sols. Today. In the first furious instants of creation, immediately after the Big Bang, immeasurably great forces were at play. Where they chanced to concentrate, they had the power to compress any amount of mass, however small, into the black hole state. It must have happened, over and over. Countless billions must have formed, a few large, most diminutive.

In the universe of later epochs, they are not stable. Quantum tunneling causes them to give off particles, matter and antimatter, which mutually annihilate. For a body of stellar size, the rate of evaporation is negligible. But it increases as the body shrinks. Ever faster and more fiercely does the radiation go, until in a final supernal eruption the remnant vanishes altogether. Nearly every black hole made in the beginning has thus, long since, departed.

This one had been just big enough to survive to the present day. Applying what theory the ship's database contained, Dorcas had made some estimates. Three or four billion years ago it was radiating with about half its current intensity. Its mass, equal to a minor asteroid's, was now packed inside an event horizon with a diameter less than that of an atomic nucleus. Another 50,000 years or so remained until the end.

Carita rallied. "A weapon?" she asked. "How could that be?"

"Your mind isn't as nasty as mine," Saxtorph replied absently. His attention was on high lattices, surrounding a paraboloid (?), which grew out of the shell where he stood. Their half-familiarity chewed at him. Almost, almost, he knew them.

"What else could it be?" Dorcas said. "A power source for peaceful use? Awkward and unnecessary when you have fusion, let alone total conversion. As a weapon, though, the thing is hideous. Invulnerable. Open a port, and a beam shoots out that no screen can protect against. At a minimum, electronics are scrambled and personnel get a lethal dose. No missile can penetrate that defense; if it manages to approach, it will be vaporized before it strikes. Sail through an enemy fleet, with death in your wake. Pass near any fort and leave corpses manning armament in ruins. Cruise low around a planet and sterilize it at your leisure."

"Then why didn't the tnuctipun win?"

"We'll never know. But they can only have had this one. That was scarcely decisive. And . . . the war exterminated both races. Perhaps the crew here heard they were last of their kind, and went elsewhere to die."

Saxtorph caught Tyra's whisper: "While the black hole, the machine, drifted through space for billions of years—" The Wunderlander raised her voice: "I am sorry. I should not interrupt. But do you not overlook something?"

"What?" Dorcas sounded edgy. As well she might be after these many hours, Saxtorph told himself.

"How could the tnuctipun bring the weapon to bear?" Tyra asked. "The black hole was orbiting free in interstellar space, surely, light-years from anywhere. The mass is huge to accelerate."

"They could have harnessed its own energy output to a polarizer system."

"Really? Is that enough, to get it to a destination fast enough to be useful?"

Smart girl, Saxtorph thought. She hasn't got the figures at her fingertips, but those fingers have a good, firm, sensitive hold on reality.

"Through hyperspace," Dorcas clipped.

"Forgive me," Tyra said. "I do not mean to be a

nuisance. You must know more about tnuctipun technology than I do. But I studied what I was able. Is it not true that their hyperdrive was crude? It would not work before the vessel was moving close to light speed. This *genstand* has ordinary velocity, in the middle of empty space."

"That is a shrewd question," Dorcas admitted.

"A real fox question," Saxtorph said. He was coming out of his preoccupation, aware how tired he was but also exuberant, full of love for everybody. Well, for most beings. Especially his comrades. "It could stonker our whole notion. Except I believe I've found the answer. There is in fact a hyperdrive engine. It's not like anything we know or much like any of the hypothetical reconstructions I've seen of tnuctipun artifacts. But I believe I can identify it for what it is, or anyhow what it does. My guess is that, yes, they could take this black hole through hyperspace, emerging with a reasonable intrinsic velocity that a gravity drive could then change to whatever they needed for combat purposes."

"How, when every ship must first move so fast?" Tyra wondered.

"I am only guessing, mind you. But think." Despite physical exhaustion, Saxtorph's brain had seldom run like this. Talking to her was a burst of added stimulation. "Speed means kinetic energy, right? That's what the Slaver hyperdrive depended on, kinetic energy, not speed in itself. Well, here you've got a terrific energy concentration, so-and-so fantastically many joules per mean cubic centimeter. If the tnuctipun invented a way to feed it to their quantum jumper, they'd be in business."

"I see. Yes. Robert, you are brilliant."

"Naw. I may be dead wrong. The tech boys and girls will need months to warm over this gizmo before they can figure it out for sure. They better be careful. Considering how well preserved the apparatus is, in spite of everything that the black hole inside and the universe outside could do, I wouldn't be surprised but what that hyperdrive is still in working order."

"More powerful than ever," Dorcas breathed. "The black hole has been evolving."

"Brrr!" Carita exclaimed. "Knock it off, will you? If the ratcats got hold of it—" She yelped. "But they were here! Weren't they? How much did they learn? How come they didn't whoop home to Alpha Centauri with this thing and scrub our fleet out of space?"

"Even taking its time, what a single expedition could find out would be limited, I should think," Dorcas said. Her tone went metallic. "We, though, the human species, we'd better make certain."

"Yah," Saxtorph concurred. He shook himself in his armor. "Listen, I decree we're past the point of diminishing returns today. Let's head back, Carita, have a hot meal and a stiff drink, and sleep for ten or twelve hours. Then I have some ideas about our next move."

"Wow-hoo!" his companion caroled, uneasiness shoved aside. "I thought you'd decided to homestead. Say, ever consider how lucky the tnuctip race was, not speaking English? Spell the name backwards—"

"Never mind," Saxtorph sighed. "Compute your vectors and boost."

Bound for *Rover*, he felt as if he were awakening from a dream. In the time lately past, he had experienced in full something that had rarely and barely touched him before, the excitement of the scientist. It had been a transcendence. How did that line or two of poetry go? "Some watcher of the skies, when a new planet swims into his ken." Or a new star, small and strange, foredoomed, yet waxingly radiant; and the archeology of a civilization vast and vanished. Now he returned to his ordinary self.

He ached, his tongue was a block of wood, his eyelids were sandpaper, but he rejoiced. By God, he had seen Truth naked, and She took him by the hand and led him beyond himself, into Her own country! It wouldn't happen again, he supposed; and that was as well. He wasn't built for it. But this once it did happen.

When he and Carita completed airlock cycle, their

shipmates were waiting for them. Dorcas embraced him. "Welcome, welcome," she said tenderly.

"Thanks." He looked past her shoulder. How bright was Tyra's hair against the bulkhead. His brain hadn't yet stopped leapfrogging. "We've got facts to go on," he blurted. "Knowing what the kzinti found, we can make a pretty good guess at what they did. And where they are. With your dad."

"O-o-oh—" the Wunderlander gasped.

He disengaged. She sprang forward, seized and kissed him.

Chapter XI

When the kzinti again drew Peter Nordbo into time, his first clear thought was: Hulda, Tyra, Ib. More than twenty years now. Do you live? I almost wish not, I who come home after helping our masters arm themselves for the enslavement of all humanity. Forgive me, my darlings. I had no choice.

"Up," growled the one that hulked above him. "The commander wants you. Why, I don't know."

Nordbo blinked, bewildered. Through the gloom in the chamber he recognized the kzin. It wasn't the technician in charge of such tasks, it was one of the fire-control ratings. Their designation translated roughly as "Gunner." What had gone on? A fight, a killing? The crew were disciplined and the discoveries at the black hole had kept them enthusiastic; nevertheless, after months in close quarters, tempers grew foul and quarrels flared.

Well he knew. He bore several scars from the claws of individuals who took anger out on him. They were punished, though no disabling injury was inflicted. Nor

246

had torture left him crippled, being carefully administered. He was too useful to damage without cause.

"Move!" Gunner hauled him from the box and flung him to the deck. There was mercy in the wave of physical pain that swept from the impact. For a moment it drowned every other awareness.

It faded, Nordbo remembered anew, he crept to his feet and hobbled off.

The corridor stretched empty and silent. How utterly silent. The rustle of ventilators sounded loud. Dread sharpened in him and cut the last dullness away. A-shiver, he reached the observation turret and entered. Only the heavens illuminated it.

No suns of Alpha Centauri shone before him, no constellations whatsoever. Around a pit of lightlessness, blue stars clustered thinly. As he stared aft he saw more, whose colors changed through yellow to red; but behind the ship yawned another darkness rimmed with embers.

Aberration and Doppler effect, he recognized. We haven't slowed down yet, we're flying ballistic at half the speed of light. Why have they revived me early? They didn't expect to. I'd served my purpose. No, their purpose. I could merely pray that when their scientists on Wunderland finished interrogating me, I'd be released to take up any rags of my life that were left. Unless it makes more sense to pray for death.

Yiao-Captain poised athwart the stranger sky. Its radiances gleamed icy on eyeballs and fangs. His ears stood unfolded but his tail switched. "You are not where you think you are," he rumbled. "Twenty-two years have passed,"—Nordbo's mind automatically rendered the timespan into human units—"and we are bound for our Father Sun."

The shock was too great. It could not register at once. Nordbo heard himself say, "May I ask for an explanation?"

Did Yiao-Captain's curtness mask pain of his own? "We were about three years en route back to Alpha Centauri." After half a year at the black hole. "A message came. It told of a fleet from Sol, invading the system and shattering our forces. Somehow the humans have gained a capability of traveling faster than light. No ship without it can win against the least of theirs. We must inevitably lose these planets. It must already have happened when *Snapping Sherrek* received the beam.

"When I was roused and informed, naturally I did not propose to continue there, bringing my great news to the enemy. I ordered our forward velocity quenched and the last of our delta v applied to send us home."

At one-half c, a trip of nearly six decades. Nordbo's thought trickled vague and slow. Can't stop at the far end. Hurtle on till the last reserve mass has been converted, the screen fields go out, and the wind of our passage through the medium begins to crumble us. Unless first another ship matches speed and takes us off. I daresay they'll try, once they have an idea of what this crew can tell.

It jolted: Faster than light? We had no means, nothing but some mathematical hints in quantum theory and the knowledge that the thrintun could do it, billions of years ago—knowledge that led this expedition to conclude that the artifact is indeed a gigantic hyperdrive spacecraft powered by the black hole it surrounds. But how did the means come so suddenly to my race?

A thunderbolt: Wunderland is free! My folk have been free for eighteen years!

Nightfall: While I am captive on the Flying Dutchman among the demons that sail it.

Yiao-Captain's voice rolled on: "If the humans do not find what we did, and if we can inform the Patriarchy of it, victory may yet be ours. Not from the alien vessel alone, irresistible though it be, but from what our engineers will learn."

Was he boasting, or trying to reassure himself? Certainly the words were unnecessary. Even without Nordbo's intellectual cooperation, the kzin known as Chief Physicist and his team had traced circuits, computed probable effects, inferred that the most plausible purpose was to achieve the relationship of wave functions which theory said *might* throw matter into a hypothetical hyperspace. They had actually identified an installation that appeared to be an activator of the entire system. Yiao-Captain had had to exert authority to keep three young members of the group from throwing what they thought was the main switch. Much more study was called for, a complete plan of the whole, before any such action was justifiable. Else they could well lose the whole treasure, construct and knowledge alike.

"We are continuously transmitting over and over, the entire set of data we did acquire, together with our ideas about it, on a beam directed forward," the commander proceeded.

The merest fraction of what is there to discover, commented the remote part of Nordbo, yet an enormous load of information, words, numbers, equations, diagrams, pictures, everything we got at a cost of seven kzinti lives and the price I paid. But perhaps the beam, dopplered though its waves are, will register on someone's communicator.

"The likelihood of its being noticed, even when it reaches Kzin, is very small, of course," Yiao-Captain said. "We send it because it does go faster than we, and may perchance convey our word, should we perish along the way. Otherwise, we shall surely be detected as we near the home planets, and receivers will be adjusted to hear what we then broadcast. Meanwhile we stand three-month watches in pairs. More would be intolerable, would lead to hatred and deadly clashes, over so long a voyage. It is again my turn. Gunner is poor company. That is best; we need not see each other much, as I would have to do where he of a rank entitled to courtesy. But the time grows wearisome. Finally I have had you wakened. Maybe we can talk. Certainly we can play chess."

Realization was draining downward from Nordbo's forebrain, along the nerves, into blood and marrow.

He barely swallowed his vomit. It burned gullet and belly.

Almost, he screamed aloud: Yes, whistle your pet monkey to you. Get what amusement you can out of the sorry creature. In the end, after he begins to bore you, disembowel him with a swipe of claws and eat the fresh, dripping meat. Enjoy.

Did you enjoy watching me under the torture? Your eyes shone, ears lay back, tongue ran over lips. No, it was not for pleasure in itself. It was to make me recant my refusal to work any more for you, after it became clear that what we were investigating was a monstrous weapon. You may have regretted it a little. But naturally the spectacle spoke to your instincts.

I cheated them, Yiao-Captain. I yielded within minutes. As for your contempt, inwardly I laughed. It was not the pain that changed my mind, nor the threat of mutilation and death. It was the hope of returning home, to stand once more between you and my Hulda, my children, my folk. Yes, also the crazy hope that somehow I might smuggle a warning off to Sol.

Afterward, yes, I worked for you again, but I told you of no more inspirations, insights, ideas worth trying. I did nothing, really, that a robot could not. What else can you expect from a slave, Yiao-Captain? Love?

The kzin's tone softened. "I know this is a stormwind upon you. You will need a while to regain balance. Go. Rest, think. Come back to me when you feel ready."

Nordbo stumbled from him.

Grief welled up: I have lost you for always, my beloved.

Bleak joy: You are free. We can outpace light. Surely our fleets went on to defeat the kzinti everywhere and ram peace down their throats.

Despair: But no secret has ever stayed long under lock and key. Someday, somehow, they too will gain the knowledge. This ship bears news that may well help them to it. We did conclude that the machine englobing the black hole is tnuctipun and is meant to pass it through hyperspace. We think we identified the activator. We could not puzzle out more than the likeliest-looking procedure for starting it up, and we have no idea how to set a course or stop a destination. But a later expedition, better equipped, with up-to-date physicists, ought to learn much more than we did.

Wrath: "We!" As if this were my band!

Shame: For a while it came near being so. I was captivated. In the work, I could forget my loss for hours at a time. But then I began to see what the thing must be—

Horror: A part of the arsenal that destroyed intelligent life throughout this galactic sector, those billions of years ago. Shall it fall into kzinti hands?

Logic: Oh, by itself it might not prove decisive, come (God take pity on us) the next war. But it would kill many. Worse, it would lead the kzinti to the hyperdrive; or, if they have that by now, it could well suggest improvements that make their ships irresistibly superior to ours. And who can be certain that that would be all it did?

Agony: And I am helpless, helpless.

Revelation: *NO!*

Through a time beyond time, Nordbo stood amidst lightnings. *And the remnant were slain with the sword of him that sat upon the horse*—

Apocalypse opened itself to metal, silence, and unseen stars; but the hand of the Lord was upon him. Somewhere a voice quavered that he had better take nourishment, sleep, recover his full strength, while watching for the best chance. He scorned it into extinction. He would never be stronger than now. Surprise, and a will that had given doubt no days or weeks to corrode it, were his only allies.

With long strides he made his way to the workshop. Every sense thrilled preternaturally keen. A bulkhead bore furrows where a kzin in a rage had scratched the facing. Air from the ventilators blew warm, a tinge of ozone cleansing a ratcat taint become slight. His feet thudded on the deck, the impacts went up through his bones. His mouth was no longer dry, but hunter-wet.

He had bitten his tongue and tasted the salt blood. His
heart beat steady, powerful. His fingers flexed, making
ready.

Though the shop was dark, cramful of stored equipment, he had no trouble finding his toolbox. Things
clattered as he went after the knife he had made and
left buried at the bottom. The kzinti had never suspected; else he would have become meat. He drew it
forth. Heavy in his grasp, blade about thirty centimeters by two, it was crude, a piece of scrap surrepti-
tiously sawed, hammered, and filed, a haft of plastic
riveted to the tang; but patience had given it a micro-
tome edge. He discarded the improvised sheath and
held the steel behind his back when he went out.
Barehanded, a kzin could take a man apart, and speed
as well as strength was why. Nordbo didn't plan to
waste time drawing.

Nor had he any qualms of conscience. The odds
against him were huge enough without the beasts he
hunted being prepared for him.

He found Gunner slumped sullen in the den that
corresponded to a human ship's saloon. The kzin watched
a drama which Nordbo recognized as classic. Maybe he'd
seen the popular repertory too often and was desperate
for entertainment. In the screen, Chrung was attacking an
enemy stronghold, wielding an ax on its parapet. Gunner
was moderately interested. He did not notice the man
who glided forward until Nordbo reached his shoulder.

The massive head turned. Lips pulled from fangs,
irritation that might flash into murder frenzy, did the
intruder not grovel and plead. Nordbo's hand came
around, machine precise. He drove his knife through
the right eye, upward into the brain.

Gunner bellowed. Nordbo cast himself against the
great body. His left hand clung to the fur while his
right twisted the knife. An arm scythed past him, reflex
that would have laid him open were he in its path. He
worked his blade to and fro. Abruptly he clutched
limpness. The kzin sagged to the deck. Death-stench
rose fetid.

Nordbo withdrew the knife and stepped aside. Not much blood ran from the socket at his feet. He had hoped for a silent kill. Well, that he had killed at all was remarkable. Next he must repeat it or die trying. He felt no fear, nor gladness or even anger. His mind was the control center of the mechanism that was himself.

He wouldn't get a second opportunity like this. A spear, a crossbow—a daydream. He glanced about. Their food being synthetic, these travelers had adopted the Wunderlander fashion of tablecloths. The gory play continued in the screen. It stirred memory of things watched or read at home, historical sociology and fiction. The trick he recalled must require long practice to be done right, but a man who had pitched tents and hoisted sails shouldn't be too inept. Heavy feet sped along the passageway outside. Nordbo took a corner of the napery in his left hand. He snapped the fabric, to gain some feeling for its behavior.

Yiao-Captain burst into the den. "What's wrong?" he roared while he slammed to a halt. His look blazed across the corpse and the man who stood beyond it, knife reddened. Insolent past belief, the man shook a rag at him and *grinned*.

For a whole second, sheer stupefaction held Yiao-Captain immobile. Then fury exploded. He screamed and leaped.

Nordbo swayed aside. The giant orange body arced across the space where the cloth rippled. It slipped aside. As the kzin passed, Nordbo hewed.

Yiao-Captain hit the bulkhead. It groaned and buckled. The kzin bounded off the deck and rushed. Nordbo was drifting toward the door. Again his capework saved him, though a leg brushed his and made him stagger. Yet he had gotten a stab into the neck.

He reached the corridor. "Blunderfoot!" he shouted in the kzinti language. "Eater of *sthondat* dung! Come get me if you dare!" His trick would soon fail him unless he kept his antagonist amok.

Yiao-Captain charged. Blood marked his trail, pumped out of the rents beneath ribs and jaws. Nordbo cut him.

Leaping by, he closed teeth on fabric. Nordbo nearly lost it. He slashed it across and saved half.

Scarlet spouted. My God, I got a major vein, Nordbo realized. Yiao-Captain turned. He lurched and mewled, but he attacked. Nordbo retreated. Flick cape over eyeballs, once, twice, thrice. Blindly, Yiao-Captain went past. Nordbo sliced his tail off.

Yiao-Captain came back around. He crumpled to his knees, to all fours. Snarling, he crawled at the man. Nordbo backed up, easily keeping ahead of him.

Yiao-Captain stopped. He stared. The raw whisper held a sudden gentleness. Or puzzlement? "Speaker for Humans, I . . . I liked you. I thought . . . you liked . . . me. . . ." He collapsed. His death struggle took several minutes.

The ship is mine, said the computer in Nordbo's head. Not that I can do anything with it. Except, of course, shut off the beamcast. And wait. Recycling is operative; plenty of food and water. Including kzin steaks, if I want. I can break into the small arms locker and shoot them where they lie. But probably that's too ugly an act. I am not a kzin, I am a man.

Otherwise I wait. Forty or more years till I reach their sun. I will occupy myself, handicrafts, study of what's in the database, love letters to Hulda. Meditation, maybe. For something may yet happen to set me free. The one sure way to lose all hope is to give up all hope.

Rationality fell apart. He retched and began to shake, miserably cold. Reaction. Let him go sleep and sleep and sleep. Afterward he would eat something, and clean up this mess, and settle down into solitude.

Chapter XII

In galactic space a sun is a mote, a planet well-nigh infinitesimal. How then to find a spacecraft falling through light-years?

"Ve haff our met'ods," boasted Saxtorph. Begin by reasoning. The kzinti would not stay longer at the black hole than it took to learn everything they were able; and they were doubtless not extremely well chosen or well outfitted for scientific research. Having shot a beam at Alpha Centauri, describing what they had done and recommending a proper expedition, they'd start after it. Presently they'd receive word that the system was falling to an armada from Sol. Consider the dates of events, assume they'd been some months at work before they set forth, figure in acceleration time, and you conclude that they got the news about a third of the way along their course. What would they then plausibly do? Why, make for 61 Ursae Majoris, the star that Kzin itself orbits, the world that spawned their breed. Just as likely, they'd spend their engine reserve boosting to a full half *c*, and now be moving at approximately that speed. Calculate the trajectory.

Your answer will reflect the uncertainties in your guesstimates. What you get is not a curve but a cone. The ship is somewhere near the top, which leaves you with a volume still so enormous that random search is a fool's errand.

However, space is not empty. The interstellar medium, mostly hydrogen with some helium and pinches of higher elements, has a mean density equivalent to about one proton per cubic centimeter. An object passing through it at 150,000 klicks per second hits a *lot* of stuff. The X-rays given off at these encounters would quickly fry the crew and their electronics, save that the screen fields keep the gas at a distance from the hull and guide it into a fairly smooth flow. Nevertheless, the perturbation is considerable. Atoms are excited and emit softer quanta. The tunnel of near-total vacuum left behind the vessel will take years to fill: which means it is correspondingly long. All this shows in the radio spectrum from that part of the sky. Sensitive instruments can detect it across quite a few parsecs.

The technique was not original with Saxtorph. The UN Navy had developed and employed it during the war. Since *Rover* was not specially equipped for it, he did have to devise modifications. In essence, he went via hyperspace from point to precalculated point. At each, his gang took readings. Dorcas had written a program that interpreted them. In due course, the seekers should get an identification. On that basis they could measure a parallax and obtain a fix.

Saxtorph and Tyra sat by themselves over beers in the saloon. Talk ransacked the past, for the future seemed like a wire drawn so taut that at any moment it would snap and the sharp ends recoil. "Oh, yes," she said, "I have been on Silvereyes. It is fascinating. A hundred lifetimes were too little for to understand those ecologies."

"You were writing about it?" he inquired.

"What else? One must pay for one's travel somehow. Of course, I knew better than to try squeezing a whole world into a book. I looked me around, but that which I made my subject was the Cyclops island."

"Really? I've got to read your book when we get back. You see, I was there myself once. A tourniquet vine damn near did for a shipmate, but we chopped her free in time, and otherwise it was, as you say, fascinating. I begrudged every minute I was on duty and couldn't explore."

"You have been everywhere, have you not?" she murmured.

"No, no, much though I'd like to. Besides, this wasn't my idea. Navy, tail end of the war, establishing a just-in-case base. Satellite, but initial supplies of air and water and such would come from the ground."

Reminiscence went on. "—boats, to check out the surrounding shoals. A simple mooring is a timber toth ered to a rock. What I could've told those clowns, because I'd been in Hawaii, was that they'd picked a chunk of volcanic pumice. But I wouldn't've known either that the log was stonewood. So they took the ensemble to the mooring place and heaved it overboard, and the rock floated while the log sank."

He always liked the heartiness of Tyra's laughter.

"Here I've gone again, blathering on about me," he said. "You're a good listener—no, a great, a vintage listener—but honest, I set out to hear about you. And I really can listen too."

She sobered. "I know. Not many men can, or will. You act very everyday, Robert, but in truth you are a deep and complicated person."

"Wrong, wrong. Never mind. I said we should talk about you. Uh, on Silvereyes, did you visit the Amanda Lakes region?"

"Of course." Tyra sighed. "Beauty that high comes near to hurt, no? At least when there is no one to share it with."

"You had nobody? You should have."

Her smile was rueful. "Well, I roomed with another woman. Although she was pleasant, finally we agreed what a shame that one of us was of the wrong sex."

"Yah, I daresay it'll become a favorite honeymoon resort." Saxtorph stared into his beer stein. "Tyra, none of my business, except we're friends. But you rate better than going through life alone the way you're doing."

She reached across the table and laid her hand on his. "You are kind." Her voice lowered. "On this journey I have discovered my father was not the only man who is a fine creature."

"Aw, hey—"

They turned their heads. Tyra pulled her hand back. Dorcas had entered. Her slenderness reared over them. "We have a decision to make about the next jump point," she said calmly. "It depends on what weight we give the last set of data. Will you come and consult, Bob?"

Saxtorph's chair scraped. " 'Scuse me, Tyra."

The Wunderlander smiled. "Why should I?" she replied. "What need? You go in my cause."

He tossed off his drink and left with his wife. When they were several meters down the corridor, she told him, "I lied, you realize. Not to make a scene."

"For Christ's sake!" he exclaimed. "Nothing was going on."

"I'd prefer to keep it that way."

"You, jealous?" He forced a chuckle. "Honey, you flatter me."

"Not exactly. I've watched where things are headed. No bad intentions on anybody's part. I continue to like her myself. But, Bob, I'd hate to see you hurt. And I've no reason—so far—to wish it on her. As for this team of ours—" She clutched his forearm. Had the muscle been less thick underneath, her fingers would have left marks.

Chapter XIII

Weoch-Captain was a thoughtful and self-controlled kzin. Much though he lusted to streak directly to his goal, first he pondered the implications of what he knew about it. Ideas came to him which he communicated to Ress-Chiuu. The High Admiral agreed that his flight plan should be changed.

Therefore *Swordbeak* cruised about, in and out of hyperspace, day after tedious day. It chewed on nerves. The crew grew restless. Quarrels exploded. A couple of times they led to fights. Weoch-Captain disciplined the offenders severely; they were long in sickbay and would bear the marks for the rest of their lives.

He had given his officers an explanation. The Swift Hunter that went to the unknown body had not been heard of again. If it found the thing, as was probable, this would have happened just about when the human armada entered the Alpha Centaurian System. That news would have taken five years to reach the ship, except that it was likely bound back. What then was its best course? Other kzin-held worlds might fall to the enemy before it could get to any of them. Wisest was to head directly for the Father Sun, especially if the expedition had made worthwhile discoveries. Assuming the crew still lived, they were now about a third of the way home. *Swordbeak* ought to search them out and learn what they could tell, before proceeding. Furthermore, such Heroes deserved to know as soon as possible that they were not forgotten.

Every basis for calculation was a matter of guessing. That included, especially, the location of the mystery object. The data that Ress-Chiuu's informant had been able to pass on were fragmentary, maddeningly vague. Thus the Swift Hunter's cone of location was immense. But the High Admiral had ordered Weoch-Captain's vessel outfitted with the best radio spectrum detectors and analyzers that its hull could accommodate.

So at length his technicians identified a tunnel of passage and placed it approximately in space. Prudence dictated that *Swordbeak* not attempt immediate rendezvous. The precise trajectory and momentary position of the other craft remained unclear; and mass moving at half light-speed is dangerous. Weoch-Captain made for a point about two light-years behind. Inside the trail, the technicians could map it exactly and pinpoint his target.

There they picked up a message.

Weoch-Captain was not totally surprised. In a like situation, he did not think he would send a radio beam ahead. The slimy humans might come upon it, read it, and jam it. However, the idea of superluminal travel would have been unfamiliar to the expedition members. They would scarcely have thought of everything that it meant. If the possibility did occur to them, they might well have discounted it, since the probability of interception was slight, while the transmission increased by a little the likelihood that the Patriarch would eventually get the news they bore. At any rate, Weoch-Captain had provided for the contingency. When he reached the tunnel, receivers were open on a wide enough band that they would register anything, Doppler-diminished though the waves be.

They buzzed. A computer got busy. A part of the message unrolled on a screen before him.

He narrowed his eyes. What *was* this? "—*material unknown. Eroded but, except where pierced, impervious to radiation*—" His finger stabbed at the intercom. The image of Executive Officer appeared. "We have evidently come in in the middle of a sending," Weoch-Captain said. "Doubtless the Swift Hunter plays a recorded beamcast continuously. I want the entirety of it. Have an acquisition program prepared."

"Immediately, sire."

"Mock me not," purred the commander. "You know full well that we shall have to leap about, snatching pieces here and there, while reception will often be poor; and the whole must be fitted together in proper sequence, ungarbled where needful, until it is complete and coherent; and the highly technical content will make this a process difficult and slow. Do you suggest I am ignorant of communications principles?"

Executive Officer was a Hero, but he remembered the punishments. "Never, sire! I misspoke me. I abase myself before you."

"Correct." Weoch-Captain switched off. He had not actually taken offense. Because he was a cautious leader, he must snatch every opportunity to assert dominance.

Alone, he rose and prowled the control cabin. Its narrowness caged him. The real mockery came from the stars in the viewport, multitudes and majesty, a hunting ground unbounded. He bared fangs at them. We shall range among you yet, he vowed; we shall do with you what we will.

First the humans—

Excitement waxed. Clearly the expedition had caught something important, something of power. He would persist until he knew everything the message told. Then he would seek out the old ship, hear whatever might remain to hear, give whatever praise and reassurance were due. And then, informed and prepared, he would be off to the goal of all this voyaging.

His ears lay back. The hair stood up on his body. Let any monkeys that he might encounter beware. The kzinti had much to avenge.

Chapter XIV

Once more *Rover* came out of hyperspace, and there the fugitive was. A computer recognized the inputs to instruments; a chime sounded; an image leaped into a screen. "That's it," said Saxtorph quietly in the command cabin. The intercom brought him a gasp from Tyra at the mass detector. Everybody else was at a duty station too. "Got to be."

He increased magnification, and the spark crawling across the constellations waxed. Tyra saw the same, on the viewer where she was. Optics set limits to what could be reconstructed at a distance of some eighty million kilometers, but he made out a blurry lancehead shape amidst a comma of bluish light, which trailed aft like a tail, the visible part of photons from excited atoms and plasma around the screen fields and aft of them. The invisible part was greater, and deadly.

"The right class of vessel, and just about where she ought to be," Saxtorph added. "Uh, what's her name? I forget."

"*Khrach-Sherrek*," Dorcas supplied. It was in the bit

of record and recollection that had survived. "A cursorial carnivore on their home planet." She didn't normally waste breath on trivia. Anticipated though it was, this culmination must have shaken her too.

"Well, well," came Ryan's voice, overly genial. "That was fun. Now what shall we play?"

"*Dada-mann,*" Tyra whispered. Saxtorph guessed it was unconscious, her pet name for her father when she was small. He imagined tears running down her cheeks, and wanted to go hold her hand and speak comfort. Her words strengthened, not yet quite steady. "Y-yes, that is the proper question. Isn't it? How shall we get him out? Have you had any more ideas, Robert?"

They had discussed it, of course, over and over, as watch after watch dragged by. Yonder vessel couldn't decelerate if the kzinti aboard wanted to, and *Rover* hadn't a decent fraction of the delta v necessary to match velocities. In the era of hyperdrive such capabilities were very nearly as obsolete as flint axes. If somebody took off in a boat, he'd still have that forward speed, and be unable to kill enough of it to help before his energy reserve was gone. Not that there'd be any point in trying. A boat's screens were totally inadequate against the level of radiation involved. He'd be doomed in a second, dead in an hour or two. The craft would become an instant derelict, electronics burned out.

The UN Navy kept a few high-boosters. They had marginal utility for certain kinds of research. "Besides," Saxtorph had observed, "all government agencies hoard stuff to a degree a squirrel or jaybird would envy. They've also got quite a lot else in common with squirrels and jaybirds."

Rigged with a hyperdrive, such as a craft could theoretically come out here, spend months building up her vector, at last draw close, mesh fields, and extend a gang tube—if the kzinti cooperated. If they didn't, an operation already perilous would become insanely so, forcing an entry under those conditions in order to meet armed resistance. Either way, the expense would be staggering. Next year's budget might even have to cut back on a boondoggle or two. Would the top brass consider it, to rescue one man, a man convicted of treason? Saxtorph's bet was that they wouldn't. If they did anything, it would most likely be to order the ship destroyed—simple and safe; leave an undeflectably large mass ahead of her—before she brought home intelligence of the black hole.

He'd not had the heart to express his opinion as more than a possibility, nor did he now. After all, in the course of time Tyra might conceivably manage to rouse public sentiment and turn it into political pressure. She was a skilled writer, and beautiful. Never had he pointed out that her success must entail mortal hazard to a number of other lives. Once he'd thought Dorcas was about to say it, and had given her their private "steer clear" sign. "She's got grief aplenty as is," he explained later.

"We start by peering, don't we?" Carita put in. Good girl, Saxtorph thought. You can always count on her for nuts-and-bolts common sense.

"Right," he said. "Not that I expect we'll learn a lot. However, let's secure every loose end we can before we decide on any further moves."

"We shall c-call them," Tyra stammered. "Shall we not?"

"Well, I suppose we should, but I want to gang mighty warily. 'Twon't be easy, you know."

Indeed not. Aberration and Doppler effect complicated the task abundantly. The speed that caused them made matters worse yet. If *Rover* sent a message, by the time a response could arrive, *Sherrek* would have passed the point where *Rover* lay. Saxtorph meant to stay always well clear. It would be nice if he could fake matched velocity by popping in and out of hyperspace. Too bad that transition between relativistic and quantum modes required time to get the wave functions of atoms into the proper phase relationships. Late in the war the kzinti had figured this out and discovered what the neutrino emission pattern was when a drive prepared itself. Warned of impending attack from an unpredictable new direction, they'd actually won a couple of engagements.

Modern vessels changed state in minutes. The engineers talked about future models that would only take seconds. *Rover*'s antiquated engine needed almost half an hour. Ordinarily that made no difference. You'd be doing something else meanwhile anyway, such as completing your climb sufficiently high out of a gravity well. But here she'd better come no closer than a quarter billion klicks ahead of *Sherrek*. Preferably much more.

"Bloody hell!" cried Ryan. "Why are we glooming and dooming like this? We've *found* her! Let's throw a proper luau."

A sob caught in Tyra's throat. "Thank you, Kam. Yes. Let us."

When she's seen the ship and doesn't know whether her father is alive or dead or worse, thought Saxtorph. That's one gallant lass. "Okay," he said. "The computers can handle the observations. We'll put other functions on auto and relax. Aside from you, Kam. We expect something special for dinner this evenwatch."

"I will help," Tyra said. "I . . . need to."

"No, you don't," Saxtorph told her. "At least, not right off. Report to the saloon. What *I* need help with is downing two or three large schooners."

She smiled forlornly as he entered, but she did smile. Quickly, before the rest arrived, he took both her hands in his. Their eyes met and lingered. Hearing footfalls, they let go. He felt a little breathless and giddy.

Either Tyra put tension aside and cheered up in the course of the next eight hours, or she did a damn good job of acting. The party wasn't riotous, but it became warm, affectionate, finally sentimental. After they started singing, she gave them several ballads from her homeland. She had a lovely voice.

Chapter XV

Effort upon effort succeeded ultimately in getting through. The first partial, distorted reply croaked forth. Dorcas heard and yelled. She, who had the most knowledge of kzin xenology, was prepared to speak through a translator for her band. What she would say, she could not foresee; she must grope forward. Could she bargain, could she threaten? To her husband she admitted that her hopes were low. He agreed, more grimly than the situation seemed to warrant as far as they two were concerned.

She was not prepared for human words.

"Sind Sie wirklich Menschen?" And what must be Tyra's own dialect: *"Gud Jesu, endelig! Hvor langt, hvor langt—"* Interference ripped the cry asunder. Static hissed and snarled like a kzin.

"Hang in there," Saxtorph said. "I'll be back." He scrambled from his seat and out of the cabin. Dorcas' gaze followed him.

Nobody else had been listening. To endure repeated failures is mere masochism, if you yourself can do noth-

ing about them. Saxtorph pounded on Tyra's door. "Wake
up!" he bellowed. "We've contacted your father! He
lives, he lives!"

The door flew open and she stumbled into his arms.
She slept unclothed. He held her tightly until she
stopped weeping and shivered only a little. She was
warm and firm and silken. "We don't know more than
that," he mouthed. Did desire shout louder in his blood
than compassion? "It's going to take time. What'll come
of it, we can't tell. But we're working on it, Tyra. We
are."

She drew herself free and stood before him. Briefly,
fists clenched at her sides. Then she remembered the
situation, crossed arms over the fairness above and
below, caught a ragged breath and blinked the tears
away. "Yes, you will," she answered before she fled,
"because you are what you are. I can abide."

She did, calmly, even blithely, while three daycycles
passed and the story arrived in shreds and snatches.
When at last the whole crew met, bodily, for they
needed to draw strength from each other, she sat half
smiling.

Saxtorph looked around the saloon table. "Okay," he
said with far more steadiness than he felt, "Peter Nordbo
is alive, well, and alone. Two years alone, but better
that than the company he was keeping, and apparently
he's stayed sane. The problem is how to debark him. I
can be honest now and tell you that I don't expect any
navy will do the job, nor anybody else that may have
the capability."

"Why not?" Carita asked. "He's got important information, hasn't he, about the black hole? That expedition checked it over as thoroughly as they could."

The captain began filling his pipe. "Yah, but you see,
their information's in the radio beam the ship was transmitting till he took over. A hell of a lot quicker, easier,
and safer to recover than by matching velocity and
boarding. Oh, I daresay what he's gone through and
what he's done will stir up a wave of public sympathy,

but unless it becomes a tsunami, that probably won't be enough."

"Among the considerations," Dorcas added in an impersonal tone, "*Sherrek* is approaching kzin-controlled space. Kzinti hyperships are bound to be sniffing about. A few of their kind did have valid reasons, from their viewpoint, to flee Alpha Centauri twenty years ago, rather than die fighting or get taken prisoner. The kzinti will search for any, as well as exploring on general principles. I agree the chance of their spotting *Sherrek*'s trail by accident is small, but it is finite, and every month that passes makes it larger. I can well imagine political objections to risking an unwanted incident, on top of every other argument."

"We can go home, report this, and agitate for help," Saxtorph said. "It's the sensible, obvious course. I won't veto it, if that's what you want."

Tyra gave him a sea-blue regard. "You have a different possibility," she said low.

His grin twisted. "You've gotten to know me, huh?"

She nodded. Light sheened across her hair.

"It's a dicey thing," he said. "Some danger to us, a lot to your father. But if it works, you'll have him back in days."

"Else years," she replied as softly as before, "or never." Only her fingernails, white where she gripped the tabletop, revealed more. "What think you on?"

"We've, uh, discussed it, him and Dorcas and me. In the jaggedy fashion you've observed. We didn't want to announce this earlier, because we had to do some figuring and would've hated to . . . disappoint you." Saxtorph put fire to pipe. "Yon ship carries a pair of flyby capsules, unpowered but made to withstand extremely heavy radiation. As much as you'd get at one-half c. He can get inside one and have its launcher toss him out." He puffed forth a cloud.

"You believe you can recover him," she said, and began to tremble ever so slightly.

"Yes. Our new grapnel field installation. If we get the configuration and timing just right—if not, you realize, he's gone beyond any catching—if we do, we can lock on. *Rover* has more mass by several orders of magnitude. We estimate that the combined momentum will mean a velocity of about 200 klicks per second, well within our delta v reserve."

"Down from . . . that speed? I should think—" she must struggle to utter it—"the acceleration overcomes your polarizers and tears your grappler out through the hull."

"Smart girl." How ludicrously inadequate that was for his admiration. "It would also reduce him to thin jelly. We can do up to fifty g. The capsules have interior polarizers with power to counteract a bit more, but we want a safety factor. Our systems can handle it too. Do you know about deep-sea fishing? Your dolphins may have told stories of marlin and tarpon."

She nodded again. "I saw a documentary once. And in the Frisian Sea on Wunderland I have myself taken a dinotriton." Ardor flamed up. "I see! You let the capsule run, but never far enough to get away, and you play it, you pull it in a little at a time—"

"Right. The math says we can do it in three and a half daycycles, through a distance of 225 billion kilometers. In practice it'll doubtless be harder." He had to have a moment's relief. "Anderson's Law, remember: 'Everything takes longer and costs more.' "

Awe struck her. She sagged back in her chair. "The skill—"

"The danger," Dorcas said. "At any point we can fail. *Rover* may then suffer damage, although if we stand ready I don't expect it'll cripple us. But your father will be a dead man."

"What thinks he?"

"He's for it," Saxtorph replied. "Of course a buck like that would be. But he leaves the decision to us. With . . . his blessing. And we, Dorcas and I, we leave it to you. I imagine Kam and Carita will go along with whatever you choose."

Abruptly Tyra's voice wavered. "Kam," she said, "you have taught me a word of yours, a very good, brave word. I use it now." She leaped to her feet. "Go for broke!" she shouted.

The Hawaiian and the Jinxian cheered.

Thereafter it was toil, savage demands on brain and body, nerves aquiver and pulled close to breaking, heedless overuse of stimulants, tranquilizers, whatever might keep the organism awake and alert.

No humans could have done the task. The forces involved were immensely too great, changeable, complex. Nor could they be felt at the fingertips; over spatial reaches, the lightspeed that carried them became a laggard, and the fisher must judge what was happening when it would not manifest itself for minutes. The computer program that Dorcas wrote with the aid of the computer that was to use it, this held the rod and reeled the line.

Yet humans must be in the loop, constantly monitoring, gauging, making judgments. Theirs was the intuition, the instinct and creative insight, that no one has engineered into any machine. The Saxtorphs were the two best qualified. Carita could handle the less violent hours. The main burden fell on Dorcas. Ryan and Tyra kept them fed, coffeed, medicated. Often she rubbed a back, kneaded shoulders, ran a wet washcloth over a face, crooned a lullaby at a catnap. Mostly she did it for the captain.

From dead *Sherrek*, the cannonball that held the living shot free. Unseeable amidst the light of lethal radiation, a force-beam reached to lay hold. Almost, the grip failed. Needles spun on dials and Dorcas cast her man a look of terror. Things stabilized. The hook was in.

Gently, now, gently. Itself a comet trailing luminance, the capsule fled. The grapnel field stretched, tugging, dragging *Rover* along, but how slowly slowing it. As distance grew, precision diminished. The capsule plunged about. The Saxtorphs ordered compensating boosts. Ideally, they could maintain contact across the width of a planetary system. In fact, the chance of losing it was large.

They played their fish.

Hour by hour, day by day, the haste diminished, the gap closed. Worst was a moment near the end, when the capsule was visible in a magnifying screen, and suddenly rolled free. Somehow Dorcas clapped the grapnel back onto it. Then: "Take over for a while, Bob," she choked, put head in hands, and wept. He couldn't recall, at that point, when he had last seen her shed tears.

Ship and sphere drew nigh. A cargo port opened. The catch went in. The port shut and air roared into the bay. Some time yet must pass; at first that metal was too cold for flesh to approach. When at length its own hatch cracked, the warmth and stench of life long confined billowed out.

A man crept after. He rose unsteadily, tall, hooknosed, bushy-bearded, going gray, though still hard and lithe. He climbed a ladder. A door swung wide for him. Beyond waited his daughter.

Chapter XVI

The song of her working systems throbbed through *Rover*, too softly for ears to hear anything save rustles and murmurs, yet somehow pervading bones, flesh, and spirit. In Ryan's cabin Carita asked, "But *why* are we headed back to the black hole? Add a week's travel time at least, plus whatever we spend there. I've *seen* the damn thing. Why not straight to Wunderland?"

She had been asleep, exhausted, when her shipmates made the decision, and had only lately awakened, to eat ravenously and join her friend. The rest had spent their remnant strength laying plans and getting on hyperspatial course. Ryan took the first mass detector watch. Tyra had it now, drowsily; when relieved, she would doubtless seek her bunk again.

"We thought you'd agree, and in any case wouldn't appreciate being hauled out to cast a vote when the count could just go one way," Ryan answered. "Wherever we picked, it was foolish to linger. Nothing else to gain, and a small possibility that a ratcat *moku* might suddenly pop up and shout, 'Boo!' Care for a drink?"

"You know me. In several different meanings of the word." Carita propped a pillow between her and the bulkhead and lounged back, her legs twin pillars of darkness on the gaudy bedspread. Ryan stepped across to a cabinet above a minifridge. He'd crowded a great deal of sybaritism into his quarters. In the screen, a barely clad songstress sat under a palm tree near a beach, plucked a ukulele, and looked seductive as she crooned. He did esoteric things with rum and fruit juices.

Meanwhile he explained: "Partly it's a matter of recuperation. Nordbo's served a hitch in Hell, and we visited the forecourts of Purgatory, eh? When we return, the sensation and the official flapdoodle are going to make what happened after the red sun business seem like a session of the garden committee of the Philosophical Society. We'd better be well rested and have a lot of beforehand thinking done."

"M-m, yes, that makes sense. But I can tell you pleasanter places to let our brains simmer down in than that black hole. You know what the name means in Russian?"

Ryan laughed. "Uh-huh. So they call it a 'frozen star.' Pretty turn of phrase. Except that this one never really was a star, and is anything but frozen."

"It's turned into a kind of star, then." For a moment they were silent. The same vision stood before them, a radiance more terrible century by century, at last day by day, until its final nova-like self-immolation. For the most part spacefarers speak casually, prosaically about their work, because the reality of the universe is as daunting as the reality of death.

"Well, but we've got a reason," Ryan continued. "Nailing down a claim of discovery. The kzinti examined the artifact as thoroughly as they could, much more than our quick once-over. Especially, of course, with an eye to the military potentials. Nordbo was there. He knows fairly well what they learned. But as you'd expect, he needs to refresh his memory. He told us the kzinti ship beamcast a full description till he got control and shut it off. But we aren't equipped to retrieve it. Think how much trouble we had communicating with him. We could waste weeks, and not be sure of recording more than snatches. Let Nordbo revisit the actual thing, repeat a few measurements and such, and he can write that description himself, or enough of it to establish the claim."

Carita raised her brows. "What claim? The government's bound to swarm there, take charge, and stamp everything Incredibly Secret."

Ryan nodded. "Does a shark eat fish? They'll be plenty peeved at us for telling the *hoi polloi* that it exists at all. We've got to do that, if only as part of Nordbo's vindication, but I'll concede that it's probably best to keep quiet about the technical details. However, he'll have priority of discovery. For legal purposes, the kzinti and their beamcast can be ignored. They shanghaied him, among numerous other unlawful acts; they've forfeited any rights, not to mention that there is no court with jurisdiction. He'll be entitled to a discoverer's award. In view of the importance of the find, and the fact that public disputes would be very awkward for the government, that award will be plenty big—and we'll share it with him."

"Ah-ha!" Carita exulted. "I see. You were right, there was no need to roll me out of the sheets to vote."

"Same thing should apply to the kzinti ship, if the Navy elects to go recover it for intelligence purposes," Ryan said. "Not likely, though. My guess is they'll simply read the message and then jam it. The black hole is our real jackpot." He finished mixing the drinks and gave her one. *"Pōmaika'i."*

"Into orbit." Rims clinked. He sat down on the edge of the bunk.

Carita turned thoughtful. "That poor man. He will be, uh, vindicated, won't he?"

"Oh, yes. If necessary, he can take truth tests, but the story by itself, with the corroboration we can give, should do the trick. His name will be cleared, his family will be reinstated in its clan, and he'll get back the property that was confiscated, or compensation for it if reversion isn't practical. He won't need any award money. I suspect he's forcing himself, for our sake."

Carita stared before her. "How's he taking all this?"

Ryan shrugged. "Too early to tell. Excitement; exhaustion; the last scrap of endurance that stimulants could give, spent on making plans. But surely he'll be okay. He's a tough cookie if ever I bit into one."

Compassion gentled her voice. "He met his little girl-child, and she was a not-quite-young woman. She told him his wife has died."

"I think I saw grief, though he was fairly stoic throughout. However, it can't have been a huge surprise. And he wouldn't be human if, down underneath, he didn't feel a slight relief."

"Yes. She'd have been old. I bet he'd have stuck loyally by her till the end, but— Well, sheer pride in his daughter ought to help him a lot, emotionally."

"A rare specimen, her." Ryan let out an elaborate sigh. "And sexy as Pele, under that brisk, sprightly, competent surface. I'd give a lot to be in the path of the next eruption. No such luck, though. In a perfectly pleasant fashion, she's made that clear. It's the single fault I find in her."

Carita drank deep, frowned, and drank again. "Her eyes are on the skipper. And his on her. They can't hide it any longer, no matter how hard they try."

"I know, I know. I'm resigned. If anybody rates that fling—more than me, that is—Bob does."

"Dorcas."

"Aw, she shouldn't mind too much. She's as realistic a soul as our species has got."

Carita's lips tightened. "I'm afraid this wouldn't be just a fling."

"Huh? Come on, now."

"You've been giving Tyra your whole attention. I've paid some to him."

"You really think—?" Flustered, Ryan took a long drink of his own. "Well, none of our business." He relaxed, smiled, leaned over, laid an arm across her waist. "How about we attend to what does concern us, firepants? It's been a while."

For a little span yet Carita sat troubled, then she put her tumbler aside, smiled back, and turned to him. The ship sailed on through lightlessness.

Chapter XVII

"No, I must speak the truth," said Chief Communications Officer. "We will continue trying if the commander orders, but I respectfully warn it will be a total waste of time and effort. The commander knows we have beamed every kind of signal on every band available to us. Not so much as an automaton has responded. That vessel is dead."

Or sleeping beyond any power of ours to disturb, thought Weoch-Captain. He stared into the screen before him as if into a forest midnight. At its distance, the runaway was a thin flame, crawling across the stars. Imagination failed to feel the immensity of its haste and of the energy borne thereby.

"I concur," he said after a minute. "Deactivate your apparatus and stand by for further orders." Rage flared. "Go, you *sthondat*-licker! Go!"

The image blinked off. Weoch-Captain mastered his temper. Chief Communications Officer did not deserve that, he thought. This past time, locked in futility, has made me as irascible as the lowliest crew member.

What, do I regret taking it out on him? I am thinking like a monkey—also by looking inward and gibing at myself. No other Hero must ever know. Yes, we are badly overdue for some action.

Weoch-Captain cast introspection from him and concentrated on the future. Not that he had a large choice. He could not overhaul *Sherrek*, board, and learn its fate. He had repeatedly suppressed an impulse to have it destroyed, that object which mocked him with silence. The Patriarchs would decide what to do about it. He could return directly to them and report. A human shipmaster would do so as a matter of course, given the circumstances.

The High Admiral has granted me broad discretion. If I come back with my basic mission half-completed, someone else may take it from me and go capture the glory. Also, I do *not* think like a monkey.

He summoned Astronomer's image. "Does analysis suggest anything new about the perturbation you noticed?" he inquired without expectations.

"No, or I would have informed the commander immediately. The data are too sparse. Something roiled the interstellar medium besides *Sherrek*, a few light-days aft of where we found it, but the effect was barely noticeable. The commander recalls my idea that a stray rock encountered the screen fields, too small to penetrate but large enough to leave a trail as it was flung aside in fragments. Further number-crunching has merely reinforced my opinion that a search would be useless."

Yes, thought Weoch-Captain. The overwhelming size of space. And if we did retrieve a meteoroidal shard or two, what of it? An improbable encounter, but not impossible, and altogether meaningless. Whatever happened to *Sherrek* happened a light-year farther back, two years in the past, which is when we established that it ceased communicating.

And yet I have a hunter's intuition—

A cold thrill passed through him. He dismissed Astronomer and called Executive Officer. "Prepare for hyperspace," he said. "We shall proceed to our primary goal."

"At once, sir!" the kzin rejoiced.

"En route, you will conduct combat drill with full simulations. The crew have grown edgy and ill-coordinated. You will make them again into an efficient fighting machine. Despite what we have learned from the beamcast, there is no foreseeing what we will find at the far end."

"Sire."

Humans? thought Weoch-Captain. Maybe, maybe. According to our information, the black hole was not their principal objective; but monkey curiosity, if nothing else, may hold them at it still. Or—I know not, I simply have a feeling that they are involved in *Sherrek's* misfortune. They, the same who destroyed Werlith-Commandant and his great enterprise.

Be there, Saxtorph, that I may take the glory of killing you.

Chapter XVIII

Stars crowded the encompassing night, wintry brilliant. Alpha Centauri was only one among them, and Sol shone small. The Milky Way glimmered around the circle of sight, like a river flowing back into its wellspring. Rifts in it were dustclouds such as veil the unknown heart of the galaxy. Big in vision, a worldlet hilled and begrown with strangeness, loomed the black hole artifact.

Rover held station fifty kilometers off the hemisphere opposite the radiation-spouting gap. "Below" her, Peter Nordbo, with Carita Fenger to help, examined a structure that he believed could throw the entire mass into hyperspace. Elsewhere squatted the robot prospector, patiently tracing a circuit embedded in the shell substance.

Aboard ship was leisure. Dorcas kept the bridge, mostly on general principles. If the robot signaled that it had finished, she would confer with Nordbo and order it to a different site. Ryan watched a show in his cabin; some people would have been surprised to know

it was *King Lear*. Saxtorph and Tyra sat over coffee in
the saloon. When Carita relieved him on the surface
and he flitted back up, he had meant to sleep, but the
Wunderlander met him and they fell to talking.

"Your dad shouldn't work so hard," he said. "Three
watches out of four, daycycle after daycycle. He ought
to take it easier. We've got as much time as we care to
spend."

"He is impatient to finish and go home," Tyra said.
"You can understand."

"Yes. Home to sadness, though."

"But more to hope."

Saxtorph nodded. "Uh-huh. He's that sort of man.
Not that I have any close acquaintance, but—a great
guy. I see now why you laid everything on the line to
buy a chance of having him again." He paused before
adding in a rush: "And with you once more in his life,
he's bound to become happy."

She looked away. "You should not— Oh, Robert, you
are too kind, always too kind to me. I shall miss you so
much."

He reached across the table and took her hand. "Hey,
there, little lady, don't borrow trouble. You know I'll
be detained on Wunderland for a goodly spell, like it or
not." He grinned. "Want to help me like it?"

Her eyes sought back to his. The blood mounted in
her face. "Yes, we must see what we can—"

Dorcas' voice tore across hers. "Emergency stations!
Kzinti ship!" Coming from every annunciator, it seemed
to roll and echo down the corridors.

"Judas priest! To the boat, Tyra!" Saxtorph shouted.
He was already on his way. His feet slapped out a
devil's tattoo on the deck. As he ran, the enormity of
the tidings crashed into him.

At the control cabin, he burst through its open door
and flung himself into the seat by Dorcas'. In the forward viewport, the shell occulted the suns of their
desire. Starboard, port, aft gleamed grandeur indiffer-
ent to them. The communicator, automatically switched
on when it detected an incoming signal, gave forth the

flat English of a translator: "—not attempt to escape. If we observe the neutrino signature of a hyperspatial drive starting up, we will fire."

Sweat shone on the woman's scalp, around her Belter crest. Saxtorph caught an acrid whiff of it, or was that his own, running down his ribs? Her fingers moved firm over a keyboard. "Ha, I've got him," she whispered. A speck appeared in the scanner screen. She magnified.

Toylike still, the other vessel appeared. Saxtorph followed current naval literature. He identified the lean length, the guns and missile tubes and ray projectors, of a Raptor-class warcraft. The meters told him she was about half a million klicks off, closing fast.

"Acknowledge!" the radio snapped.

"Message received," he said around an acid lump in his gorge. "What do you want? We're here legitimately. Our races are at peace." Yah, sure, sure.

"Oh, God, Bob," Dorcas choked while the beam winged yonder. "The call was the first sign I had. She may have emerged a long distance away. If we'd spotted her approaching—"

He squeezed her arm. "We didn't keep an alert, sweetheart. We didn't. The bunch of us. What reason had we to fear anything like this?"

"Weoch-Captain of Hero vessel Swordbeak, speaking for the Patriarchy." Now, behind the synthetic human tones, were audible the growls and spits of kzinti. "You trespass on our property, you violate our secrets, and I believe that in the past you have been guilty of worse. Identify yourself."

Saxtorph stalled. "Why do you ask that? According to you, no human has a real name."

Can we cut and run for it? he wondered. No. The question shows how kicked in the gut I am. She can outboost us by a factor of five, at least. Not that she'd need to. Even at this remove, her lasers can probably cripple us. A missile can cross the gap in a few minutes, and we've nothing to fend it off. (Grab it with our grapnel, no, too slow, and anyway, there'd be a second or a third missile, or a multiple warhead, or—) She herself, at her acceleration, she'll be here in half an hour. But how can I think about flight? Carita and Pete are down at the black hole.

It had flashed through him in the short seconds of transmission lag. "Do as you are told, monkey! Give me your designation."

No sense in provoking the kzin further by a refusal. He'd soon be able to read the name, jaunty across these bows. "Freighter *Rover* of Leyport, Luna. I repeat, our intentions are entirely honest and we can't imagine what we may have done that you could call wrong."

Silence crackled. Dorcas sat stiff, fists clenched.

"*Rover*. Harrgh! Saxtorph-Captain, is it? Give me video."

Huh? The man sat numbed. The woman did the obedience.

Weoch-Captain evidently chose to make it mutual. His tiger head slanted forward in the screen, as if he peered out of his den at prey. "So that is what you look like," he rumbled. Eyes narrowed, tongue ran over fangs. "How I hoped that mine would be this pleasure."

"What do you mean?" Dorcas cried.

Silence. The heart drubbed in Saxtorph's breast.

"You know full well," said Weoch-Captain. "You killed the Heroes and destroyed their works at the red sun."

So the story had reached Kzin. Not too surprising, as spectacular as it was. Saxtorph had been assured that the Alpha Centaurian and Solar governments had avoided being very specific in their official communications thus far. They wanted to test ratcat reactions an item at a time. But spacefarers, especially nonhuman spacefarers with less of a grudge or none, traveling from Wunderland to neutral planets, might well have passed details on to their kzin counterparts in the course of meetings.

"Through my whole long voyage, I hoped I would find you," Weoch-Captain purred. His flattened ears lifted and spread. "A formidable opponent, a worthy one. If you behave yourselves and do as you are told, I promise you deaths quick and painless. . . . No, not

quite that for you, Saxtorph. I think you and I shall
have single combat. Afterward I will take your body for
my exclusive eating, fit nourishment for a Hero, and
give your head a place among my trophies."

Saxtorph braced himself. "You do us great honor,
Weoch-Captain," he croaked. "We thank you. We praise
your large spirit." What else could I say? Keep them
happy. Kzinti don't normally torture for fun, but if this
one got vengeful enough he might take it out on Tyra,
Dorcas, Kam, Carita, Peter. At the least, he might
bring them, us, back with him. Unless we kill ourselves
first.

In the magnifying viewport the Raptor had percepti-
bly gained size, eclipsing more and more stars.

Weoch-Captain flexed claws out, in, out again. "Good,"
he said. "But I still will not talk at length to a monkey.
Stand by. You will receive your final instructions when
I arrive."

The screen blanked.

"Bob, darling, darling." Dorcas twisted about in her
seat to cast her arms around him.

He hugged her. As always in crisis, confronting the
worst, he had grown cool, watchful but half detached, a
survival machine. Not that he saw any prospect of living
onward, but— "We should bring the others up," he
reminded her. "We can have a short time together."
Before the kzinti arrive.

"Yes." He felt how she quelled her shuddering. Steady
as he, she turned to the communicator and directed a
broad beam at the sphere. "Carita, Peter, get straight
back to the ship," she said crisply.

"*Was ist*—what is bad?" sounded Nordbo's hoarse
bass.

"Never mind now. Move, I tell you!"

"*Jawohl.*" And: "Aye, aye, ma'am, we're off," from
Carita.

Dorcas cut transmission. "I want to spare them while
they flit," she explained. "They'll worry, but if they
don't happen to make the enemy out in the sky, they
won't be in shock."

"Until we meet again," Saxtorph agreed. "What about . . . Tyra and Kam? Shall we keep them waiting too?"

"We may as well, or better."

"No. Maybe you weren't being kind after all. I think Tyra would want to know right away, so she can, well, she can—" kiss me goodbye?—"prepare herself, and meet the end with her eyes wide open. She's like that."

Dorcas bit her lip. "I can't stop you if you insist." Her words quivered a little. "But I thought you and I, these fifteen minutes or so we have left before we must tell them—"

He grinned, doubtless rather horribly. " 'Fraid I couldn't manage a quickie."

She achieved a laugh. "Down, boy." Soberly: "Not to get maudlin either. But let me say I love you, and thank you for everything."

"Aw, now, the thanks are all due you, my lady." He rose. She did. They embraced. He damned himself for wishing she were Tyra.

She kissed him long and hard. "That's for what we've had." The tears wouldn't quite stay put. "And for, for everything we were going to have—the kids and—"

Yah, he thought, our stored gametes. We never made provision for exogenesis, in case something clobbered us. They'll stay in the freeze, those tiny ghosts of might-have-been, year after year after year, I suppose, forgotten and forsaken, like our robot yonder.

Saxtorph lurched where he stood. "*Fanden i helvede!*" he roared.

Dorcas stepped back. She saw his face, and the breath whistled in between her teeth. "What?"

The Danish of his childhood, "The Devil in Hell," his father's favorite oath, yes, truly, for a devil did squat just outside the hell star awaiting his command. His revelation spilled from him.

Fierceness kindled in her, she shouted, but then she must ask, "What if we fail?"

"Why, we open our airlocks and drink space," he answered. He had dismissed the idea earlier because he knew she wouldn't want suicide while any chance of being cleanly killed remained. "Though most likely the kzinti will be so enraged they'll missile us on the spot. Come on, we haven't got time to gab, let's get going."

They returned to their seats and controls. An order went out. On the tnuctipun structure, the robot prospector stirred. Cautiously, at minimum boost, it lifted. When it was well clear, the humans accelerated it harder. They must work fast, to have the machine positioned before the enemy came so near that watchers at instruments might notice it and wonder. They must likewise work precisely, mathematically, solving a problem of vectors and coordinates in three-dimensional space. "—line integral of velocity divergence dS—" Dorcas muttered aloud to the computer while her fingers did the real speaking. There passed through the back of Saxtorph's awareness: If the scheme flops, this'll be how we spent our last moments together. Appropriate.

A telltale blinked. Nordbo and Carita had arrived. "Kam, our friends are back," the captain said through the intercom. "Cycle 'em through and have them sit tight. Tyra, I think we can cope with our visitors."

Except for Ryan's "Aye," neither of them responded. The quartermaster knew better than to distract the pair on the bridge. The woman must have understood the same on her own account. She isn't whimpering or hysterical or anything, Saxtorph thought—not her. Maybe, not being a spacehand, she won't obey my order and stay at the boat. It's useless anyway. But the most mutinous thing she might do is walk quietly, firmly through my ship to meet her dad.

"On station," Dorcas sighed. She leaned back, hands still on the keys, gaze on the displays. "It'll take three or four mini-nudges to maintain, but I doubt the kzinti will detect them."

The Raptor was big in the screen. Twin laser guns in the nose caught starlight and gleamed like eyes.

"Good." Saxtorph's attention skewered *Rover*'s control board. He'd calculated how he wanted to move, at full thrust, when things started happening. Though his

present location was presumably safe, he'd rather be as
far off as possible. Clear to Wunderland would be ideal,
a sunny patio, a beer stein in his fist, and at his side—

"Go!" Dorcas yelled. She hit the switch that closed
her last circuit. *"Ki-yai!"*

Afloat among stars, the robot prospector received the
signal for which the program that she sent it had waited.
It took off. At a hundred gravities of acceleration, it
crossed a hundred kilometers of space in less than five
seconds, to strike the shell around the black hole with
the force of a boulder falling from heaven.

It crashed through. White light was in the radiation
that torrented from the hole it left and smote the kzinti
ship.

Chapter XIX

"Put me through again to the human commander," said Weoch-Captain.

"Yes, sire," replied Communications Officer.

Human, thought Weoch-Captain. Not monkey, whatever my position may require me to call him in public. A brave and resourceful enemy. I well-nigh wish we were more equally matched when I fight him. But no one must know that.

His optics showed *Rover*, an ungainly shape, battered and wayworn. Should he claim it too for a trophy? No, let Saxtorph's head suffice; and it would not have much meaning either, when he returned in his glory to take a full name, a seat among the Patriarchs, the right to found a house of his own. Still, his descendants might cherish the withered thing as a sign of what their ancestor did. Weoch-Captain's glance shifted to the great artifact. Power laired there, power perhaps to make the universe tremble. "Arrh," he breathed.

The screens blanked. The lights went out. He tumbled through an endless dark.

"Ye-a-a-ach, what's this? What the venom's going on?" Screams tore at air that had ceased to blow from ventilators. Weoch-Captain recognized his state. He was weightless.

"Stations, report!" No answer except the chaos in the corridors. Everything was dead. The crew were ghosts flapping blindly around in a tomb. Nausea snatched at Weoch-Captain,

He fought it down. If down existed any more, adrift among stars he no longer saw. He shouldn't get spacesick. He never had in the past when he orbited free. He must act, take charge, uncover what was wrong, rip it asunder and set things right. He groped his way by feel, from object to suddenly unfamiliar object. "Quiet!" he bawled. "Hold fast! To me, officers, to me, your commander!"

The sickness swelled inside him.

He reached the door and the passage beyond. A body blundered into his. Both caromed, flailing air, rebounding from bulkheads, all grip on dignity lost. "My eyes, arh, my eyes," moaned the other kzin. "Did the light burn them out? I am blind. Help me, help me."

An idea took Weoch-Captain by the throat. He bared teeth at it, but it gave him a direction, a quarry. Remembrance was a guide. He pushed along corridors where noise diminished as personnel mastered panic. Good males, he thought amidst the hammerblows of blood in ears and temples. Valiant males. Heroes.

His goal was the nearest observation turret. It had transparent ports for direct viewing, backup in case of electronic failures, which he kept unshuttered during any action. He fumbled through the entry. A blue-white beam, too dazzling to look near, stabbed across the space beyond. It disappeared as *Swordbeak* floated past. Weoch-Captain reached a pane and squinted. Stars clustered knife-sharp. Carefully, fingers hooked on frames, he moved to the next.

A gray curve, a jutting tower, yes, the relic of the ancient lords, the end of his quest. *Swordbeak* slipped farther along. Weoch-Captain shrieked, clapped palms to face, bobbed helpless in midair.

Slowly the after-images faded. The glare hadn't blinded him. By what light now came in, he discerned metal and meters. He understood what had happened.

Somehow the humans had opened a new hole in the shell. Radiation tore the life from his ship.

Sickness overwhelmed him. He vomited. Foul gobbets and globules swarmed around his head and up his nostrils. He fled before they strangled him.

Yes, death is in my bones, he knew. How long can I fight it off, and why? You have conquered, human.

No! He shoved feet against bulkhead and arrowed forward. The plan took shape while he flew. "Meet at Station Three!" he shouted against night. "All hands to Station Three for orders! Pass the word on! Your commander calls you to battle!"

One by one, clumsily, many shivering and retching, they joined him. Officers identified themselves, crew rallied round them. Some had found flashlights. Fangs and claws sheened in the shadows.

He told them they would soon die. He told them how they should. They snarled their wrath and resolution.

Spacesuits were lockered throughout the ship. Kzinti sought those assigned them. In gloom and free fall, racked by waxing illness, a number of them never made it.

Air hung thick, increasingly chill. Recyclers, thrusters, radios in the spacesuits were inoperative. Well, but the pumps still had capacitor power, and you wouldn't have use for more air than your reserve tank held. You had your legs to leap with. You knew where you were bound, and could curse death by yourself.

Weoch-Captain helped at the wheel of his airlock, opening it manually. Atmosphere howled out, momentarily mist-white, dissipated, revealed the stars afresh. He followed it. *Rover* wasn't in sight. It must have scampered away. Maybe *Swordbeak*'s hull blocked it off. The artifact was a jaggedness straight ahead. He

gauged distance, direction, and velocities as well as he
was able, bunched his muscles, and leaped, a hunter at
his quarry.

"Hee-yaa!" he screamed. The noise rattled feebly in
his helmet. Blood came with it, droplets and smears.

Headed across the void, he could look around. Except for his breathing, the rattle of fluid in his lungs, he
had fallen into a silence, an enormous peace. Here and
there, glints moved athwart constellations, the spacesuits of his fellows. We too are star-stuff, he thought.
Sun-stuff. Fire.

Hardly any of them would accomplish the passage,
he knew. Most would go by, misaimed, and perish
somewhere beyond. A lucky few might chance to pass in
front of the furnace mouth and receive instant oblivion.
Those who succeeded would not know where to go.
There had been no way for Weoch-Captain to describe
what he had learned from long days of study. A few
might spy him, recognize him, seek him, but it was
unlikely in the extreme.

No matter. Because of him they would die as warriors, on the attack.

Swordbeak receded. It had still had a significant
component of velocity toward the sphere when the
flame struck, though it was not on a collision course. It
left him that heritage for his flight.

Rover hove into view. Saxtorph was coming back to
examine the havoc he had wrought, was he? Well, he'd
take a while to assess what his screens and instruments
told him, and realize what it meant and then—what
could he do? Unlimber his grapnel and collect dying
kzinti?

He can try raying us, Weoch-Captain thought. He
must have an industrial laser. I would certainly do it in
his place. But as a weapon it's slow, unwieldy, and—I
am almost at my mark.

The shell filled half of heaven. Its curve now hid the
deadly light; only stars shone on spires, mazes, unknown engines. Weoch-Captain tensed.

A latticework seemed to spring at him. He grabbed a

member. His strength ebbing, he nearly lost hold and shot on past. Somehow he kept the grip, and slammed to a halt. He clung while he got his wind back. Rags of darkness floated across his eyes.

Onward, though, lest he die unfulfilled. It was hard, and grew harder moment by moment as he clambered down. With nothing left him but the capacitor supplying the air pump and a little heat, he must by himself bend the joints at arms, legs, and fingers against interior pressure. With his mind going hazy, he must stay alert enough to find his way among things he knew merely from pictures, while taking care not to push so hard that he drifted away in space.

Nevertheless he moved.

A glance aloft. Yes, *Rover* was lumbering about. Maybe Saxtorph had guessed what was afoot. Weoch-Captain grinned. He hoped the human was frantic.

He'd aimed himself carefully, and luck had been with him. His impact was close to the activator. He reached it and went in among the structures and darknesses.

On a lanyard he carried a flashlight. By its glow he examined that which surrounded him. Yes, according to Yiao-Captain's report, this object like a lever and that object like a pedal ought to close a connection when pushed. The tnuctipun had scarcely intended any such procedure. Somewhere must be an automaton, a program, and shelter for whatever crew the black hole ship bore on its warfaring. But the tnuctipun too installed backup systems. Across billions of years, Weoch-Captain hailed them, his brother warriors.

This may not work, he cautioned himself. I can but try to reave the power from the humans.

I do not know where it will go, or if it will ever come back into our space. Nor will I know. I shall be dead. Proudly, gloriously.

A spasm shook him, but he had spewed out everything in his stomach before he left *Swordbeak*. Parched and vile-tasting mouth, dizziness, ringing ears, blood coughed forth and smeared over faceplate, wheezing breath, shaky hands, weakness, weakness, yes, it was good to die. He got himself well braced against metal—to be inside this framework was like being inside a cane-brake at home, he thought vaguely, waiting for prey—and pushed with the whole force that remained to him.

Aboard *Rover*, shortly afterward, they saw their prize disappear.

Chapter XX

Regardless, the homeward voyage began merrily. When you have had your life given back to you, the loss of a treasure trove seems no large matter.

"Besides, a report on *Sherrek* and her beamcast, plus what we collected ourselves, should be worth a substantial award by itself," Saxtorph observed. "And then there's the other one, uh, *Swordbeak*." Dorcas had read the name when they flitted across and attached a radio beacon, so that the derelict would be findable. "In a way, actually, more than the black hole could've been. Your navy—or mine, or the two conjointly —they'll be overjoyed at getting a complete modern kzinti warcraft to dissect."

"What that artifact, and the phenomenon within, should have meant to science—" Peter Nordbo sighed. "But you are right, complaining is ungrateful."

"No doubt the authorities will want this part of our story hushed up," Saxtorph went on. "But we'll be heroes to them, which is more useful than being it to the public. I expect we'll slide real easy through the bureaucratic rigmarole. And, as I said, get well paid for it."

"I thought you were a patriot, Robert."

"Oh, I s'pose I am. But the laborer is worthy of his hire. And I'm a poor man. Can't afford to work for free."

They sat in the Saxtorphs' cabin, the most spacious aboard, talking over a beer. They had done it before. The instant liking they took to one another had grown with acquaintance. The Wunderlander's English was rusty but improving.

He stroked his beard as he said slowly, "I have thought on that. Hear me, please. My family shall have its honor again, but I disbelieve our lands can be restored. The present owners bought in good faith and have their rights. You shall not pity me. From what I have heard since my rescue, society is changed and the name of Landholder bears small weight. But in simple justice we shall have money for what they stripped from us. After I pay off Tyra's debt she took for my sake, much will stay with me. What shall I then do? I have my science, yes, but as an amateur. I am too old to become a professional in it. Yet I am too young to . . . putter. Always my main work was with people. What now can I enjoy?" He smiled. "Well, your business has the chronic problem that it is undercapitalized. The awards will help, but I think not enough. How would you like a partner?"

Saxtorph goggled. "Huh? Why, uh, what do you mean?"

"I would not travel with you, unless once in a while as a passenger for pleasure. I am no spaceman. But it was always my dream, and being in an enterprise like yours, that should come close. Yes, I will go on trips myself, making arrangements for cargoes and charters, improvements and expansions. Being a Landholder taught me about business, and I did it pretty well. Ask my former tenants. Also, the money I put in, that will make the difference to you. Together we can turn this very profitable for all of us.

"You cannot decide at once, nor can I. But today it seems me a fine idea. What do you think?"

"I think it's a goddamn supernova!" Saxtorph roared.

They talked, more and more excitedly, until the captain glanced at his watch and said, "Hell, I've got to go relieve Dorcas at the mass detector. I'll send her down here and the pair of you can thresh this out further, if you aren't too tired."

"Never for her," Nordbo replied. "She is a wonderful person. You are a lucky man."

Saxtorph's eagerness faded. After a moment he mumbled, "I'm sorry. I often bull ahead with you as though you hadn't . . . suffered your loss. You don't speak about it, and I forget. I'm sorry, Peter."

"Do not be," Nordbo answered gently. "A sorrow, yes, but during my time alone, assuming I would grow old and die there, I became resigned. To learn I missed my Hulda by less than a year, that is bitter, but I tell myself we had already lost our shared life; and God has left me our two children, both become splendid human beings."

The daughter, at least, for sure, Saxtorph thought.

Nordbo smiled again. "I still have my son Ib to look forward to meeting. In fact, since Tyra tells me he is in naval intelligence, we shall be close together—Robert, what is wrong?"

Saxtorph sat moveless until he shook himself, stood up, tossed off his drink, and rasped: "Something occurred to me. Don't worry. It may well turn out to be nothing. But, uh, look, we'd better not discuss this partnership notion with Dorcas or anybody right away. Let's keep it under our hats till our ideas are more definite, okay? Now I really must go spell her."

Nordbo seemed puzzled, a bit hurt, but replied, "As you wish," and left the cabin with him. They parted ways in the corridor and Saxtorph proceeded to the detector station.

Dorcas switched off the book she had been screening. "Hey, you look like a bad day in Hell," she said.

"Out of sorts," he mumbled. "I'll recover. Just leave me be."

"So you don't want to tell me why." She rose to face him. Sadness tinged her voice. "You haven't told me much lately, about anything that matters to you."

"Nonsense," he snapped. "We were side by side against the kzinti."

"That's not what I meant, and you know it. Well, I won't plague you. That would be unwise of me, wouldn't it?" She went out, head high but fingers twisting together.

He took the chair that was not warm after her, stuffed his pipe, and smoked furiously.

A light footfall raised him from his brooding. Tyra entered. As usual, her countenance brightened to see him. "Hi," she greeted, an Americanism acquired in their conversations. "Care you for some company?"—as if she had never before joined him here for hours on end, or he her when she had the duty. "Remember, you promised to tell me about your adventure on—" She halted. Her tone flattened. "Something is woeful."

"I hope not," he said. "I hope I'm mistaken."

She seated herself. "If I can help or console, Robert, only ask. Or if you wish not to share the trouble, tell me I should hold my mouth."

She knows how to be silent, he thought. We've passed happy times with not a word, listening to music or looking at some work of art or simply near each other.

"You're right," he said. "I can't talk about it till—till I must. With luck, I'll never have to."

The blue eyes searched him. "It concerns you and me, no?" How grave and quiet she had become.

Alarmed, he countered, "Did I say that?"

"I feel it. We are dear friends. At least, you are for me."

"And you—" He couldn't finish the sentence.

"I believe you are torn."

"Wait a minute."

She leaned forward and took his free hand between hers. "Because you are a good man, an honest man," she said. "You keep your promises." She paused. "But—"

"Let's change the subject, shall we?" he interrupted.

"Are you afraid? Yes, you are. Afraid of to give pain."

"Stop," he barked. "No more of this. You hear me?" He pulled his hand away.

An implacable calm was upon her. "As you wish, my dear. For the rest of the journey. You have right. Anything else is indecent, among all of us. But in some more days we are at Wunderland."

"Yes," he said, thickly and foolishly.

"You will be there a length of time."

"Busy."

"Not always. You know that. We will make decisions. It may take long, but at last we must. About the rest of our lives."

"Maybe."

"Quite certainly." She rose. "I think best I go now. You should be alone with your heart for this while."

He stared at the deck. "You're probably right."

Steadiness failed her a little. "Robert, whatever happens, whatsoever, you are dear to me." Her footfalls dwindled off into silence.

A squat black form stood at a distance down the passage, like a barricade. "Hallo," said Tyra dully.

Carita fell into step with her. "That was a short visit."

Tyra bridled. "You watched?"

"I noticed. Couldn't help it. Can't, day after day. A kdat would see. I want a word with you."

Tyra flushed. "Please to be polite."

"We're overdue for a talk," the Jinxian insisted. "This is a loose hour for both of us. Will you come along?" Although tone and gait were unthreatening, the hint lay beneath them that if necessary, she might pick the other woman up and carry her.

"Very well," Tyra clipped. They walked on mute to the pilot's cabin and inside.

Carita shut the door. Eyes met and held fast. "What do you want?" Tyra demanded.

"You know perfectly well what," Carita stated. "You and the skipper."

"We are friends! Nothing more!"

"No privacy aboard ship for anything else, if you're civilized. Sure, you've kept out of the sack. A few kisses, maybe, but reasonably chaste, like in a flirtation. Only that's not what it is any longer. You're waiting till we get to Wunderland."

Tyra lifted her arm as if to strike, then let it fall. "Do you call Robert a *schleicher*—a, a sneak?" she blazed.

Carita's manner mildened. "Absolutely not. Nor you. This is simply a thing that's happened. Neither of you would've wanted it, and you didn't see it coming till too late. I believe you're as bewildered, half joyful and half miserable, as he is."

Tyra dropped her gaze. She clenched fists against breasts. "It is difficult," she whispered.

"True, you being an honorable person."

Tyra rallied. "It is our lives. His and mine."

"Dorcas saved your father's," Carita answered. "Later she saved all of us. Yes, Bob was there, but you know damn well he couldn't have done what he did without her. How do you propose to repay that? Money doesn't count, you know."

"*Ich kann nicht anders!*" Tyra cried. "He and I, we are caught."

"You are free adults," Carita said. "You're trapped in nothing but yourselves. Tyra, you're smart, gifted, beautiful, and soon you'll be rich. You've got every prospect bright ahead of you. What *we've* got is a good marriage and a happy ship. Bob will come back to her, if you let him go."

"Will he? How can I? Shall I leave him hurt forever?"

Carita smiled. She reached to lay an arm around the taller woman's shoulders. "I had a hunch that'd be what makes you feel so helpless. Sit down, honey. I'll pour us a drink and we'll talk."

Chapter XXI

The Jinxian relieved Saxtorph at the end of his watch. Lost in tumult, he barely noticed how she regarded him and forgot about it as he went out.

Oh, hell, he thought, I'm getting nowhere, only churning around in a maelstrom. Before it drags me under, I'd better—what? Have a bite to eat, I guess, take a sleeping pill, go to bed, hope I'll wake up clear-headed.

That he came to the place he did at the minute he did was coincidence. Nobody meant to stage anything. It made no difference, except that he would otherwise have found out less abruptly.

The door to Tyra's cabin stood half open, Kamehameha Ryan in it. His hair was rumpled, his clothes hastily thrown on, his expression slightly dazed. Saxtorph stopped short. A tidal wave surged through him.

The quartermaster said into the room: "—hard to believe. I never would have—I mean, Bob's more than my captain, he's my friend, and—"

Her laugh purred. "What, feel you guilty? No need. I enjoy his company, yes, and I had ideas, but he is too much married. Maybe when we are on Wunderland. Meanwhile, this has been a long dry voyage until now. Carita was right, she told me you are good."

He beamed. "Why, thank you, ma'am. And you are terrific. Tomorrow?"

"Every tomorrow, if we can, until journey's end. Now, if you excuse, I am ready for happy dreams."

"Me too." Ryan blew a kiss, shut the door, and tottered off. He didn't see who stood at his back.

After a space Saxtorph began to think again. Well. So that is how it is. *Du kannst nicht treu sein.*

Not that I have any call to be mad at either of them. I've got no claim. Never did. On the contrary.

Even so—

Vaguely: That's the barbed wire I've been hung up on. Because the matter, the insight that hit me, touches Tyra, no, grabs her with kzin claws, I couldn't bring myself to consult Dorcas. I couldn't bring myself to see that she is the one living soul I must turn to. Between us we'll work out what our course ought to be.

Later. Later.

He walked on, found himself at Peter Nordbo's quarters, and knocked. The Wunderlander opened the door and gazed at him with surprise. "Hi," Saxtorph said. "Am I disturbing you?"

"No. I read a modern history book. Thirty years to learn about. What is your wish?"

"Sociability. Nothing special. Swap stories of our young days, argue about war and politics and other trivia, maybe sing bawdy songs, definitely get drunk. You game? I'll fetch any kind of bottle you like."

Chapter XXII

Both suns were down and Munchen gone starry with
its own lights. Downtown traffic swarmed and throbbed
around the old buildings, the smart modern shops.
Matthiesonstrasse was residential, though, quiet at this
hour. Apartment houses lined it like ramparts, more
windows dark than aglow, so that when Saxtorph looked
straight up he could make out a few real stars. A breeze
flowed chilly, the first breath of oncoming fall.

He found the number he wanted and glanced aloft
again, less high. Luminance on the fifth floor told him
somebody was awake there. He hesitated. That might
be a different location from the one he was after.

Squaring shoulders, setting jaws: Come on, boy, move
along. Rouse him if need be. Get this goddamn thing
over with.

In the foyer he passed by the *fahrstuhl* and took the
emergency stairs. They were steep. He felt glad of it.
The climb worked out a little of the tension in him.
Nonetheless, having reached the door numbered 52, he
pushed the button violently.

After a minute the speaker gave him an uneven *"Ja, was wollen Sie von mir?"* He turned his face straight toward the scanner, and heard a gasp. *"Sie!"* Seconds later "Captain Saxtorph?" sounded like a prayer that it not be true.

"Let me in," the Earthman said.

"No. This is, is the middle of the night."

Correct, Saxtorph thought.

"You had not even the courtesy to call ahead. Go away."

"Better me than the patrol," Saxtorph answered.

He heard something akin to a strangled sob. The door opened. He stepped through. It shut behind him.

The apartment was ascetically furnished and had been neat, but disorder was creeping in. The air system failed to remove the entire haze and stench of cigarette smoke. Ib Nordbo stood in a civilian jumpsuit. His hair was unkempt, his eyelids darkly smudged. Yes, thought Saxtorph, he was awake, all right. I daresay he doesn't sleep much any more.

"W-welcome back," Nordbo mumbled.

"Your father and sister were disappointed that you weren't there to greet them personally," Saxtorph said.

"They got my message. My regrets. They did? I must go offplanet, unfortunately, at that exact time. A personal difficulty. I asked for compassionate leave."

"Except you holed up here. I figured you would. No point going anywhere else in this system. You'd be too easily found. No interstellar passenger ship is leaving before next week, and you'd need to fix up identity documents and such." Saxtorph gestured. "Sit down. I don't enjoy this either. Let's make it as short as possible."

Nordbo retreated, lowered himself to the edge of a chair, clutched its arms. His entire body begged. Saxtorph followed but remained standing above him.

"How long have you been in kzinti pay?" Saxtorph asked.

Nordbo swallowed dryness. "I am not. I was not. Never."

"Listen, fellow. Listen good. I don't care to play

games. Cooperate, or I'll walk right out and turn this
business over to the authorities. I would have already,
if it weren't for your sister and your father. You damn
near got them killed, you know."

"Tyra— No, I did not know!" the other screamed.
"She lied to me. If I knew she was going with you, I
would have gotten your stupid expedition stopped. And
my father, any reasonable person believed him long
dead. I did not know! How could I?"

"Bad luck, yah, but richly deserved," Saxtorph said.
"I might not have guessed, except that a clue fell my
way. At that, the meaning didn't dawn on me till a
couple days later."

He drew breath before driving his point home. "You'll
have followed the news, as much of our story as has
been released. Before then, being who you are and in
the position you are, you'll have been apprised of what
we told the Navy officer we requested come aboard as
we approached. A kzinti warship caught us at the black
hole, later than you expected it might, but still something you knew was quite likely."

"I—no, you misjudge me—"

"Pipe down till I give you leave to speak. The encounter *could* have been by chance. The kzinti might
have happened on the beamcast from the earlier ship
and dispatched this one at the precise wrong moment
for us. Her captain knew who I was and what vessel I
command. He *could* have heard that on the starvine or
through his intelligence corps. *Rover*'s name wouldn't
matter to that mentality and would scarcely have been
in any briefing he got, but conceivably he'd heard it
somehow, lately, and it was fresh in his mind. Yah. The
improbable can happen. What blew the whistle, once I
realized what it meant, was that he told me he'd hoped
to find me. He believed it was entirely possible we'd be
there, we of all humans, *Rover* of all ships.

"We'd never disclosed where we were bound for or
why. Nobody else knew, besides you. Nobody but you
could have sent word about us to Kzin.

"I imagine you informed them as soon as Tyra discovered your father's notes and showed you. The matter would be of interest to them, and might be important. When she got serious about mounting a search, you did everything you could to discourage her, short of telling your superiors. You dared not do that because then they might well order an official look-see, which could open a trail to you and your treason. They aren't as stodgy about such things as you claimed. The disclosure about Markham had cast suspicion your way, and you must be feeling sort of desperate. When we made clear that we'd embark in spite of your objections, you got on whatever hyperphone you have secret access to and alerted the kzinti. If they scragged us, you'd be safe.

"Okay, Nordbo. How long have you been in their pay?"

"Tyra," the seated man groaned. He slumped back. "I did not know, I swear I did not know she was with you."

"Just the same," Saxtorph said, "betraying us to probable death was not exactly a friendly act. For her sake and your father's, I just might be persuaded to . . . set it aside. No promises yet, understand, and whatever mercy you get, you've got to earn."

For their sakes, grieved a deep part of him. Yes, Peter has suffered, has lost, quite enough. He's so happy that Dorcas and I will take him on as a partner. Christ, how I'd hate to dash the cup from his lips.

He wouldn't be ruined. His vindication, the reparation to him, the family's restoration to the clan, those will stand, because *he* was and is the Landholder, not this creature sniveling at me tonight. I think he has the strength to outlive it if he and the world learn the truth about his son, his only son, and to get on with his work. But if I can spare him—if I can spare him!

Nordbo looked up. He was ghastly haggard. The words jerked forth: "I never did it for money. I got some, yes, but I did not want it, I always gave it to the Veterans' Home. Markham was like a, a father to me, the father I had worshipped before he— Well, what could I believe except that my real father turned collab-

orator and died in the kzinti service? I thought Tyra
was a wishful thinker. I could not make myself say that
openly to her, but I thought my duty was to restore the
family fortune and honor by my efforts. Markham was
faithful in those first years after the trial, when many
scorned. He helped me, counseled me, was like a new
father, he, the war hero, then the brilliant administrator. When at last he asked me to do something a, a
little irregular for him, I was glad. It was nothing harm-
ful. He explained that if the kzinti knew better how our
intelligence operations work, they would see we are
defensive, not aggressive, and there would be a better
chance for lasting peace. What should I trust, his keen
and experienced judgment or a stupid, handcuffing regulation? That first information I gave him to pass on to
the kzinti, it was not classified. They could have collected it for themselves with some time and trouble.
But then there was more, and then more, and it grew
into real secrets—" Again he covered his eyes and
huddled.

Saxtorph nodded. "You'd become subject to black-
mail. Every step you took brought you further down a
one-way road. Yah. That's how a lot of spies get
recruited."

"I love my nation. I would never harm it." Nordbo
dropped fists to knees and added in a voice less shrill,
"Even though it did my father and my family a terrible
injustice."

"You got around to agreeing with Tyra about that,
eh? And what you were doing couldn't possibly cause
any serious damage. Such-like notions are also usual
among spies."

Nordbo raised his head. "Do not insult me. I have
my human dignity."

"That's a matter of opinion. Now, I told you to listen
and I told you I want to make this short so I can get the
hell out of here and go have a hot shower and a change
of clothes. Snap to it, and perhaps, I'll see if I can do
anything for you. Otherwise I report straight to your

superiors. For openers, how many more are in your ring?"

"N-no one else."

"I'd slap you around if I had a pair of gloves I could burn afterward. As is goodnight."

"No! Please!" Nordbo reeled to his feet. He held his arms out. "I tell you, nobody. Nobody I know of. One in my unit at headquarters, but she died two years ago. An accident. And Markham is dead. Nobody more!"

Saxtorph deemed he was telling the truth as far as possible. "You'll name her," he said. "That, and what else you tell, should give leads to any others." If they existed. Maybe they didn't. Markham had been a lone wolf type. Well, investigation was a job for professionals. "You will write down what you know. Every last bit. The whole story, all you did, all you delivered personally and all you heard about or suspected, the works. You savvy? I'll give you two-three days. Don't leave this apartment meanwhile."

Nordbo's hands fell to his sides. He straightened. A sudden, eerie calm was upon him. "What then?" he asked tonelessly.

"If I judge you've made an honest statement, my wife and I will try to bargain with the authorities, privately, when we bring it to them. We can't dictate what they do with you. But we are their darlings, and the darlings of the public and the media more than ever. Our recommendations should carry weight. The Markham affair has shaken and embarrassed a lot of the brass pretty badly. They'd like some peace and quiet while they put their house in order. A sensation involving the son of hero-martyr Peter Nordbo is no way to get that. Maybe we can talk them into accepting your resignation and burying the truth in the top secret file. Maybe. We'll try. That's all I can promise. And it's conditional on your writing a full and accurate account."

"I see. You are kind."

"Because of your father and your sister. Nothing else." Saxtorph turned to go.

"Wait," said Nordbo.

"Why?" Saxtorph growled.

"My memory is not perfect. But I need not write for
you. I kept a journal of my, my participation. Everything that happened, recorded immediately afterward.
I thought I might want it someday, somehow, if Markham or the kzinti should— *Ach*, let me fetch it."

Saxtorph's heart banged. "Okay." He hadn't hoped
for this much. He wasn't sure what he'd hoped for.

Nordbo went into an adjacent room. He strode reso-
lutely and erect. Saxtorph tautened. "If you're going for
a gun instead, don't," he called. "My wife knows where
I am."

"Of course," the soft voice drifted back. "No, you
have convinced me. I shall do my best to set things
right."

He returned carrying a small security box, which he
placed at the computer terminal. He laid his palm on
the lid and it opened. Had anyone else tried to force it,
the contents would have been destroyed. Saxtorph moved
closer. He saw a number of minidiscs. "Encoded,"
Nordbo said. "Please make a note of the decoding command. A wrong one will cause the program to wipe the
data. You want to inspect a sample, no?"

He stooped, inserted a disc, and keyed the board. A
date three years past sprang onto the screen, followed
by words. They were Wunderlander, but Saxtorph's
reading knowledge sufficed to show that the entry did
indeed relate an act of espionage. Copies of photo-
graphs came after.

"You are satisfied?" Nordbo asked. "Want you more?"

"No," Saxtorph said. "This will do."

Nordbo returned the disc to the box, which he relocked
and proffered. "I am afraid you must touch this," he
said matter-of-factly.

Sudden pity welled forth. "That's okay." In several
ways he resembled his sister: eyes, cheekbones, flaxen
hair, something about the way he now stood and faced
his visitor. "We'll do whatever we can for you, Ib."

"Thank you."

Saxtorph took the box and left. *"Gute nacht,"* Nordbo said behind him.

The door closed. Saxtorph went the short distance along the hall to the stairwell and started down. Whatever I can for you, Tyra, he thought.

His mind went on, like himself speaking to her, explaining, though they were not things she would ever hear.

I'm not mad at you, dear. Nor at Kam, as far as that goes. You weren't deliberately playing games with me. You honestly believed you were serious—confusing horniness with love, which God knows is a common mistake— till the impulse itself overwhelmed you.

Or so he supposed. Nothing had been uttered, except in the silent language. They simply understood that everything was over. Apart from friendship. Already he hurt less than at first. He knew that before long he'd stop altogether and be able to meet her, be with her, in comradely fashion. Dorcas would see to it.

I do wish you'll find a man you can settle down with. I'd like you to have what we have. But if not, well, it's your life, and any style of living it that you choose will be brave.

Saxtorph had reached the third-floor landing when he heard the single pistol shot.

Experience the bestselling worlds of

JERRY POURNELLE